FRED VARGAS

THIS POISON
WILL REMAIN

TRANSLATED FROM THE FRENCH BY
Siân Reynolds

VINTAGE

1 3 5 7 9 10 8 6 4 2

Vintage
20 Vauxhall Bridge Road,
London SW1V 2SA

Vintage is part of the Penguin Random House group
of companies whose addresses can be found
at global.penguinrandomhouse.com

Penguin
Random House
UK

Copyright © Fred Vargas and Flammarion, Paris, 2017
English translation copyright © Siân Reynolds, 2019

Fred Vargas has asserted her right to be identified as
the author of this Work in accordance with the Copyright,
Designs and Patents Act 1988

First published with the title *Quand sort la recluse* in France
by Flammarion, Paris in 2017

First published by Vintage in 2020
First published in the UK by Harvill Secker in 2019

penguin.co.uk/vintage

A CIP catalogue record for this book is available
from the British Library

ISBN 9781784708290 (B format)

Printed and bound in Great Britain by Clays Ltd, Elcograf S.p.A.

Penguin Random House is committed to a sustainable future for
our business, our readers and our planet. This book is made
from Forest Stewardship Council® certified paper.

MIX
Paper from
responsible sources
FSC
www.fsc.org   FSC® C018179

FRED VARGAS

Fred Vargas was born in Paris in 1957. A historian of the medieval period and archaeologist by profession, she is now a bestselling novelist. Her books have sold over 10 million copies worldwide and have been translated into 45 languages. She has been awarded the CWA International Dagger a record four times.

SIÂN REYNOLDS

Siân Reynolds is a historian, translator and former professor at the University of Stirling.

THIS POISON WILL REMAIN

I

JEAN-BAPTISTE ADAMSBERG, SITTING ON A ROCK AT THE QUAYSIDE, watched the Grimsey fishermen return with their daily catch, as they moored their boats and hauled up their nets. Here, on this tiny island off the coast of Iceland, people called him simply 'Berg'. An onshore breeze, temperature 11 degrees, hazy sunshine, and the reek of discarded fish entrails. He had forgotten that, not so long ago, he was a commissaire, the police chief in charge of the twenty-seven officers of the Paris Serious Crime Squad, based in the 13th arrondissement. His mobile phone had fallen into some sheep dung, and the ewe had trodden it firmly in with its hoof, no malice intended. That was a novel way to lose your phone, and Adamsberg had appreciated it as such.

Gunnlaugur, the landlord of the little inn, was just arriving down at the harbour, preparing to choose the best fish for the evening meal. Adamsberg waved to him with a smile. But Gunnlaugur did not look his usual jovial self. He was heading straight for Adamsberg, ignoring the fish market just getting under way. Frowning under his blond eyebrows, he held out a piece of paper.

'*Fyrir þig,*' he said – with a gesture. *For you.*

'*Ég?*' *Me?*

Adamsberg, who was normally incapable of memorising the most basic rudiments of any foreign language, had inexplicably amassed a stock of about seventy words of Icelandic, in just seventeen days. People spoke to him as simply as possible, with a lot of sign language.

From Paris, the message must be from Paris. And they wanted him back, that must be it. He felt combined sadness and anger and shook his head, refusing to look, turning towards the sea. Gunnlaugur insisted, unfolding the paper and thrusting it into his fingers.

Woman run over. Husband or lover. Not straightforward. Your presence required. Details follow.

Adamsberg looked down, opened his hand and let the paper blow away in the wind. Paris? How could it be from Paris? Where was Paris, anyway?

'*Dauður maður?*' Gunnlaugur asked. *Someone's died?*

'*Já.*' Yes.

'*Ertu að fara, Berg? Ertu að fara?*' *So you're leaving us, Berg? You're leaving?*

Adamsberg drew himself up wearily and looked towards the pale sun.

'*Nei.*' No.

'*Jú, Berg,*' Gunnlaugur sighed. *Yes you are, Berg.*

'*Já,*' Adamsberg admitted.

Gunnlaugur shook his shoulder, pulling him along.

'*Drekka borða,*' he said. *You must eat, drink.*

'*Ja.*' OK.

The shock, as his plane's wheels touched down on the tarmac at Roissy-Charles de Gaulle airport, triggered a sudden migraine such as he had not had for years, and at the same time he felt as if he were being battered all over. Back to base, all that aggression, Paris, city of stone. Unless it was the number of glasses downed the night before, at his farewell party at the inn in Iceland. The glasses had been very small. But numerous. And it was his last night. And it had been *brennivín*.

He gave a furtive glance out of the window. Not to get out. Not to have to go anywhere.

But he was there already. *Your presence required.*

II

BY NINE O'CLOCK ON TUESDAY 31 MAY, SIXTEEN OF THE SQUAD'S officers had gathered in their council chamber, armed with laptops, folders and cups of coffee, ready to fill the commissaire in on the business they had been dealing with in his absence, under the leadership of Commandants Mordent and Danglard. By the relaxed and suddenly chatty atmosphere, the team was expressing its pleasure at seeing him back, seeing once more his face and mannerisms, without wondering whether his stay in the north of Iceland, on that little island of mists and pounding waves, had altered his approach in any way. And if it had, so what? Lieutenant Veyrenc was saying to himself. He, like Adamsberg, had grown up in the rocky Pyrenees and understood the boss well. He knew that when the commissaire was in charge, the squad was like a tall sailing ship, sometimes with a brisk wind behind it, other times becalmed and its sails drooping, rather than a powerful speedboat churning up torrents of spray.

Commandant Danglard, on the other hand, was perpetually worried about something. He was forever scanning the horizon, on the lookout for threats of all kinds, flaying his skin on the rough surface of his fears. Following Adamsberg's departure for Iceland, at the end of a particularly trying case, apprehension had already gained the upper hand. For an ordinary mortal who was simply tired, going off for rest and recuperation to a cold land of mist and fog might seem appropriate. Better than chasing the southern sun, where the relentless light would illuminate the slightest relief, the sharp edges of a gravel chip, no, that was not at all relaxing. But for someone whose mind was already full of mist to go off to a similarly mist-shrouded country seemed to him on the contrary dangerous, potentially heavy with consequences. Danglard feared difficult, possibly irreversible results. He had seriously wondered whether, through some kind of chemical fusion between a country's fogs and those of a human being, Adamsberg might be swallowed up in Iceland and never come back. News of the commissaire's return to Paris had somewhat reassured him. But when Adamsberg had come into the room, with his usual slightly rolling gait, smiling round at everyone, shaking hands, Danglard's anxiety immediately revived. More vague and elusive than ever, with his wandering gaze and absent-minded smile, the commissaire seemed to have lost touch with the precisely carpentered joists which had always, in spite of everything, underpinned his approach, like a series of supporting beams, infrequent but reassuring. He's looking invertebrate, boneless, Danglard deduced. Amusing, still damp from the north, thought Lieutenant Veyrenc.

Junior officer Estalère, who specialised in preparing the squad's ritual coffee, a task he accomplished faultlessly – indeed it was the only area in which he excelled, according to most of his colleagues – immediately served one to his chief, with just the right amount of sugar.

'OK, go ahead,' said Adamsberg in a gentle, faraway voice, much too relaxed for a police chief dealing with the death of a woman of thirty-seven who had been run over – twice – in the street by a 4x4, which had broken her neck and legs.

This had happened three days earlier, on the previous Saturday night, in the rue du Château-des-Rentiers. What château, what rentiers? Danglard wondered, since that name sounded very odd in the less-than-well-heeled 13th arrondissement where they were based. He promised himself to check what its origin was, since no detail of knowledge was too trivial for the commandant's encyclopedic mind.

'Did you read the file we sent for you to pick up at Reykjavik airport?' asked Mordent.

'Of course,' said Adamsberg with a shrug.

And indeed he had read it during the flight from Reykjavik to Paris. But in reality, he had found it hard to concentrate. He knew that this woman, Laure Carvin – a pretty woman, he had noted – had been killed by the 4x4 between 22.10 and 22.15. The precision about time of death resulted from the victim's extremely regular routine. She sold children's outfits in a luxury boutique in the 15th arrondissement between 14.00 and 19.30. Then she did the accounts and pulled down the shutters at 21.40. She crossed the rue du Château-des-Rentiers every evening at the same time, at the same traffic lights, very near her home. She was married to a rich 'self-made man', but Adamsberg could not now remember what line he was in, or what his bank account looked like. It had been the husband's 4x4, the rich guy's – what was his first name? – that had run the woman down, there was no doubt about that. There was still blood in the treads of the tyres and on the bodywork. The same night, Mordent and Justin had retraced the tracks left by those killer wheels, taking with them a sniffer dog from the canine squad. Which had led them directly, via a set of side streets, to the small car park of a video games centre, a mere three hundred metres from the scene of the crime. The rather high-maintenance police dog had demanded many pats for his performance.

The proprietor of the centre was well acquainted with the owner of the bloodstained vehicle: a regular who frequented the games room every Saturday evening from about 9 p.m. until midnight. If he was out of luck, he might well stay until closing time, 2 a.m. He had pointed the man out: in a tailored suit and with loosened tie, he was easy to spot among the other players who wore hoodies and held beer cans. The man was furiously battling with huge cadaverous figures speeding towards him on screen, and he had to mow them down with a machine gun, in order to force a passage to the labyrinthine Mountain of the Black King. When the officers had interrupted him by touching his shoulder, he had shaken his head frantically, without lifting his hands from the controls, and shouted that there was no way he was going to stop now, at 47,652 points, almost the level needed for the Bronze Route, no way! Raising his voice above the noise of the machines and the loud voices of the customers, Mordent had managed to communicate to him that his wife had been killed, knocked down on the road, a mere three hundred metres away. The man had collapsed on to the console, cancelling the game. The screen carried the message 'Too bad, you've lost!' with appropriate music.

'So according to the husband, he hadn't left the games room?' asked Adamsberg.

'If you've read the report –' Mordent began.

'I'd prefer to hear it from you,' Adamsberg said, cutting him off.

'That's right, he'd been there all evening.'

'So how does he explain that the tyres of his own 4x4 are covered in blood?'

'Because there's a lover in the picture. The lover must have known the husband's habits, come and borrowed the car, driven it at his mistress, then parked it back in its place.'

'So as to make it look as if it was him?'

'Yes, because the police always accuse the husband.'

'How was he?'

'What do you mean?'

'How did he react, the husband?'

'Taken aback. He seemed more shocked than distressed. He recovered somewhat when they took him to the station. The couple were apparently considering divorce.'

'Because of the lover?'

'No,' said Lieutenant Noël with a sneer. 'Because a man like him, a

7

jumped-up fancy lawyer, thought his lower-class wife was a drag on him. If you read between the lines of what he says.'

'And his wife,' chimed in fair-haired Justin, 'was humiliated to be left out of all the cocktail parties and grand dinners he gave in his suite of rooms in the 7th arrondissement, for his clients and contacts. She wanted to come along, but he refused. They had a number of scenes about it. She'd have been "out of place", according to him, she "wouldn't have fitted in". He's that kind of man.'

'Unbelievable – eh?' said Noël.

'He gradually regained control,' said Voisenet, 'and then he started protesting as if he'd been forced on to a Go to Jail route in his video game. He started speaking in more and more complicated and incomprehensible sentences.'

'It's a simple strategy,' said Mordent, jerking his long thin neck from his collar, having in no way over the past fortnight altered his appearance of an old heron, disillusioned with the trials of existence. 'He's banking on the contrast between himself, a lawyer handling big business, and the lover.'

'Who is?'

'An Arab, as he insisted on telling us at once, a guy who repairs drinks machines. And he lives in the adjoining building. Nassim Bouzid, Algerian but born in France, married, two children.'

Adamsberg hesitated, then did not speak. He couldn't decently ask his officers how the interrogation of Nassim Bouzid had gone, because it must have been in the report. But he couldn't remember anything about this man.

'What impression did you get of the lover?' he asked casually, while signalling to Estalère to fetch him another coffee.

'Good-looking guy,' said Lieutenant Hélène Froissy, pushing towards Adamsberg her laptop, which showed a photo of a miserable-looking Nassim Bouzid. 'Long eyelashes, honey-coloured eyes, looks like he's wearing make-up, very white teeth and a charming smile. Everyone adores him in the building, and they all use him as their handyman. Nassim will change a light bulb for you, fix a leaking pipe, Nassim never says no.'

'Which makes the husband conclude that he is a weak and servile creature,' said Voisenet. 'Come from nowhere, going nowhere, was how he put it.'

'Unbelievable,' said Noël again.

'And the husband is jealous?' asked Adamsberg, who had started to take a few scribbled notes.

'He says not,' said Froissy. 'He thinks the affair's beneath his contempt, but it would have suited him because of the divorce.'

'So?' asked Adamsberg, turning to Mordent. 'You mentioned strategy, commandant.'

'He's banking on police reflexes. He thinks we're all uneducated, racist and stereotypical: if we're faced with a high-status lawyer who uses language so sophisticated as to be incomprehensible, and an Arab handyman, the cops will always go for the Arab.'

'So what are these sophisticated and incomprehensible words he uses?'

'Hard to say,' said Voisenet, 'because I didn't understand. Words like "aperception", or wait, hetero-something, "heteronomous". Does that mean something to do with sexual deviance? He used it about the lover.'

All eyes turned to Danglard for help.

'No, it means "other-directed", the opposite of autonomous, which means "self-directed". It would be worth trying to play him at his own game,' said Danglard.

'I'll count on you to do that, commandant,' said Adamsberg.

'If you say so,' said Danglard, cheering up somewhat at this thought, and for a moment forgetting Adamsberg's perplexing absent-mindedness and his current uninformed approach. It was clear that the commissaire had not retained much from the report over which he, Danglard, had taken such trouble.

'He quotes a lot of stuff too,' said Mercadet, surfacing from a short nap.

Mercadet was one of the squad's two brilliant IT experts, just a little behind Hélène Froissy, but he suffered from narcolepsy and his fellow officers all respected and even covered up for their colleague's handicap. If it had come to the ears of their hierarchical superior, the divisionnaire, Mercadet would have been sacked on the spot. What can you do with a cop who falls uncontrollably asleep every three hours?

'And this lawyer, Maître Carvin, expects us to react to his damn quotations,' Mercadet went on. 'He wants us to recognise – or rather, *not* to recognise – where they're from. He's banking on us being ignorant, playing at humiliating us, no question.'

'For instance?'

'Well, take this,' said Justin, flicking open his pad. 'About Nassim Bouzid, again: "Men do not flee from deception so much as from being damaged by deception." '

They were once more expecting to hear from Danglard, who would save them from the repeated disdain of the lawyer, but out of delicacy, Danglard refrained from identifying the author of the quotation, so as to put himself on an equal footing with his more ignorant colleagues. This modesty was not understood, but they readily forgave him, since you can't ask anyone, however frighteningly learned, to know every quotation in literature.

'What it means in plain language,' said Mordent, 'is that Carvin is kindly providing a motive for Bouzid to murder: killing his mistress to escape the damage caused by the adultery and so avoid the break-up of his family.'

'And who's the quotation by, Commandant Danglard?' asked Estalère, breaking with the general reluctance and demonstrating his usual lack of tact, or possibly his incurable stupidity, as some thought.

'It's by Nietzsche,' Danglard finally admitted.

'Is he someone important?'

'Very.'

Adamsberg went on sketching for a moment, wondering, as he often did, what deeply entrenched mystery accounted for Danglard's phenomenal memory.

'Oh, right!' said Estalère, looking stunned, and opening wide his big green eyes.

But Estalère was always wide-eyed, as if he could never get over his stupefaction at everything in life. And no doubt he was quite right, Adamsberg thought. The fate of this poor woman, atrociously crushed to death, was certainly enough to leave anyone staring, perplexed, into the night.

'Because,' Estalère went on, concentrating hard, 'you don't have to be important to know that we're scared of the result of telling a lie. Otherwise it wouldn't matter, would it?'

'Very true,' Adamsberg agreed, ever ready to defend the young man, something the others could never understand.

Adamsberg lifted his pencil. He had been sketching the outline of his friend Gunnlaugur watching the fish market on the quayside. Plus the seagulls, flocks of seagulls.

'Well,' he said, 'what are the arguments one way or the other?'

'The lawyer has his alibi, the video games place,' said Mordent. 'But it isn't worth a damn, because with the crowd of other players shouting and getting excited, and riveted to their screens, who would miss him if he nipped out for a quarter of an hour? And he has a vast amount of money in the bank. If he was to divorce, he'd stand to lose half of his four million two hundred thousand euros.'

'Four million two hundred thousand?' asked a timid junior officer, Lamarre, speaking for the first time. 'How many years' pay would that mean for us?'

'Don't go there, Lamarre,' said Adamsberg, raising his hand. 'It'd be too painful. Carry on, Mordent.'

'But then again, there's no particular evidence against him. Nassim Bouzid looks in a trickier position, because there are some material elements. In the 4x4, they found three white dog hairs near the passenger seat and a scrap of red thread on the brake pedal. According to the preliminary forensics, the hairs are indeed from Bouzid's dog. And the thread matches the kilim in his dining room. As for the car keys, he could have got the spare any time from his mistress. All their keys hang up in the entrance hall of their flat.'

'So why would he take the dog with him, if he wanted to kill his mistress?' asked Froissy.

'Well, Bouzid is married himself. It would be a good excuse to his wife to say he was taking the dog round the block to do its business.'

'And what if the dog had already been round the block?' asked Noël.

'No,' said Mordent. 'It was his regular time for taking the dog out. Bouzid readily agrees he left the house about that time, but he totally denies ever having been Laure Carvin's lover. He says he didn't even know the woman. Maybe by sight in the street. So if he's telling the truth, Carvin the lawyer must have singled him out as a fall guy, somehow got hold of some dog hairs and fibre from the carpet, because where Bouzid lives, the front-door lock would open with a hairpin. Don't those two details look a bit over the top to you?'

'Exactly. Just one bit of evidence would have done,' Adamsberg agreed.

'That's a failing of people who are too proud of their own intelligence,' said Danglard. 'Their infatuation blinds them, they can't gauge what other people might do, they go too far one way or another. So contrary to what they imagine, their judgement isn't infallible.'

'And,' said Justin, putting his hand up, 'Bouzid says when he takes the dog in his own car, he always puts him in a holdall. And we didn't find any dog hairs at all in his car. Or fibres from the carpet.'

'Are the two men the same height?' Adamsberg asked, turning his portrait of Gunnlaugur face down on the table.

'Bouzid is shorter.'

'So he would have had to adjust the driving seat and the mirrors? How were they?'

'In position for someone taller. He could have readjusted them afterwards, or else the lawyer could have left them as they were. You can't be certain either way.'

'Fingerprints in the car? Steering wheel, controls, doors?'

'Had a nice nap on the plane, did you?' said Veyrenc with a grin.

'Yes, maybe I did, Veyrenc. And it stinks.'

'Too right, it stinks – we're getting nowhere with this.'

'No, I meant it stinks here, in the room. Can't you smell anything?'

His colleagues all raised their heads at once to sniff the air. Funny thing, Adamsberg thought, humans always instinctively lift their heads up about ten centimetres when they are trying to smell something. As if ten centimetres were going to alter anything. Driven by an animal reflex established back in the mists of time, the group of police officers looked like nothing so much as a mob of meerkats trying to pick up the scent of a predator on the wind.

'Yeah, smells a bit of fish,' said Mercadet.

'Smells like a whole *fish market*,' Adamsberg said.

'I can't smell a thing,' said Voisenet, rather firmly. 'Well, it can wait.'

'Where were we?'

'Fingerprints,' said Mordent, who, since he was sitting at the far end of the long table by Danglard, couldn't smell anything odd.

'OK, go ahead, commandant.'

'Well, the fingerprints,' he said, pecking away at his notes like a heron, 'give us nothing conclusive. Because everything had been wiped. Either by Bouzid or by the lawyer who wanted to incriminate Bouzid. Not so much as a hair on the headrest.'

'Not so simple,' murmured Mercadet, to whom Estalère had now served two very strong cups of coffee.

'That's why we decided to call you back a bit early,' said Danglard.

So it was *him*, Adamsberg deduced. It was Danglard who had brought him back, as if it were a real emergency, tearing him away from his relaxed spell in Iceland. The commissaire observed his oldest colleague through narrowed eyes. Danglard had been afraid *for* him, no doubt about it.

'Can I see what these two men look like?' he asked.

'You've seen the photos,' said Froissy, moving her laptop towards him again.

'I'd like to see a video, from the questioning.'

'Which bit of the questioning?'

'Doesn't matter. And you can turn the sound down. I just want to get an idea of their expressions.'

Danglard stiffened. Adamsberg had always had a detestable tendency to judge people by their faces, separating the good from the bad, something Danglard considered totally reprehensible. Adamsberg knew this quite well, and sensed his colleague's apprehension.

'Sorry, Danglard,' he said with one of his lopsided smiles, which often seduced reluctant witnesses, or disarmed his opponents. 'But this time, I've got a quotation in my defence. I found it in a book someone had left on a seat at Reykjavik airport.'

'Well, tell us all about it then.'

'One moment, I don't know it by heart,' he said, feeling in his pocket. 'Here we are: "Everyday life shapes the soul, and the soul shapes the physiognomy."'

'Balzac,' muttered Danglard.

'Exactly. And you're an admirer of Balzac, aren't you, commandant?'

Adamsberg's smile grew broader and he folded up the scrap of paper.

'What book is it in?' asked Estalère.

'Who cares which book?' snorted Danglard.

'It was,' said Adamsberg, coming to Estalère's defence, 'a story about this priest, honest but not very bright, and some nasty individuals get the better of him. It happens in Tours, I think, on the Loire.'

'What's it called?'

'That, Estalère, I've forgotten.'

Disappointed, Estalère pushed away his pencil. He venerated both Adamsberg and the massive police lieutenant, Violette Retancourt, who was the exact opposite of the chief. He tried to imitate Adamsberg in every respect, such as reading this book for example. On the other hand, he had instinctively given up trying to imitate Retancourt. Because no man or woman was her equal, and even the arrogant Noël had finally realised as much. In the end, Danglard came to the young man's rescue.

'It's called *Le Curé de Tours*, The Priest of Tours.'

'Thank you,' said Estalère warmly, noting it down clumsily, because he was dyslexic. 'Still, Balzac didn't bust a gut making up the title, did he?'

'Estalère, one doesn't say of Balzac that "he didn't bust a gut".'

'Of course, commandant, I won't say that again.'

Adamsberg turned to Froissy.

'OK, Froissy,' he said, 'let's have a look at these two guys. While I'm doing that, the rest of you can take a break.'

Ten minutes later, sitting alone in front of the computer screen, Adamsberg suddenly realised that apart from the first few moments of Carvin's interview, he had seen and heard nothing. Brestir, his friend in Iceland, had invited him to go fishing, with the approval of the others on the quay. A great honour for a foreigner without doubt, an honour granted to the man who had overcome the perils of the Devil's Island, a few kilometres out to sea, its black and sinister profile visible from the harbour. Adamsberg had been allowed to help sort out the fish caught in the nets, throwing back juveniles, pregnant females and non-edible species. He had spent the last ten minutes on the slippery deck, his hands plunged into the nets, scratching himself on the fishes' scales. He returned abruptly to the image of Maître Carvin's face, paused the computer and went out to rejoin his colleagues, who were now scattered around the large open-plan office.

'Well?' asked Veyrenc.

'Too soon to say,' Adamsberg hedged. 'I'll need to take another look.'

'Yeah, naturally,' remarked Veyrenc, with a smile. He's still clammy with Icelandic fog, he thought.

Adamsberg signalled to Froissy that he was going back to the video, then stopped short.

'It really stinks!' he said. 'And it's coming from in here.'

Lifting his nose ten centimetres in the air, he went round the room, following the trail of the horrible smell, and like a police dog, stopped at Voisenet's desk. Voisenet was a cop and a very good one, but he had been frustrated in his youth from pursuing a career as an ichthyologist: his father had strictly forbidden him to do so, but he had carried on with his passion in secret. Adamsberg had finally managed to learn by heart that word, *ichthyologist*. Voisenet was an expert on fish, particularly freshwater fish. His fellow officers were used to seeing journals and articles of all kinds on the topic lying on his desk and Adamsberg allowed this to go on, if kept within limits. But it was the first time that an actual and fetid smell of fish had spilled out of Voisenet's workspace.

Going swiftly round the desk, Adamsberg pulled from under the chair a large plastic freezer bag. Voisenet, a small short-legged man, with a shock of black hair, a prominent stomach and round rosy cheeks, drew himself up with all the dignity his shape allowed him. A man unjustly accused, held up to ridicule, his attitude said.

'That's personal, commissaire,' he said loudly.

Adamsberg undid the clips on the top of the bag and opened it wide. He gave a jump and dropped the whole thing which flopped heavily to the floor. It was years since the commissaire had been so startled. His cool, even ultra-cool temperament was usually proof against it. But apart from the pestilential odour coming from the bag, the hideous sight inside had caused the shock. The head of a repulsive creature, with staring eyes and an enormous mouth bristling with terrifying teeth.

'What kind of shit is this?' he cried.

'My fishmonger –' Voisenet began.

'It's not your fishmonger!'

'No, it's a moray eel, *Uropterygius macularius*, a marbled moray from the west Atlantic,' Voisenet replied haughtily. 'Or to be more precise, the *head* of a moray eel and about sixteen centimetres of its body. And no, it's not a piece of shit, it's a magnificent male specimen, 1m 55 long when it was alive.'

For Adamsberg to show anger was so rare that the other officers, fascinated, all crowded round murmuring, peering in to see the creature, holding their noses, then quickly turning away. Even the hard-boiled Lieutenant Noël said, 'I guess nature slipped up there.' Only the massive and muscular Retancourt displayed no emotion at the sight of the repugnant head and went back calmly to her workstation. Danglard smiled discreetly to himself, delighted at this outburst, which, he thought, would bring Adamsberg back sharply to the real world, with real feelings. Adamsberg himself felt rather ashamed. He regretted leaving the island of Grimsey, he regretted leaping in the air and having raised his voice, and he felt ashamed that he could not work up more interest in the terrible murder of a poor woman under the wheels of a 4x4.

'Wow, a moray eel, that's really something!' said Estalère, looking more astonished than ever.

Voisenet picked up his bag with dignity.

'I'm taking it home,' he said, facing his colleagues as if they were a gang of ignorant enemies, prisoners of their preconceived ideas.

'Excellent idea,' said Adamsberg, who was now calmer. 'Nice present for your wife.'

'I'm going to take it over to my mother's to get it boiled.'

'Good thinking. Only mothers are ready to forgive anything.'

'I paid a lot for this,' Voisenet claimed, anxious to stress the significance of his specimen. 'My fishmonger sometimes gets in unusual species. Last month, he had a whole swordfish with a sword a metre long. Fantastic! But I couldn't afford it. I got a special rate for the moray eel, because it was starting to go off. So I jumped at the chance.'

'Yes, I can well understand,' said Adamsberg. 'Get that horrible thing out of here right away, Voisenet. You could have left it outside in the yard. It'll take three days to get rid of the smell.'

'In the yard? Someone might pinch it.'

'All the same,' Estalère repeated, 'that's quite something, isn't it, a moray eel?'

Voisenet shot him a grateful glance, then slipped behind his desk and rapidly, almost furtively, switched off his computer screen. After which, he left the room, not exactly gracefully, which was impossible for him, but with a certain bravado, carrying his heavy trophy at arm's length and leaving behind the ignorant company of police officers. What could you expect from a bunch of cops?

'Now open all the windows, everyone,' Adamsberg ordered. 'Froissy come with me, we'll try that video again from the beginning.'

'Did you notice anything special?'

'Possibly,' Adamsberg lied. 'Wait, just a sec.'

The commissaire, feeling suspicious, went to stand behind the desk of his fish-loving colleague once more. Why had Voisenet turned off his screen so quickly before going out? He switched it back on and looked at the last site consulted. Nothing there about either moray eels or police business. Instead, a photo of a small brown spider, of no apparent interest. Feeling puzzled, he flicked back, one by one, to Voisenet's last internet searches in the computer's history. Spider, spider, always the same one, specialist articles, distribution in France, feeding habits, harmful effects, reproduction and a few recent newspaper articles with alarmist titles: 'Return of the recluse spider?', 'Man bitten by spider in Carcassonne', 'Should we be worried about the brown recluse spider?', 'Second death in Orange'.

Adamsberg paused the computer. Froissy stood waiting beside him, elegant, upright and slim. Given the amount of food she ate (in secret, she firmly believed) because of a deep-seated fear of going hungry, her perfect figure was an enigma.

'Lieutenant,' said Adamsberg, 'can you check out and download all these files consulted by Voisenet over the last three weeks. About some spider.'

'What kind of spider?'

'Something called the recluse, or the brown recluse or the violin recluse – ever heard of it?'

'No, not at all.'

'Spiders aren't his usual terrain. He's held forth often enough about hooded crows, dormouse droppings, and – of course – fish. But spiders, never. I'd just like to know where our lieutenant is going with this.'

'Sir, it's not proper to look into a colleague's computer.'

'No, it isn't very. But I want to know. Can you transfer the files to me?'

'Yes, of course.'

'Perfect, go ahead, Froissy, and don't leave any footprints.'

'I never do. But what will I tell the others, if they see me working on Voisenet's computer?'

'Say he asked you to take a look, because of some bug. And you're fixing it while he's away.'

'His desk stinks to high heaven.'

'I know that, Froissy.'

III

THIS TIME, ADAMSBERG MANAGED TO CONCENTRATE ON THE interrogations of the proletarian, Nassim Bouzid, and the arrogant lawyer, Maître Carvin. He replayed several times passages where the lawyer shamelessly sought to deploy his superiority and cynicism. His 'strategy', as Mordent had called it, but above all his personality. Adamsberg decided that his commandant had misunderstood the exact nature of the strategy.

> *Mordent:* Your bank account shows you have savings of four million, two hundred and seventy-six thousand euros. But they weren't there as recently as seven years ago.
>
> *Carvin:* Have you heard of the mass return of the tax exiles? Trying to negotiate the best terms for making their peace with the Revenue? A windfall for lawyers, believe me. But you have to have the right kind of knowhow. You need to be familiar with the law, that goes without saying, but you need to know all the loopholes as well. Spirit of the law and letter of the law, have you heard of that? Myself, I'm in favour of the spirit, an infinitely flexible concept.
>
> *Voisenet:* . . . ?
>
> *Carvin:* But I don't see what this has to do with my wife's death.

Mordent: Well, I'm wondering, for example, why, with all that money, you continue to rent a three-room apartment on the ground floor in a gloomy little side street like the Impasse des Bourgeons.

Carvin: What does that matter? I spend all day in my chambers, weekends too. I come home late, and I just sleep there.

Mordent: Do you come home for dinner?

Carvin: Not often. My wife is a good cook, but one has to cultivate one's networks. Networks are my garden.

'Clumsy allusion to Voltaire,' muttered Danglard, who had slipped in behind Adamsberg. 'As if this pompous ass had any right to quote him.'

'He's unbelievable,' said Adamsberg.

'But he got the better of Voisenet.'

Voisenet: . . .

Carvin: Just move on, lieutenant. I'm still waiting for you to explain what connection any of this has with my wife's death.

Mordent: So like Louis XIV, you've 'almost been kept waiting'.

The tape showed Carvin shrugging his shoulders contemptuously. Danglard pulled a face.

'Nice try,' he said, 'but they didn't score. He's outfooted them both.'

'So why didn't you handle this interrogation, Danglard?'

'I wanted Carvin to reveal the extent of his strategy of condescension towards us. Towards the cops, and maybe towards his wife. So that he would reveal his concealed potential for violence. But I don't see where he's going. Humiliating the police won't help him get them on his side – on the contrary.'

'He's not humiliating them, Danglard, he's dominating them. Different thing. Our local zoologist Voisenet would say that the whole pack of cops would implicitly obey the alpha male – Carvin. Because

Carvin has dominated the alpha male of the squad, that is Mordent, in terms of rank. You wouldn't have been so vulnerable to Carvin's attacks, because you're an alpha male yourself.'

'Me?' said Danglard.

'*Já*,' said Adamsberg.

Danglard was taken aback, since he considered his own life, apart from his five children, to be an alternating sequence of anguish and impotence.

'It was probably a mistake not to have taken over the interrogation yourself, Danglard. You'd have crushed this lawyer and the squad would have felt strengthened. It's all very well sneering that he's "unbelievable", which is true, but they're all to some extent under his sway. So they can't apply reason to the question of who is guilty of this murder.'

'It's not being an alpha male to quote a bit of Nietzsche or Voltaire now and then.'

'Depends on the context. Here he's banking on the fact that a police station is unlikely to be a hothouse of high culture. So he's using that weapon to get at us, find our weak spot. Oh, for pity's sake, Danglard, you should have gone in to fight for us!'

'I'm sorry, I didn't see it like that.'

'It's still not too late.'

Mordent: But what about your wife? She spent every evening and morning there. For how many years?

Carvin: Over fifteen years.

Mordent: And you never thought of offering her somewhere with more light, in a less lonely district when she came home at night?

Carvin: Commandant, you don't try to dislodge a limpet from its rock.

Mordent: Meaning?

Carvin: If I had made the mistake of forcing my wife to leave the flat, I'd have been uprooting her, as surely as if I had taken an axe to her. It was for her sake that I kept the apartment on. She would have quite lost her psycho-social bearings in some place with high ceilings on one of the West End boulevards.

Voisenet: You don't believe in the power of adaptation then? One of the signs of human intelligence?

'Voisenet is trying to haul him in – he's on his own ground here, the natural world,' said Adamsberg.

'Won't work.'

'As I saw. I watched this bit twice.'

Carvin: My wife was not intelligent, lieutenant.

Mordent: Why did you marry her, then?

Carvin: For her laugh, commandant. I'm not a man who laughs. And her laugh, which was a joyful sound, attracted everyone, including even that Arab. Not a vulgar laugh, a cackle or a peal, it was a series of little chuckles, like a Seurat painting, so to speak.

Mordent: . . .

Carvin: And I'm going to miss her laugh.

Voisenet: Not as much as you'd miss the two million euros she could have walked away with if you'd divorced.

Carvin: A life-giving laugh has no price on it. Even if we had divorced – and we hadn't reached that stage anyway – I would have carried on being able to hear it.

'I've seen enough,' said Adamsberg stopping the video sharply.

'What about Nassim Bouzid?'

'Seen that too.'

'And what would you say about the two of them? How do their "looks" strike you?'

'Signs, wrinkles, marks, gestures. Not enough, though. This morning before coming to work, I walked the route you'd tracked from the tyres, between the video shop and the murder scene, through the back streets. I found something interesting.'

'We've already timed the journey.'

'Not that, Danglard. The gravel chippings on one street, where there'd been roadworks.'

'What about them?'

'We're agreed, are we, that of the billions of dandelions growing on this earth, no two are identical?'

'Of course.'

'Same thing with drivers. No two alike. Summon Dandelion No. 1, Carvin, for 2 p.m. and Dandelion No. 2, Bouzid, for 3 p.m. We'll take a little drive. And get the fingerprint team to be there when I get back.'

'All right. We've time for lunch.'

'*Drekka borða*,' said Adamsberg with a smile. 'Drink, eat.'

OK, said Danglard to himself. Adamsberg could speak Icelandic – and how had he managed to learn his few words? But since the business over the moray eel, he did seem to have his feet more firmly on the ground.

'One more thing, Danglard,' said Adamsberg, standing up. 'At about two thirty, when I come back with Carvin, put him through another round of questioning. But this time, beat him at his own game. I want him taken down a peg or two. And let the squad see the recording. That'll cheer them up a bit. I want every officer to feel on an equal footing with both him and Nassim Bouzid. Use his own weapons and crush him.'

Danglard went out with a less lacklustre step than usual, holding himself straighter and rendered more cheerful by his new status as 'alpha male' – in which he did not believe at all.

And he had no idea what was going on with the gravel chippings.

IV

MAÎTRE CARVIN WAS A COOL CUSTOMER, NEITHER IMPATIENT NOR hot-tempered, and when Lamarre and Kernorkian came to his chambers to summon him over to the station, interrupting him when he was busy at work, he merely asked for five minutes to clear his desk, and followed them without demur.

'What's it about this time?' he asked.

'The commissaire . . .' Kernorkian began.

'Ah, him. He's back then? I've heard a bit about him.'

'He wants to see both of you, you and Nassim Bouzid.'

'Perfectly normal. I'm quite willing to speak to him as much as he wishes.'

'I don't think he wants to talk, he wants to take you for a drive.'

'That's a little less normal, but I assume he knows what he's doing.'

Adamsberg had eaten lunch in his office, this time rereading the report he had received at Reykjavik airport. He stood to read it, as was his habit, pacing round the room. The commissaire rarely sat down to work if he could help it. As he read, murmuring every word out loud – which took some time – he could not help seeing Voisenet's little spider running across his thoughts from left to right. It was advancing prudently, as if it didn't want to be noticed, or to disturb anyone. But it *was* disturbing him, since Adamsberg now knew, thanks to Froissy's efficiency, that the spider was in his own computer. He put down the report and switched on his screen. Better get to the bottom of it and brush the damn spider out of the way. Better find out what Voisenet was doing with this creature, even this morning, when he should have been concentrating on the approaching meeting and indeed thinking about how to deal with his pestilential fish. So why had he, all the same, called up yet another picture of the recluse spider?

Still standing, he opened the file Froissy had sent and checked back through it. Voisenet had been calling up information about this spider for the last eighteen days. This very morning, he had consulted the main local newspapers in Languedoc-Roussillon in southern France, and followed the subject on social media. There was a lot of passionate debate about this recluse spider, engaged in by people who were variously panic-stricken amateurs, pseudo-experts, pragmatists, ecologists and alarmists. Voisenet had even downloaded some news from last summer when, in the same region, there had been six recluse-spider bites, none of them fatal, but they had caused panic, even in certain national weeklies. And all this because of a rumour, coming from who knew where, spreading its scary breath: had the *American* brown recluse spider been sighted in France? That species was undoubtedly considered dangerous. But where was it, and how many of them could there be? There was a total outbreak of panic until a real specialist stepped in and closed the debate. No, the American variety had never set foot in France. But one of its relations had always been native to the south-east of the country, and was not lethal. Indeed it was a particularly timid creature, not aggressive, living in its hole, and the risk of it meeting a human was correspondingly small. This must be the one in question then, and none other, *Loxosceles rufescens* – Adamsberg couldn't pronounce this Latin term. And that was the end of it.

Until this spring, when this same little spider had bitten two elderly men. And this time, they had both died. This time, the recluse spider had actually killed people. Some commentators argued that the deaths could be explained by the advanced age of the victims. At any rate, these two deaths had launched a polemic stretching to over a hundred pages, as far as Adamsberg could hurriedly estimate. He checked the time on the computer, 13.53, so Maître Carvin would be here any minute. He crossed the large office (still stinking of fish, despite the wide-open windows) and took from the cupboard the keys of the only top-of-the-range car to which the squad had access. But what the hell was Voisenet interested in this spider for? All right, two people had died, and presumably their weakened physical condition had not been enough to protect them from a dose of poison, but did that mean his lieutenant had to keep track of the situation every day for the last eighteen days? Unless, perhaps, one of the victims was a relative of his, or a friend? Adamsberg expelled the recluse from his mind and set off to intercept the lawyer on the pavement, before his officers, who might be forgetful, could let him enter the putrid atmosphere inside the police station.

'You're taking him out in our best car, are you, commissaire?' remarked Retancourt as he went past. 'So you're impressed by Maître Carvin and his haughty ways, too.'

Adamsberg smiled as he looked down at her, head on one side.

'Have you forgotten what I'm like, Retancourt? In just seventeen days?'

'No. I must have missed something.'

'Yes indeed. The gravel chippings, on the way back to the video games centre.'

'Gravel chippings,' she said thoughtfully. 'And you can't tell me any more than that?'

'Yes, I can. No two dandelions and no two drivers are identical on this earth, that's all.'

'That's all? And Danglard was afraid you'd changed. Huh.'

'I'm probably worse than before, but nothing to worry about. Tell me,' he said, swinging the keys from the end of his finger, 'what are your views about losing one's spare car keys? This is a serious question.'

'Simple. You should never lose your spare car keys, commissaire.'

'What if you do?'

'You go in desperate search of them. Spare car keys are something that turns us all into idiots.'

'I lost my mobile phone on Grimsey.'

'Where?'

'In a field, and a sheep trod it into some shit.'

'And you didn't make desperate efforts to get it out?'

'Never underestimate the strength of a sheep's hoof, Retancourt. It will have been shattered.'

'So now you don't have a phone?'

'I've taken the cat's phone. You know, the one that sits on the photo-copier next to the cat. It doesn't work properly though, I think the cat must have pissed on it. All my phones must have some excremental destiny. I don't know how to take that.'

'The cat hasn't done anything to the phone,' Retancourt objected, defending the cat (Snowball) which was the apple of her eye. 'But it's true that when you're texting, that one does "r" for "c" and "p" for "n".'

'Right. So if you get a message saying "Bark soop", you'll know it's from me.'

'That'll make things easier. Not to worry.'

'No.'

'How are they all?' she went on, lowering her voice. 'Gunnlaugur, Rögnvar, Brestir . . .'

'They sent you their fond regards. Believe it or not, Rögnvar has carved your portrait on to the blade of an oar.'

Adamsberg was happy to be back in the company of Retancourt, although he hadn't been able to express this to her, except by a few gestures. This polyvalent goddess as he called her, standing 1m 85, weighing 110 kilos and endowed with the strength of ten men, impressed him enough to make him lose his usual sangfroid. She had unrivalled physical capacity and imperturbable mental equilibrium. To Adamsberg, Retancourt seemed like some tree in a folk tale, on whose branches the entire squad, if lost at night in a dense and storm-tossed forest, would find complete safety. A Druidic oak. Naturally, with all her unusual attributes, the lieutenant did not pretend to have feminine graces, as Noël sometimes vulgarly reminded her. Although, in fact, Retancourt had delicate features in a face which was, it is true, almost square in shape.

He parked the shiny black limousine in front of the station, just as Kernorkian and Lamarre were escorting Carvin towards him. The lawyer shot a quick glance at the commissaire. Shabby dark jacket and trousers, a faded T-shirt that might once have been grey or blue, none of this fitted the idea Maître Carvin had of the rather celebrated chief of this unit. He held out his hand.

'Apparently, monsieur le commissaire, you are going to take me for a drive?'

Without waiting for an answer, Carvin headed for the passenger seat.

'No, maître,' said Adamsberg, handing him the keys, 'I'd like *you* to drive.'

'Oh, you want to test my competence?'

'Something like that.'

'As you wish,' said the lawyer, coming back round the car.

Carvin could not rid himself of his slightly provocative attitude, but Adamsberg noted that he was being more affable towards him than to his colleagues. As far as this man was concerned, a man who strove untiringly to dominate those around him, Adamsberg was boss class. Instinctively, therefore, he considered it more prudent to maintain a respectful distance. Just because a man is shorter than you and is wearing a shabby linen jacket doesn't mean you should underestimate him, if he's the chief.

'I imagine,' the lawyer said, sliding behind the steering wheel, 'that this car doesn't belong to the squad? Or perhaps the public has been misled about the resources at the police's disposal?'

'It belongs to the divisionnaire,' said Adamsberg, fastening his seat belt. 'I get the feeling you drive well, but fast. I've got to get it back to him tonight without a scratch, so I'd ask you to be careful.'

Carvin switched on the engine and smiled.

'Trust me. Where are we going?'

'The car park outside the video games place.'

'And then to the spot where someone killed my wife?'

'To start with, yes.'

The lawyer drove off, flicked the indicator without looking for it first and turned left.

'I suppose you're going to play this game with that Bouzim character as well?'

'*Bouzid*. Yes, of course.'

'I confess I can't see where you're heading with this, commissaire.'

'I still don't know myself, if that's any comfort.'

'I'm not worried. Nice car, this. Very nice.'

'You like cars?'

'What man doesn't?'

'Me for a start, they leave me cold.'

After first parking the car opposite the games arcade, then driving to the rue du Château-des-Rentiers, Carvin stopped at the traffic light where his wife had been run over by his own 4x4.

'Here we are, commissaire. What next?'

'Back to the games room, just as the killer did.'

Adamsberg could read on the lawyer's sardonic lips his scorn for the simplistic stratagem of the commissaire.

'Which way should I go?'

'Go through the side streets. Take the first right, then the next three right turns, and it'll bring us out there.'

'Very well.'

'Be careful, there are roadworks on the rue de l'Ormier, the surface is uneven.'

'Don't worry, I won't damage your car,' said Carvin, moving off.

Four minutes later, they were back at the games arcade. Adamsberg signalled to Carvin to carry on back to the police station.

'Come inside, please,' he said. 'The commandant would like a word with you.'

'Not you?'

'No, not me.'

'The commandant? But I've already talked to him any number of times.'

'This is a different one.'

'It smells of something in here,' said Carvin, wrinkling his nose.

'Yes, we had a delivery,' said Adamsberg.

Danglard introduced himself. Maître Carvin registered the well-cut, English-tailored suit worn by this tall man of unprepossessing looks, with his very pale blue eyes, bent legs and hunched shoulders. But Adamsberg noticed a slight sign of apprehension in the lawyer, not inspired simply by Danglard's choice of clothes. He had recognised in Danglard an enemy of a different calibre from those he had so far faced.

'Nassim Bouzid has already arrived, commissaire,' said Danglard.

'Fine, I'll take him out at once.'

The two suspects came face-to-face in the hall, one following Danglard, the other Adamsberg.

'You bastard, Bouzim!' shouted the lawyer. 'What had she ever done to you? You piece of shit! Barbarian! What tribe do you belong to, the dopeheads? Hashish-eaters . . . !'

Adamsberg and Danglard each took hold of their man by the arm, aided by Retancourt and Lamarre who had run up to assist. Bouzid was the one dealt with by Retancourt, who propelled him back a full six metres, though no one quite understood how she managed it.

'I've never even *met* your wife!' shouted Bouzid.

'Filthy liar! Doesn't the Koran tell you lying is a sin?'

'What makes you think I read the Koran? I don't even believe in God, you ignorant scumbag!'

'I'll kill you, Bouzim!'

They managed to keep the two men apart, and Adamsberg took a good five minutes to calm Nassim Bouzid down, as they stood on the pavement: the other man kept repeating in a shaken voice: 'He started it!' – the way children talk. The commissaire installed him in the driving seat and waited for a while until he felt he had settled down emotionally enough to drive.

Adamsberg made him follow the same circuit as the lawyer, only asking him to do it twice. Before setting off, Bouzid had taken a few minutes to check the positions of the controls, and unlike the lawyer, he talked the whole time during their drive – while asking for instructions, as Carvin had – about his family, his work, that lawyer bastard, this woman who'd been run over, who was *not* his mistress, whom he'd never seen. Terrible thing to run a woman down like that, isn't it? No, Bouzid didn't cheat on his wife, never, when would he have had the time? And anyway, his wife, she was the suspicious kind, she watched him like a hawk. So? How could he possibly have done what they said? He'd never been called to do repairs in the shop where the murdered woman worked. He was too good-natured, that was the problem, always obliging people, he even offered his services free to Adamsberg if the drinks dispenser at the station was out of order. (As a matter of fact, it no longer dispensed soup, but nobody cared.)

On his return, Adamsberg passed the car over to the fingerprint team, explaining precisely what he wanted them to look for, both on the divisionnaire's car and on Carvin's 4x4. Just one thing, which could be quickly checked. Danglard was coming out of his office, his cheeks slightly pinker than usual, as he accompanied the lawyer to the door. Carvin stalked out, his jaw set, avoiding any eye contact and shaking hands only with the commissaire when he came face-to-face with him. Clearly the score was 10–nil to Danglard, an execution carried out with consummate skill, Adamsberg was sure. Who lives by the sword perishes by the sword.

Arms folded, Adamsberg paced round the office. Voisenet had now returned to work, and had realised, as he entered the room, that it did indeed smell like a fish market. With all the windows wide open, there was a ferocious draught and everyone had had to pin down paper files with whatever came to hand, pencil cases, shoes, tins nabbed from Froissy's reserve-food cupboard – wild boar pâté, duck parfait with green pepper. This assortment of contrivances made the office look like a cross between a car boot sale and a charity bazaar, and Adamsberg hoped the divisionnaire would not make a surprise visit to come and fetch his car, and find half the squad minus their shoes in a room stinking of fish.

'Froissy,' he said, 'download the interrogation of Carvin by Danglard to everyone. It'll be entertaining, don't miss it. But first, can you make for me an enlargement of Carvin's hands during his first interrogation, as close up as you can get it, of the ends of his fingers, the fingernails?'

Froissy was a fast worker and a few minutes later she sent Adamsberg a picture of the lawyer's left hand. 'I get best results one hand at a time,' she explained.

'Can you turn up the contrast?'

She did so.

'And enlarge it again.'

Adamsberg looked for a long while at the screen before sitting back up, looking pleased.

'Can you do the same for the right hand?'

'It's on the way, sir. What are you looking for?'

'Do you see, he has round nails? I mean the ends of his nails curl over like a shell at the end of the finger. See? That's the kind of nail us cops particularly like, because they are more likely to capture substances than other types.'

'What substances?'

'I'm looking for earth, some nice brown earth.'

'Right, I'll work on it.'

'What do you mean?'

'To bring up the brown. There you are.'

'Excellent, lieutenant! Now, where can you see the dirt?'

'Under the nails on the thumbs and the ring fingers.'

'Yes, and he still had a bit on his thumbnail even today, one of the corners hardest to clean, especially if it's soft, clinging soil and especially with that shape of nail.'

'Could it be engine oil?'

'No,' said Adamsberg tapping the screen, 'it's earth. But either way, earth or oil, do you think that's normal for a man as fastidious about his appearance?'

'Perhaps he was planting something in the garden – it'll soon be June.'

'That's the kind of thing he'd leave to his wife. Can you print off the close-ups, please? Then get on with the Danglard video. That'll cheer them all up.'

The fingerprint team was putting away its equipment in the back courtyard.

'Sorry, commissaire,' said their leader, stretching his arms. 'We got a print, two actually, thumb and index, on the windscreen of your divisionnaire's car, but nothing on the 4x4. Can't win 'em all.'

'That's fine. Send me the report as soon as you can, with pictures of both windscreens.'

'Not till tomorrow, sir. Two more jobs to do by tonight.'

The office was emptying out as the video began in the chapter room. Adamsberg grabbed Voisenet as he was leaving.

'Voisenet, get your camera, a trowel, gloves and an evidence bag. I'm taking the metal detector. We're not going far, just to the Impasse des Bourgeons.'

'But, commissaire,' Voisenet protested, wondering whether this was some kind of disciplinary action, 'I wanted to see Danglard crushing that lawyer guy.'

'You can look at it afterwards on your own, you'll enjoy it even more.'

Voisenet looked at Adamsberg's face: by his expression, he seemed to have completely forgotten the moray eel business, for good or ill, and was moving on to other things. The eel on the other hand hadn't forgotten *them*, because it had taken care to leave its atrocious smell behind. Although Voisenet well knew that the commissaire did not nurse a grudge, he found it hard to accept, since he was inclined to do so himself.

Once they were in front of the building where the Carvins lived, Adamsberg walked up and down the street – it was a cul-de-sac, wide but not long, so it looked more like a small square.

'Three chestnut trees,' he remarked. 'That's handy.'

'I was just going to tell you, sir. If you want to search their house, I would remind you that we still don't have permission from the examining magistrate. It was the weekend when it happened, and now he's digesting the file.'

'Let's leave him to his digestion, Voisenet, I don't need to go inside.'

'So what are we doing here?'

'Tell me, Voisenet, are you any kind of expert on spiders?'

'Not my field, commissaire. And it's a huge field. Forty-five thousand species in the world, just think of it.'

'Pity. Not that it's important, but I had hoped you could help me, lieutenant. Since I got back from Iceland, I've been checking back over the news. Apart from various murders and galloping pollution, I was intrigued by a little story about spiders.'

Voisenet's dark eyebrows contracted in a frown: he was immediately on his guard.

'What little story, sir?'

'Something called the recluse spider, apparently there've been some cases when it's bitten people in Languedoc-Roussillon, and now, there have been two deaths,' said Adamsberg, as he hauled the metal detector from the boot of the car. 'Let's try that tree first, Voisenet, the one in the middle. Pull up the grids around it.'

Voisenet watched Adamsberg activate the detector without replying. He was a little lost as he listened to the commissaire's remarks, switching between the chestnut trees and the recluse spider. Pulling himself together, he began to follow the circular path of the machine, step by step.

'Nothing under this one,' said Adamsberg, standing upright again. 'Carvin is less subtle than I thought. Let's try the other one, right opposite his building.'

'What are we looking for?' asked Voisenet. 'A metal spider?'

'You'll see, Voisenet,' Adamsberg said with a grin. 'You won't regret missing the video. So this recluse spider and its bites, that doesn't ring any bells?'

'Well, yes, in fact it does,' said Voisenet, still moving round the base of the tree. 'I followed that story up a bit.'

'You followed it up a lot, you mean. Why, Voisenet?'

'A long time ago, my grandfather was bitten on the leg by a recluse spider. Gangrene set in, and the leg had to be amputated below the knee. Well, he survived, but he'd lost his leg. And he used to like going jogging in the evening, even when he was eighty-six. I used to go with him. "Listen, son," he would say, "it's the time of day when everything tilts over. Listen to the sounds: some animals going to sleep, others waking up. Listen to the flowers folding their petals." '

'Flower petals?'

'Yes.'

'And they make a sound when they close up?'

'No. Anyway, he couldn't go jogging any more, he wasted away and died nine months later. That's why I hate recluse spiders.'

The two men froze. The detector had just pinged.

'A coin, maybe,' said Voisenet.

'Pass me your gloves.'

Adamsberg carefully examined the earth in the quarter-circle they had covered.

'See there,' he said, pointing. 'No dead leaves on that bit. Someone's been digging there recently.'

'But what are we looking for?' Voisenet persisted.

The commissaire gently removed the topsoil on a patch about ten centimetres wide and about eight centimetres deep. Then he stopped and looked up at Voisenet with a smile.

'Spare car keys are objects that can turn us all into idiots. You really don't want to lose them.'

Moving more earth aside, he cleared the earth from around the object his fingers had encountered.

'And what do we have here, my dear Voisenet?'

'Some car keys.'

'Right, photograph them in situ. Close-ups, middle distance and wide angle.'

Voisenet obeyed and then Adamsberg used two fingers to extricate the keys, holding them by their ring. He dangled them in front of his lieutenant.

'Pass me the evidence bag, Voisenet. We'll leave the earth on the keys, don't brush it off. Now we put the grids back and pack up. Call the squad, and get them to haul Carvin out of his chambers again. He's to be taken into custody.'

Adamsberg stood up, brushed the knees of his trousers, then pushed back his hair, leaving bits of earth in it.

'Sometimes, Voisenet, weak and passive individuals who never say no to anyone and fall over themselves to help others, can kill in a sudden outburst of frustration. It could have been that way with Bouzid.'

'Passive-aggressive types.'

'Yeah, right. But sometimes the opposite kind, the arrogant, over-confident ones, who look dangerous, really are dangerous. That's Carvin. Their greed is like a demon, it grows a new mouth every year.'

'News to me.'

'Well, it's true, Voisenet,' said Adamsberg taking off the gloves. 'It gets to the point where everything in their path has to be crushed. Literally crushed, in this case. Is your moray eel as aggressive as that?'

Voisenet shrugged.

'It's a timid creature,' he said. 'It hides in crevices.'

'Like the recluse.'

'Commissaire, what is it with the recluse?'

'Well, you followed it up, didn't you, Voisenet?'

'I already told you why *I* was interested. But what about you?'

'Wish I knew, lieutenant.'

V

THE NEWS — WITHOUT FURTHER EXPLANATION — THAT CARVIN WAS TO be taken into custody immediately, on a charge of murder, had preceded the two men by the time they returned to the squad's headquarters. Still smelling strongly of fish, the large open-plan room was buzzing, none of the officers sitting at their desks. They were all on their feet, arguing, debating, wondering. How had Adamsberg managed this, when he'd only just returned from the fogs of the north? It was the fingernails, someone said, he asked to see the man's nails. No, it was when he viewed the guys being questioned, he read it in their faces. What about the windscreen, there was all that stuff about the windscreen, wasn't there? Yeah, but look, what was there on the windscreen of the 4x4? Nothing at all, in the end. The officers were divided between relief that there was an outcome, and frustration, as if the carpet had been pulled from under their feet far too quickly, without explanation, and with no time to anticipate how it would end. Adamsberg had arrived back only that morning, not having bothered to read the report – that much was clear to them all, though no one had said anything – and now, at seven in the evening, the curtain had come down suddenly, in a confusing welter of acts and questions.

Danglard and Retancourt both invariably deplored this kind of confusion. Leaders of the pragmatic branch of the squad, believers in linear logic and rational calculation, they were annoyed at the way Adamsberg had conducted the day's work, pursuing his haphazard inquiries, with few words to anyone. Even if there was a result – as it now seemed – the commissaire's methods of operation always seemed erratic to them, quite the opposite of their Cartesian approach. But this evening, Danglard made no objection, since he was still on a high after his victorious joust with Maître Carvin – which had earned him a memorable success with the team, when they watched the video. As for Retancourt, her double satisfaction at seeing Adamsberg again and learning that Rögnvar, back in Grimsey, had carved her portrait on an oar, prevented her from voicing any criticism. She could still hear in her head the voice of the crippled fisherman in that inn in Iceland on their last day, she could still see his hand, gripping her knee. *'Listen to this, Vióletta, listen carefully. No, don't write it down, you'll always remember it.'* Rögnvar, the anti-positivist par excellence, Rögnvar, the crazy man, the weirdo. And at that moment at least, she had loved him, with his long, matted blond hair, his weather-beaten wrinkles and his missing leg.

Adamsberg walked across the room, specks of earth in his hair, and smudges of dirt on his trousers. His eyes now showed marks of fatigue. He wedged himself upright against a table, and Estalère instinctively hurried to fetch him a coffee. The boss might do things slowly, without saying much, he might seem all over the place, but days like that can wear you out. In the young man's view, wandering about and jumping from one thing to another was more tiring than going in a straight line.

'I'll just take a couple of minutes to fill you in,' Adamsberg began. 'There was a little dirt in the corners of Carvin's fingernails, on the thumbs and the ring fingers, and it seemed out of place for a man like that. But you already knew that.'

'No, commissaire, we didn't know about that,' Retancourt interrupted him.

'Yes, you did, lieutenant,' said Adamsberg with a sigh. 'I didn't make a secret of it. I told Lieutenant Froissy about it, because I wanted enlargements of the photographs showing his hands. Keep each other in the picture, I can't talk to everyone individually about every detail. So, dirt then, and in my view it was probably earth. Because Carvin's spare car keys were nowhere to be found. As *you* knew, Retancourt, because we'd had a word about it. And you said, "Our spare car keys turn us all into idiots." If we lose them, we get distraught, it's as if some safety barrier has collapsed. Many people would think that to chuck them in the Seine would be too painful. And Maître Carvin is the kind of man who takes a shower, not a bath. An action man, always in a hurry.'

'Excuse me, commissaire,' said Mercadet.

'Excuse you for what?'

'The shower?'

'A shower is less efficient at getting ingrained dirt out than a bath, which soaks everything away. Carvin had to lose his spare car keys so that he could accuse Bouzid of taking them. But why actually throw them away, if he could find some other way to keep them? If he could find a hiding place that would be inexpugnable – is that the right word, Danglard?'

'Yes.'

'Thanks. Well, of course, he couldn't hide the keys at home, or in his chambers. And the idea of hiding something usually suggests burying it. A simple but excellent idea. Bury the keys in the earth under the chestnut tree opposite his windows. Covered by the grid. A very good plan. If it hadn't been for the little residue of earth under his nails, it would never have occurred to me. If it was me, I'd have thrown the keys away. Lamarre and Kernorkian, when Carvin gets here, take samples of the matter under his fingernails, so that we can get it analysed and compare it with the earth still attached to the keys. The spare keys were luckier than the wife: he wanted to save his own life, but not his wife's. There are men like that, who have a talent for making choices.'

Voisenet brought out the evidence bag from his rucksack and passed it round. 'Take care,' he warned them, 'don't rub the earth off the keys.'

'But what about the windscreen?' asked Justin. 'We didn't know anything about the windscreen.'

'Oh really, Justin? But I told you about the gravel chippings, on a section of road that we knew the 4x4 had travelled. I told you, Danglard, and I told you too, Retancourt. Dammit all, why don't you pass things on? And I did say that just as there are no two dandelions alike, there are no two motorists alike. Didn't I? So it was easy enough to see why I took Carvin and Bouzid both out in a car, to see how they would drive when they reached the gravel.'

'I still don't get it,' said Lamarre frankly, twisting a button on his jacket, always the same one.

Lamarre, who was diffident, and had retained from his time in the gendarmerie a painful military stiffness, was honest to the point of blundering, and readily admitted that he couldn't follow a train of thought, a confession many others preferred to avoid. In this, he was a valuable asset, because, like Estalère, he saved his colleagues from asking a lot of foolish questions.

'We'd checked the 4x4 inside out,' Adamsberg said. 'But we didn't bother with the windscreen, because normally no one touches the windscreen.'

'I still don't get it,' said Lamarre.

'Gravel chippings, windscreen, what do drivers do about them?'

Lamarre remained for a moment head down and his clenched fist against his mouth.

'Oh,' he began slowly, 'you mean people that when they're driving over gravel, put a finger on the windscreen, in case bits jump up, to reduce the impact? I've got an uncle does that.'

'Well, that's what Bouzid does too. A careful, almost nervous driver. He puts his fingers on the windscreen, though actually no one knows if that does any good. Everyone has their own little ways.'

'Well, I do that too,' said Justin. 'You don't think it works?'

'Never mind whether it works or not, Justin, you're still going to do it, aren't you?'

'Oh. OK.'

'I had Bouzid drive over the route twice. And both times, he put his fingers on the windscreen when we drove over that stretch of gravel, even though he was talking a lot, and thinking about other things. It was a pure reflex action.'

'And Carvin?'

'Well, of course, he's a fast, aggressive, show-off sort of driver. He doesn't bother putting his fingers on the glass. He likes making the gravel fly.'

'Lots of people like that,' remarked Danglard. 'It's a nice noise.'

'And the inside surface of a windscreen,' Adamsberg went on, 'is usually both greasy and dust-covered. If you put a finger on it, even wearing a glove, it's going to show up. And there was nothing at all on the 4x4. Which means Bouzid never drove it.'

'But why use the divisionnaire's fancy car?' asked Retancourt. 'To impress the lawyer?' She was annoyed with herself for not having noted the detail of dirt under Carvin's fingernails, when she had had him sitting in front of her. And for not having pieced together the elements of evidence Adamsberg had given her. But while the commissaire may have thought he was speaking clearly, he was wrong, since you couldn't spend all your time trying to work out his incomplete riddles.

'Because that car is the same make as the 4x4. Same angle of windscreen. We have to be as precise as possible, so that they can't pick holes in it. Our evidence is actually pretty weak. The spare car keys for instance: a good defence lawyer could say that Bouzid had buried them to incriminate the husband. Which wouldn't have been very clever of him, since the hiding place is hard to find. But then Bouzid has no dirt under his fingernails. And he takes showers too.'

'How do we know that?'

'Because I asked him, Retancourt,' said Adamsberg, a little surprised.

'Well, with luck then,' said Justin, 'we'll have Carvin's prints on the keys, not Bouzid's.'

'Whatever we've got,' said Danglard, 'at least we know now for sure that Bouzid wasn't driving the car. No human hairs, no fingerprints on the windscreen, plus some extra dog hairs when there aren't any in his own car. We'll get Carvin.'

'*You'll* get him, commandant,' said Adamsberg, 'by extracting a confession from him. And for reasons you well know, you're the one who's going to make him spit it out. This man who doesn't shrink from crushing a woman to death in the street. Here he is, command- ant, this is your moment. Take your time, I'll be watching through the screen.'

'He's going to say it stinks in our offices,' said Noël.

'He's already noticed that. If he mentions it again, you can tell him we went fishing for a repulsive creature, a moray eel.'

'No, don't do that!' protested Voisenet.

'All right, we won't say its name. What's happening to it now?'

'My mother will just have finished boiling it.'

'There you are then, all in order.'

Adamsberg disappeared into his office at the back of the big room. Voisenet followed him straight inside.

'There's been another one, sir,' he whispered, as if they were sharing a dangerous secret.

'Another what?' asked Adamsberg, carelessly slinging his jacket over a chair.

'Another victim of the recluse.'

The commissaire spun round sharply, his eyes more focused than they had been all day.

'Tell me.'

'A man, same area.'

'How old?'

'Eighty-three. He's not dead, but he's already developed septicae-mia. The outlook's not good.'

Adamsberg took a few paces across the office then stopped short, folding his arms.

'Well, we don't want to miss Danglard questioning the lawyer,' he said.

'No, absolutely.'

'Tell me about it later, with all the details. This evening perhaps? Are you tired?'

'No, commissaire. Well, I'm not tired of the recluse.'

'Did you give Froissy the photos of the car keys?'

'Yes.'

'Right, fine. Better talk about it outside the office.'

'About what? Froissy and the keys?'

'No, about the recluse spider. After we've heard Danglard do the questioning, come round to my place, I'll rustle up something for you to eat.' Adamsberg thought for a moment, head on one side.

'Pasta OK for you?'

Even before entering the interrogation room with Danglard, the silent and unexplained procedure of taking samples of dirt from under his fingernails had unsettled the lawyer. Adamsberg had been present, and Carvin's features were transformed by fear. People who have a highly elevated idea of themselves have never envisaged falling one day. And when it happens, they collapse, they're stunned, unprepared for it, all their substance vanishes in the stupor of failure. They have no middle ground, no shades of grey, no capacity for anticipation. That's the way they are.

'No, Maître Carvin,' said Adamsberg as he walked behind the lawyer, 'don't go thinking I'll be searching for similar earth samples all over France – it is earth, isn't it? It's just to confirm something. I've already found your spare car keys. Those damned keys. How childish to want to hang on to them, don't you think? Little children are like that, they want to own everything, hold on to it, not lose it, little trifles, bits of string. And that desire can move them to violence. But when they're about eight, it seems to go away. They've developed more of a sense of security. Not in every case though. A child can be willing to kill for a glass marble. But he *doesn't* kill anyone, he shouts, he has a tantrum. An adult, who is greedy for possession, *can* kill: he can run over – twice! – a woman who weighs fifty-two kilos, a woman with a charming laugh. But that's because the marble has turned into two million, one hundred and thirty-eight thousand, one hundred and twenty-three euros. And fourteen centimes. Let's not forget the centimes. Because they are the surviving echo of that glass marble.'

The commissaire left the interrogation room and went to sit behind the one-way mirror, where over a dozen colleagues were already crammed together, driving up the temperature in the little viewing room. It was hot and sweaty and the persistent aroma of moray eel didn't help. Froissy, who was a sensitive soul, was sitting on a chair and fanning herself. Retancourt remained impassive, showing no sign of sweat. Just another of her many extraordinary qualities. Adamsberg tended to say that Retancourt could convert her energy into as many different capacities as the circumstances warranted. He supposed that just now she had converted it into cooling down her organism and suppressing her sense of smell.

Danglard began courteously, without irony or aggression.

' "Ah money! Whether you have it or whether you don't, it's always the root of all evil." No, don't bother chasing up that quotation, maître, it's from a popular author, writing for ordinary people. "Whether you *have* it" – in my view, that's when it does much more damage. We need some kind of vigilant sensor, calibrated to react when our fortune and our power increase, so that it can scan any modifications in our brain cells, and set off alarm signals. What do you think about that, Maître Carvin?'

Carvin did not move a muscle, or even shiver. The looming spectacle of his defeat had plunged him into a catatonic state. Danglard took over three hours to extract his confession, through the use of a thousand banderillas. It was a dazzling display of carefully thought-out questions, contrasting and unpredictable, and they finally got the better of the lawyer's last defences. It was 22.35 when the commandant came out of the room, his leg muscles trembling with the effort.

'I'm starving,' he said simply. 'He is too. Did you hear him? He wants some grated carrot. Grated carrot!'

'He's in shock,' said Adamsberg.

Danglard headed quickly to his own office where he poured himself a glass of white wine, then another, without taking the time to sit down.

'Anyone coming for supper?' he asked. 'Drinks on me at the Brasserie des Philosophes. Champagne for starters.'

About ten of his colleagues went out with the commandant, as the night shift arrived, and Adamsberg slipped away, saying he needed some sleep.

VI

AS HE TAPPED QUIETLY ON ADAMSBERG'S FRONT DOOR, VOISENET HAD
the sensation, both amusing and worrying, that he was taking part in
a minor conspiracy. And also a sudden feeling that he must be an
idiot. Fretting over this spider, sneaking out at night to discuss it in
private, none of that made sense. He was still thinking about Carvin's
collapse, about Danglard's brilliant show of intellect, and the discovery of the car keys. All of that existed, and justified their efforts and
their motivation. But this spider, well, no.

Adamsberg was watching the pasta cooking and motioned to his
lieutenant to sit down.

'There's someone in your garden, commissaire.'

'It's just my neighbour, old Lucio. Every night, he goes out there
under the beech tree with his beer. God protects him from spiders.
When he was a child, he lost an arm during the Spanish Civil War.
But on the arm he lost, he'd been bitten by a spider, and he's forever
telling me the arm was lost before he could finish scratching the bite.
So it carries on itching. He's turned this into a saying that applies to
every life situation, according to him. Never let an itch persist, give it
a good scratch, draw blood if you have to, or it will go on itching all
your livelong days.'

'I don't get it.'

'Never mind,' said Adamsberg, putting some tomato sauce and cheese on the table. 'Get two plates out of the cupboard, will you, it's nearly ready. Cutlery in the drawer, glasses up above.'

'There's wine?'

'Bottle under the sink. Help yourself to the pasta, it cools quickly.'

'So my mother always says.'

'Did she finish boiling that eel?'

'All I need to do now is disengage the skeleton. It's going to be a whopper.'

'You said it.'

Adamsberg uncorked the bottle of wine, opened the jar of tomato sauce, and thought for a moment before passing it to the lieutenant.

'You don't know what's in this stuff. Forty-three kinds of pesticide, crude oil, additives, colouring, bit of horseflesh, nail varnish. We have no idea what we're putting in our mouths.'

'The recluse doesn't either.'

'What do you mean?'

Voisenet realised that the light bulb that had switched on in Adamsberg's head was still there. His expression was usually so vague that you couldn't miss it when the spark appeared in his eyes.

'It eats insects, like birds do. So it must eat insecticides. That's part of the big debate on the internet to explain the deaths.'

'Go on.'

'I don't know whether I ought to "go on", sir. What are we up to with this recluse spider? What business is it of ours?'

'Put it another way. What is the recluse up to?'

'It's biting people, and by bad luck it chanced on some old men. And they died.'

'And why did it attack just old people?'

'I think it might have bitten anyone, but we only noticed the old men. Usually, like all spiders, the recluse gives a harmless bite. That's to say, it doesn't inject any venom at all. The bite's to warn you off, but the spider doesn't want to waste venom on humans, we're not her food supply. With a mild bite, all you see is two little red spots on your skin and nobody bothers about them. Someone who's bitten doesn't even know he's come across a recluse. See? Or else, another possibility, it only empties one of its two venom glands, to save its supply. And the reaction will still be quite minor. Same result, no one's bothered. And there are some people who don't react to spider bites at all. They might have a little pink mark, followed by a swelling, coming to a bit of a head, but it all goes away on its own.'

'So?'

'Well,' said Voisenet, refilling their glasses, 'that could mean that fifteen people have been bitten since the warm weather started, but they never noticed. Except for these three men.'

Adamsberg shook his head.

'But you said, didn't you, that the recluse spider isn't aggressive?'

'No, that's right, it hides away in holes, it's timid. Hence its name. It cloisters itself from the world. It doesn't spin a web in the corner of a window like the big spiders you see round the house.'

'Big black ones, yes?'

'Yes. Harmless by the way. But the recluse just comes out prudently at night to feed and once a year to mate.'

'So it rarely bites anyone?'

'Only if it has no choice. You could have recluse spiders in your house for years and never see one or get bitten. Unless you happen to put your hand on it as it creeps along in its timid way.'

'Right. So a bite is very rare. And how many bites were recorded last year?'

'Something like five or seven for the whole season.'

'And now we've had three, these old people, in three weeks. Not to mention the fifteen others that might not have been noticed, and the season's only just beginning. Do we have any statistics about recluse bites?'

'No, because nobody's ever been bothered about them. Their bite isn't fatal.'

'We're getting to it now, Voisenet. Were there any elderly victims last year?'

'Yes.'

'And did they die?'

'No.'

'Young victims?'

'No, they didn't die either.'

'Did everyone who was bitten have the same reaction, what you call a minor one?'

'According to what I read, yes.'

'See what I'm getting at, Voisenet? There's something wrong. Three old men have been bitten, and three have died, or as good as. And that's something new. Sorry, there's no dessert, no fruit or anything.'

'Well, fruit is stuffed as full of pesticides as spiders are. As is wine,' added the lieutenant, examining his glass before taking another sip.

Adamsberg cleared the table, pulled his chair up in front of the empty grate, and sat down with his feet on the fender.

'Three dead, or as good as,' Voisenet repeated. 'Agreed, it isn't normal. And that's exactly what people are talking about.'

'What's it like, a *bad* reaction to a recluse bite? Why would you die?'

'Well, its venom isn't neurotoxic, which is the case for most spiders. It's necrotic. That's to say, it decomposes the flesh around the wound. The necrosis can spread up to twenty centimetres long and ten across.'

'I've seen some photos of the wounds online,' Adamsberg said. 'Black, deep and repulsive. Like gangrene.'

'That's right, it is a kind of gangrene. But with antibiotics, it regresses, and can be healed. Sometimes the necrosis is serious enough for plastic surgery to be needed, to get the limb looking more or less normal. One time, this guy lost his ear. Eaten away.'

'Sounds atrocious.'

'Ah, you see, my moray eel seems nice and clean by contrast.'

'Yes, I guess so.'

'Although an eel's bite can cause a bad infection too, because of the bacteria between its teeth. And that's the point, sir, the necrosis caused by the spider can trigger a general sepsis or reach vital organs. Or it can destroy the red blood corpuscles, and damage the liver and kidneys. But for heaven's sake, that's extremely rare! Only in the case of very young children or very old people. Whose immune system has either not got going properly or has started to fail.'

Voisenet stood up in turn, took a few steps, then leaned on his chair.

'That's what we have, sir. Three men, whose bites were fatal because they were old. And that's it. End of story.'

'Because they were old, end of story?' repeated Adamsberg. 'But in that case, what are all these people discussing on the internet?'

'Well, everything. Except that there's no police investigation going on.'

'What are they talking about then?' Adamsberg insisted.

'The cause of death. There are two theories. The one that's causing the most panic online is that the spiders have somehow mutated: because they've absorbed so many insecticides and other rubbish that changes their organism, the venom of recluse spiders may have mutated to become deadly.'

Adamsberg left the hearth to fetch a packet of cigarettes left by his son Zerk on the sideboard. He pulled out a crumpled one.

'And the other theory?'

'Global warming. The power of the venom is increased by heat. The most dangerous spiders in the world live in hot countries. Last year, France had one of its hottest summers ever. Then the following winter wasn't wintry at all. And now, it's already been abnormally warm for three weeks. So the toxicity of the venom could have increased, possibly the size of the creatures too, and their glands.'

'That's not daft.'

'Daft or not, commissaire, it's nothing to do with us.'

'I need to know more. About the victims and about the recluse.'

'About the victims? Are you serious?'

'Something's wrong somewhere, Voisenet. It isn't normal.'

'OK. Global warming, pesticides? Do you find it normal that we can't eat apples any more?'

'No, I don't. Is there somewhere in Paris where I could find some specialists on insects?'

'Spiders *aren't* insects.'

'Ah yes, of course, Veyrenc already told me that.'

'In the Natural History Museum, there's a lab devoted to spiders. But please don't go dragging me over there, sir.'

After his lieutenant had left, Adamsberg went back to sit down, rubbing his neck to get rid of a vague tension. This feeling had come over him for the first time when he was looking at Voisenet's computer screen and had come face-to-face with the recluse spider. The tension had been accompanied by a slight malaise. A minor, passing trouble, that surfaced if he talked about the spider, then disappeared. It would go over, it was going over already. Something itching, as Lucio would undoubtedly have said.

VII

TWO DAYS AFTER CARVIN'S ARREST, THE SERIOUS CRIME SQUAD WENT into paperwork mode, something that was always accompanied by a nervous silence, with people tiptoeing round the office, shoulders bent, faces tense and concentrated, or sitting with eyes glued to their screens. In the same way, the cat, curled up on the warm photocopier, its head scarcely visible and its fur laid down flat, seemed to have shrunk by a third of its normal size. Retancourt, who was the cat's principal carer, assisted by Mercadet, had noted that the creature seemed sensitive to paperwork phases, as others were to those of the moon, and tended to curl into a tight ball more often than during the active stage of an investigation. Not that Retancourt watched it constantly. But she did fill its bowl three times a day. And three times a day she had to take the cat up to the first floor, into the room with the drinks machine. Because the cat refused to eat anywhere else, and would have allowed itself to starve to death rather than eat a meal on the ground floor. One had to carry it upstairs at such times, even though in its infrequent playful moods, it was quite capable of climbing up and coming down the stairs in a sprightly fashion. The cat dictated, Retancourt obeyed, because this great ball of fluff had once saved her life. During the paperwork phase, Retancourt did not even try to unfold the creature, but picked up its soft bulk in two hands, like an offering.

The previous day had brought the squad the last elements of the investigation, like the last wayward surges of a falling tide. Analysis had confirmed that the earth under Carvin's fingernails and clinging to the car keys was identical. At six in the evening, the lawyer had been transferred to temporary custody at the Santé prison. A prison where, inmates claimed, the courtyard walls were so filthy you were afraid to lean against them, in case you got stuck.

The paperwork phase always followed the same protocol. Each officer involved had to write up his or her own actions. These reports went to Commandant Mordent, who took it upon himself to sort out this disparate mass of paper, while Froissy and Mercadet assembled the photographic evidence and forensic reports. The whole lot was then delivered to Commandant Danglard, who would be responsible for the final draft of the official report, its completeness, accuracy, coherence and readability. By some good fortune, since this was an exhausting task, Danglard, who had a quasi-neurotic passion for paperwork and the written word in all its forms, was the only member of the squad who actually liked this stage. His reports were regarded as outstanding by the hierarchy and contributed, alongside their detection results, to the reputation of the squad.

In his capacity as an officer concerned in the investigation, Adamsberg too was supposed to give an account of his actions and words. Avoiding writing himself, he dictated an oral account to Justin, who tidied it up for him. At the end of the process, all Adamsberg had to do was sign Danglard's report, which was known as The Book, on account of the perfection of its form.

For the third time, the commissaire called a thirty-minute halt with Justin. He switched on his computer and plunged back into the web of the recluse spider. The third victim had died in the night at the hospital in Nîmes, carried off by one of the worst consequences of the venomous toxins: necrosis of the vital organs.

Adamsberg had already noted, under the heading 'Recluse or Violin Spider', a few facts about the two previous victims.

Albert Barral, born in Nîmes, died three weeks ago, 12 May, aged 84; insurance broker, divorced, two children.

Fernand Claveyrolle, born in Nîmes, died a week after Barral, on 20 May, aged 84; art teacher, twice married and divorced, no children.

To whom he now added: *Claude Landrieu, also born in Nîmes, died 2 June, aged 83; shopkeeper, married three times, five children.*

And that very day, a local newspaper reported that a woman, Jeanne Beaujeu, who had just returned from three weeks' holiday and heard about the deaths, had gone to hospital in Nîmes asking to have her own wound, now healing, to be examined. She stated that she had been bitten by a spider on 8 May, but since the bite had not spread beyond a slight irritation, she had merely taken the medicine prescribed by her doctor. She was forty-five.

Adamsberg stood up and went to gaze at the lime tree outside his window. So it wasn't just old people. As Voisenet would no doubt point out to him. Sure enough, returning to his desk, he found an email from the lieutenant:

See that? A woman of 45 had a non-fatal bite. It's because they were old!

To which Adamsberg replied:

Thought you were dropping the whole subject. You should be sweating over your report.

You too, sir.

Justin, punctual as ever, turned up at the door that moment, the half-hour pause being up. Back to the report. Adamsberg closed down the screen and, still standing, described to the junior officer his two car journeys with Carvin and Bouzid.

'Just as there are no two identical dandelions in the world,' he added.

'I can't write that,' said Justin, shaking his head. 'It'll only get us into trouble.'

'As you like.'

Then Adamsberg sent Justin across to the forensic team which had examined the windscreens, and immediately went back to his computer, plunging into the social media which had sprung into activity once more, following the report of a fourth spider bite. The polemic inspired by this non-harmful case centred on the existence or otherwise of some kind of mutation in the recluse spider.

At 6.06 p.m., there was a sudden aggressive post from someone writing as Léo.

Léo: *You're pissing us all off with this ageist stuff. I'm 80 years old, I got bitten by a spider on 26 May, and I didn't make a big fuss about it, didn't even see the doc. And here I am.*

Arach: *Good on you, Léo. That's reassuring.*

Léo: *Just got a little blister, that's all.*

Mig: *No mutation then?*

Cerise33: *Nobody suggested they'd all mutated.*

Zorba: *Whatever, there are still way too many bites. Either the spiders have got more aggressive, cos of the insects they eat, or there are more of them cos of the heat. Or maybe cos there's not so many birds around these days.*

Craig22: *Zorba's right. It's 2 June today and there've been 5 bites. That's a lot. In 3 months how many will there be? 40? And people have died!*

Frod: *Yeah but they were old.*

Léo: *Can you just stop this shit about the old? You'll be old one day too.*

Arach: *Calm down, Léo, no one's getting at you. But maybe you've got a good constitution.*

Léo: *39 years working a crane, all weathers. So what does that tell you about my constitution, eh?*

Adamsberg added to his list:

Jeanne Beaujeu, 45, first victim in order of date, bitten on 8 May, healing up.

Léo, 80, crane operator, bitten on 26 May, just a blister, healed itself.

Then he read another email from Voisenet.

Seen that site with the guy Léo? Not all the old people die. But Craig22 is right. Too many bites, it isn't even high summer.

Adamsberg replied:

Thought you were dropping it.

Yes I am!

Doesn't look like it. But there are years when we get plagues of ladybirds, aren't there?

Must be something like that. A plague of recluses. Many more bites, and three old guys who couldn't fight off the venom. That's it. You should drop it too, commissaire.

I'm not following this, I'm doing my report.

Me too.

Adamsberg leaned back in his chair. Perhaps the spider had bitten him too. Just its *name* seemed to trigger something in him, piercing his thoughts, mingling with that first memory of looking at Voisenet's computer screen while smelling the awful stink of his moray eel. The stiff neck had come back and gone again several times over the last three days, a fleeting visitor but a persistent one.

And all that because of a word, a sound. Which had nothing to do, for instance, with the Lac de Cluses, where his father used to take the family paddling, a dazzling memory of being soaking wet. Unlike the grey floating cobwebs this spider seemed to bring with it, concealing perhaps some hidden fear. Adamsberg sat upright. It would pass. He had completed the report with Justin's help by eight thirty. Most of the officers had left for home by then. Not Danglard though. The commandant had wandered into his office while he was still dictating to Justin, leaning on the open window. And Adamsberg had not had time to hide his note with the names of the spider's five victims. Danglard had seen it. And the commissaire knew that when Danglard saw something written down, he read it, and when he'd read it, he'd remember it. And he was certainly not going to appreciate the heading 'Recluse or Violin Spider' at the top of the sheet. He would know that the boss must already have done an internet search for it.

Adamsberg sensed that Danglard would surely be waiting for him this evening. He quickly telephoned Lieutenant Veyrenc.

'Louis, still here?'

'Just leaving.'

'Anything on this evening?'

'Remains of shepherd's pie.'

'Home-made?'

'No, shop-bought.'

'So, how about supper with me at La Garbure?'

'You're after local atmosphere, are you? And you need me?'

Garbure is a traditional dish of the Pyrenees region, and you probably have to have grown up there to like this cabbage soup mixed with other home-grown root vegetables, and if possible some pork shank. At the restaurant called La Garbure, they usually added duck leg confit. What was more, the proprietress had a weakness for Veyrenc's chiselled face, his rather feminine lips and the fourteen russet locks contrasting with the rest of his dark hair.

'I just might bring along an extra diner,' Adamsberg explained. 'Who won't be in too good a mood, I fear.'

'Danglard?'

'How did you guess?'

'He's been traipsing round the office muttering to himself for the last hour, preoccupied, anxious even. But no one knows why.'

'I do.'

'Ah. Where is the wind blowing you this time, Jean-Baptiste?'

'Towards the recluse spider.'

'The one there's been stuff about in the papers, down south? Biting people?'

'The very same.'

'I see,' said Veyrenc.

Not that Adamsberg presumed that Louis Veyrenc de Bilhc (to give him his full name) would defend his cause, or in any way support his curiosity about the wicked doings of the spider. But the thought of having to justify himself under Danglard's disapproving and piercing gaze bothered him, the more so since he could not really explain it. Still, Danglard, however upset he was, would never pick an open fight with Veyrenc. No one did. Or any other kind of fight. Not that they feared a violent response from Veyrenc, such as might come from Retancourt or Noël. He was a calm person. But his face and body expressed a kind of granite density, against which you would dash your teeth and claws to no effect. And the quickness of his mind adapted to every bend in the road, without ever seeming surprised or taken aback.

Both natives of the Béarn region, Adamsberg and Veyrenc had inherited from their mountain childhood some unbreakable material – suppleness in one case, stability in the other. Whereas a puff of air could waft Danglard into the wastelands of anguish.

VIII

DANGLARD HAD VEHEMENTLY REFUSED TO SWALLOW A SINGLE HELPING of garbure, which to him meant a soup concocted from leftover vegetables, fit only for hardened mountain-dwellers. He was delicately making his way through some stuffed suckling pig. Since the first course (duck liver pâté) accompanied by a glass of Jurançon, his mood had lifted. The best way to nip in the bud any of the commandant's growing objections to something was to take him out to dinner, and make sure it was a good one. But for all that, he never lost sight of the trajectory he was launched on. Just as wine had never made him forget anything. And he could not be intimidated by other people. He was the only person who could fill himself with dread.

'Don't beat about the bush, Danglard,' said Adamsberg, who was feeling more light-hearted. 'Come on, let's have it.'

'I'm not beating about any bush. I'm eating my food while it's hot.'

'As Voisenet's mother recommends.'

'As everyone's mother recommends,' said Veyrenc, helping himself to more garbure.

'It's called a recluse spider, also known as the violin spider, because of its markings,' Adamsberg insisted.

'Its Latin name is *Loxosceles rufescens*,' said Danglard with precision.

'*Loxosceles reclusa* in the Americas, but *rufescens* over here. There are hundreds of species.'

Estelle, the proprietress of the restaurant, a woman of forty or so, came over to ask Veyrenc whether he wished her to warm up the garbure, because it was not a good idea to eat it cold. She did so while laying a hand on his shoulder. Veyrenc refused with a smile, a smile that with an almost magnetic effect prevented her lightly posed hand leaving his shoulder. Adamsberg's glance met Veyrenc's brown eyes. The days when they had crossed swords over a woman were long gone.

'Known to you, commandant?' Adamsberg asked.

'Who, the woman who owns this place? Vaguely. You've tried to make me eat that soup here before.'

'No, I meant the recluse spider. It's known to you?'

'No, but I've read about it.'

And Adamsberg knew that Danglard would have been able to read, in two hours, thirty times more than he had now read himself.

'And why did you read about it?' he asked, while signalling to Estelle that she could bring them their cheese: a mature ewe's milk Tomme. 'Creepy-crawlies aren't your thing.'

'Just a minute, commissaire. I'd like red wine with the cheese.'

'Here, that'll be Madiran.'

'Yes, I know about your regional specialities.'

Once his glass was full and the cheese in front of him, Danglard became visibly more relaxed.

'Because I saw that note lying on your desk,' he replied.

'I know. And that's why you're here.'

'Names of the "victims", ages, occupations, dates of death, makes it look like the start of an investigation, doesn't it? I should be informed if there are upcoming jobs for the squad.'

'You don't mean that, Danglard. It isn't an investigation.'

'In that case, I was mistaken. If it's a game, then that's another matter.'

Adamsberg's expression suddenly darkened.

'No, it's not a game.'

'Well, what is it then?'

'Five victims, three deaths,' said Veyrenc. 'In such a short space of time. There might be –'

'Might be?' Danglard interrupted him.

'– some shadow looming over that.'

'One that might spread its wings,' Adamsberg added.

Danglard shook his head and pushed back his empty plate.

'Three deaths. Correct. But that's a matter for doctors, epidemiologists and zoologists, not for us. No way. It's well outside our competence.'

'That's something we need to check out,' said Adamsberg. 'Which is why I've got an appointment tomorrow with a specialist on spiders, no idea what you call someone like that, a spiderologist or an arachnologist or something, never mind what, at the Natural History Museum.'

'I don't believe it,' said Danglard. 'Well, I don't *want* to believe it. Come back to earth, commissaire. Good grief, what kind of fog is blinding you now?'

'I can see perfectly well in a fog,' said Adamsberg curtly, putting his hands palm down on the table. 'Better than elsewhere in fact. So I'll be clear, Danglard. I don't believe there's been a sudden increase in recluse spiders. I don't believe their venom has mutated. So seriously and so abruptly. I think these three men were murdered.'

There was a silence before Danglard, looking stunned, spoke again. Adamsberg's large hands remained firmly down on the table.

'*Murdered?*' repeated Danglard. '*By recluse spiders?*'

Adamsberg took his time to reply. His hands left the table and fluttered a little in the air.

'In a way, yes.'

*

Veyrenc and Adamsberg were walking back, jackets unbuttoned in the warm air of early June, having taken the precaution of accompanying Danglard home, dazed as he was, not by the wine, but by the commissaire's declaration.

'This appointment at the museum, Jean-Baptiste, the word is indeed arachnologist.'

'Wait a bit, I'd better write that down.'

Adamsberg took out his notebook, wrote the word, spelled out for him by Veyrenc, and accompanied it with a rapid sketch of a spider.

'No, spiders have eight legs. I already told you that.'

'And insects six,' said Adamsberg correcting his drawing. 'I remember now.'

He put the notebook back in his pocket and his fingers encountered a crumpled cigarette stolen from his son Zerk. He brought it out, half empty of tobacco, and lit it.

'So you can see *that* far through the fog,' said Veyrenc calmly, as they walked on.

'Yes. What should I do?'

'What you're doing. I can't see through fog. But I can sometimes see a little ahead.'

'And what can you see ahead?'

'That shadow, Jean-Baptiste.'

IX

AT 1.50 P.M., ADAMSBERG, A LITTLE AHEAD OF TIME, WAS WAITING FOR his appointment with Professor Pujol, the arachnologist – he checked the word one last time in his notebook. Eight legs. *Loxosceles rufescens.* Last night, on the way home, Danglard had mused out loud about the etymology of the word *Loxosceles,* although no one had asked him to. It must come from *loxo,* meaning oblique and, by extension, devious or walking crookedly. Possibly also from *celer,* one who hides. A crab-wise walker that hides. But Danglard was not satisfied with derivations that mixed Greek and Latin roots.

The commissaire was sitting on a rickety wooden bench, in a room that smelled of old parquet floors, dust, formalin and possibly dirt. He wondered how he was going to justify his visit, and found no answer.

A plump little woman of about seventy, walking with a stick, approached the bench. Either because she was anxious or distrustful, she took care to sit down over a metre away from the commissaire. She tucked the stick alongside her, but it fell to the floor. All the walking sticks in the world do that, Adamsberg said to himself, immediately jumping to pick it up. He handed it back to the woman with a smile. She was wearing a flowered blouse, an old-fashioned cardigan and oversized jeans, the legs rolled up over grey trainers. Since he too took no trouble over the way he dressed, Adamsberg could spot a 'provincial' outfit, as they would say in the great stone city. She reminded him of his mother who wore bulky woollen jackets, their buttons sewn firmly on, with too much thread, so that they wouldn't come off. This woman was not particularly pretty, but she had a friendly round face, permed hair dyed some shade of blonde, and heavy-framed glasses that didn't suit her. And like his mother, she had two deep lines between her eyebrows, from too much frowning; she must have been rather strict bringing up her children.

Adamsberg wondered what this woman could be doing on this bench, why she had come this far. She was holding a small black bag on her knees and opened it to take out a plastic box, which she examined, then put back. She checked at least four times that she hadn't forgotten the box. This was why she was here.

'Excuse me,' she said. 'Would you be kind enough to tell me the time?'

'Sorry, I don't have it.'

'So what are those two watches doing on your wrist?'

'Yes, they are watches, but they don't work.'

'Why are you wearing them then?'

'I don't know . . .'

'Sorry, sorry, it's none of my business. Excuse me.'

'Not to worry, no harm done.'

'No, but it's just I don't like being late.'

'You've got an appointment here? What time?'

They could have been two patients in a dentist's waiting room, chatting to cover their apprehension. But since this was not a dentist's surgery, each was also curious about the motives of the other. And concerned that the other person might jump the queue.

'Two o'clock,' she said.

'Same as me then.'

'Who with?'

'Professor Pujol.'

'Same as me,' she said with a frown. 'So he's seeing us together. That doesn't sound right to me.'

'Perhaps he's a busy man.'

'But what do you want to see him about? If that isn't being too nosy? To get your watches repaired?'

She gave a merry little laugh, without malice, then choked it off quickly. She had nice teeth, still white for her age, and looked ten years younger when she smiled.

'I'm sorry, I'm sorry,' she said. 'I just like my little joke.'

'No harm done,' Adamsberg said again.

'But what are you here for?'

'Well, let's say I'm interested in spiders.'

'You must be, if you're coming to see Professor Pujol. Are you some kind of amateur arachnologist?'

'You could say that.'

'And you've got a problem with a spider?'

'Yes, I suppose so. What about you?'

'Oh, I'm bringing him one. Sometimes they like to have specimens. Because this one's rare.'

Then the little woman seemed to think, looking straight ahead, and weighing up gravely the pros and cons of what she was about to do. She looked hard at her companion, without being nosy, she hoped. A little man, dark, thin, with muscles as tight as sinews. A head . . . but what could one say about his head? Very irregular features, high cheekbones, hollow cheeks, a large Roman nose and a crooked smile that was quite attractive. Having thought about the smile, she took a decision, brought out her precious box and held it out to him.

Adamsberg looked closely at the brown creature curled up behind the yellowing plastic. A dead spider doesn't look like anything at all. If you squash a huge house spider, what's left is a little lump. Today, talking about the recluse, even seeing it for the first time, did not trigger any alarm bells in his head. Same thing the previous evening at dinner. He had no idea why, and didn't try to work it out. He must just be getting used to it.

'You don't know what it is?' asked the woman.

'I'm not sure.'

'Never seen a dead one perhaps?'

'No.'

'But you can see its back?'

'Yes.'

'Doesn't anything strike you about the cephalothorax?'

Adamsberg hesitated. He had read something about this. The other name for the recluse was the violin spider. Because apparently there was a violin shape on its back. He had looked at the pictures online, but frankly he hadn't seen anything like a violin.

'It's the pattern, is it?'

'I hope you don't mind my saying so, but if you're an arachnologist, then I'm the Pope.'

'True,' said Adamsberg, handing her back the box.

'Which spider is it that interests you?'

'The recluse.'

'The recluse? So you're the same as everyone else? You're scared?'

'No. I'm a cop.'

'A *cop*? Let me get this straight.'

The little woman stared ahead of her again, then turned to Adamsberg.

'When people die, the cops get involved. But you're not going to arrest recluse spiders for murder, are you?'

'No.'

'Mind you, they'd love it in a prison cell, if you just gave them a little pile of wood to hide in. Sorry, sorry, just joking.'

'Not at all, no harm done.'

'Wait for me to work it out. Now, I get it. When people start panicking, *then* the police get involved. To bring things under control. So what you're doing, you've come to get information, so that you can tell your bosses or your juniors what they need to do to reassure people.'

Adamsberg realised that this little woman had just provided him with the perfect explanation to justify his request for an appointment with Professor Pujol.

'That's right,' he said with a smile. 'Orders from my bosses. As if we didn't have enough to do.'

'You should have phoned me, you could have saved yourself a lot of time.'

'But I didn't know you!'

'No, of course not. You didn't know me. This one in the box is a recluse spider. Sometimes they need to extract its venom.'

'Is it dangerous, the recluse?'

'What do you think? Of course, with old people, it's worse. But especially if people wait days and days. They're so ignorant. They don't know that if you get a little blister, it could be a recluse bite. Best to go to the doctor and get antibiotics. But no, they wait, especially if they're old. Because that's what old people do, they don't rush. If it's swollen, they say, "Oh, it's just an insect bite, it'll go over." And normally, fair enough, they're not wrong. What if we rushed off to hospital every time we saw a pimple? But a recluse bite doesn't always go over. Of course, when they see a big black patch, *then* they rush off to hospital. And sometimes, well, it's too late.'

'You seem to know a lot about the recluse spider.'

'That's because I've got quite a few in my house.'

'And you're not scared?'

'No, I know where they live, I don't disturb them, that's all. I wouldn't disturb any spider. I like all kinds of creatures. Oh, well, there is one, one I can't stand. A nasty creature, the cellar beetle. You know about it? I say, this professor's late, he's not bothered, is he? With all the trouble I took to get here. I don't know if I will give him my spider in the end. So, anyway, the horrible stinking cellar beetle, know what that is?'

'No, never heard of it.'

'Oh, you must have. It's a big black beetle, but a kind of dirty black. Like shoes that've never been cleaned. It's got lots of names, stink beetle, stink bug, angel-of-death beetle.'

'What's it done to deserve that?'

'It likes dark places, cellars, dirty places. Oh, it's a filthy creature. And if you disturb it, instead of running away, it lifts up its bum, oops, language, please excuse me, sorry, sorry, it lifts up its back end, and it squirts out nasty smelly stuff. It's itchy too, if you get it on you. They're quite big, four centimetres long where I live. You must have seen them. Where are you from?'

'The south-west, Béarn. What about you?'

'Cadeirac, near Nîmes. But you *must* have seen them. Wherever there's shit, you'll find these beetles. Oh, language, excuse me, sorry.'

'OK, no harm done.'

'Well, if I see one of *those*, I squash it with a piece of wood or a stone, before it gets time to squirt at me. What worries me, I've seen two of them recently, not in the cellar but in the house. And I don't like that.'

'Because it's an angel of death?'

'I don't know about death, but they certainly bring bad luck. No one wants to see one of them. The first one crawled out from behind my gas cylinder. And the other out of my *boot*. Bold as brass. And you know what they feed on? Rat droppings, no, I'm not joking.'

Professor Pujol was coming to meet them, his white lab coat flapping open, a large bearded man with rimless glasses, a bald head, and the stern expression of someone who has been disturbed in his serious work. He held out his hand to Adamsberg first.

'Commissaire Jean-Baptiste Adamsberg?'

'Himself.'

'I must admit that receiving a visit from a senior police officer because of a few recluse spider bites does surprise me a bit.'

'Me too, professor. But I'm under orders.'

'And you obey them. What a job! No opportunity to think for yourself, believe me, I feel sorry for you.'

You couldn't make this guy up, Adamsberg thought. Then Pujol turned to stare at the little woman who was hauling herself to her feet with some difficulty, hampered by her bag and her walking stick. Adamsberg helped her, gently taking her arm, and picking up the bag.

'Sorry, please excuse me, it's my arthritis.'

The professor had not lifted a finger to help and waited until the woman was standing up before extending his hand.

'Irène Royer-Colombe? Is that right? Follow me, please, both of you.'

Pujol set off at a smart pace along the corridors, while Adamsberg, slowed down by the little woman, whose elbow he was still holding, couldn't keep up.

'Take your time,' he said to her.

'No manners, has he? But perhaps I'm wrong, jumping to conclusions. I didn't know you were a police chief, and I said "cop". Please forgive me, I'm so sorry.'

'No harm done, I said "cop" before you did.'

'Ah, that's true.'

Seven minutes of corridors, at the slow pace of Irène Royer, creaky parquet floors, formalin, various jars on shelves, until they reached the very small office of Professor Pujol.

'Go ahead, ask your questions,' he said, even before sitting down. 'I should warn you, my speciality is the Salticidae family, nothing to do with your recluse. I've heard of it, of course. It's this business about it biting people in Languedoc-Roussillon, isn't it? Commissaire?'

'The rumours all over the internet, after five bites in three weeks and three fatalities – all old men – are starting to make people come up with theories and spreading panic. The police hierarchy doesn't like panic, because it could lead to violence.'

'And I'll tell you something,' Irène Royer added, 'you don't know the half of it up here in Paris. But down there, there's a kind of witch-hunt. Sales of vacuum cleaners have shot up, to get them out of their little haunts.'

'Good for business then,' said Pujol, picking up a toothpick and fiddling with his jaw.

'Witch-hunts of all kinds. In my village, people know that I don't kill recluses.'

'That's commendable.'

'It may be commendable but I've already had a stone through my window. I told the gendarmes, but they don't know what to do, or what to think: should they be helping to get rid of these so-called "mutant" recluses, or cut the numbers of "invaders"? Or just do nothing at all? They've no idea.'

'That's where you can help us,' put in Adamsberg. 'My superiors want a scientific opinion, so as to advise the local authorities.'

'An opinion on what?'

'Well, has there been a sudden increase in the number of recluse spiders? Because, some say, of climate change.'

'Out of the question,' said Pujol, with a disdainful curl of his lip, disdain for the ignorant and credulous. 'Arachnids aren't rodents. They don't suddenly multiply as spermophiles do for example.'

'Well,' Adamsberg insisted, 'some people are saying that the fall in bird numbers, because of insecticides, and pollution, might have meant more small spiders are surviving.'

'As with all species, if some disappear, others take their place. When the passerines' numbers drop for instance, that's sparrows, blue tits and so on, other hardier species move in and prosper. Crows for example. So the small spiders are still going to get eaten in the same quantity. Next question?'

Adamsberg took a moment to note this down. You couldn't make him up, he thought again.

'Well, there's another hypothesis doing the rounds: mutation,' he went on. 'What people are saying –'

'What people are saying! You mean on social media?'

'Yes.'

'In other words, idiots, ignorant people, who get steamed up over some crackpot hypothesis, about things of which they know nothing.'

'Well, professor, the social media are places that start humming and spread rumours. Like I said, my superiors don't like rumours. And as I told you, what they want is a firm opinion before they put out official denials.'

'I've been arguing with people for three weeks on social media,' Irène Royer put in. 'It was a waste of time. I might just as well have been . . .'

'. . . pissing in the wind,' she was going to say, Adamsberg thought.

'. . . pouring water into a funnel,' was what she actually said. 'Only a scientific announcement can deal with them.'

'And what do you say to these people, Madame Royer, on these networks?'

'Madame Royer-Colombe actually, but all right, it's easier just to say Royer, everyone else does. I tell them that the recluse spiders hide themselves away, it's not often you see them. They're not aggressive, they don't jump or anything. And their venom isn't fatal, well, OK, perhaps it could be for very old people with a failing system –'

'An immunodeficient system,' Pujol interrupted.

'And it's the time they wait too, before they go to the doctor, because they don't know how to recognise a recluse spider bite.'

'Well, roughly speaking that's right. I might phrase it differently.'

'But you didn't answer my question about mutation,' Adamsberg pressed him. 'This terrifies people, but it fascinates them too, they want it to be true and fear it at the same time. They say that spiders eat huge quantities of insects.'

'Which is correct.'

'And that since insects these days are pumped full of insecticides, the spiders are absorbing toxins that could affect their venom.'

'Mutations, that is to say modification of DNA information, happen all the time. The flu virus mutates every year. But it's still flu. There's never a mutation that totally modifies an animal organism.'

'But you get children born with four arms and stuff like that,' said the woman.

'That's an individual chromosome anomaly, nothing to do with mutation. Do you think, Madame Royer, that a mutant spider with eighteen legs and super-powerful venom is suddenly going to materialise and go chasing after humans? Don't confuse genetic reality and horror movies. You follow me? Well, to close the subject, yes indeed, spiders *are* full of insecticide from their diet. As we are, too. As are insects, which die of it. And birds, which also die of it. Well, so do the spiders. There's more likely to be a drop in their population than a rise.'

'So, mutation is out of the question?' asked Adamsberg, still taking notes.

'That's right, no mutation. If you really want to invest resources in this, commissaire, get the Ministry of the Interior to analyse the toxin present in the blood of victims who have died of loxoscelism.'

'Loxoscelism?' said Adamsberg, pen raised.

'That's what we call the morbid strain present in the recluse. So you should apply to the APC –'

'The APC?'

'The Anti-Poison Centre in Marseille.'

'Oh, right.'

'You ask them at the APC to do a comparison with the venom of the recluse from last year, and measure the rise in toxicity. The patients must have had blood tests which will have been preserved. You follow me? Do that if you want. That'll be fun, believe me.'

'Very well, that's good news on the whole,' said Adamsberg closing his notebook. 'No population increase and no mutation. So how would you explain the fact that already this summer, by the second of June, we've seen five recluse bites and three actual fatalities?'

'Well, the fatalities, as madame here suggests, probably result from an unfortunate delay in seeking treatment, on the part of immuno-deficient individuals, who fell victim to haemolysis or sepsis. As for the other two cases, it's the rumours, and the to-do in local papers and the internet that have prompted the people concerned to come forward. If there hadn't been this ridiculous scare last year about the American recluse spider – now that one *is* dangerous – spreading to France, this wouldn't be happening. As a rule, if someone is bitten by a recluse, the bite is harmless, no venom is injected, or very little. In the rare cases where it injects all the venom from both glands, the person will notice it and go straight to the doctor who will prescribe antibiotics. But people don't seem to know this. Is that all?'

'Not quite, professor. Is it possible that an individual, let us say with malicious intent, could introduce a whole lot of recluses into some-one's house?'

'In order to kill some other person?'

'Yes.'

'You must be joking, commissaire.'

'I have my orders.'

'Ah, I was forgetting, your orders. You must be better placed than me to know that there are a thousand infinitely simpler ways of murdering someone. Let's suppose – though it's ridiculous, isn't it? – that your psy-chopath wants to use some kind of animal toxin. Well, he'd choose to take it from vipers, for heaven's sake! A single viper can deliver, if it wants to, 15 milligrams of venom. I'll spare you its LD 50, that is, the lethal dose that's 50 per cent efficient on a group of mice, weighing 20 grams per individual. You follow me? So to kill a man with viper venom, he'd have to be bitten four or five times. And if you know how to get four or five vipers to do that, please tell me, that would be fun. So just think about the little recluse. Its stock of venom is tiny. Even if it empties both glands in a single bite, which, I repeat, is actually rare, you'd need, let me think, we don't have a LD 50 rate for recluses, just glandular estimates . . .'

There was a silence while the professor did some calculations in his head. 'Right,' said Pujol finally, with a smile, 'you'd need the equivalent of forty-four recluse glands to be sure of killing someone. That would be twenty-two spiders, all biting this victim, which would be quite an achievement for a solitary non-aggressive species of spider. And you'd probably have to have about sixty, in practice, to take account of the harmless bites. To kill three men, 180 recluses. So your psychopath would have to get hold of almost two hundred recluses, and then let them loose on his intended victims, his enemies presumably, and just hope they'd do the job. But why *would* they, I ask you! Two hundred! And I'd remind you that they're hard to find. They aren't called recluses for nothing.'

'Quite,' said Irène Royer. 'Hard to catch too, even if you know where they are. You know what I had the privilege of seeing one day? A whole swarm of baby spiders flying away with the wind on their gossamer.'

'You were lucky, madame, it's a fine sight. But let me pursue the commissaire's theory about a group attack. Don't you think that after having been bitten, let's say three times, the victim would realise something was wrong and get out of bed, if that's where it happened? Would he wait to be bitten sixty times? So you see, commissaire, the suggestion's preposterous. But if you ever find this extraordinary aggressor, please bring him here . . .'

. . . and it'll be fun, Adamsberg mentally finished Pujol's sentence.

'Well, as far as I'm concerned, professor, that's the end of it. Thank you for your time.'

And he stood up, followed by Irène Royer.

'And you too, madame? You're satisfied?'

'Yes, likewise. Thank you. Excuse me, I'm sorry to have bothered you.'

'You didn't need to apologise,' said Adamsberg when they were back in the corridor, 'not to someone as . . .'

Adamsberg tried to think of what Danglard would say.

'Boorish . . . someone as boorish, self-important and rude. But never mind that, we've got our answers.'

'Well, *you* got them and I did, thanks to you. Because I'm sure he wouldn't have bothered to explain it to me. But when it's for the cops, I mean the police, and especially a commissaire carrying out orders, he's got to take notice, all right, that's understandable. Good thing I didn't give him my little box. He'd just have laughed.'

'Now, Madame Royer, a warning. Please, I beg you, do not go spreading it on Twitter or whatever that my superiors sent me on this mission.'

'Why not? For once, when the cops, I mean the police, do something useful for a change, you should tell people about it. Why shouldn't I tell them?'

'Because it wouldn't be true. Nobody sent me on this mission.'

They had just come out of the museum entrance and the woman stopped short on the rue Buffon.

'What? You're not even a policeman? This was all a pack of lies? Well, I don't approve of that, no indeed I don't.'

'I *am* a cop,' said Adamsberg, showing her his card.

The little woman looked at it carefully then tilted her chin.

'So you just came off your own bat? You didn't really have any orders. You got some fixed idea in your head, did you? Seems like it to me. That's why you asked all those questions about the poison, so you looked like you were totally ignorant.'

'That doesn't bother me, I'm used to it.'

'Well, it does bother me. I could have explained it to you. You can't kill people with recluses. They don't want to bite, like I said. I couldn't have given you all those figures the prof had. But it comes to the same thing. It's not possible, just not possible.'

'Yes, maybe. But I didn't know you, did I?'

'Yes, I was forgetting you didn't know me.'

'Madame Royer-Colombe,' said Adamsberg who was extremely

anxious not to have his name and his action bruited abroad on social networks, 'why don't we go for a coffee? The Étoile d'Austerlitz is just along the street. Then we could talk more openly.'

'Madame Royer will do,' said the woman, 'it's simpler, most people call me that. I don't like coffee, thank you.'

'Tea, or hot chocolate, then.'

'All right, I'm going that way in any case.'

Veyrenc phoned him, as they were making their way slowly along the street, Adamsberg still holding her arm and with her bag slung on his shoulder.

'Nothing suspicious,' Adamsberg reported to Veyrenc. 'The professor is odious, but he knows his onions.'

'That's the least he could do,' muttered Irène Royer from beside him. 'It's his *job*, isn't it? You don't want to come all this way to listen to rubbish, eh?'

'No, Louis,' Adamsberg went on. 'No sudden increase in numbers, no mutation, and absolutely no way you could use these creatures to kill anyone. That makes it clearer anyway.'

'Are you disappointed?'

'No.'

'Well, *I* am, a bit. Oh, it's nothing really.'

'The shadow?'

'Maybe. But we can make mistakes about a shadow, can't we?'

'Like we can make mistakes about the fog.'

'Yes, we'll just have to admit that's the end of it.'

'No, it's not the end of it, Louis. Don't forget: what's the global statistic? Ten deaths a year caused by spiders. None to date in France.'

'But you just said "absolutely no way".'

'Yes, looking at it from this angle. But what if one approached it from another one? Remember the different ways you can climb the Pic de Balaïtous in the Pyrenees? There are some routes to the top where you're more likely to fall, others that work fine.'

'I know them, Jean-Baptiste.'

'Just a question of the right route, Louis. The angle of approach. The right track.'

Sitting in front of her hot chocolate, Irène Royer pointed at the mobile.

'You've got a funny way of talking. Sorry, sorry, not my business, but "shadow", "route", "angle of approach"?'

'He's a childhood friend. And a colleague.'

'He's from the Béarn then, like you.'

'Precisely.'

'They say people from there have hard skulls, because of the mountains. Like Bretons, with the sea. Just one little slip and the mountain lets you fall or the sea gets you. They're elements too big for us, so you need to have a hard skull, I suppose.'

'Possibly.'

'But you *are* making your little slip, you know. You're clinging on to your rock, and you might find yourself falling down, over the cliff.'

'No, I'll climb down from this rock and try another.'

'I suppose your bosses, they don't know anything about all this? That you're getting worked up about the recluse? Without rhyme or reason.'

'No, they don't.'

'And if they did know, you'd be in hot water?'

Adamsberg smiled. 'Yes.'

'That's why you're buying me a hot chocolate. So I won't go spreading it on social media that this Paris commissaire is off his trolley, all on his own and his bosses don't know. That's why you're being nice to me.'

'But I *am* nice.'

'And obstinate. That's pride. You've got your little hunch, without knowing anything about this spider, less than a kid would know, and the prof showed you you were wrong. Yes or no?'

'Yes.'

'But you tell your friend, no, it's not the end of it. When you've got everything there under your nose. So that's what I call pride.'

Adamsberg smiled again. This little woman appealed to him. She had insight and summed things up well. He put a finger on her shoulder.

'I'll tell you what it is, Madame Royer. I'm not proud. But I just had my own little hunch, as you put it, that's all.'

'Well, now, I've got my own little hunch too. Because the recluse spider isn't a killer. And because there have been three deaths. And because we've never seen anyone killed by a recluse before, in France. And for another reason, too. But so what? We all have our little hunches, especially when we're lying awake at night, don't we? But I'm not crazy like you. When it's not possible, it's not possible, and that's it, as far as I'm concerned.'

'So,' said Adamsberg leaning back and crossing his legs, 'what's this "other reason"?'

'Oh, this is just silly,' she said with a shrug. 'They do a good hot chocolate here, I have to say.'

'Come on, what other reason, Madame Royer?' Adamsberg insisted.

'Look, you might just as well call me Irène, it's quicker.'

'Thank you. All right, Irène, what risk is there? You'll never see me again. You can tell me your little hunch. I like hunches, especially little ones and especially when they come to you at night.'

'Well, I don't. They bother me.'

'OK then, pass it on to me, I don't often get bothered. Otherwise it'll go on bothering you.'

And inevitably, Adamsberg thought of his old neighbour Lucio, who would say: 'You've always got to finish scratching it.'

'It's nothing, really, it's just that when the second death was in the papers, I thought there was something fishy about it.'

'Something moray-eelish.'

'I *beg* your pardon!'

'Sorry, I was thinking of something else.'

'Look, do you want to hear about my hunch or not?'

'Yes, of course I do.'

'Well, those first two old men that died, they knew each other. Had done, since they were kids.'

'Ah, did they now?'

'Before I retired to Cadeirac, I lived in Nîmes.'

'And they did too?'

'If you keep interrupting me, I'll lose the thread and the something fishy will get lost.'

'Sorry.'

'We lived not far from each other, just a couple of streets away. Now me, at 7 p.m., I like a little glass of port. Sorry if that shocks you, but that's all I ever drink. A little glass sees off the worms, as my mother used to say, but I think that's probably a load of cobblers. Oops, pardon me, sorry.'

'It's all right, no harm done,' said Adamsberg for the nth time that afternoon.

'What it does, for sure, it helps the arthritis,' she said, pulling a face. 'It's the damp. I'm better in the south. So, my little glass of port. And those men used to go to the same café as me, La Vieille Cave. Because a glass of port at seven is all very well, but it's a bit sad to drink it all by yourself at home, isn't it? You follow me? As that prof kept saying. I think I'll use that myself. What do *you* drink?'

'I have a beer after supper with my old neighbour, under a tree.'

Adamsberg could see the little hunch, the fishy thing, disappearing under a rock, like a moray eel sliding back into its hole. He realised he had better not interrupt the flow, then she'd get to the point. Otherwise her little hunch would go on irritating her, itching forever, and she didn't seem entirely unwilling to unburden herself by passing it on to him.

'Well, in my case, not under a tree, at La Vieille Cave café. And those two old men were always there, all the time. And I'll tell you, they had more than a little glass of port. Pastis after pastis, and talking non-stop. That's the way it is when you've been through hell, you can't stop talking about it, it's like you've got to bury it once and for all. You follow me? Sometimes people joke about it, as if it was paradise. The good old days and all that. But *their* time in hell was this orphanage. They called it La Miséricorde. Not far from Nîmes. That had made them mates for life, and what they liked doing was talking about all the naughty things they had done when they were little. And what I heard, when I was sitting there, doing my crossword – one day I won an electric blanket for the crossword, but it was a piece of sh— oops, sorry, excuse me, language.'

'No harm done.'

'What I mean is, it could set fire to your bed, couldn't it? So they were telling each other all about the bad things the naughty boys at the orphanage got up to. They pissed (their word, not mine) in the director's cloakroom, they did their number twos in his briefcase, they climbed out at night, they tied another kid up in his bedsheets, they pinched another one's trousers, they pulled down some kid's shorts playing football, they beat someone else up, locked up another, you see the kind of thing. Bad blood, a bad lot, and they liked doing *evil* things. And they weren't alone, there was a whole gang of them. At the same time, I guess they can't have been happy at all in that place, poor kids. You can bet on that. But these two still used to have a laugh about it over their pastis. Sometimes, though, it wasn't just a laugh, they kept their voices down so you couldn't hear, and they were smirking. Must have been even worse things.'

'So what you've been thinking as you lie in bed, unable to sleep, is that someone is taking some sort of revenge on them?'

'Yes.'

'And making it look as if it was a bite from a recluse?'

'Yes. But seventy years on, what sense would that make?'

'You said it yourself. If you've been through hell, you can't stop talking about it. Which means you can't stop thinking about it. Even sixty years on.'

'But they did die from spider poison, didn't they? And we keep coming back to the same thing: you can't force a recluse to bite someone.'

'What if you put it in someone's bed? Or their shoe?'

'That doesn't work. Because the first old man was bitten out of doors, by his woodpile. And the other one, he was outside too, opening his front door. So the recluse must have been hiding under some stones.'

'It doesn't make sense.'

'Like I said.'

'What about the third man, did you know him?'

'No, never seen or heard of him. Have you got the time?'

Adamsberg showed her his two wristwatches.

'Oh, I'd forgotten,' she said. 'But I need to go, I'm staying with a friend here.'

'I've got my car nearby, I can give you a lift.'

'It's on the Quai Saint-Bernard.'

'All right, I'll drop you off.'

Outside her friend's flat, Adamsberg passed Irène her bag and her walking stick.

'Now don't go chewing away on this forever,' she said, before leaving.

'And don't you put my name out on social media!'

'I'm not going to ruin your career, I'm not a bad lot, like those boys.'

'Would you perhaps let me have your phone number?' asked Adamsberg, taking out his mobile.

Irène thought for a moment in her usual way, staring straight ahead, then dictated a string of numbers, after consulting a little notebook.

'Just in case you hear anything,' she said.

'Or in case you do.'

Adamsberg was already back in the driving seat, when the little woman tapped on his window.

'Here you are, you can keep this,' she said, passing him the yellowed plastic box.

X

IT WAS LATE BY THE TIME ADAMSBERG RETURNED TO HEADQUARTERS, which now smelled only moderately like a fish market. The windows were still wide open, and the haphazard collection of objects designed to keep papers from blowing away still sat on the desks. There was an undertow of odour though, but now combined with some kind of rose or lilac perfume, sprayed round the room by Lieutenant Froissy – who else? – driven by her uncontrollable desire to care for everyone's welfare. The resulting mixture was somewhat nauseating and Adamsberg would have preferred an honest smell of fish.

'It was Froissy,' said Veyrenc, coming over to him.

'Thought so.'

'Can't say anything, it's well meant. She's used up two cans of air-freshener, no one dared discourage her. But as ever, there's no point trying to cover up a bad smell.'

'Perhaps we should bring in another moray eel to cover up the rose and lilac. Or this, perhaps.'

Adamsberg brought the little plastic box out of his pocket.

'This is a recluse spider, and it was a gift. Admire it. I must say nobody has ever made me a present of a dead spider before. It doesn't smell of anything though. Unlike a cellar beetle.'

'You mean the stinking cellar beetle?'

'Correct. Harbinger of death.'

'And who was the thoughtful person who gave you a dead spider?'

'This little old lady I met at the Natural History Museum. She'd come all the way from Nîmes to offer it to the spider expert.'

'The arachnologist.'

'Indeed. And since she took a dislike to him, she gave it to me instead. It's an offering, an honour, Louis. Like when Rögnvar carved a portrait of Retancourt on to a wooden oar.'

'He did what?'

'You heard. Finished the report, have you?'

'Yes. It's with Mordent now.'

'I need to have a word with you about something this woman told me. In private. Come and find me in my office, but be discreet. How's Danglard?'

'I think his passion for paperwork and having to compile The Book is melting his bad temper.'

Adamsberg put the spider down on an already cluttered desk. He opened the box, picked up a magnifying glass stolen from Froissy and examined the creature's back. What was that other word for it that arachnologists would use? He looked in the notebook. He had written it down somewhere. Ah yes, the cephalothorax. OK. Why not just call it the back? And however hard he looked at the creature's back, nothing like the shape of a violin seemed to emerge. Hearing footsteps, he hastily closed the lid. Not that he was afraid of his fellow officers, but he didn't want to upset Danglard again.

It was Voisenet, who immediately spotted the box and peered into it.

'A recluse! How did you get hold of this?' he asked in a tone of envy. 'They're rare.'

'Someone gave it me.'

'Who? What do you mean?'

'In the Natural History Museum.'

'You're not giving up then, commissaire?

'Yes, in fact I am. There has been no increase in spider numbers and no mutation. That's a blind alley.'

'But three deaths, all the same.'

'I thought *you'd* given it up, lieutenant. You kept on saying it was just because they were old.'

'I know. It's just that the recluse has never killed anyone in France before. No mutation then, you're sure about that?'

'Yes.'

'Right. Anyway, it's none of our business.'

Adamsberg sensed his lieutenant wavering between logic and temptation.

'I came to see you about the report.'

Voisenet tapped his bulging stomach, an unfortunate tic of his, betraying either embarrassment or satisfaction, so he did it quite often.

'The interrogation of Carvin,' he began. 'I came to ask, um, how can I put this? Would it be possible to cut the places where he makes fun of me, with all those bloody *aperceptions* and quotations?'

'What's come over you, Voisenet? You want us to cut up the tape and stick it together again?'

'Those bits aren't necessary for the investigation.'

'Yes they are, because they reveal Carvin's personality. Since when have you had the idea of falsifying our case records?'

'Since the word "aperception". Can't get over it.'

'And what about me? I've had to cope with an arachnologist and a cephalothorax. Just swallow your aperception, digest it and that's an end to it.'

'But the cephalothorax isn't in any report.'

'Who knows, Voisenet?'

Just then, Veyrenc telephoned and Voisenet left the room, still massaging his belly.

'I heard Voisenet in your office,' said Veyrenc, 'so I walked past. Maybe somewhere else?'

'Where?'

'We could go back to La Garbure? Danglard rather spoilt our appetites yesterday.'

Estelle, Adamsberg thought at once. Her hand on Veyrenc's shoulder last night. Veyrenc had been on his own for a while, since his extremely demanding set of requirements in a woman reduced his choice considerably. Adamsberg had the opposite problem, because of his low expectations. It's Estelle, he thought again. He's going back there to see her, and not for cabbage soup, even if it's a Pyrenean speciality.

XI

BECAUSE IT WAS THEM, VEYRENC AND ADAMSBERG, BUT PARTICULARLY Veyrenc, Estelle put the soup tureen containing the garbure over a little burner on their table, so that they could take their time without it getting cold. Veyrenc had somehow changed places, and unlike the previous evening, he was now facing the counter, instead of turning his back on it.

'You did tell me the recluse spider has never caused any deaths in France,' Veyrenc began.

'That's right. Whereas vipers account for between one and five deaths a year.'

'That alters things.'

'You're not with me now?'

'I didn't say that. Tell me about this woman who gave you a dead spider.'

'Men give fur coats to women, don't they? What a thought. Having your arms round a woman wearing sixty dead squirrels on her back.'

'Are you going to have this spider on your back?'

'I've already got it on my shoulders, Louis.'

'And I've got some leopard skin on my head,' said Veyrenc, running his fingers through his thick thatch of hair.

Adamsberg felt his stomach clench, as it did every time Veyrenc referred to this. They had both been children back then, in the mountains. Little Louis Veyrenc had been attacked by some other boys who had given him fourteen penknife cuts on the head. Over the scars, his hair had grown again, but this time reddish, and strikingly so. It was very noticeable, which was one reason you didn't send Veyrenc out to shadow anyone. This evening, under the restaurant's low-hanging lamps, the bright locks gleamed against his dark hair. Yes, kind of leopard skin, but the other way round.

'What did this woman say?' Veyrenc asked.

Adamsberg pulled a face and leaned back, tilting the legs of his chair and laying his hands on the table.

'It's difficult, Louis. I have this impression, no, it's more than an impression. I've got this déjà vu sensation.'

'Who about, the woman?'

'No, the recluse.'

This time the stiffness was back in his neck, and Adamsberg shook his head to try and make it go away.

'Of course, I've never seen one. Or perhaps I have. Or something like it. A long time ago.'

'Of course you've seen one, but only in the last three days, it's all over the internet.'

'And the day before, I saw a picture of one on Voisenet's computer. And it made me feel strange, a kind of nausea.'

'Spiders make a lot of people feel sick.'

'Not me. Not normally.'

'Remember, the room was full of that terrible stink of fish.'

'Well, that somehow got mixed up with it. The smell and the spider. I know the smell must have had something to do with it, I'm sure of that.'

'Can you remember exactly what you saw on Voisenet's computer?'

'I can never remember words, but I can recall images, yes. I could give you a whole list of the things people have put on their desks to keep their papers from blowing away. I could even draw that tree up in the hills where you . . .'

'Forget that one. My hair's fine like it is.'

'OK.'

'So, on Voisenet's computer. What did you see?'

'Nothing special. An enlarged photo of the spider, light brown, head down, and across the top in blue letters "The European Recluse, aka the Violin Spider". And that's all.'

Adamsberg rubbed the back of his neck energetically.

'You got a pain?'

'Just a bit. It's when I hear that word, sometimes.'

'And when you see it. In the little box.'

'No,' said Adamsberg with a shrug. 'Funnily enough, that doesn't bother me at all. Legs, back, no problem. Or it's a different shape.'

'What kind of shape?'

'No idea.'

'You see a shape? Like in a dream, a nightmare, real, or when you're asleep?'

'I just don't know. Maybe it's a spectre,' said Adamsberg with a smile.

'A dead person perhaps?'

'No. Or maybe, a dead person dancing. You know, like in old pictures that scare kids, the dance of death.'

Adamsberg twitched his head. The stiffness had vanished.

'OK, forget my questions,' said Veyrenc. 'Tell me what this woman told you.'

Adamsberg let his chair fall back down, took a spoonful of soup and summarised the conversation in the Étoile d'Austerlitz.

'The same orphanage, you say?'

'It's what she said.'

'Bad blood, a bad lot?'

'That was the way she put it.'

'They might have carried on like that afterwards. But what were these evil deeds?'

'I'd like to go and see the director of the orphanage.'

'Who must be about a hundred and twenty by now.'

'Well, whoever took it over, I mean.'

'On what pretext? You can't go round saying again you're just obeying orders from on high. You're lucky that woman is going to keep quiet about it. If she is. You're sure of her, are you?'

'Since I bought her a hot chocolate in the Étoile d'Austerlitz.'

'Making up to old ladies, that's not a very proper thing to do, as she might have told you.'

'Oh, don't worry. She was well aware what I was up to, and she told me so. And she asked me to let her know if I discovered anything new. But I didn't promise anything,' Adamsberg added, with a smile.

'Except that you would look after this dead spider for her. That's something. What kind of new, Jean-Baptiste?'

Adamsberg shrugged.

'Nothing,' he said. 'You can't make two hundred recluses march off and attack someone.'

'Out of doors, what's more. I can't see why hordes of spiders would come out of the woodpile to attack a man.'

'No, it's impossible, they're solitary creatures. They just wait timidly until people have gone away.'

'We're getting nowhere, Jean-Baptiste.'

'That's why we have to try another route. Leading to the orphanage. We know its name: "La Miséricorde". Somebody must have kept its old records, wouldn't you think? You don't chuck out piles of papers containing piles of orphans.'

'And then what?'

'We find the names of the kids who were at La Miséricorde in the same years as our first two victims, and we try to reconstitute the "little gang" she talked about.'

'If you're going that far, Jean-Baptiste, you'll have to inform the squad.'

Veyrenc poured out a second glass of wine each, as they both reflected in silence, going over what very little they had in the way of data. Adamsberg staring at his empty plate, Veyrenc observing Estelle, who was that evening making more of an exaggerated display of waiting on the tables.

'But why?' Adamsberg said. 'Do you want to get Danglard worked up again? We could easily manage without making it a big production. We could ask Froissy to research the three men who died and the orphanage, and she'd do it. We could probably count on support from Voisenet. You and I could carry out some visits. Mercadet, no doubt.'

'So that way, we'd be a cosy little group of conspirators inside the squad. Danglard already knows what you're up to, and he's watching your every step, as if he thinks you're about to fall off a cliff. We'd have to sneak off to the drinks machine room to have a chat. How long do you think that would last?'

'Louis, what do you want me to tell them?' Adamsberg reacted vigorously. 'That I'm investigating three deaths by recluse bite, because recluses don't kill? Because they never attack humans spontaneously? They'll all say, like Voisenet did, those people were all very old. No dossier, not a shred of evidence of any kind. Then what will happen? Remember the last time they mutinied? When three-quarters of the team decided they wouldn't go along with me? The squad almost disintegrated. This will be worse. I've no wish to go through that again. And I don't want to drive them into a brick wall.'

'But that's where you're going?'

'I've no choice, Louis.'

'Well, OK,' said Veyrenc after another silence. 'Just do what you have to.'

They had finished their meal. Adamsberg prepared to leave. They were the last customers.

'Already?' asked Veyrenc. 'Did I say something to offend you?'

'Not at all.'

'I'd quite like a coffee.'

'It won't bother you if leave you to it?'

'No, off you go.'

Adamsberg left his share of the bill, put on his jacket, and as he went past, quickly took hold of Veyrenc's arm.

'I'm going to have a think,' he said.

Veyrenc knew that Adamsberg was not going to have a think. Because he didn't know how. He was incapable of sitting by his fireside, meditating, sorting out the evidence, weighing up the pros and cons. In his case, his thoughts were, so to speak, formed before he realised it. The commissaire was departing so that Veyrenc would be left alone with Estelle.

Once at home, Adamsberg took a half-smoked cigarette out of an old packet belonging to Zerk. He was missing his son. When they had been on the point of leaving Iceland, Zerk (real name Armel, and only known to Adamsberg once he had reached the age of twenty-eight) had announced that he had a mind to stay there. He had met a girl who was taking her sheep up to the summer pastures. Coming back without him had aggravated Adamsberg's wish not to be in the city. And what was he going to do for cigarettes now? He didn't smoke, except when he pinched one from Zerk's packets. Which wasn't really smoking, just stealing. Well then, he would buy a packet for his son, and now and again take one from it. So that was settled, at least.

He missed Lucio too. He would have adored this story about spiders. But Lucio had left that very morning to visit family in Spain. Adamsberg opened the door on to the little garden they shared, and looked at the old packing case they used as a seat, under the tree. He sat down on it, lit Zerk's cigarette, and tried in spite of everything to think. Perhaps it was just as well, all things considered, that his son was away, so he wouldn't witness his father's confusion of mind and those spider legs waving about for no reason in a terrible atmosphere of stinking moray eel. He wasn't going to tell his fellow officers about those images to explain the start of his investigation. He leaned back against the tree trunk, and stretched out his legs on the packing case. Should he disguise the truth to smooth over the rough edges? But even smoothed over, those rough edges wouldn't pass muster. Think. He must think.

XII

NEXT MORNING, FROISSY EYED ADAMSBERG ANXIOUSLY, IMMEDIATELY diagnosing the source of his trouble.

'You haven't had any breakfast, have you, commissaire?'

'Not important, lieutenant.'

Heading towards his office, he motioned to Veyrenc to join him.

'I went straight off to sleep, Louis. But I woke up at five o'clock, under the tree, and wrote this. Just two pages, summarising what we've got so far: the deaths, the orphanage and the conclusions of Professor Pujol. Could you type it out for me, put it into decent French and tidy it up a bit?'

'Give me ten minutes.'

'Who's on duty today?' Adamsberg asked, glancing up at the noticeboard.

'Not all that many. Last Saturday and Sunday, a lot of people put in overtime because of the 4x4. So they're taking time off.'

'So who's in?'

'Justin, Kernorkian, Retancourt, Froissy. Mordent is working on phase 2 of the report, but at home.'

'Call in all the others, Louis. Better it should come from you.'

'You're going to inform the squad?'

'That's what you advised me, isn't it? And you were right. Get them together, Danglard of course, Mordent, Voisenet, Lamarre, Noël, Estalère and Mercadet. Make enough copies of my text to go round when you've got it into shape. Meeting to start at eleven, no point getting them out of bed and have them arriving here in a bad mood. They'll have a chance to change their minds during the meeting.'

'That's possible,' said Veyrenc, glancing down at Adamsberg's notes.

'The usual photocopier isn't working – we'll have to lift the cat off the other one.'

Just then Froissy arrived, carrying a full breakfast tray, her hands shaking slightly which made the cups tinkle.

'I've wrapped the coffee pot in a tea towel,' she explained, 'so it won't get cold. I added a cup for you, lieutenant,' she said before leaving.

'What did you tell her?' asked Veyrenc, eyeing the excessively large pile of croissants. 'That you hadn't eaten for five days?'

The lieutenant made space on the desk, pushing the recluse spider's box aside, and began pouring out the coffee.

'Not as good as Estalère's,' he commented. 'But that's between ourselves.'

'She's on edge, isn't she? She was looking very pale.'

'Yes, very, and she's lost weight.'

Retancourt appeared in the doorway. And when Retancourt appeared in a doorway it was difficult to see anything either behind her or above her.

'Come in, lieutenant, join us,' said Adamsberg. 'Froissy provided the croissants.'

Retancourt helped herself without speaking and sat down in the seat vacated by Veyrenc, who had gone off to edit Adamsberg's notes. She never worried about her weight – which was considerable – since she seemed able to convert any fat into pure muscle.

'Can I have a word with you?' she asked. 'Because this is something that normally wouldn't be any business of ours.'

'We've got a little time, lieutenant. I've called a meeting for eleven.'

'What about?'

'About something that normally wouldn't be any business of ours.'

'Oh really?' said Retancourt suspiciously.

'But obviously I'm not alone. Tit for tat, tell me about yours.'

'It's a case of sexual harassment. Possibly. But the person concerned lives in the 9th arrondissement, out of our area.'

'Has this person been to complain to the police?'

'No, she wouldn't dare. And I have to say there isn't any firm evidence, nothing that would justify going to the cops. She says it's nothing. But really, she thinks the worst, she's withdrawn into herself, she can't sleep.'

'And you think she has good reason? Why?'

'Because it's something vicious, commissaire, something invisible and incomprehensible.'

'Well, so is my case. Invisible and incomprehensible. It happens. What else?'

'There have been two rapes in the 9th in the last month. Only three hundred metres and five hundred metres from where she lives.'

'Get to the point, give me the story.'

'It's when she goes into the bathroom. Not a threat, not a stalker, no phone calls. But just the damn bathroom. The room doesn't look out on anyone else. It only has a window on to the courtyard, frosted glass.'

Retancourt hesitated.

'And?' said Adamsberg.

'Commissaire, if you smile, even a shadow of a smile, I'll tear you to shreds.'

'Sexual harassment isn't something I find remotely amusing, lieutenant.'

'But there's only one thing to report, and it's inconclusive.'

'As you said. Go ahead.'

'The minute she goes into her bathroom, the neighbour starts running water, on the other side of the wall that separates their flats. Every time. That's all. Think that funny?'

'Do I look as if I think it funny?'

'No.'

'What do you mean, runs water?'

'Flushes the toilet.'

Adamsberg frowned.

'And this woman lives alone?'

'Yes.'

'And how long has it been going on?'

'Over two months. It might sound like nothing at all, but . . .'

'No, it doesn't sound like nothing at all.'

The commissaire stood up and walked around, arms folded.

'It's like a signal of some kind? As if every time she goes in, her neighbour says "I'm here, and I know you're there".'

'Or worse, "I can *see* you."'

'Is that what she thinks? A hidden camera, CCTV?'

'Yes.'

'And that's what you think too?'

'Yes.'

'So it could be taking images? There was a case like this a few months ago, it started in Romorantin. A flush that kept going. And a little later, it was all over the internet. The victim's face was easily identifiable. She was spared nothing, the toilet being in the bathroom too.'

'Same here.'

'And that woman killed herself.'

Adamsberg walked round a bit more, arms tightly folded.

'But you're right,' he said. 'Complaining to the police because the neighbour flushes the toilet isn't going to be followed up. Does she know the neighbour?'

'No, never seen him.'

'How does she know it's a man then?'

'Because his name's on the letter box in the entrance: Rémi Marl-lot, with two *l*s.'

'One second, let me note it. So he must be avoiding meeting her face-to-face. Not leaving the house until after she does, and getting home before her. Does she keep regular hours?'

'No.'

'So he's probably stalking her. What about weekends?'

'He's there the whole time. Flushing his fucking toilet.'

'Is this woman a friend of yours, Retancourt?'

'You could say that. If I have any friends.'

'I'm surprised you're even telling me this. Knowing you, you'd have dealt with it yourself. You'd have gone over there, ripped out the camera, found the images, grabbed the guy and torn him limb from limb.'

Veyrenc came into the room, and put the photocopies on the desk, glancing with surprise at Retancourt's tense expression.

'Did you contact them?' Adamsberg asked him.

'Yes.'

'Who's coming?'

'Everyone.'

'Perfect. We've got another twenty minutes.'

'I did go there one evening,' Retancourt admitted, when Veyrenc had left again. 'I did a thorough search of the bathroom – I was look-ing for the camera. I examined the walls, the radiator, the hairdryer, the mirror, the towel rail, the piping and even the light bulbs. Nothing.'

'Is there a ventilator outlet?'

'Yes, of course, on the outer wall. I dismantled it. Nothing.'

'Then you, er, entered the neighbour's flat?'

'Yes. It was filthy and stinking. It doesn't look like he's really moved in, it's just a temporary campsite. I checked out the bathroom too:

nothing. No porn magazines or DVDs, no photos, nothing on the computer. Perhaps it really is a toilet cistern that's out of order,' she said with a wry smile.

'No, that can't be it. He's keeping the images somewhere else.'

'But how would he get any images? Like I said, I really searched the place. Nothing.'

'That's all to the good, Violette.'

Adamsberg occasionally addressed his lieutenant by her first name, out of a sudden surge of affection: 'Violette' – perhaps the least appropriate name for someone of Retancourt's stature.

'If you'd touched the camera,' he said, 'he'd have noticed. He'd have dismantled his sensor quickly and disappeared with the images. Anything on the bathroom ceiling?'

'Nothing special. Two spotlights, ordinary bulbs, and a smoke detector.'

'A smoke detector? In the bathroom?'

'Yes,' said Retancourt with a shrug. 'The installing guy told her it was compulsory because she keeps her washing machine in there, which she's not really supposed to, plus a wall-mounted hairdryer.'

'Installing guy? What guy?'

'Well, there's a big market for this kind of thing, because people don't know how to install them themselves,' she said, with the puzzled air of someone who had been born with an adjustable spanner in her hand. 'A fitter came round the whole building, putting them in. For people who were no good at DIY. Or old people who didn't want to get up on a ladder with a drill. I had someone come round too, it's quite common.'

'So what does the detector look like?'

'Like a regular one, far as I know. I haven't bought mine yet. Grooves for taking in the air, a perforated disc that lights up for the alarm, and a little indicator for the battery.'

'Is the indicator black?'

'Yes, black, normal. It's supposed to light up when the battery runs out.'

'Yes, it should go red. I need this woman's name,' said Adamsberg sternly, 'and her address.'

Retancourt hesitated.

'It's kind of awkward,' she said.

'Oh for God's sake, why come to me then, Violette, if you don't want to tell me? I've never known you so slow off the mark.'

This comment appeared to stimulate the lieutenant, whose anxiety for 'the woman' had indeed seemed to absorb her normal energy.

'Froissy,' she murmured.

'What did you say?'

'Froissy,' she repeated quietly.

'Are you telling me we need Froissy to help, or that she *is* this woman?'

'It's her.'

'Good God!'

Adamsberg pushed his hair back from his brow and started pacing again. A fit of anger made him clench his arms.

'Right, we'll sort this out, Violette, believe me.'

'Without getting the cops in? Nobody must ever know about this, *ever.*'

'Without the cops.'

'But we *are* the cops.'

Adamsberg brushed away this paradox with a wave of his hand.

'These images must never find their way into the hands of anyone,' he said. 'People think that voyeurs are just passive observers, but plenty of rapists have spent hours watching images. We've only got six minutes before the meeting. Could you nip down into the courtyard and check, wearing gloves, whether anyone has put a GPS trace on her car? If so, just leave it there.'

'I *could* suggest Froissy goes to spend the night at a hotel.'

'No, no, absolutely not. We don't want to do anything to alert this guy. She should carry on as usual. Which direction is the dividing wall between the bathrooms? North, south, east or west?'

'North.'

'Right. During the meeting, sit down next to her. Find some way of pinching her house keys out of her bag, then drop them in my jacket pocket. I'm going to go over there and take a look. I've got work for Froissy that will keep her here for quite a while. Anyway, she'll be in no hurry to go home.'

'Thanks, commissaire,' said Retancourt, standing up.

'And one more thing, lieutenant. During this meeting about to take place, if you smile, even the shadow of a smile . . .'

Retancourt frowned.

'Blackmailing me, eh?'

'Fair exchange is no robbery, lieutenant.'

The meeting opened on time in the council chamber, the rather pompous name Danglard had given the room where the squad held general assemblies, and which had become part of its everyday vocabulary. People said 'See you in the council chamber', or 'in the chapter room', if they meant a smaller office used for more intimate meetings. Adamsberg greeted everyone, especially Danglard, as if to put him on guard for what was to come, then, with a smile, he distributed the photocopies of his text, now elegantly edited by Veyrenc. Which did not on that account make it any more like police business.

'I'll give you a few minutes to take it in, without me, while Estalère serves up some coffee.'

Before going out he shot a glance at Retancourt who gave him a brief nod.

So, yes, there was indeed a goddam GPS trace under Froissy's car.

Good grief. Retancourt ought to have told him her story before this. While he walked round the outer office waiting for his colleagues to read the text, he was not yet thinking about how he was going to handle the session. For the moment, he was thinking about Froissy, and how to give her absolute protection, while informing the police in the 9th arrondissement. And now he began to hear exclamations from the council chamber, as lively arguments started breaking out.

He went into his office, noted Froissy's home address and returned to face his team. He sat down without taking any notice of the various movements of the officers nor of the sudden silence that fell. He noted how Froissy was looking thinner and more fragile, her fingers tense on the keyboard of her laptop.

XIII

ADAMSBERG HAD NO NEED TO LOOK AT THE MEMBERS OF HIS TEAM TO identify the nature of this silence. It was composed of perplexity, lassitude and fatalism. He did not sense any temptation on their part to react aggressively, nor even any desire to ask him questions. This meeting, he predicted, would be one of the shortest in their history. They all seemed to have thrown in the sponge, in a spirit of sad resignation, which had the result of abandoning the commissaire to his lonely course. Except for Veyrenc, Voisenet, possibly Mercadet, and Froissy – simply because the spider story was the least of her worries. Danglard, however, was eyeing the commissaire with a combative and disappointed expression.

'I'm listening,' said Adamsberg.

'Oh, what's the point?' said Danglard, firing the first shot. 'You know quite well what we think. This is absolutely no business of ours.'

'That's your view, Danglard. What about the others?'

'Same goes for me,' said Mordent wearily, twisting his long neck.

There were several nods of approval – the opinion of the two senior commandants was influential – and a few faces did not dare to look up.

'Let's be clear about this,' said Adamsberg. 'I understand your doubts, I'm not forcing anyone to join me in this investigation. I'm simply keeping you informed. As you read in my notes, the first two victims had known each other since childhood.'

'Nîmes isn't that big a place,' remarked Mordent.

'No, it isn't. Secondly, according to Professor Pujol, the venom of the recluse spider can't have mutated. And people only die from its bite in extremely rare cases.'

'But they were *old*,' said Kernorkian.

'Yes, they were,' Mordent agreed.

' "Investigation"?' said Danglard. 'Did I just hear you say this was an "investigation"? With victims and a murderer?'

'Yes, that's what I said.'

'They'll need three pairs of handcuffs when they catch the killer,' guffawed Noël. 'One for each pair of legs.'

'Four, you mean, Noël,' said Adamsberg. 'Spiders have eight legs.'

The commissaire got to his feet and spread his arms in a gesture of helplessness.

'OK, you can all go,' he announced. 'Froissy and Mercadet, I need you for a spot of research.'

The council chamber emptied with a sound of shuffling feet. The meeting had lasted less than six minutes. Gradually the officers who had been roused from their beds disappeared. Adamsberg grabbed Mercadet by the arm.

'Lieutenant, can you give me five minutes?'

'Froissy's on duty, sir,' said Mercadet. 'I'm dropping off to sleep.'

'It's something I can't ask Froissy to do. I need you, Mercadet. This is an emergency.'

The lieutenant rubbed his eyes, shook his head and stretched his arms.

'What's it about?'

'Here's an address: 82 rue de Trévise, staircase A, third floor, flat 5, I've written it all down. I want to know everything you can find out about this tenant's neighbour on the north side. Well, at least his name, age, occupation and family situation.'

'I'll do my best, sir.'

'Thank you. This is just between ourselves, understood?'

The appeal to secrecy seemed to wake Mercadet up, and he went off towards his computer holding his head a little higher. Adamsberg signalled to Estalère that he should provide the valiant lieutenant with some coffee, then went to see Veyrenc.

'Are you still so sure it was a good idea to tell them?'

'Yes.'

'Ever see such discouraged faces? I think I've plunged three-quarters of the squad into an immediate depression.'

'They'll get over it. Are you getting Froissy to look into the orphanage?'

'Yes, and into the victims.'

Adamsberg entered Froissy's office as if tiptoeing into a hospital ward. For once, she was doing nothing, just chewing gum and rolling a little ball between her fingers. Probably one of those gadgets that are meant to soothe bad nerves. No, he realised, it was the cat's woolly ball, made for it by Mercadet. It was blue, since the cat was a male. An undoctored male, which nevertheless showed no sign of sex drive. One day, maybe, Froissy would go and curl up like the cat on top of the photocopier.

'Thank you for the breakfast,' he said. 'I really needed it.'

This acknowledgement drew a smile from the lieutenant. In that respect at least, things were in order. He must get rid of the extra croissants, Adamsberg thought, so that she would think he had eaten them all.

'Lieutenant, I've got these three guys and I know nothing at all about them.'

'And you want to know everything?'

'Correct. It's to do with the recluse spider. And I've given everyone permission *not* to join in this investigation.'

'The right to go on strike or something? I suppose you mean the three men who died?'

Froissy had dropped the woollen ball. That was a good sign. He was banking on her help. Not that she had made up her mind about the relevance of this project and chosen her camp. That kind of thing was of little importance to her. What did animate her intensely was the chasing up of secret data hidden deep within her computer. The deeper buried it was, the more the chase seemed to galvanise her.

'I hope this is a difficult one,' she said, but her fingers were already hovering over the keyboard.

'You've got the three men's names on the note I gave you all earlier.' Fair skin flushes easily, and Froissy went crimson.

'I'm so sorry, sir, I don't know what I've done with it.'

'Not to worry, the meeting was unpleasant, that's all. I'll give you their names right now. Ready? Albert Barral, born in Nîmes, died 12 May, aged eighty-four, insurance broker, divorced, two children. Fernand Claveyrolle, born in Nîmes, died 20 May, aged eighty-four, art teacher, twice married and divorced, no children. And Claude Landrieu, born in Nîmes, died 2 June, aged eighty-three, shopkeeper.'

Froissy had already encoded this information and was waiting for the rest, hands hovering, and a more relaxed expression on her face.

'The first two, Barral and Claveyrolle, were fellow pupils at La Miséricorde orphanage just outside Nîmes. They got up to all kinds of mischief there. Not on their own, they had a little gang. What kind of mischief? Who else was in the gang? Try looking there. The third victim who died, Claude Landrieu – where did he go to school? Did he know the others? What's their point of contact? And for all three, try to find out if they were ever found guilty in later life of any crime or wrongdoing.'

'So you want to know if they could have made enemies? And whether their schoolboy mischief was just the result of their difficult childhood or whether they turned into really bad guys, temporarily or permanently?'

'Exactly. Find out as well who was running the orphanage back then. Are there records for those years? You're with me?'

'Yes, of course. Where else would I be?'

Back in the bathroom, Adamsberg thought.

'Something else, but probably impossible. I won't get the go-ahead from the divisionnaire to start a formal investigation.'

'No, we shouldn't count on that,' said Froissy.

'So I don't have any right to question the medics who treated these patients. I'm not a family member.'

'What is it you want to know?'

'The general state of health of these men, in the first place. But there's probably no way we can find that out.'

'Up to a point. I can get the names of their local doctors through the social security records. But then I'd have to go deeper into those records, to know what treatment they received. From which one could deduce their possible pathology. Not exactly legal. I'd better tell you, we'd be operating in the realms of piracy.'

'*Seas* of piracy. Pirates, seas.'

'If you like. You're getting like Danglard,' she said with a smile, 'playing on words.'

'Who on earth could get like Danglard, Froissy? It's just that I like the idea of sailing on the high seas.'

'That's because you're just back from Iceland. And there'll be mists on those seas. Well, what do we do? We go right ahead with this?'

'Yes.'

'Very well.'

'Can you cover your tracks afterwards?'

'That goes without saying. Otherwise I'd never suggest it to you.'

'I'd also like to know the dates they were admitted to hospital, that is, how many days after the spider bite. And how the infection developed. Wait a second.'

Adamsberg brought out his notebook, where nothing was written in order, and leafed through it.

'I need to know how their loxoscelism developed.'

'How do you spell that?'

'There's an s between loxo and celism,' said Adamsberg, showing her the page.

'And it means?'

'That's the name of the illness caused by the venom of the recluse spider.'

'Right. You want to know if this loxoscelism developed as normal, or if there was anything abnormal about it.'

'Correct. And if they had any blood tests, what the results showed.'

'Uh-oh,' said Froissy, leaning back from her keyboard and rolling her chair to the side. 'We'd really be on the high seas there. You'd need to know the names of the doctors who treated them in hospital. Well, that's easy enough. But then it means getting into confidential data.'

'So it can't be done?'

'Won't make any promises. Anything else, sir?'

'That's all for now. But it will probably give you more than one day's work. Take your time.'

'I don't mind too much coming in on a Sunday to work, like tomorrow. If needed.'

No, I guess you don't, thought Adamsberg, it would be the ideal refuge for Froissy to come into headquarters, where no crazy neighbour was going to work the lavatory flush every time she turned a tap on.

'That's perfectly OK. I'll add you to the duty roster. Thank you, lieutenant.'

'In fact, if my work keeps me far into the evening,' she said, with a slightly more shaky voice, 'could I perhaps sleep on the cushions in the upstairs room?'

This was the small office with the drinks machine, where three large foam cushions had been installed so that Mercadet could take a nap in his narcoleptic phases.

'It's no problem as far as I'm concerned. Gardon will be on duty downstairs with Estalère. But I don't want you to overdo things.'

'I'm not short of sleep, it'll be fine. I have a little overnight case here – I always keep one for emergencies.'

'It'll be fine,' Adamsberg echoed her.

Now for Mercadet. The commissaire was annoyed with himself for having asked him to do some research when the man was dropping with fatigue. His guilt magnified several times when he saw the grey face of his officer, who was propping his chin up with one hand while he tapped away on the keyboard with the other.

'Stop, lieutenant,' he said. 'I'm very sorry, go and get some sleep.'

'No, no,' said Mercadet in a faint voice. 'I'm just being a bit slow.'

'Mercadet, that's an order.'

Adamsberg helped the lieutenant up by the arm and pulled him towards the stairs. Step by step, he helped him on the long climb up to the first floor. Mercadet collapsed on to the providential cushions. Before he closed his eyes, he raised his arm.

'Commissaire, the neighbour's name is Sylvain Bodafieux. One "f". Aged 36, bachelor, dark hair, balding. He rented the ap . . . um, the ap . . .'

'The apartment.'

'Just three months ago. Door code 3492B. Moves from place to place. Works for a removal firm, he's a s-stepialist . . .'

'Specialist?'

'Yeah, specialist in moving antique furniture, upright pianos, grand pianos, baby grands . . .'

'It's OK, lieutenant, you can go to sleep now.'

'. . . and boudoir grands,' Mercadet murmured, as he dropped off.

*

Bodafieux. Not Marllot. The man was using a false name. Retancourt came into the little room just then, carrying the cat draped over her arm like an old cloth, paws dangling. Stretched out like that, it looked as big as a young lynx. Time for din-dins. Adamsberg put a finger to his lips.

'Got the keys?' he whispered.

'In your left pocket.'

'I'm off. Froissy's going to spend the night here, and all day tomorrow.'

'I'd better go and park her car outside her flat. So the neighbour doesn't smell a rat.'

'If everything goes to plan, there's no need for that.'

Retancourt nodded, looking relieved. Although she was a systematic opponent of Adamsberg's methods, his calming approach sometimes rubbed off on her like a soothing balm. Though as Danglard said, you had to watch out with the commissaire's silent waters, and not let them swirl around you and engulf you along with him.

Adamsberg put on his jacket, felt the keys in the pocket, mixed up with three ragged cigarettes belonging to Zerk. Last stop: Danglard's office. The latter, entrenched behind his desk, was relieving his distress with a steady stream of white wine, which did not prevent him making progress with his draft of The Book.

'This isn't about the recluse,' Adamsberg said as he walked in.

'No? You mean you have some other thoughts, commissaire?'

'Now and then. Danglard, the police commissaire in the 9th.'

'What about him?'

'Name, character, career. This is urgent.'

'Nothing to do with *Loxosceles rufescens*?'

'I just told you, no.'

'Hervé Descartier. He's about fifty-eight.'

Commandant Danglard's memory was not confined to erudition.

He had at his fingertips the names of all the commissaires, commandants and captains in the French gendarmerie, and kept up to date with transfers, promotions and retirements.

'I think I've met him before,' said Adamsberg. 'I must have been a junior and he was already a young lieutenant.'

'What was it about?'

'A naked man found dead on the line of the Paris–Quimper express.'

'Paris–Deauville,' Danglard corrected him. 'Yes, years back. Nice enough guy, quite sharp, gets to the point fast. Sensitive, intelligent, sense of humour, likes word games and tricks. He's not tall, quite slim, a ladies' man, and will be till his last breath. There's a problem, though, that nearly cost him his career.'

'Corruption?'

'Absolutely not. But he bends the rules, if he thinks it'll be more effective to take a short cut.'

'Give me an example, Danglard. Just one will do.'

'Let me see. Well, there was the case of a rapist in Blois, when Descartier kicked the door in without a warrant, and beat the guy up. It wasn't self-defence, and actually they didn't have definite proof he was guilty. The man almost lost an eye.'

'I see.'

'Yes. Descartier got off because, in the end, it *was* the right guy. But they slapped a six-month suspension on him.'

'And when was that?'

'Eleven years ago.'

'Thanks a lot, commandant,' said Adamsberg, making haste to leave, since he had no wish for Danglard to change the subject and get on to the recluse.

'Wait a minute. If you want to contact him you probably won't find him at work on a Saturday. I may have a home phone number for him.'

Danglard leafed through a large folder of handwritten papers on a shelf.

'Got a pen?'

Adamsberg wrote down the number, thanked him again and left. He rarely hurried. But he now crossed the big room quickly, nodding discreetly to Retancourt and, a few minutes later, was driving off towards the 9th arrondissement with a screwdriver in his pocket.

XIV

ADAMSBERG SAT DOWN AT A SIDE TABLE, IN A BRASSERIE ALMOST opposite Froissy's building. It was already nearly four o'clock, and despite his morning croissants, he was hungry. He ordered a sandwich and a coffee, and tapped in the office number of the 9th arrondissement police headquarters. As Danglard had predicted, Hervé Descartier wasn't there. To call him at home made matters more delicate. He considered again the different reactions he might get, but called anyway.

'Commissaire Descartier?'

'He's not here,' replied the breaking voice of a teenager.

The son obviously had his instructions. But the note of uncertainty in his voice indicated that Descartier was indeed at home.

'One second, young man, before you hang up. I know your dad, we've worked together. He is your father?'

'Yes, but he's not at home.'

'Just try this. Tell him it's Commissaire Adamsberg, can you remember the name?'

'Wait while I write it down. But he's not here.'

'Yes, I know. And tell him that I can help him find the man he's after at the moment. That it's urgent.'

'Do you mean the rapist?'

'Since you know all about it, yes. Written all that down?'

'Yes.'

'I know he's not there, but will you go and show it to your father. Can you do that?'

Adamsberg heard the youngster running and a door banged.

'Descartier speaking. Adamsberg? Is that really you?'

'Remember me?'

'Say something else for me to be sure.'

'We worked on the case of the naked man. Found on the track between Paris and Deauville. Contusions on his shoulders and a head injury. For some people, such as you and me, it meant someone had knocked him out first and pushed him on to the tracks. But for other people, such as our boss, whose name was something like Jardion or Jardiot, his death was simply the result of falling on to the rails.'

'Yeah, right, Adamsberg, I do recognise your voice now. Jardiot he was called, Jardiot as in idiot.'

'If you say so.'

'Not that I give a damn about him. OK, I'm listening.'

'Sorry to trouble you at home.'

'If it's about this bastard we're after for rape, you're not troubling me. We're getting nowhere with it.'

'Do you have any DNA?'

'A fingerprint *plus* some DNA. Stupid bugger left a few drops of sperm in the car park when he took off his condom. Talk about a cretin.'

'But you don't have a name?'

'No, he wasn't on the database.'

'Well, I have a suspect, fairly strong case. And I've got a name, Sylvain Bodafieux, lives at 82 rue de Trévise. Temporary lease, under a false name, Rémi Marllot. Self-employed, removals specialist. Interested?'

'Don't wind me up. Why have you fingered this bloke?'

'That's just it. I can't tell you.'

'Thanks a lot. What the fuck am I supposed to do about your "suspect", if I've got nothing to go on? No evidence, no warrant. Forgotten the rules, have you? Why are you keeping it secret? Want the credit for your people?'

'No, not at all. Not bothered about that. But if a whisper of this gets out, even to you, a woman might die. Which I'm anxious to avoid.'

There was a silence, and Adamsberg heard the sound of a cigarette lighter. He got up in turn, made a sign to the waiter and went out on to the pavement to light one of Zerk's cigarettes.

'You smoke now?' asked Descartier.

'No, I'm smoking one of my son's.'

'When I knew you, you didn't have any son.'

'No, I only got to know him when he was twenty-eight.'

'You haven't changed much, I see. So what are you suggesting here?'

'Got the time?'

'It's 4.15.'

'How long would it take you to get six men to the rue de Trévise? You'd need that many, the building might have two exits, best to check.'

'Twenty minutes from when I end this call.'

'OK, say in thirty minutes, you get your men posted. Discreetly, plain clothes in the first place. When I know that the guy is about to come out into the open, I'll call you – give me your mobile number. That's if it *is* our man.'

'And?'

'And then they quickly put on their hi-vis jackets, whip out their guns, act as conspicuous as possible. If you see a guy about mid-thirties, dark hair, thin on top, exiting the building, either quickly or furtively, looking round, and carrying a rucksack or whatever, that's him. If he starts to run when he sees you, it's even more likely to be him.'

'And you're planning to dislodge him somehow?'

'That's right. But I need you to be there to grab him.'

'And how are you going to work this? I know, you can't tell me. OK, understood. This woman, you know her?'

'No.'

'Liar!'

'Yes. Now listen, I can't be sure he's home right now. Normally, he's in the flat all weekend. If you don't see anyone come out, wait – until the evening if necessary. If he's out now, but comes home, believe me he won't take long to come dashing out again.'

'OK, got it. But how am I going to justify having six men hanging around the building?'

'Make something up. You got a phone call from someone in distress, you think someone has been attacked, whatever, you sort that out. And then by pure chance, seeing a man who tries to run away as soon as he catches sight of the cops, you lay hands on him. You take him to the station, flagrant case of evading police pursuit, and you take his prints.'

'Might work, but it's a bit irregular.'

'Since when has that bothered you? Since you kicked in a door and almost put out someone's eye, I seem to recall.'

'Never mind, it was the right guy. Either that or we lost him. The judge didn't want to listen.'

'That's life.'

'Yeah.'

'So are you on?'

'Yes.'

'One more thing, and this is important. In his bag, you'll probably find a laptop, a CCTV receiver and some images on a hard disk.'

'What kind of images?'

'What do you think? Peeping Tom pictures.'

'And?'

'And you pass them to me.'

'You're making a monkey of me, Ad,' said Descartier, reverting involuntarily to the way he had addressed his fellow officer back in the day. 'What evidence have *I* got then? What are you going to do with my evidence?'

'You'll have his prints and his DNA – isn't that enough for you?'

Adamsberg went back inside the café, holding the phone to his ear.

'All right, let's do it,' said Descartier.

'Mind, this is all if it *is* him. I can't promise. But I'm pretty sure I'm right.'

'Why do you want the recordings?'

'To destroy them.'

'Or else she might kill herself? That it? OK, Ad, understood.'

'What time's it now?' asked Adamsberg.

'Haven't you got a watch?'

'Two, but they don't work.'

'You really haven't changed, have you? That's the only reason I'm trusting you on this.'

'Thanks.'

'It's 4.23 now.'

'OK, get going. I'll phone you, don't switch it off for a second.'

Adamsberg finished his sandwich unhurriedly, his eyes on the clock in the café which he had just noticed. He broke camp only at 4.35.

He crossed the rue de Trévise calmly. No one could have taken him for a policeman. He tapped in the door code, went up to the third floor and quietly opened Froissy's door. He went through the sitting room (impeccable, of course), noticed the enormous refrigerator in the kitchen, holding her backup food store, and sat down to take off his shoes. But he didn't think there would be a hidden audio sensor. All spy cameras with 360-degree visibility are equipped with a motion sensor which is more efficient. The world of hidden cameras has made huge progress. They could nowadays be concealed inside pens, light bulbs, cigarette lighters, watches, and sold like harmless toys over the internet under the unambiguous name 'spy camera'. Sent under plain cover, however, and with the pious injunction 'protect your house' – in other words, spy on people. Still, just in case his target was still using sound, he tiptoed on stockinged feet towards the bathroom.

Placing himself outside camera range, climbing on a chair from the sitting room, close against the door jamb, he gently pushed the door open, looked round the room to note the walls, the tiling, the shower, the piping and finally the ceiling. From the side, he could see the smoke detector, with its grooves and battery indicator, a flat round object about 150 millimetres across. Black, but in the centre, something shining like a marble. Shining like a camera lens.

He got down from the chair, grinning to himself and went into the kitchen, closing the door and making no more noise than Snowball the cat on its photocopier, then checked the time on his mobile, which he had set in the café. 4.52. After waiting a minute or two, he called Descartier.

'Are you in position?'

'Just got here. Are you?'

'Yes, I'm on the spot. How long would it take your men to put on their police gear?'

'Two minutes.'

'OK, I'll launch things here. Good luck, Descartier.'

'You too, Ad.'

This time, Adamsberg went into the bathroom without any precautions, carrying his chair, turned on the taps in the basin and washed his hands quite naturally. The next-door toilet flush was immediately activated. The neighbour wouldn't bother filming a man of course. But he was likely to be very cautious. If he wanted to make anyone think it was just some mysterious faulty plumbing, and at the same time to alarm Froissy, while leaving a frightening doubt in the air, he had to set off his waterworks whoever was in the bathroom. In the mirror, Adamsberg watched the 'smoke detector', which was detecting nothing except poor Hélène Froissy. In daylight, Retancourt wouldn't have missed the camera lens, but she had inspected the bathroom at night, looking up, and would have been blinded by the spotlights on the ceiling surrounding the sensor.

Adamsberg switched the lights on, and looked at the false smoke detector. Now you couldn't see the camera lens gleam. With a sense of intense satisfaction, he climbed on the chair and unscrewed the fixture. Now, this very second, the guy must realise what was happening. He put his ear against the north wall, through which he could hear only muffled sounds, but someone was moving about in the next-door flat, pushing aside furniture, opening cupboards.

Precisely eleven minutes later, a man left the building looking wary. Peering out of the window, having raised the blind, Adamsberg watched Descartier's men, who quickly became highly visible with their police jackets and guns. Rémi Marllot (or whatever his real name was), a short fat little man, carrying a rucksack, chose to run as soon as he saw them. Straight into the arms of Commissaire Descartier.

'Whoa! Where do you think you're going?' the commissaire shouted, very loudly, so that witnesses would hear. 'What's your problem? Scared of the cops? Start running when you see us?'

'Got something to hide?' chipped in a lieutenant.

'No! What is this, bloody hell, why are you stopping me?'

'Just asking why you were running.'

'Because I'm in a hurry.'

'You didn't look in a hurry when you came out of the building. Only started running when you saw us.'

'What's in the bag? Weed?'

'No, never touch the stuff.'

'Like touching something else, do you?'

'Get off, what do you want with me?'

'We're just wondering, sir, why you started to run.'

Reassured, Adamsberg pulled down the blind, and removed all traces of his presence in the flat. Froissy must never, ever know that anyone had removed that fitting from her bathroom. A new smoke alarm – a real one – would have to be installed urgently. Adamsberg called Lamarre, a man capable of fixing anything, since he'd built a house for his mother in Granville. Who said he'd have a new one fitted in a couple of hours. Adamsberg sent him a photo of the false detector, so that he could procure a similar model. Although Lamarre did not yet know that he would be operating in Froissy's flat, the commissaire insisted that this was totally confidential, and Lamarre was indeed a little shocked that his discretion should be in doubt. After all, he had once been in the French Army, where secrets remained secret, and it showed in his everyday demeanour. But if Lamarre was somewhat lacking in imagination, he was a man to count on absolutely for the execution of a practical task. Whereas imaginative people – well, it was their job – would be asking questions all the time about the propriety of the procedure.

All that remained was for Descartier to keep his word. Adamsberg felt sure he would.

XV

THE COMMISSAIRE HAD ARRANGED TO MEET RETANCOURT IN THE courtyard behind headquarters. As soon as she heard his car door slam, she was approaching with her large guardsman-like strides.

'All done and dusted,' said Adamsberg calmly. 'She won't know a thing about it.'

He felt in his inside pocket and pulled out the false smoke alarm.

'Take a look,' he said, showing her the little black camera lens, curved and shining in the sun.

'God Almighty,' said Retancourt, frowning with irritation.

'It's over, Violette,' he said gently.

'But it isn't, she'll notice the smoke alarm's gone.'

'As we speak, Lamarre's busy fixing a new one. It'll look almost identical, but this time it's genuine.'

Retancourt did feel admiration for Adamsberg, an emotion she was very bad at expressing, among others.

'I thought the detector looked absolutely normal,' she said, through clenched teeth and still frowning. 'Like it seemed perfectly normal that Froissy had it put in as soon as possible. Shit. I should have spotted it.'

'No.'

'Yes. But I didn't imagine you could fit a spy camera so quickly to a new fixture. How long is it? Only six months they've been compulsory.

That's what fooled me, must have distracted me. But shit, all the same I should have spotted it,' she repeated.

'No, you couldn't. Not when the spotlights were on. It doesn't shine at all then, I tried it out.'

Adamsberg sensed that his lieutenant was relaxing a little, as her regrets could be explained.

'And as I said, "that was all to the good", Violette. Because the guy has now been collared by Descartier's men, that's the chief in the 9th.'

'Jesus, you didn't tell him what it was about, did you?'

'Retancourt!' said Adamsberg simply.

'Sorry, sorry.'

'Like I just said, she won't know a thing. Here are her keys. Get them back into her handbag somehow. I'll be picking up the man's laptop and the images as soon as I can. Meanwhile, just get rid of this piece of shit for me,' he said, passing her the fitting. 'And while you're at it, the pile of croissants Froissy gave me as well.'

'Croissants?'

'So she won't know I didn't eat them all this morning. That matters too.'

'Oh, you're right, it does.'

'When she gets home, she'll notice that the flush next door isn't going off. All will be well.'

'She's scared to go inside the bathroom any more. So how will she know?'

'That's a point.'

'I can only see one solution. I'll invite her round for a meal tomorrow night.'

'And?'

'And when I pick her up, I'll go and wash my hands. And I'll tell her it's all quiet on the bathroom front. I'll try it out several times. Nothing. So the guy must have got his faulty plumbing fixed, it must have been triggered by vibration from the floor in her flat.'

'Is that possible?'

'No, of course not, but I'll convince her, I'll do my utmost.'

'I'm counting on you.'

'The thing is, I've never before asked her to dinner. But I think I can see a plan,' she went on after a moment's thought. 'She's keen on Vivaldi, isn't she?'

'How would I know?'

'Yeah, she is, I've heard her say. Just round the corner from me, there's a little church, and this Sunday there's a Vivaldi concert on there. I could say I don't want to go on my own. I think that would work.'

'Because you were going to go to it anyway?'

'No, what do you think!'

'How are you going to explain that you'll pick her up, instead of her coming over to yours?'

'I won't explain, I'll convince her.'

'Of course.'

'Commissaire, just one thing. This spider. I'm against it, totally against it.'

'I know that, lieutenant. Do we have to get into a discussion about that again? Not that there was any discussion.'

'No, no point.'

'End of conversation, then.'

'Just this, commissaire. If you *do* need anyone to help out over this fucking spider, I'll be there.'

Adamsberg walked back towards the main building, hands in pockets and a smile on his lips. He went into Froissy's office: she was too absorbed in her research to be aware of any movement. He had to put a hand on her shoulder, making her jump when she realised he was there.

'You can switch off for a bit, lieutenant. Time for a break.'

'But I've just started finding things out.'

'All the more reason. Let's go and take a stroll round the courtyard. Have you noticed the lilac is out now?'

'You're asking *me*?' said Froissy, a little offended. 'Who kept it watered during the dry spell when you were in Iceland?'

'You did, lieutenant. But there's something else as well. Remember that pair of blackbirds that nested in the ivy three years ago? Well, they've come back, and the female is on the nest.'

'You think they're the same ones?'

'I asked Voisenet. Yes, he's sure they are – the male is very thin. You wouldn't have a bit of cake, would you? They just love it. Actually, Froissy, what I want is not to talk about the recluse in these offices.'

'I understand. Wait for me in the corridor. I must just finish something off.'

Adamsberg went out. Everyone knew that Froissy wouldn't open the cupboards where she kept food, if anyone else was there – imagining it was a well-kept secret. While being aware at some level that it wasn't. She joined him a moment later with two slices of cake in one hand, and her laptop under her arm.

'Look, there they are,' said Adamsberg, once they were in the yard, pointing to a dense mass of twigs in the ivy on the wall, about two metres up. 'See her? The female? Don't go too close. Here comes the male.'

'You're right, he does look thin.'

Froissy carefully set her laptop down on a stone step and began to crumble one of the cake slices.

'I found out about the orphanage,' she said. 'It was called La Miséricorde Children's Home, back then. It was converted into a youth club twenty-six years ago. So its records may have been destroyed, or transferred somewhere else.'

'Our bad luck then,' said Adamsberg as he scattered more cake crumbs.

'No, wait. The director at the time is dead – well, he would be well over a hundred now! – but he had a son who was brought up inside the orphanage. Not exactly with the orphans, not in the dormitories, but he attended the same lessons and sat with them for meals. He seems to have followed in his father's footsteps, because he became a child psychiatrist. Children's psychological problems. Give me a second.'

Froissy wiped her hands clean of grease from the cake, using a white cotton handkerchief, and opened her laptop.

'I can't remember the title of his book,' she explained, as Adamsberg wiped his own hands on his trousers.

'Your trousers will be ruined.'

'No, they won't. What book?'

'Here we are. The son published a book, privately, just a little brochure: *Father of 876 children*. The text's on open access on the internet, I didn't have to work hard to find it,' she added, a little disappointed. 'He describes the life there, the other boys, the crises, the festivities, the fights, how they sneaked out to peep at the girls through the high fence that separated their quarters. But it's mostly about the subtle methods his father used to care for these abandoned children. Then he analyses the different effects of parental absence. It's insightful and a hard read, but there's nothing to help us there. Except that it proves the son obviously knows a great deal about La Miséricorde, and is closely attached to it. There are loads of precise events, notes, with names and dates, that can only come from the records. He must have them, sir.'

'Excellent, Froissy. And can we somehow contact this son?'

'He lives in Mas-de-Pessac, seventeen kilometres outside Nîmes. His name is Roland Cauvert, he's seventy-nine now. Piece of cake to find him. 5 rue de l'Église. I've got his phone number, email, all you need to get in touch.'

Adamsberg caught Froissy by the arm.

'Don't move. See the male? He's already daring to pick up crumbs, although we're here.'

'Want some cake yourself? I know Zerk stayed behind, in Iceland. And I get the feeling you've not been eating properly since then. I've got something on the third man who died, Claude Landrieu. It's not much. And he wasn't at La Miséricorde.'

'Landrieu, the shopkeeper?'

'Owner of a chocolate shop, to be precise. When he was fifty-five, he was questioned about a rape in Nîmes.'

'Got a date for that? The rape?'

'30 April 1988. Victim's name, Justine Pauvel.'

'And Landrieu was a suspect?'

'No, he turned up spontaneously next day as a witness. He knew the girl well, saw her almost daily. Her parents both worked and Justine came to his shop to do her homework, long-standing family friend, kind of godfather. He knew the names of most of the boys in her class, which was why he went to the police. But none of the leads took them anywhere.'

'Find out where the victim lives today, if you can. I'm always suspicious of spontaneous witnesses. They come running to help the cops without being asked. Have either of the others been suspected of rape?'

'I've begun looking in the court records for the Gard département – nothing so far. I'll extend it to all of France, though as a rule rapists tend to attack on their own ground. And these guys don't seem to have left their département. Still, they could have gone away on holiday or for a weekend, who knows?'

'In the case of the first two, one might suspect revenge for their "mischief" at the orphanage. But seventy years later? And for Landrieu, it could be revenge for a rape. But almost thirty years later? Is someone trying to wipe out these stink bugs?'

'These *what*, sir?'

'They're a kind of horrible smelly beetle, they've got lots of names, but that's the best one. Apparently they eat rat shit, and maybe these three men who died were like that: stink bugs. Still, we keep coming back to the same thing. Can you kill anyone with recluses? No, it's impossible.'

'So it's no use, what I've found?'

'On the contrary, Froissy. Keep on digging and save anything you can find. Impossible or not, there are stink bugs somewhere in this story.'

Adamsberg received the text message from Commissaire Descartier an hour later, as he was about to leave the office.

Prints identical. He's the one.

He replied quickly:

Got the laptop and images?

Yes. Nobody else knows. Fetch when you want.

Then a final message:

Cheers, Ad, and thanks.

Adamsberg put his phone down on Retancourt's desk. She read what it said in silence.

'I won't be in tomorrow, Retancourt. Quick trip to the provinces. I'll be reachable though.'

'Taking Sunday off, are you?'

Adamsberg could hear in her voice the relief she was feeling on Froissy's behalf.

'Yes, that's right. A walk in the country.'

'Languedoc perhaps? Nice area.'

'Very. I plan to go to a little village near Nîmes.'

'Careful, commissaire, they say there are recluse spiders in the area. Apparently they've been biting people.'

'You seem well informed, lieutenant. Want to come too?'

'Can't, I've got Vivaldi tomorrow, remember.'

'Ah yes. Well, that'll be very nice too.'

Adamsberg put his head in at Veyrenc's door.

'Tomorrow morning, 8.43 train to Nîmes? Suit you?'

'I'll be there.'

'And tonight 8.30 at La Garbure?'

'I'll be there too.'

Veyrenc had been right. The investigation into the recluse, even now it was known about, had turned into a sort of plot, obliging Adamsberg to keep his voice down in the office or escape into the courtyard. Which was noticed of course. The atmosphere of secrets and whispers wasn't good for anyone. They needed more troops, and to pool their knowledge.

'Shall we ask Voisenet along?' suggested Veyrenc.

'You're recruiting? I've already got Retancourt onside.'

'Retancourt? How did you manage that?'

'A miracle.'

'So, Voisenet, for tonight?'

'Why not?'

'*We set off only two, but at once by our side, / As we came to the port, hundreds more for us cried. / And while we marched onward, with our hearts full of zeal, / The timid among them found their nerves turned to steel.*'

'Is that one of your Racine imitations?'

'No, it's genuine Corneille, well, twitched a bit. From *Le Cid*.'

'Yes, I thought it sounded a bit better than usual. Do you think Voisenet is one of "the timid among them" about this recluse business?'

'Not a bit of it. Anyone who can deal with a moray eel isn't going to be scared of a spider.'

'OK, invite him then.'

Adamsberg was preparing to drive away when Danglard appeared alongside his car. He lowered the window and put the handbrake on.

'See the little blackbird, Danglard? She's returned to nest here again. Perhaps she'll bring us good luck.'

'They've just arrested the rapist in the 9th,' said the commandant, sounding quite excited.

'Yes, I know.'

'And a few hours ago, you asked me how to get in touch with Descartier.'

'True.'

'So it was you? This arrest?'

'Yes.'

'Without telling anyone? All on your own?'

'I *am* all on my own, aren't I?'

That was below the belt, Adamsberg thought, as he saw Danglard's features collapse. Emotions appeared on Danglard's face like chalk on a blackboard. Adamsberg had just wounded him. But Danglard was beginning to create serious problems for the team. With the weight of his knowledge and the logic of his arguments – for who would believe those men had been killed with recluse spiders as the murder weapon? – Danglard was undermining the cohesion of the squad. He was creating a majority group opposed to the commissaire. For the second time in a year. Good grief, yes, the second time! Of course, Danglard had some right on his side. But on the other hand, he was losing his faculty of imagination, or at any rate his open-mindedness, and even his tolerance. Putting him, Adamsberg, in danger. Danger of losing his authority, though he cared little for that. Danger of appearing insane, but he cared little for that either. Danger of being mocked by his officers, and he did care somewhat about that. Danger that all this would come out, and it *was* coming out, danger of being sacked as incompetent or wayward, and yes, he did care about that. Besides which, if Danglard was going to carry on like this, a confrontation would be inevitable. Him or me. Two stags clashing antlers. His oldest friend. One way or another, he was going to have to settle this.

'We'll talk some more about this, Danglard.'

'What about, the rapist in the 9th?'

'No, you and me.'

And Adamsberg drove off, leaving the commandant standing in the yard with a disconcerted expression on his face.

XVI

FOR THE THIRD NIGHT IN A ROW, ESTELLE SAW OFFICERS FROM THE Crime Squad come into her restaurant. This time, the two from the Béarn were accompanied by a little man with a shock of dark hair and a ruddy complexion, whom she did not know. The policeman with russet highlights had seemed to be showing some interest in her the night before, staying behind after his friend had left, smiling and chatting to her about the mountains back home. But these repeated meetings around the soup tureen were clearly not just a ruse to see her. No, they obviously had some problem, which was obliging them to meet and discuss it every evening. The three men said little until she had brought their food over to the table.

'You don't *have* to eat garbure, Voisenet,' said Adamsberg.

'Aha,' said Voisenet, patting his stomach. 'Since you invited me here, I might have thought this was a ritual initiation to join the secret society. It's that soup you have in your region, isn't it – chuck everything in?'

'Not everything,' Veyrenc corrected him. 'Cabbage, potatoes, shin of pork if there is any.'

'That'll do fine,' said Voisenet, 'I'm not fussy.'

'As for the secret society, or at least the discretion required,' Adamsberg said, 'you're not wrong there. And that's a great pity. The atmosphere in the office is unhealthy.'

'You're telling me. Three factions again. The antis, and facing them, not exactly anyone who's *for*, but the fellow travellers, so to speak. Because – are any of them entirely in favour? And then there's a group that haven't made up their minds, or don't want to get involved. But some of the neutral ones can be well disposed, like Mercadet, or more hostile, like Kernorkian. Is that what you're trying to find out? What's going on inside the squad? But you know that as well as I do.'

'Yes indeed, and I've no intention of using you as a spy, lieutenant. I asked you along to tell you a few new details.'

'Why me?'

'Because you were the first to spot the way the recluse was behaving.'

'I already told you why it interested me.'

'Never mind. Apart from your grandfather, it obviously bothered you.'

'Yes, the thought that the recluse could actually kill someone did bother me. All those rumours about mutations, insecticides, increased numbers, makes you think, doesn't it? It's not bad, your garbure, by the way. So what are these new details, sir?'

'The two men who died, Claveyrolle and Barral, had known each other all their lives, they used to sit and chew the fat, while downing a few Pernods.'

'Nîmes isn't a very big place, as Mordent pointed out. Still, it is a bit odd.'

'Especially when you know they had both been part of a gang of "bad boys" at their orphanage.'

'The sort that bully you in the playground, if you're too fat, or too skinny, or just look helpless? Believe me, I had my share of those. What would I have given to see them dead, back then! But returning to murder my old tormentors, years and years later? No! Was that what you were thinking, sir?'

'Well, it's a possibility,' said Veyrenc. 'In an investigation, we don't ignore coincidences, as you well know.'

'Investigation? When Danglard heard that word, he went ballistic.'

'But in any case, nothing proves they didn't carry on being bastards all their lives.'

'Stink bugs,' said Adamsberg.

'Stink bugs?' said Voisenet. 'Oh, you mean cellar beetles, ones that make a bad smell?'

'Yes.'

'But the third man who died, Landrieu, he wasn't from the orphanage.'

'Maybe they knew each other all the same?'

'And,' said Veyrenc, 'this same Landrieu had come forward as a witness in the case of the teenager who was raped.'

'Uh-oh, spontaneous witnesses who come forward, don't like the sound of that,' said Voisenet.

'As I was about to say,' Adamsberg agreed.

'Did they get the rapist?'

'No.'

'And when was this?'

'Twenty-eight years ago.'

'Ah, well, that's a long time back as well,' said Voisenet, holding out his plate for a second helping. 'But it's not unthinkable. A young woman, who never recovers and decides when she's older she's going to kill the man who raped her. After all that time, who would think of her? Especially if the death is camouflaged by other victims. Of spider bites.'

'We keep coming back to that,' said Adamsberg. 'You can't order a recluse spider to bite, and certainly not sixty of them.'

'Sixty?'

'Do you know how much recluse venom it would take to kill a man, Voisenet?'

'Let's think,' said the lieutenant. 'Three to five vipers I think, at fifteen milligrams per snake. So for a tiny little recluse, five times more, surely?'

'You're close. You'd need the content of forty-four venom glands, or twenty-two spiders.'

'Not counting the times the bites didn't cause any harm.'

'Exactly.'

'But still,' said Voisenet, 'I have to say it again, these guys were *old*. You could imagine that, say, three bites might destabilise the immune system of very old people. It's not a mild poison, you know. Necrosis, septicaemia, haemolysis. Why not three bites?'

'I hadn't thought of that,' said Veyrenc.

'Well, it would be possible,' said Voisenet, warming to his subject and holding out his glass. 'What's this wine?'

'Madiran.'

'Very good. So let's say someone works out a technique for trapping a whole lot of recluses. At night, in the shadows.'

'Or perhaps,' said Veyrenc, 'using a vacuum cleaner to suck them out of their holes, spiders can survive that. Then all you have to do is empty out the vacuum bag and catch them.'

'Good thinking,' said Adamsberg.

'Yes, I could go along with that,' Voisenet said. 'They'd still be alive in the bag. Suppose our killer – well, I say "our", but it doesn't mean I believe in him . . .'

'Yes, we gathered that,' said Veyrenc.

'Let's suppose our killer makes a collection of recluse spiders. He puts three or four inside a shoe, or a pair of trousers – trousers would be good, because they'd stay there – or in a sock, or in an old geezer's bed, well, there's a fair chance the man would squash them, and they'd bite him.'

'The problem with that,' said Adamsberg, 'is that in two of the cases, the victim was outside the house.'

'Ah, shit!' said Voisenet.

Adamsberg and Veyrenc exchanged glances. If Voisenet was put out at the idea that his theory wouldn't work, it was a good sign.

Anyone who's constructed a theory, even on the spur of the moment, will be unhappy to see it demolished. The pathway was opening up, just a little, but opening.

'Or,' said Adamsberg slowly, 'of course the two old men could have been lying. Perhaps they were bitten indoors.'

The three men sat silently pondering this new hypothesis. Estelle brought over their cheese course, Tomme again.

'But I don't see why they *would* lie about that,' Voisenet said at last.

'No, nor do I,' said Adamsberg, who had in fact thought of one reason why that might be the case, but preferred to let Voisenet pursue the train of thought for himself.

'It's a bit unlikely,' said Voisenet at last. 'But let's suppose they were lying because they *knew*.'

'Knew what?' said Adamsberg.

'That someone was taking revenge on them. And in that case, you might not want to tell other people you'd done something bad enough to deserve vengeance.'

'With recluse spiders?' said Adamsberg.

'We'd also have to imagine,' Voisenet went on, 'that the recluse was some kind of *sign* of vengeance. For instance, that they had already done some harm with recluse spiders back in the orphanage. Suppose when they found a spider, they put it in the bed of some poor little boy they were picking on?'

Voisenet sat up, took another mouthful of wine and grinned, proud of his performance. Adamsberg and Veyrenc exchanged glances again.

'Of course,' Voisenet went on, 'you'd need to find out what happened in the old days in the orphanage. But how would you do that? It's over seventy years ago!'

'Froissy has traced the son of the former director of the orphanage. He's now a child psychologist. She thinks it's highly likely he's kept the records.'

'So Froissy's one of us, is she?' said Voisenet, using a conspiratorial formula. 'She's doing a search for you?'

'She doesn't mind what the subject is. The chase is what lights her fire.'

'Well, this guy should definitely be interviewed then,' said Voisenet firmly.

'That's tomorrow's programme,' said Adamsberg. 'Veyrenc and I are going to Nîmes in the morning.'

'What about the woman who was raped?'

'I'm not forgetting her. But there are just two of us.'

'This woman, does she live far from Paris?'

'No, not all that far. She works in Sens now.'

Voisenet finished his glass, looking thoughtful. Adamsberg silently passed him a note with the address of the woman, Justine Pauvel. The lieutenant nodded.

'Leave it to me,' he said.

XVII

'I DON'T HAVE EVERYTHING, MESSIEURS, FAR FROM IT,' DR CAUVERT said, waving his arms as though trying to dispel a crowd of gnats. 'Just think, the orphanage, as it was called in those days, was founded in 1864. So, you see!'

This man was astonishingly fidgety, walking round the room with little jumps or fast footsteps by turns, shaking his head to throw back his long white hair, and all with a lively air that took ten years off his age. It was a long time, he had explained as he warmly welcomed them, since anyone had shown any interest in the records. 'A veritable gold mine, though,' he explained, 'so vast and rich that I won't manage to exploit it all in my lifetime. Just think, 876 children in all, their lives, from birth or early childhood until the age of eighteen. And for each orphan's life, my father noted down every detail, night after night. Thirty-eight years, thirty-eight volumes.'

Then the doctor seemed to realise he had not yet invited his visitors to sit down, or offered them any refreshment, in the 33-degree heat of the day in Nîmes. He moved the piles of books from two chairs, and hurried into the kitchen to fetch something to drink.

'Dynamic, isn't he?' said Veyrenc.

'Very,' said Adamsberg. 'You'd think a psychiatrist would be sitting down calmly, not jabbering away and hopping about like that.'

'Perhaps he wasn't like that with his patients. He seems really glad to see us, as if he hadn't talked to anyone for years.'

'Could be the case.'

Froissy had sent them a short message while they were on the train: *Dr Roland Cauvert, only child, bachelor, no children. Aged 79. Working on a second book entitled 876 Orphans, 876 Destinies.*

Then they had received a text from Voisenet at 2.20 p.m.

Just arrived, sir.

Where? Adamsberg had texted back.

Sens.

'Well, he didn't waste time,' Veyrenc had commented.

'You'll see everything, in the fullness of time,' Dr Cauvert continued enthusiastically, with an expansive gesture of his arms. 'If divine providence gives me another five years, I shall have produced the definitive work on the paedopsychiatry of abandoned children. I have already devised an analysis based on the daily trajectories of 752 of them – I've got 124 to go. And then, of course, I'll have to factor in peer-group pressure, paradoxes and similarities, syntheses, and their adult careers, whenever I've been able to trace them, their occupations, their marriages, and whether they turned out to be satisfactory parents. Oh yes, this'll make him rise from the grave and bow down.'

'Who?' asked Veyrenc, though he knew the answer.

'Why, my father!' cried the doctor, laughing out loud. 'I've only got tap water and apple juice in the house, nothing else, I'm afraid. Because, as you can imagine, what with all these maladjusted kids, my father had precious little time for me. I was his only child, but he hardly saw me. The invisible child – that was me. He never remembered a single one of my birthdays. But thanks be to divine providence' – here he laughed again – 'I had my mother, and she was a saint. Ice? I didn't ever want to have children myself. I've seen too many orphans to believe that fathers stick around for ever, as you might imagine. Well, anyway,' he said, passing them drinking glasses, 'that's not why you're here. So go ahead, be my guest, dig into this big cauldron where all those unfortunates are preserved. What names was it, and which years?'

'Just two, doctor. A boy aged eleven in 1943, Albert Barral, came to –'

Dr Cauvert laughed again, but this time it was a short, sharp laugh.

'Well I never! Young Barral, you say? Barral, Lambertin, Missoli, Claveyrolle, Haubert . . . !'

'Claveyrolle interests us as well.'

'Oh, the whole gang then? The worst group of boys my father knew in his thirty-eight years in post. The only ones he couldn't master, the only kids he ever wanted to send somewhere else. There was the very devil in them. I know as a psychiatrist I shouldn't say that, but it's what my father used to say, and when I was little I thought it was the truth. He tried everything. He talked to them at length, he listened to them, trying to understand, he brought in doctors, medicine. And he handed out punishments too, keeping them in, stopping treats. Tried everything. Was it all predestined? Would things have been different if it hadn't been for that little demon, Claveyrolle? Because he was the ringleader, the boss of the gang, the dictator, call him what you like. There's always one. But I'm so stupid! Marie-Hélène brought me some apple tart with cinnamon, and it's four o'clock. That woman is a gift from heaven.'

The doctor shot off again into the kitchen, excited by the thought of the tart.

'Claveyrolle and Barral. Stink bugs,' said Adamsberg.

'Don't go saying that kind of thing to a child psychiatrist.'

'He already called Claveyrolle a demon, and said they all had the devil in them. I envy this doctor, he seems to have a great relish for life. I don't think I'm in his league. An apple tart would never get me so excited.'

'He must be a little unbalanced, Jean-Baptiste. Imagine, being the invisible son of his perfect father. And still wanting his father's approval today – that's why he's doing all this.'

'Perhaps he's never really left the orphanage.'

Cauvert bustled back in cheerfully, served out the tart on plates for the visitors. He ate his own standing up, with voracious bites.

'Ah, well, you're in luck, because my father had a special file on Claveyrolle's gang. What a little shit! I can see him now. Impossible to get rid of him – well, to transfer him somewhere else. It was wartime, there were plenty of orphans, and you can imagine the other children's homes weren't exactly welcoming kids like that with open arms. He spread terror throughout La Miséricorde. I think Missoli and Torrailles were his lieutenants. I was five years younger than them, but they didn't come near me. Son of the director, no, they wouldn't touch me. Anyone who spoke to me was treated as a toady and threatened by the gang of bullies. Nobody ever touched a hair of my head, true, but I never had a single friend either. My bad luck, eh? How's the apple tart?'

'Excellent,' said Veyrenc.

'Thanks, commissaire.'

'He's the commissaire,' said Veyrenc, pointing to Adamsberg.

'Oh, sorry, I didn't imagine. No offence?'

'None taken,' said Adamsberg, standing up, feeling he'd been sitting long enough. 'So your father had gathered some documentation on this Claveyrolle gang?'

'Can you do me a favour, commissaire? Tell me what Barral ended up doing. I know about Claveyrolle – art teacher. A teacher, that's ironic, isn't it? But he had a gift, that's true enough, especially for caricaturing the teachers, or drawing naked women on the playground walls. There was one time – you'll see, it's in the file – he managed to get inside the girls' dormitory, and covered the walls with paintings. Paintings of what, do you think? Cock and balls, times fifty! But what about Barral?'

'He worked in insurance.'

'Ah, he settled down then. Unless of course he was a crook. Married?'

'Divorced. He had two children. Claveyrolle was married and divorced twice, no children.'

'Couldn't forge a proper relationship – that will have been true of a lot of them. How can you create a family, when you have no idea what it's like?'

And as Veyrenc had predicted, Dr Cauvert, once he was on professional ground became quite calm, concentrated indeed, and almost sad. Perhaps he had learned to laugh a lot and take pleasure in apple tart, in order to forget for a while the 876 damaged lives he had been following, step by step.

'They kept in touch with each other all their lives.'

'Really? So the gang didn't break up when they were older?'

'No, they used to meet again over a few drinks, well, two of them did.'

'And now they're dead,' said Veyrenc.

'I should have guessed. You're cops, after all. Someone must be dead. What happened?'

'They died last month, a week apart,' said Adamsberg. 'Both as the result of a bite by a recluse spider.'

Dr Cauvert's face suddenly froze. Without a word, he stacked the plates, collected the glasses, and then abandoned this diversionary activity to go over to his bookcase, from which he took down a faded blue cardboard folder. With a serious expression, he placed it on the table in front of the two officers, without taking his eyes off them. The folder carried a large label, stuck on and fixed back again many times, after years of use. Written on it in black ink was the heading 'The Recluse Gang' and underneath in smaller letters: 'Claveyrolle, Barral, Lambertin, Missoli, Haubert and Co.'

'What does this mean?' asked Adamsberg, after a good minute of silence.

'It means "live by the recluse and die by the recluse" – doesn't it?'

'But you can't die by a recluse,' said Veyrenc.

'No, but you can do a lot of damage with one. That was one of their favourite tricks, apart from all the other brutal attacks, not to mention being sex pests.'

Cauvert pulled from the file a series of photographs of some very young boys which he spread out on the table, flipping through them as if they were playing cards.

'Here's what they did,' he said with disgust. 'Eleven other kids, eleven victims of their cruelty – and their recluses. These four,' he said, pointing to their pictures, 'only received harmless bites. And these two only got slightly infected – here, you can see on Henri's arm, a purple patch about nine centimetres across. He recovered, and so did this one, Jacques. But on the other five, just take a look at the damage.'

Adamsberg and Veyrenc passed the five photographs to each other. One showed a small boy of about four whose leg had been amputated, another a boy who had lost his foot.

'Those two were bitten by spiders in 1944. Louis and Jeannot, aged four and five. In those days, penicillin was only just starting to appear. And the first serious consignments went as a priority to the troops in Normandy after the D-Day landings. It wasn't possible to treat the children, or to save their limbs from the gangrene that developed. They had to amputate. My father went to court about it. Claveyrolle, Barral and Lambertin spent eight months in a boys' reformatory. So then what was known as the "recluse nightmare" went quiet for a while. But as soon as they got out, they started it again.'

Looking serious, the doctor fetched the three glasses from the tray and refilled them with apple juice.

'Sorry,' he said as he passed them across, 'the ice cubes have melted.'

He drank his own juice off in one gulp, and returned to the photographs.

'This one here is Ernest, aged seven. He has a wound almost ten centimetres long and five across. It was 1946, so this time, the doctors were able to save his arm. Also in 1946, here we have Marcel, aged twelve: look, half his face is eaten away. Yes, he was cured too, but disfigured, with a horrible scar, as indeed was Ernest's arm. Finally we have Maurice, aged eleven in 1947, bitten on the left testicle. Just a little marble left, see, and in fact the necrosis spread to the penis, so he became impotent. In 1948, the attacks using recluse spiders came to an end. Claveyrolle turned his attention to sexual abuse. Along with the others of course. He was the leader of a little gang of eight other little bastards who stuck as close to their hero as they did to their shadows.'

Adamsberg quietly put down the abominable photographs of mutilated children.

'How did they do it, doctor?'

'They would go out at night, and there were plenty of places they could collect the creatures: under the eaves, in the playground, the barn, the woodpile, the toolshed. These spiders were quite plentiful in summer round here. What we gathered afterwards was that they lured them with other insects they'd collected, flies, crickets especially, laid out on the ground in a likely place. Did you know that the recluse spider feeds on the corpses of other insects?'

'No,' said Veyrenc.

'Well, it does, so that made it easier for them. They just put a few flies down on the ground and waited with their pocket torches.'

'But how did they catch the spiders without being bitten themselves?' asked Adamsberg naively, in the manner of Estalère.

Dr Cauvert looked at him in puzzlement.

'You've never caught any spiders?' he asked.

'No, just toads.'

'You just need a glass and a bit of cardboard. You trap the spider under the glass and you slide the cardboard underneath and there you are.'

'Oh, it's simple,' Adamsberg agreed.

'Not that simple, actually. Recluses are timid creatures. They didn't catch very many, eleven in four years. But that was already too many. They would choose their victim, and at night, they'd slip the spider into a shirt or a pair of trousers. And then the inevitable happened. The creature was cornered and it bit. What bloody little savages! When I think that after that, you could get to be an art teacher and walk around in a three-piece suit.'

'You're not trying to take a medical approach?' Veyrenc enquired.

'No, I'm not,' said Cauvert sharply. 'Don't forget, I knew them and I knew their victims. I hated the Recluse Gang with all my heart. My father did what he could. He had the dormitory doors watched more closely, he shook out the children's clothes every morning, he closed off the yards. But it wasn't enough. These boys were wicked, and proud of being so, arrogant about their virility, and high on their power inside the Miséricorde community. And they got what they wanted, because sadism always generates plenty of energy and ideas. Lights out was at 9 p.m., so how did they get out at night? Some of them were even seen in town after nightfall. They'd gone there on bicycles, after forcing the bike shed. You can have the whole file – make a copy and look after it carefully. If one of their little victims has finally taken his revenge on them in his old age, messieurs, an eye for an eye and a tooth for a tooth, a recluse for a recluse, well, just let him be! That's the only thing that would give me pleasure.'

Adamsberg and Veyrenc walked together back up the long rue de l'Église without speaking, too stunned to raise at once the subject of recluse spiders, those of today and those of the past, meeting up after an interval of seventy years.

'Pretty little street, this,' remarked Veyrenc.

'Yeah, it is.'

'See that niche over the door? With the statue of a saint? Danglard would say it was sixteenth century.'

'He would.'

'He'd say the stone is very worn down, but you can recognise a dog beside him. So it must be St Roch who protects people from the plague.'

'Yes, indeed. And to make him happy, I would ask, "Why is St Roch shown with a dog alongside?"'

'And he'd explain that St Roch caught the plague and took refuge in a forest, so as not to contaminate anyone else. But the dog belonging to the lord of the local manor brought him food it had stolen every day. And he got better.'

'Do you think he'd protect people from recluse spider bites as well?'

'Absolutely.'

'And what would Danglard say about recluse bites?'

'Knowing what we know now, he'd be in quite a fix what to say.'

'Deep in shit is what you mean. Because there really *is* a case here with these recluses, isn't there? Yes or no?'

'Yes.'

'And it all began from *this* rock. The orphanage. Do you think Danglard will admit to being mistaken?'

'He's going to have to admit to more than that. I found something out yesterday.'

'And you didn't tell me?'

'Danglard was intending to take his concerns to Divisionnaire Brézillon, so as to get the recluse trail completely closed off.'

Adamsberg stopped still and stared at Veyrenc.

'What did you say?'

'You heard.'

'Talk to Brézillon! And why not get me suspended while he was at it? With a reprimand for incompetence?' said Adamsberg, speaking quickly, his top lip trembling with surprise and anger.

'That wasn't what he was after. He thought the squad was being led in the wrong direction. He said as much to Mordent. Who told Noël. And Mordent and Noël, yes, Noël, our own local bully, marched round to Danglard's office, where Noël put an end to the plan by banging his fist on the table. It is said some of the pages of The Book fell to the ground. And Noël threatened – you know how tactful he is – to lock Danglard in his office if he made the slightest attempt to contact the divisionnaire.'

'Who told you all this?'

'Retancourt.'

'But why? Why did Mordent and Noël take my side?'

'Instinctive protection of the herd from the top brass. Defence of our squad, defence of our territory. You could add a poetic note actually.'

'You think this is really the moment, Louis?'

'We know that Mordent was totally opposed to following up the recluse business. But he's also a fanatic about fairy tales. And believe me, there's so much that's improbable and unreal in the story of our recluse that it isn't unlike some kind of fairy tale.'

'A *fairy* tale?'

'All fairy tales are cruel by nature, that's their distinguishing feature. And something about it, perhaps without his realising it, must be attracting Mordent to this business.'

'Not Danglard, though. He began by creating division in the squad then he tried to get me locked up. Louis, is Danglard becoming a stink bug?'

'No. He's frightened.'

'What of?'

'Of losing you perhaps. And then losing himself. He thought he was saving you both.'

'But his fear, if that's what it is,' said Adamsberg, gritting his teeth, 'has turned him into a traitor.'

'That's not the way he sees it.'

'Well, don't tell me he's simply lost his wits.'

Veyrenc hesitated.

'I could be wrong,' he said, 'but I think it might be some deeper kind of fear.'

XVIII

DURING THE SHORT DRIVE TO THE STATION, IN AN OVERHEATED BUS, Adamsberg remained silent, sending texts from his phone. Veyrenc did not interrupt him, waiting for him to calm down. His dark mood was quite understandable. But Adamsberg was not a man to remain angry for long. His wayward mind prevented him from travelling far down the clear trajectory of rage.

'You should get another phone,' Veyrenc finally remarked.

'Why?'

'Because if you keep typing the wrong letters, p for n and all that, you'll end up being infected.'

'What do you mean?'

'You'll start talking like it, saying "soop" for "soon". Change it.'

'Another day,' said Adamsberg, pocketing his mobile. 'We're meeting someone at the station buffet.'

'If you like.'

'You don't want to know who?'

'Yes, tell me.'

'Remember Irène Royer, the woman I met in the Natural History Museum?'

'The one who offered you a fur coat full of dead recluses?'

'The one who overheard Claveyrolle and Barral talking when she went out for a glass of port. She might be able to recall more of their conversation. She lives locally, in Cadeirac.'

'Well, since she's local . . . Is she making the journey for your sake?'

'No, for the recluse's sake, Louis.'

Irène Royer was waiting impatiently for them at the bus station, waving her walking stick in the air to greet them.

Adamsberg had told her he had some news. In the southern heat, she had exchanged her jeans for an old-fashioned flowery dress, but was still wearing ankle socks and trainers.

'Must be her, I guess,' said Veyrenc looking out of the bus window, 'Exactly the kind of person to offer you dead recluses in all innocence.'

'Admit it, Louis, you're jealous of my dead spider.'

While Irène Royer was moving to shake hands with the commissaire – apparently pleased to see him again, or perhaps to hear his news – her eyes alighted on Veyrenc's hair: the russet patches were particularly visible in the glaring sunshine of Nîmes, and her hand halted. Embarrassed, Adamsberg grabbed the hand in mid-air and shook it.

'Thank you for coming, Madame Royer.'

'You were calling me Irène last time.'

'Yes, true. And let me introduce my colleague, Lieutenant Veyrenc. He's helping me on the recluse case.'

'Ah, but I never said *I* was going to help you with it.'

'No. I know. But as we happened to be just round the corner from you, I wanted to come and thank you.'

'Is that all?' asked Irène. 'So you haven't got anything new to tell me? Commissaire, you never seem to tell the truth.'

'Let's go into the café here. That bus was like an oven.'

'I like the heat, it's good for my arthritis.'

As if it had become a habit by now, Adamsberg took Irène's elbow and steered her to a distant table overlooking the railway tracks.

'No more stones through your windows?' he said as they sat down.

'No. No new spider bites, so the ignoramuses are giving up. They've forgotten about it. But you haven't, have you? What exactly are you doing in Nîmes, if that's not being too nosy?'

'We followed the trail you pointed out, Irène. Would you like a hot chocolate?'

'You're going to try and get me to promise something again, aren't you?'

'Well, to keep a secret, yes. Or I can't tell you what we've found. A cop isn't supposed to divulge information about an investigation.'

'Ah, keeping a secret, that's quite normal. I'm sorry.'

Irène's gaze had once more diverted quite openly towards Veyrenc's variegated hair, and it wasn't clear whether she was more interested in hearing the news or in finding out how he had acquired these striking highlights. Adamsberg glanced at the café clock – their train would leave at 18.38. He was wondering how to regain the attention of the little woman, when she came out bluntly with a question:

'Do you dye your hair, Lieutenant? It's the fashion, isn't it?'

Adamsberg had never heard anyone dare ask Veyrenc to his face about his hair. People noticed it, but said nothing.

'It was when I was a kid,' Veyrenc told her, without embarrassment. 'This gang of boys cut my scalp in fourteen places, and when the hair grew again it was ginger.'

'That can't have been much fun!'

'No.'

'Kids, rotten kids, nothing between the ears, they do something like that for fun, not thinking it could last a lifetime.'

'Yes, indeed,' said Adamsberg, signalling to Veyrenc to bring out Dr Cauvert's folder. 'I was just saying that we followed your trail.'

'What trail?

'The secret link, like an eel hiding under a rock.'

'Your *moray* eel under a rock, you mean.'

'Well remembered. Anyway, the first two old men who died. The ones you saw in the café, when you went out for your port.'

'Just *one* glass,' Irène made it clear, for Veyrenc's benefit. 'At 7 p.m., not before and not after.'

'Well, you said they were talking about the mischief they got up to,' Adamsberg insisted, 'and that was the eel I followed.'

'Well?'

'And it was indeed a moray eel.'

'Can you stop talking in riddles please, commissaire?'

'The son of the former director of the orphanage has kept his father's archives. Including a whole folder about the "bad boys". And mischief, well, they did a lot of that – really nasty things. So you were right. Claveyrolle was the ringleader and Albert Barral followed his lead. A whole gang of stink bugs.'

'Stink bugs?'

'Don't you remember? It was *you* that told me about them. Cellar beetles. Little bastards. I hope you're not squeamish?'

'Oh, yes, I am.'

'Have a sip of your chocolate then, to give yourself courage.'

Adamsberg put on the table one after another the photos of the victims of recluse bites, starting with those whose bites had become necrotic, but who had survived.

'Do you know what these are, Irène? You recognise the signs?'

'Yes,' she said in a low voice. 'That's what happens if a recluse bite goes necrotic. Oh my God, that one has a terrible wound.'

'And this one,' said Adamsberg, 'has had a third of his face disfigured. Eleven years old.'

'Oh my God!'

Then he gently put in front of her the photos of the two children who had had limbs amputated. Irène gave a little cry.

'I'm not trying to upset you. But I *am* telling you where this eel under the rock led to. In the case of these two children, penicillin wasn't yet available. Little Louis, four years old, lost a leg, and Jeannot, who was five, his foot.'

'Holy Mother of God. So that's what they called getting up to mischief?'

'Yes. And they had a name: the Recluse Gang. Claveyrolle, Barral and the others. They caught spiders, and hid them in clothes of other children they'd decided to persecute. Eleven victims in all, two amputations, one disfigured, and one who became impotent.'

'Holy Mother of God. But why are you showing these to me?'

'To help you understand, and I'm sorry to have given you a shock like this, that the two old chaps sipping their drinks in La Vieille Cave, were the lowest of lowlifes. Louis and Jeannot were their first victims, but that didn't stop them, they carried on doing the same thing for four years.'

'When I think,' muttered Irène, 'when I think I was sitting alongside them, sipping my port, alongside those bastards, sorry, language, excuse me. When I think back.'

'That's just what I'm asking you to do, to think back, and to try really hard.'

'Ah now, I told myself you'd be wanting something from me. But wait a minute,' she interrupted herself. 'Does that mean you were right? That these two were killed deliberately with a spider bite, because one of these poor kids was taking revenge? And what about the third man who died? What was his name?'

'Claude Landrieu.'

'Was he in the orphanage too?'

'No. We're just at the beginning of this, Irène.'

'But you *can't* kill someone with a recluse, there's no getting away from that.'

'What about if you had a few of them? Let's say three or four, hidden in someone's trousers? And then if the person was very old . . .'

'. . . they might die?' Irène finished the sentence.

'You follow me? As Professor Pujol would say.'

'Still, all the same, *three* old men died. That means if someone killed them, they'd have had to find, ooh, nine to twelve recluses. Not so easy.'

'It's true,' Veyrenc said, 'that those kids only managed to catch eleven in four years. And there were nine of them in the gang, and they were used to it.'

'What about someone breeding them? What if the killer was breeding spiders?' asked Adamsberg.

'Begging your pardon, commissaire, but I can see you still don't know much about spiders. You think maybe they lay eggs, and then you can collect them when they hatch, like baby birds? No, no, it doesn't work like that. When baby spiders are born, they fly, they're carried away by the wind on gossamer, like little specks of dust to take their chances, if they don't get snapped up by birds. Out of a couple of hundred, maybe two or three remain – have you ever tried to catch a speck of dust?'

'I have to say, no.'

'Well, that's what little recluses would be like.'

'What about if you put them in a box, so they couldn't fly away?'

'They'd eat each other. The mothers would start on the little ones.'

'What do they do in scientific labs then?' asked Veyrenc.

'No idea. I dare say it's very complicated. Labs are always complicated places. You think your killer has lots of special equipment?'

'If he happened to work in a lab, why not?' said Veyrenc.

'Anyway, your idea doesn't work. You're forgetting that the old men were bitten out of doors in the evening, not because there was a spider in their trousers when they got up. I already told you about that.'

'What if they were lying?' said Adamsberg.

'Why would they do that?'

'Because they *did* know. If they got three recluse bites, from inside their trousers, they'd know what that meant. And they wouldn't want anyone else to know that someone was taking revenge. They wouldn't want anyone to know that they were persecuting little kids back in the orphanage.'

'Oh, I see what you mean. I think I'd have lied too.'

'So, Irène, please, can you concentrate and think back? Can you remember any more precise details of their conversations?'

'Yes, but if it was one of the little kids getting back at them, I wouldn't want him to be caught.'

'Well, we all think that. I didn't say I was going to catch him. But if it is one of them, I might be able to persuade him to stop before he spends the rest of his life in jail.'

'Oh, I see. I suppose you could be right.'

Irène, as Adamsberg had already seen her do, leaned her head back to think, eyes staring straight ahead, out of the window.

'There might be something,' she said, finally. 'Wait a minute. It was something they said about this car boot sale there'd been in Écusson, oh, ten years ago or so now, on the main square. Those sales, there's nothing much worth buying, just old shoes going cheap, you know, but people like to come out and chat. Mind you, this dress is from a car boot sale, and it's fine.'

'Very becoming,' said Veyrenc quickly.

'One euro,' said Irène. 'Now just a minute, wait while I think. It was the big one who was talking.'

'Claveyrolle.'

'Right, Claveyrolle. He was saying something like, "Guess who I saw at the fucking car boot sale." I'm sorry, forgive me, really, language! But I have to tell it the way they were talking.'

'That's fine.'

'So he said that. And then he said. "Little Louis. The so-and-so recognised me, no idea how." Is Little Louis one of those children?'

'Yes, the one who lost a leg.'

'Well, the other one, Barral, he said to the big one, Claveyrolle, yes? That maybe it was because of his *teeth* that Louis recognised him.

Because even when he was a kid, Claveyrolle was missing some teeth. That's what they thought anyway, Little Louis had spotted him and the big one wasn't at all pleased about that. Oh no, not at all. He was very grumpy. Oh yes, he said something else, that the little so-and-so (I won't say what he really called him) was as skinny as ever with stick-out ears, but he'd had the cheek to threaten him. So he'd told him to piss off (sorry, that's what he said). But this Little Louis had said, "You better watch out, Claveyrolle, I'm not alone." '

'Not alone? So the victims might have carried on seeing each other?'

'How would I know? But you know, these days, with all that stuff on the internet, social media, Friends Reunited, School Mates and so on, everybody seems to like catching up with everybody else. So why shouldn't these men?'

Then Irène gave a jump.

'Your train!' she cried. 'It's at the platform, I heard a whistle.'

Adamsberg just had time to gather up his photos. Veyrenc grabbed the folder and they both ran to the platform.

Adamsberg sent Irène a text: *V. sorry about the chocolate, no time to pay.*

Irène texted back: *Don't worry, I'll get over it.*

Two new texts were awaiting him. One from Retancourt: *Have a nice time?* and Adamsberg showed it to Veyrenc with a smile.

'Retancourt is moving our way,' he said. 'We'll soon be four, instead of three. What was that Racine poem?'

'Corneille, you mean.'

'You'll have to change it.'

'*We set off only* four, *but at once by our side, / As we came to the port, hundreds more for us cried –*'

'So there you are,' Adamsberg interrupted him, raising his hand. 'With *four* of us working, we'll be able to question the five victims.'

'Eleven victims.'

'Yes, but four of the eleven didn't get infected at all, and two only slightly. They didn't suffer like the others.'

'Still, absolutely not a reason to rule them out. They were part of the target group, they'd take the side of the ones who were badly affected. And the ones who got off with no harm might feel guilty about the others. It's called "survivor guilt". They might even become *more* vengeful and aggressive than the others.'

'All right, eleven. We'll have to ask Froissy to trace them for us.'

Adamsberg replied to Retancourt: *Very. An intensely relaxing day.*

Interesting?

VERY interesting.

'There's a message from Voisenet too. He'll be at the station waiting for us. What time do we get in?'

'21.53.'

'He says shall we go for a garbure?'

Veyrenc nodded.

'Yes, they're open on Sundays.'

'You know that?'

'Yes. Shall we ask Retancourt to join us? Swell the ranks?'

'No, impossible, she's at a Vivaldi concert tonight.'

'And you know that?'

'Yes.'

Adamsberg typed a last text, slipped his phone into his pocket and went straight off to sleep. Veyrenc stopped short in mid-sentence, always taken aback by the commissaire's ability to sleep suddenly. His eyelids were closed, but not quite, leaving a narrow slit like in a cat's eye. Some said you couldn't always tell whether the commissaire was asleep or awake, even when he was walking along, and that he hovered between the two states. Perhaps it was during those moments, Veyrenc told himself, as he opened Dr Cauvert's folder, that Adamsberg was thinking. Perhaps those were the mists through which he could see clearly. He lowered the tray at his seat and drew up a list of the nine members of the Recluse Gang. Then a list of their victims, Louis, Jeannot, Maurice . . . where were they now? The one without a leg, the one without a foot, the one without a cheek, the one without a testicle, and the one with the hideous-looking arm?

He read the rest of the report carefully, shaking his head. All the members of the Recluse Gang had fetched up in the orphanage as a result of tragic circumstances. Their parents had died, or been deported during the war, the father had been murdered by the mother, or vice versa, a parent had been imprisoned for rape or murder, a whole litany of tragedy. After the time with the recluse spiders, came the time they attacked girls. They'd managed on only one occasion to get inside the girls' dormitory (supposed to be 'inviolable') and the janitor had stopped them as they started pulling off blankets and sheets from the beds. As Dr Cauvert had said, these kids had managed to get in everywhere.

'He's neurotic,' said Adamsberg quietly, without opening his eyes.

'Who?'

'Cauvert, you said so yourself.'

'Jean-Baptiste, get it into your head once and for all that every one of us is neurotic. It all depends on the balance we manage to work out afterwards.'

'Me too? I'm neurotic?'

'Certainly.'

'Ah, good.'

Adamsberg went back to sleep, while Veyrenc went on taking notes. The closer the train got to Paris, the more Danglard's face loomed up before him. For heaven's sake, what had got into him? Adamsberg's anger had faded, he hadn't mentioned it again. But Veyrenc knew that he was heading for some kind of showdown.

XIX

VEYRENC STOPPED ON THE PLATFORM, ABOUT FIFTEEN METRES AWAY from Voisenet, who was smoking an illicit cigarette in one of the best ventilated sites in Paris.

'Does Voisenet smoke?' he asked.

'No. Perhaps he pinched it from his son.'

'He doesn't have a son.'

'Then I don't know.'

'Ever see Balzac?'

'No, Louis, the occasion never arose.'

'Well, take a look at Voisenet, and you see Balzac. He doesn't have the frowning eyebrows. And he's not quite as fat yet, but add a black moustache and then you have Balzac.'

'So Balzac's not dead, all things considered?'

'Correct.'

'That's good to know.'

Estelle welcomed the three police officers with no sign of surprise. For as long as their problem lasted, she'd be seeing the policeman with the russet streaks every night. It was starting to feel like a habit, and the habit was turning into a vague desire. When their case was solved, they'd vanish, and he would go with them. She decided to withdraw a bit, and make herself less welcoming this evening.

'For a change,' said Voisenet, 'I'm going to order the suckling pig tonight. Is that a good idea?'

'In Danglard's opinion, certainly,' said Veyrenc.

'But what weight should be put on Danglard's opinion now?' asked Adamsberg. 'On pork, yes, agreed, but not beyond. You've had some echoes of it, Voisenet, have you? Apparently, Noël thumping the desk caused a bit of a stir.'

Voisenet lowered his head and clasped his hands on his stomach. Veyrenc stood up and went to the counter to order. It had not escaped Adamsberg's attention that Estelle was avoiding looking at his Béarn colleague. She was moving one of her pawns back, so Veyrenc was moving one forward.

'I guess he thought he was doing the right thing,' said Voisenet.

'I don't care what he thought. If Mordent and Noël hadn't intervened, I'd be getting a reprimand by now. It's what *you* think that I care about.'

'He'd had a lot to drink, for sure.'

'That's no explanation, he's always had a lot to drink.'

'He thought he was doing the right thing.'

'He was doing the wrong thing.'

Voisenet remained head down, and Adamsberg gave up. He didn't want to torment his lieutenant, putting him between a rock and hard place.

'Is that,' Voisenet suddenly replied, 'because you've found something to *prove* he's done the wrong thing? You've seen the archives?'

'Yes, the lot. The "bad boys" had all been in a gang in the orphanage. And the gang had a name.'

Veyrenc, back at the table, took out the folder from his bag and laid it in front of the lieutenant. With its label uppermost: 'The Recluse Gang: Claveyrolle, Barral, Lambertin, Missoli, Haubert and Co.'

Voisenet didn't notice as Estelle brought over his dish of pork, not even acknowledging her with a nod. His eyes were riveted on the label.

'God in heaven,' he said in the end.

It seemed to Adamsberg that everyone made an appeal to God or his Holy Mother when they discovered these recluses from seventy years back.

'More like the Devil,' he said. 'The former director said that the Devil had got into them. Claveyrolle, Barral and the rest.'

'But what the hell were they doing with recluses? Were these real recluses, I mean spiders, or women?'

'What do you mean, women?' asked Adamsberg.

'Well, you know, in medieval times, there were these women who shut themselves up to offer their lives to God. Recluses they were called.'

'No, no, we're talking about spiders. Eat your food before I show you the pictures, Voisenet. Veyrenc will give you a rundown of what we found – he read the whole folder in the train.'

'How do you know? You were asleep.'

'Very true.'

Veyrenc summarised their discoveries to Voisenet, who was eating mechanically, without seeming to taste his dish, concentrating on what his colleague was telling him. He hadn't even touched his glass of Madiran.

'Now, take a sip of wine, Voisenet, because I'm going to show you the photos.'

Which once more fell on the table like a set of sinister playing cards. Voisenet obeyed and took several mouthfuls of wine. At the sight of the little amputees, the boy without a testicle, the one without a cheek, and the one with the hideous arm, he grimaced in horror. Then he pushed the pictures away, finished his glass and put it down firmly on the table.

'So you were right, commissaire. There really was a recluse spider affair. Long ago. And it's come back to life, eight legs and all. The descendants of the spiders of the past, returning in the hands of one of the ex-victims.'

'Yes, Voisenet.'

'Or,' added Veyrenc, 'it could be several ex-victims. Maybe even all of them acting together.'

'About ten years ago, in a café in Nîmes, Claveyrolle mentioned meeting Little Louis. The one who lost his leg. And Little Louis had threatened him. Claveyrolle had told him to piss off, like in the past, but Louis said to look out, he wasn't alone.'

'You think the victims might have formed a gang too?'

'Why not?'

'All right, but Landrieu, the third man who died, he's not in the gang. That's like an *étoc*, as we say in Brittany. A reef you don't see till you hit it.'

A reef, the hidden rock on which ships founder. Voisenet had grown up in Brittany.

'Not necessarily,' said Adamsberg. 'Claveyrolle and company went over the wall at night. They might have met up with Landrieu wandering round Nîmes. In fact, it's quite probable. So what about this woman who was raped, Voisenet? Justine Pauvel?'

The lieutenant sighed, rubbed his forehead, reliving the difficult two hours he had spent with the woman.

'We get a bit of training for this in the police, don't we?' he said. 'How to talk to women who've been raped, and above all get them to talk. But not enough, really, sir. It was over an hour before I could get past her resistance. She clammed up, she didn't want to say a word. And you know, I did do the training, and I think I can be tactful. I respect women, but they don't seem to want to talk to me. Maybe it's the way I look.'

'What's wrong with the way you look?' asked Veyrenc.

'I'm heavy-looking and heavy-handed,' said Voisenet. 'That may have made a difference for this woman.'

'Perhaps it was simply that you're a *man*, Voisenet,' said Adamsberg, touched by Voisenet's negative judgement of himself.

'Yes, we should have sent a woman to see her,' Voisenet said. 'They tell us that too in training. Anyway, this Justine, she was shattered, really shattered. In the end, she did agree to talk. Since if she'd agreed to see me in the first place, it must have been that she wanted to, one way or another. What did I do? I dressed correctly, as you can see, I took her flowers and a dessert, just a light one, chocolate mousse with fruits. That probably sounds stupid, but perhaps it helped a bit. She's totally turned off men, that's true, she doesn't want to see them at all. She's remained frightened and ashamed, because she never got justice. Well, we learn that in training too. But I lied to her, I said we'd get her justice. And that calmed her down.'

'We might be able to, lieutenant.'

'I'd be surprised.'

'Has she any idea who did it?'

'She swears she didn't recognise anyone, and that she couldn't give any description. If only there had just been the one! But there were three of them. Three! She was only sixteen, a virgin.'

Voisenet stopped, rubbed his brow again and took some pills from his pocket.

'Headache, 'he said, '*she* gets one every day apparently.'

'Eat something,' said Veyrenc, pushing the cheese board towards him.

'No thanks, Veyrenc, sorry, but this isn't easy for me.'

'Three?' said Adamsberg. 'A gang rape then?'

'Yes. In a van – classic ploy. One driving. Two to pick the target. The driver stops to ask the way, the other two jump on the girl and drag her into the van. She gave me a newspaper article about her "godfather", in case I wanted to speak to him. This man, Claude Landrieu, our spontaneous witness. Apparently she doesn't know yet that he's dead. It's just an interview with the paper, in which he says he's terribly shocked. Of no interest for us.'

'With a picture of his shop, perhaps?' asked Adamsberg.

'Yeah, sure, why not, he would get some free publicity that way.'

'Show it to me, lieutenant. I find it strange that she should have given it to you.'

Without understanding, Voisenet fished out the old newspaper cutting from his wallet. Veyrenc poured out some more wine, and this time Voisenet drank it with pleasure. He was feeling better.

'You got involved, Voisenet,' said Adamsberg.

'Yes, a bit.'

Adamsberg concentrated on the old press cutting, with its photograph of Landrieu, a middle-aged man with a bloated face, in his luxury *chocolaterie*, where an assistant in overalls was serving a line of customers. He frowned, reopened the folder belonging to Dr Cauvert, and took out the photos of the nine members of the Recluse Gang, a series taken from when they arrived at the orphanage until they reached the age of eighteen, when they left. Veyrenc let him study the pictures, without asking any questions.

Several long minutes later, the commissaire looked up with a smile, almost a triumphant grin, as if he'd been in a fight. He hadn't noticed any movement around him and looked at his full glass in surprise.

'Did I pour this out?' he asked.

'No, I did,' said Veyrenc.

'Ah, I didn't notice.'

He put his large hands flat down on the table, one on the press cutting, the other on the photos.

'Bravo, Voisenet!' he said.

He raised his glass to his lieutenant who nodded, still without understanding.

'Here's Claude Landrieu,' he said. 'OK, we know that. And here's his shop, his customers, his assistant. And the newspaper dates from two days after the rape. As does the photo.'

'It doesn't have a date on it.'

'We know the rape happened on 30 April. On 1 May, the shop would have been closed, it's a public holiday, but the police station would of course have been open. So Landrieu rushes over there with the list of boys he says his "god-daughter" might have known. The newspaper, must be an evening one, must date from 2 May. And so does the photo. On the counter, if you look carefully, you can see the sprays of lily of the valley, still looking fresh, because they'd have been delivered, shops get them in for the holiday. Yes, that photo was taken *very* soon after the rape. Not that Landrieu would have been best pleased about it.'

'Why not?'

'Because here,' said Adamsberg, pointing to one of the customers, 'we can see Barral. And this one is Lambertin.'

Veyrenc shook his head and seized the photograph.

'I don't see it,' he said. 'The last snaps you got of Barral and Lambertin are from when they were eighteen. How can you identify them in their fifties? Voisenet?'

Veyrenc passed the lieutenant the press cutting and the photographs of Barral and Lambertin when young. Adamsberg drank a mouthful of Madiran, sitting patiently and quite serene.

'No,' said Voisenet, passing the photographs back. 'I don't see it either.'

'Good grief, use your eyes! I'm telling you those two are not in that queue to buy chocolates. It's Barral and Lambertin.'

Neither Voisenet nor Veyrenc contradicted him. They knew that the commissaire's visual acuity was unusual.

'All right,' said Voisenet, with a burst of energy. 'Let's say it's them. What the hell are they doing there, anyway?'

'Two days after the rape?' said Adamsberg. 'They're coming round to see if there's any news. They want to know how the "spontaneous witness statement" went. The one their pal Landrieu gave the local cops.'

'So why didn't they come the day before then? It was 1 May, they'd have had the day off work.'

'Not very discreet. Better to turn up in the shop once it opened, and exchange a quick nod and a wink. That's probably how they got in touch. A word, a sign, in the shop.'

'What for?'

'To go out and find a girl. I'm telling you Justine Pauvel was raped by this so-called "friend of the family", a guy she'd trusted since she was a child. She would have got in his van without hesitation. Then she was raped by the three of them, Landrieu, Barral, Lambertin.'

'So she must *know* them.'

'Of *course* she knows. At least about the "godfather". That's why she gave you the cutting. She's never been able to bring herself to tell anyone. Doesn't prevent her wanting revenge. Another point. Thirty years on, the Recluse Gang was still in existence. As well as Claveyrolle and Barral, we can add Lambertin and Landrieu.'

'Yeah, right,' Veyrenc agreed.

'Neither dispersed, nor reformed. The young stink bugs from the orphanage had grown up. No more slipping spiders into the pants of some poor little kid. When stink bugs grow up, they turn to sex attacks, like they tried in their last years at the orphanage.'

'But how?' asked Voisenet. 'If they couldn't get into the girls' section?'

'Not in the playground,' Veyrenc said. 'Because it seems there was a big fence between boys and girls, just ordinary wire netting. Either they flashed at the girls, or maybe they even poked their peckers through the mesh and ejaculated on some girl who'd been unwise enough to get close. Or they scribbled pornographic graffiti on the walls. A janitor stopped them when they managed to get into the girls' dormitory, just the once. And they'd already started pulling off the bedclothes.'

'And what's to say they didn't manage it on other occasions?' said Adamsberg. 'Carried out rapes? Which the girls never told anyone about, like eighty per cent of women who are raped? The Recluse Gang turned into the Rapists' Gang. But it didn't break up after La

Miséricorde. Just went on committing more outrages. As in their youth.'

'But where are we going to look for the killer?' said Veyrenc. 'And who wants a coffee?'

Both Adamsberg and Voisenet raised their hands. It had been a long and difficult day for them all. Veyrenc went back up to the counter to order.

'Where indeed?' he repeated as he sat back down. 'Could it be the boys who were bitten by recluse spiders? Or the girls who were raped? We don't know how many there were of them, we just know the one.'

'Could be any and every one of those, Louis.'

'But why would girls who had been raped use *spider* venom, since it would mean going in for some very complicated process? You could argue the boys might have thought of that. Poison for poison. But rape victims? They could just pick up a gun and have done with it.'

'There's another possibility,' said Voisenet, 'but you'll say I've got my zoologist's hat on, or that I'm thinking like Danglard.'

'Go ahead anyway.'

'It means penetrating deep into the recesses of the primary thoughts of human beings.'

'All right,' said Adamsberg, 'down you go.'

'I'm not sure how to begin. Primary instincts are very complicated.'

'Start with "Once upon a time". Veyrenc says these recluse creatures remind him of fairy tales.'

'All right, that'll do. Once upon a time, venom was possessed by certain creatures. It has always had a special place in the human imagination. People came to think of poison, venom, as endowed with all kinds of magical properties, beneficial or prophylactic, and it was used by herbalists, for instance, on the principle that what can kill can also cure.'

'What's "prophylactic" mean?' asked Adamsberg.

'Anything that prevents an illness, or protects you from it.'

'OK.'

'So poisonous creatures, snakes, scorpions, spiders, what have you, were all seen as the enemies of mankind. To meet one was a fatal sign. But if you managed to *master* them, you could "cast the spell back". So you would be stronger than the poison, stronger than death, invincible. Stop me if I'm boring you.'

'No, not at all,' said Adamsberg.

'I'd add that there was an unconscious link between this venom, the poison that a creature could spit or inject, and human sperm. Especially for snakes, the kind that rear up before they strike, or worse, the kind of snake that spits. So you *might* imagine that a woman who's been raped, and soiled by her aggressor's sperm, *might* have the idea of vengeance of the same kind. For her, snake venom would be the liquid nearest to the sperm she hates.'

'That figures,' said Veyrenc.

'But I'll concentrate on the spider. With the idea that you could master the toxic poison, and become strong by overcoming it, the spider you've now controlled might bring you good luck and protection. People have made all kinds of concoctions from spiders to treat illnesses – they sometimes gave them to patients by mouth, in the olden days, to cure all kinds of diseases, intermittent agues, haemorrhages, bleeding from the womb, arrhythmia, senile dementia, impotence –'

'Impotence?'

'It's quite logical, commissaire. Like I said, there's a link between the poisonous fluid and spermatic fluid.'

'But why wouldn't you try to treat impotence by using real animal sperm direct?'

'Because that would be the same as ours, no more, no less. You need some kind of superior fluid. But men do yield to big animals if they're dangerous. Bulls' testicles were used for instance. Can I get back to the spider?'

'Yes, go on, Voisenet.'

'Not all that long ago, people said if you carried around on you a spider you'd subdued – in a locket, say, or in a nutshell if you were poor, or sewn inside your clothes – it would protect you from all kinds of sickness, bad luck or the perils of war.'

'Really?'

'Yes, really. So let's imagine a woman who's been raped, and she somehow manages to tame some spiders. She becomes the master of the poisonous liquid, and she can dominate the offensive human sperm. So that way, she could be victorious, and kill someone, with the spider and thanks to the spider.'

'Well, to think up all that,' Veyrenc observed, 'you'd have to be a woman who's seriously disturbed.'

'Rape is seriously disturbing.'

'Even today, Voisenet, in our time? Who's going to believe in all that poison stuff?'

'Our time, sir? What time are we talking about? Civilised? Rational? At peace? Our time is still prehistory, it's the Middle Ages. Human-kind hasn't changed one iota. And primal thoughts certainly haven't.'

'Very true,' said Veyrenc.

'And when the little stink bugs were attacking kids with their recluses, that was really, deep down, a kind of *sexual* attack. The law of the strongest, injecting venom, animal liquid.'

'Eleven victims of bites,' said Adamsberg, 'and God knows how many women raped. And there are just five of us.'

'Five?' said Voisenet.

'You, Veyrenc, me, Froissy, and add Retancourt.'

'No, not Retancourt.'

'Yes, Voisenet. She's on our side, she doesn't believe in it, but she's not opposing us. Five.'

'So we're nowhere near winning.'

'But we've made a start, lieutenant.'

XX

FOR ONCE, ADAMSBERG ACTUALLY REMEMBERED HIS DREAM. SITTING IN front of his bread and coffee, and reflecting that the bread wasn't as interesting these days without Zerk cutting big uneven slices for him, he remembered that in his dream he had become impotent. And a feeling of devastation had sent him towards the only possible remedy: recluse spiders. He had searched through piles of logs and stones, without finding a single one to eat.

It was with his mind full of these jumbled stones, and the unpleasant idea that he had wanted to eat spiders, that he now crossed the large workroom in the squad headquarters, as The Book was finally being completed. People were coming and going, bringing their final drafts, while the printers were spitting out their first copies. He stopped Estalère who, with the help of Veyrenc, was carrying piles of papers to Danglard's office, taking all the precautions one would have used for an ancient and precious manuscript. It could all have been done by sending attachments to his computer, but Danglard insisted on paper versions, which made the whole thing more long-winded.

'Meeting at eleven this morning, council chamber. Estalère, can you spread the word? And call anyone who isn't on duty today.'

'You mean wake them up?' asked the young officer, always worried that he might not have quite understood his orders. 'Like the other time when it didn't get anywhere?'

There was no criticism in his remark. There was no crack in his veneration of Adamsberg through which the slightest negative thought could slip.

'Exactly. Like the other time when it didn't get anywhere.'

'Even Commandant Danglard?'

'Especially him. Louis, you're going to fill in the team, if we can still call them a team. With Voisenet explaining about the fluids. Can you show them the photos by PowerPoint on the big screen, the torturers and the victims?'

Veyrenc nodded.

'But why don't you want to speak yourself?'

'Because I'm afraid Danglard is going to counter-attack, with Mordent backing him up,' said Adamsberg with a slight shrug. 'And I don't want to cross swords this morning. Today, those two are not the ones who matter, it's the team as a whole. I'll just say a few words to kick off, then you can take over.'

But what words? he asked himself. He had not given it any thought. He moved off towards Froissy's office.

'Lieutenant, it's a fine day, the steps in the yard are probably warm by now.'

'Shall I bring some cake?' asked Froissy, immediately switching off her computer.

Once in the yard, she sat down on the steps, laptop on her knee, while Adamsberg crumbled the cake a few metres from the blackbirds' nest.

'Your trousers really will be ruined,' Froissy muttered to herself, as Adamsberg came back across to her.

She was looking better. Retancourt must have done what she intended, washing her hands in the bathroom and noting that no further sound could be heard. He had never imagined that Retan-court would not succeed.

'Any luck, lieutenant? With the doctors?'

'I got through to their report. I must say, I felt guilty.'

'But satisfied.'

'Well, firstly,' said Froissy with a slight smile, 'all three of these men were still in good health, no heart trouble, though they did have serious liver problems. Arising from alcohol, in all cases. One of them was taking something for high blood pressure, another something for cholesterol, and the third Nigradamyl.'

'What's that?'

'It's to treat impotence.'

'Well, well. Which one was that?'

'The eighty-four-year-old, Claveyrolle.'

'It would be.'

'My cousin's a doctor. He says the number of old men who don't give up is impressive.'

'And old Claveyrolle hadn't given up.'

'So,' said Froissy, 'on the face of it, no reason they would be extra-vulnerable to a spider bite. Or that their loxo . . . whatever . . .'

'Loxoscelism,' Adamsberg proposed.

He now felt quite confident about this word, not having to look it up yet again in his notebook.

'Right. Or that their loxoscelism would develop so fast. The first one, Barral, turned up at the hospital on the morning of 10 May. He'd been bitten the night before, when he was clearing nettles near his woodpile. I'll read you the doctor's report: "*Patient felt stinging sensation lower left leg, not much pain, possible nettle sting.*" Then "*11.30: sting giving cause for concern. Purplish patch, 7 x 6 cm, early sign of necrosis. Suspected recluse bite. Anti-venom ordered from APC Marseille. Amoxicillin drip prescribed + local shot of midocaïne*" – that's a painkiller. Then here's the note in the evening: "*20.15: Alarming progress of wound. Necrotic extension to 14 x 9 cm. Temperature 39.7. Treatment modified: Rocephin"* – that's a much more powerful antibiotic – *"plus an antihistamine."* Next day, 11 May: *"7.05: Temperature 40.1. Leg necrotic 17 x 10 cm. Wound 7 mm deep. Additional quarter-dose of Rocephin. Blood test result: level of immunity satisfactory. Presence of haemolysis"* – a fall in proportion of red corpuscles – *"and necrotic development in left kidney. Patient put on dialysis. 12.30: injection of anti-venom. 15.10: Temperature down to 39.6. Unprecedented speed of toxicity. 21.10: Temperature 40.1. Rapid rise in haemolysis, septicaemia diagnosed, visceral infection of right kidney, liver affected."* 12 May: *"Patient died 6.07. Cause of death: haemolysis, septicaemia, kidney failure and cardiac arrest. The case appears to be one of rapidly developing loxoscelism of a kind never previously recorded. Stocks of anti-venom ordered."* '

'Never previously recorded,' Adamsberg repeated. 'Death occurred in the space of two days and three nights. Actually it's less than that, Froissy, two days and two nights.'

'How do you make that out?'

'Because Barral must have been lying. I think he must have been bitten in the morning, when he put his trousers on. Not the night before by the woodpile. What about the other two?'

'I could read you the same kind of text – I've already sent you them by attachment. The development of the poisoning and the treatment were similar. Except that the anti-venom was administered as soon as the patient showed up, and they were put on a Rocephin drip straight away. Didn't make any difference though. So what now?'

Adamsberg pulled two crumpled sheets of paper from his pocket.

'Here's a list of the nine boys in Claveyrolle's gang in the orphanage, plus Landrieu.'

'Right.'

'Three of them are dead, so seven are left. And here are the names of their eleven victims. Kids.'

'Back at the orphanage?'

'Yes. Forgive me, lieutenant, I haven't time to give you all the details, I know that you'll be working in the dark. You'll hear everything in the meeting. But I need to find out where all these people are right now, all of them. Mercadet can check out all the reported rapes in the Gard département. But I won't know if he'll be willing to do this until we've finished the meeting.'

'*Rapes*? More than one?'

'When they grew up, these stink bugs went in for a new distraction. I'd be very surprised if they were guilty of just one rape.'

'Because the rape of that girl, that was him, Landrieu?'

'Landrieu, Barral and Lambertin. Three of them together.'

'How many?' said Froissy in a faint voice. 'How many of us are with you, now, and believe in you?'

'With me, five. Believing me, four.'

Adamsberg's call to Professor Pujol was quickly answered. However insufferable one might be, one usually replies promptly to a call from the police.

'I won't keep you long, professor. Do you think that, say, two to four bites from recluse spiders, suffered simultaneously, could trigger a rapid case of loxoscelism?'

'Recluses are solitary spiders, you wouldn't find several of them biting at once.'

'This is just in theory, professor.'

'Very well, I'll repeat what I told you. A lethal dose of the venom from recluse spiders has been calculated as forty-four glands, i.e. twenty-two recluses, so work it out. Your three or four theoretical bites wouldn't do it. To kill your three men, you'd have needed something like two hundred recluses. Or sixty to seventy spiders for each man. I told you that before.'

'Yes, I've got your figures. But if these men died with unprecedented toxic poisoning in the space of a couple of days, what does that suggest to you?'

'They must have been eating recluse spider pâté, to give themselves an erection, because they confused it with the black widow,' said Pujol, laughing in his casual and disagreeable manner.

You really couldn't make him up.

'Thank you, professor.'

He had some thirty minutes before the meeting. Pujol's obscene joke had revived his thoughts about impotence and spider venom. Obscene but scientific. 'They confused it with the black widow,' he'd said. Adamsberg typed in 'spider venom' and 'impotence' and grabbed his notebook to see which sites came up first. On the question: 'Can spider venom cure impotence?' he found dozens of websites. Nothing to do with the ancient beliefs Voisenet had talked about. But completely serious articles about current research, suggesting that scientists had discovered that the bites of certain spiders could provoke a long and painful episode of priapism. On account of that, medical researchers were now at work identifying, sorting and weakening the toxins responsible, with the hope of being able to extract a new drug, to treat impotence without risk. He copied down laboriously the following sentence: 'Some components of the toxin act by stimulating production of a remarkable amount of nitrogen monoxide, which is implicated in the mechanism of the male erection.' From the analysis of 205 species of spider, eighty-two of them had been shown to display the right kind of toxin, but three of them were ahead of the rest: the Phoneutria, or Brazilian wandering spider, the Australian funnel-web spider, and the black widow.

But not the recluse.

Adamsberg opened the window and looked out at the latest state of his lime tree. The black widow spider, of course he'd heard of that, everyone had. Among other places, it was known to inhabit the warm regions of the south of France. A pretty little creature with its red or yellow heart-shaped spots. Much more visible, and easier to collect than the recluse hiding away in the depths. And you couldn't possibly confuse it with the recluse either. Unless you were stupid enough to think that one spider's much like another, and try to use the recluse for the erectile properties of the black widow.

He looked in on Voisenet.

'Lieutenant, might one possibly mix up the effects of a recluse bite and a black widow bite.'

'No, impossible. The black widow injects a neurotoxic venom, the recluse a necrotic one, nothing in common.'

'OK, I believe you. Where are they all going?' he asked as he saw the officers leaving their desks.

'To the meeting you called, sir.'

'What's the time?'

'Five to. Did you forget? About the meeting?'

'No. Just the time.'

Adamsberg went unhurriedly back to his desk to pick up his confused notes. He preferred to get there once they were all settled, like two days ago. Two days ago? Heavens above, only two days since his squad had been split down the middle. Still, he had not been wasting his time. He'd discovered the meaning of the word loxoscelism, he'd dealt with Lieutenant Froissy's terror, he'd found out why St Roch is accompanied by a dog, he'd fed some blackbirds and remembered a dream.

Was it possible, he wondered, that those old bastards, Claveyrolle, Barral and Landrieu, had been trying to regain their virility by injecting themselves with recluse venom? Supposing one spider is as good as another?

XXI

ADAMSBERG ALLOWED THE MEETING TO SETTLE DOWN, WITH THE USUAL clatter of coffee cups and spoons, before speaking. He had not chosen to keep silent to increase the tension, which was quite high enough already. It was simply because he wanted to write a sentence in his notebook: *'If it's possible to weaken the virulence of a given spider venom, in order to extract from it a drug to treat impotence, is it possible the other way round, to amplify it, like a wine that can be distilled to 70 degrees proof?'*

He shook his head and dropped the pen, glancing quickly at the two commandants, Danglard and Mordent, who were sitting together at the other end of the table. Mordent was looking determined, very concentrated, as he often appeared. Danglard had changed his demeanour. Pale and stiff, he was affecting the phlegmatic air of someone above all tedious contingencies. But of course, Danglard had never been able to place himself above all contingencies, even for a few minutes, and certainly not in a phlegmatic way. He was assuming this pose to resist the attacks of the commissaire, and to defend his attempt to approach the divisionnaire. Adamsberg had always been able to interpret the complexities of his long-standing deputy, but this time something was escaping him. Some new element.

'I am going to persist,' Adamsberg began, in a voice as calm as usual, 'in keeping you informed of the affair under consideration, as I am also going to persist in calling it an investigation, and as I am persisting in calling these three deaths in the south of France, three murders. There are only four of us working on it, which isn't many. I'll remind you of the names of the first three victims: Albert Barral, Fernand Claveyrolle and Claude Landrieu.'

'When you say "the first three victims",' Mordent asked, 'does that mean you're expecting others?'

'Yes, exactly, commandant.'

Retancourt lifted one massive arm, and then let it fall on the table.

'Five working on it,' she said. 'I've already committed myself, and I'm not going back on that.'

This was an incomprehensible declaration from the implacable positivist they knew Retancourt to be. It plunged into disbelief all those who had opted for the invalidity – and indeed the absurdity – of the investigation into deaths by recluse spider bite. Adamsberg gave a slight smile to the majestic Violette. Danglard – although remaining above contingencies – could not help pulling a face. The unexpected support from Retancourt was a major advantage for the chief.

'La Miséricorde orphanage, or children's home, in the Gard département, near Nîmes. That's where we'd got to. Here's a file put together by the former director, covering the years 1944 to 1947. Go ahead, Veyrenc.'

'I beg your pardon,' said Lamarre, 'but *what* dates did you say?'

'1944 to 1947. Or seventy-two generations of recluse spiders before we get to ours.'

'We're measuring time in recluse generations now, are we?' asked Danglard.

'Why not?'

Veyrenc projected on to the big screen a slide of the cover of Dr Cauvert's folder: 'The Recluse Gang. Claveyrolle, Barral, Lambertin, Missoli, Haubert & Co.' The title in large, carefully written letters generated a small shock wave in the room, punctuated by murmurs, a few groans, and the scraping of chairs. Veyrenc left the text on the screen, to allow time for the improbable truth to get through to the officers.

'But what does it mean, "Recluse Gang"?' asked Estalère. 'A gang of spiders attacking the orphanage?'

Once more, Estalère's question suited everyone, because they were no wiser than he was. Veyrenc turned towards the junior officer. His face that morning resembled more than ever an antique bust carved in bright marble, with his straight nose, prominent lips and curly locks on his forehead.

'No,' he explained. 'A gang of kids who attacked weaker children, using recluse spiders. There were nine boys in the gang, including the two who have now died, Barral and Claveyrolle, and they had eleven victims back then. These four boys,' Veyrenc went on rapidly, show-ing photographs, 'Gilbert Preuilly, René Quissol, Richard Jarras and André Rivelin, were all bitten, but without serious consequences. We shouldn't neglect them all the same. When it came to the next two, Henri Trémont and Jacques Sentier, the spiders didn't release a full dose of venom. Still, even in this black-and-white photo, you can see a dark circular patch, which would have been purple, marking the inflammation from the bite. These two got better without treatment. Louis Arjalas, known as "Little Louis", wasn't so lucky. He was bitten on the leg, and with both venom glands. He was four years old,' he added, pointing to the damaged leg with his finger.

There were further groans and movements of revulsion. Veyrenc didn't allow them to take breath.

'This was 1944, there wasn't any penicillin.'

'In 1944,' Justin objected, 'penicillin already existed.'

'But it was very new, lieutenant. And the first stocks were sent to Normandy for the Allied landings.'

'Oh, all right,' said Justin, in a smaller voice.

'He had to have his leg amputated. This one is Jean Escande, known as "Little Jeannot", who was bitten the same year. He lost his foot. He was five years old. Next boy, Ernest Vidot, seven, bitten in '46, he got a big wound on his arm. This time, penicillin *was* available, and they saved his arm, but with a scar described as "hideous-looking". Tenth victim, Marcel Corbière, eleven, whose cheek, as you can see, was eaten away down to the jawbone. People would look aside when they met him. What you need to know is that recluse venom is necrotic, which is to say it consumes flesh. Finally we have Maurice Berléant, twelve years old, bitten on the left testicle in 1947. The flesh was eaten away and the penis damaged, leaving him impotent.'

Adamsberg watched Veyrenc's face, now resolutely stony, a man who could change his expression so radically with half a smile. But the lieutenant was making this tragic presentation without offering an instant's respite to the assembled officers. The photographs of Marcel's ravaged cheek and of Maurice's private parts had taken them to an emotional plane where the theoretical question of whether or not the recluse spider was worth an investigation was just then a million miles from their preoccupations. It wasn't a moment for abstract theorising.

Veyrenc now developed the hypothesis that one or more of the victims might have been turning the recluse attack back on their former tormentors, mentioning the threat Little Louis had made to Claveyrolle, ten years previously.

'So long?' said Estalère. 'I mean, they waited seventy years?'

'So long,' said Adamsberg, who was drawing something in his notebook. 'According to the notes taken by Cauvert's father, the victims were shy, passive, timid little children, more like ladybirds than stink bugs. But the Recluse Gang were aggressive and mean. Stink bugs.'

'*Stink bugs*? What do you mean?'

'Like this,' said Adamsberg, showing them his drawing, which was very lifelike, of the large fat black beetle, collecting little black pellets with its long legs. 'The stink bug,' he announced, 'more commonly known as the cellar beetle or harbinger of death.'

'What are the little black things?' asked Estalère.

'Rat droppings. Which is what they eat. And if you go near them they squirt a toxic liquid out of their backsides. So there you have it, the Recluse Gang were like these nasty stink bugs.'

'Oh, OK,' said Estalère, satisfied.

'But not the group of victims, of course,' said Adamsberg. 'Still, when one's time on earth is almost up, perhaps some things become possible that weren't before.'

'What about the third death?' asked Kernorkian.

'Claude Landrieu.'

'Was he in the gang too? You didn't mention him.'

'No, he wasn't. Over to you, Voisenet.'

The lieutenant started his explanation, about Landrieu and his visit to Justine Pauvel, the woman who had been raped. Veyrenc showed the photo of the chocolate shop.

'Here,' said Adamsberg, pointing with his pencil, 'is the shop's owner, Claude Landrieu, this is in 1988, and two days after the rape of Justine Pauvel. The thing to note is the queue of customers. Here, and here, are two men, apparently waiting to be served. They are Claveyrolle and Lambertin, no less. These were the three men who raped Justine Pauvel. The Recluse Gang never disbanded. But they weren't interested in recluse spiders any more. They were into sex attacks, rapes.'

'Do we know anything about their victims?' asked Mordent, who was torn between his initial opposition and the fact that he had prevented Danglard from taking his objections to a higher authority.

'Only the one.'

'So how do you know they had committed other rapes?'

'Because from their adolescent years, the Miséricorde stink bugs were already harassing and trying to rape the girls in the orphanage.

They drew penises on the dormitory walls, and no doubt flashed at the girls or ejaculated through the fence in the playground. They broke out at night and went into Nîmes by bike. To look for girls, it seems fairly certain. The Recluse Gang turned into the Rapists' Gang.'

'But you've only got the evidence of a single rape,' Mordent insisted. 'As for the men in that photo of the shop, they're in their fifties, and the image is fuzzy.'

Adamsberg made a sign to Veyrenc, who projected photographs of Lambertin and Claveyrolle aged eighteen, face and profile.

'Frankly, I don't see it,' said Noël.

'It is them, no question,' said Adamsberg calmly.

Silence fell once more. They were yet again coming up against the commissaire's unfounded statements.

'Froissy will demonstrate this to you,' he said. 'You can't judge by the jawline, which has become jowly, or by the neck, which has thickened, or by the eyes, because they now have bags under them. But what always remains is the high line of the profile, running from the forehead to the base of the nose. And one absolutely unchanging element, it could almost be made of rubber, is the shape of the ear. When she's enhanced the quality of the newspaper cutting, Froissy can compare the heads of the two men to their profiles at eighteen. It's them.'

Mercadet nodded conspicuously. He had just come over to their side. Six.

'I'm working on it,' said Froissy, plunging into her laptop.

'All right,' Mordent conceded, 'one could accept that the victims of the bites might want to use recluses to get revenge. But in practical and scientific terms, the thing's impossible.'

'Agreed,' said Adamsberg.

'That's the hidden reef we keep hitting,' said Voisenet.

'And we can't rule out vengeance by a woman who had been raped, either,' added Veyrenc.

'But that's even less likely,' said Mordent. 'Why would a woman choose some impossible procedure, by recluse venom, when there are a thousand easier ways of killing a man?'

'Over to you, Voisenet,' said Adamsberg.

As at La Garbure, Voisenet took his time to develop his account of the legendary significance of poisonous creatures, the invincible strength they conferred in turn on anyone who had mastered them, the unconscious links between venomous liquid and the power of human sperm. It was certainly true, Adamsberg thought, that Voisenet changed in stature and vocabulary once he was launched into the animal kingdom. Against his will, Danglard was paying attention, realising he had always considered Voisenet's piscatorial obsession as on the level of that of a Sunday fisherman. Mistakenly.

'And finally,' said Adamsberg, when Voisenet had finished, 'we have the reports Froissy has obtained on the three dead men, which say they died of catastrophic or galloping loxoscelism, that is the sickness caused by the venom of the recluse. The doctors called it "never previously recorded".'

'Got them,' Froissy now interrupted, 'their ears, yes, and their profiles. If there are no two dandelions alike, there are no two ears alike either, are there?'

Adamsberg reached for the laptop and smiled.

'Yes, that's them. Thank you, Froissy.'

'Don't mention it, you knew already.'

'Yes, but the others didn't.'

The computer was passed around, each officer nodding before handing it to the next.

'Agreed?' said Adamsberg. 'It's Claveyrolle and Lambertin, coming to their meeting with Landrieu after the rape.'

'OK,' Mordent conceded.

'I'll carry on from where I left off. Catastrophic attacks of loxoscelism. What killed these men was no natural recluse bite. Their abnormal and violent reaction wasn't because of their age either. Apart from their livers, which had suffered from too much pastis, their immune systems were judged good. They were murdered.'

'Well, if there is a murderer,' Mordent began, this time much more prudently, 'how did he manage it? By collecting a few recluses?'

'No, commandant. The recluse is a timid creature, quite hard to catch. And to be sure of killing just one man, you'd need twenty-two at full strength. But, half of them would only bite without venom, others only using one gland, so you would need as many as sixty to be sure. And for three men, about two hundred.'

'And is that possible?'

'No, it isn't.'

'What about extracting the venom?'

'That's possible with a viper, but not with a spider, unless you have access to some sophisticated apparatus in a laboratory. And even then, the amount of poison it spits is so tiny, it would dry on the test tube before you could collect it.'

Mordent stretched his neck and threw out his arms.

'Well then?' he said.

'Well then, we're up against a particularly vicious reef, what they call in Brittany an *étoc*.'

Adamsberg glanced at Voisenet. He liked that word.

'Well then?' repeated Danglard.

'Well then, we are going to *investigate*, commandant,' said Adamsberg, stressing the sensitive word. 'We'll try to find the survivors of the Recluse Gang. They're the only ones who understand what's happened to their three pals. And for the first time in their lives, they're scared to death. It's up to us to save their skins.'

'And why would we do that?' said Voisenet, pulling a face.

'Because it's our job, stink bugs or no stink bugs. And because they might lead us to unknown rape victims.'

'What about the kids who were bitten?' asked Kernorkian.

'Froissy will make a list for us of the ones who are still with us. We'll also have to check any unresolved cases of rape, let's say between 1950 and 2000, if we assume the rapes might have stopped when the men hit about sixty-five. Mind, we don't know that. Apparently Claveyrolle was still taking anti-impotence pills at eighty-four.'

'Ha! Kept at it, the old rogue,' said Noël.

The meeting was now reaching a critical moment, the time for decisions, and Adamsberg signed to Estalère to fetch another round of coffee. A breathing space before the home straight. Everyone understood the nature of the pause, and no one interrupted this short delay for reflection. For once they would have wished Estalère's careful preparation of their coffees to take longer, since they all felt the time had come for a showdown between Adamsberg and Danglard. Adamsberg looked at his flock with a determined casualness, not lingering on anyone's face to search for signs of positive or negative reaction.

He waited until the coffee ritual was well launched before speaking, as he gathered together all the documents that had been presented, replacing the photos of the eleven victims carefully inside Dr Cauvert's folder.

'This folder can be copied for anyone who's interested,' he said, fastening the strap that held it together.

They had been expecting some declaration, an offensive, or the taking up of a position. But that wasn't Adamsberg's way, as the team well knew.

'Hands up if you want it sent to your computer.'

And that was all. No summary of the meeting, no rhetorical speeches. After a moment's hesitation, Noël was the first to raise his hand. As Adamsberg had often noted, Noël might lack many essential qualities, but courage was not one of them. Following him, more arms went up, all in the end except Danglard's. They waited a few instants for some sign, a movement. But the commandant, as if made of plaster, did not budge.

'Thank you,' said Adamsberg. 'You can all go to lunch.'

The room emptied and faces reflected the same paradoxical thoughts. Regret at having missed a showdown between Danglard and the chief, but also the ambiguous satisfaction of being confronted by an insoluble problem. The thoughts were accompanied, with sidelong glances and discreet nods, towards Adamsberg's tenacity. They often thought him too dreamy and absent-minded, for good or ill, and attributed to that anomaly the improbable success of today. Without understanding that he was simply looking into the mists.

Danglard was leaving the room too, his stiff pose slightly dented.

'All except you, commandant,' said Adamsberg. As he spoke, he sent a quick text to Veyrenc: *Listen outside.*

XXII

'IS THAT AN ORDER?' ASKED DANGLARD, TURNING BACK.

'If that's what you want to call it, feel free.'

'And if I'm starving hungry?'

'Don't make things more difficult. If you really were hungry, I'd let you go. I don't want you running to Brézillon complaining I'm a torturer on top of everything else.'

'Very well, in that case,' said Danglard, making for the door again.

'I said I'd like you to stay, Danglard.'

'So it *is* an order.'

'Because I know perfectly well you're not starving to death. You're not going for lunch, you're running away. And I know you well enough by now to predict that running away will ruin your soul. Sit down.'

Danglard did not take a chair facing Adamsberg, but strode rather fast – hastened by anger – to his original seat about five metres away.

'What are you afraid of, commandant? That I'm going to run you through with a sword? I already asked you, Danglard: have you forgotten what I'm like, after all these years? But if you're opting for prudence, it's up to you.'

'*True prudence means seeing from the start of something what its end will be.*'

'Another quotation. It's easy to wriggle out of anything with a quotation, especially when you know about a thousand.'

'That way you understand everything.'

'So you're predicting a sorry end to this investigation.'

'I should be sorry to see you fall headlong into the sands.'

'In that case, explain yourself, Danglard. Explain why you went right ahead and split the squad down the middle. Explain why you were going to complain about my wanderings to the divisionnaire. Explain why I'm going headlong into the sands.'

'As regards Brézillon, it's very simple: *We are not obliged to praise or honour our leaders, we have to obey them at the time of obedience and check them when the time comes to check them.*'

'You're beginning to get on my nerves with your quotations. You're sticking to your guns, are you, after what you've just heard? Which convinced the whole of the rest of the squad? So please, for the love of God, *explain* yourself, Danglard.'

'It's impossible.'

'Why?'

'*Because something that can be explained in several ways does not merit any explanation.*'

'Well, when you've returned to your normal self, let me know,' said Adamsberg, standing up.

The commissaire left the room, slamming the door and grabbed Veyrenc by the arm.

'Let's go into the yard,' he said. 'It's become a habit, and I have blackbirds to feed. There's a female nesting in the ivy.'

'Blackbirds are quite capable of feeding themselves.'

'Birds are dying in their millions, Louis. Do you ever see any sparrows in Paris now? It's a wholesale slaughter. And the male is very thin.'

Adamsberg made a detour to call on Froissy.

'She keeps the victuals,' he explained.

'I've made some progress on the eleven victims,' said Froissy, without turning her head, as they came in. 'Six of them are already dead. Gilbert Preuilly, André Rivelin, Henri Trémont, Jacques Sentier, Ernest Vidot, the one with the bad arm, and Maurice Berléant, the one who was impotent. There are five left: Richard Jarras and René Quissol, who had harmless bites, both live in Alès. Louis, the one who lost a leg, Marcel, whose cheek was damaged, and Jean, who lost a foot, are all in the Vaucluse département: Louis and Marcel live in Fontaine-de-Vaucluse and Jean lives in Courthézon, about fifty kilometres away.'

'So the three who suffered the most are still close together. And not that far from Nîmes. How old are they now?'

'Louis Arjalas is seventy-six, Jean Escande is seventy-seven, and Marcel Corbière is eighty-two.'

'Send me their addresses, family situation, state of health, anything you can find.'

'Already sent.'

'Got their former occupations?'

'Of the five, in no particular order, one sales rep, one antiques dealer, one restaurant owner, one in hospital admin and one primary teacher.'

'What about the stink bugs? How many of them are left to kill?'

'Well, if you put it that way,' said Froissy with a sigh. 'Four of them have died: César Missoli, Denis Haubert, Colin Duval and Victor Ménard. Then there are the three who died as a result of the recluse bites.'

'So there are three left.'

'Alain Lambertin, Olivier Vessac and Roger Torrailles.'

'And where do these ones live?'

'Lambertin's in Senonches, near Chartres, Vessac in Saint-Porchaire, near Rochefort, and Torrailles at Lédignan, near Nîmes. I've sent all this to your phone.'

'Thanks, Froissy. We'll wait in the corridor, if you can find some cake. We might have a bite too, as we haven't had anything to eat.'

'What are we doing hanging about in the corridor?' asked Veyrenc.

'You know perfectly well Froissy doesn't open her food store in front of anyone. She thinks no one knows about it.'

After several long minutes, Froissy emerged with a heavy basket covered with a tea towel, saying, 'Can I come with you? I like feeding the birds.'

As he followed the lieutenant, food provider for the whole squad, Adamsberg repeated: 'Little Louis, little Jeannot, little Marcel.'

'Worrying, eh?'

'Yeah. And they're living near each other. Reminds you of the other gang, doesn't it?'

'Not necessarily. They've stayed in touch because they're locked together by the same memories – understandable.'

'But ten years ago, Louis threatened Claveyrolle, and said "I'm not alone".'

'I haven't forgotten that.'

'It's really not easy to put recluse spiders in someone's trousers. Getting in the house while he's asleep. Old people are light sleepers.'

'You could always slip something into their drinks.'

'But we come up against the same old *étoc*,' said Adamsberg, as they reached the courtyard. 'You'd have to be able to slip sixty goddam spiders into their goddam trousers. And get them all to bite at the same place. Would you be able to do that?'

Adamsberg sat on the stone steps facing the courtyard and let his neck and shoulders relax in the warm air. Froissy crumbled the cake on the ground under the nest.

'What's she got in the basket?' asked Veyrenc.

'It'll be our lunch, Louis. On china plates with proper knives and forks. A high-quality cold meal, wild boar pâté, leek quiche, guacamole, fresh bread, or whatever. You didn't seriously think she was just going to give us some cake?'

The two men ate their lunch – which was indeed delicious – in a few minutes, and Froissy, looking pleased, collected the plates, leaving them two bottles of water.

'Danglard's going off the rails,' said Veyrenc.

'He's not the same man. He's changed, there's something new going on. It's as if we've lost him.'

'I think it's something personal.'

'Against me? That would be new, Louis.'

'Against you because you're launching *this* investigation, not the same thing. He really doesn't want this investigation to go ahead. Today, he *should* have accepted that he was wrong. He's perfectly capable of doing that normally. He only had to raise his arm.'

'You think there's something lurking in the depths?'

'Something nasty, like that eel. And it matters desperately. If he's reached this stage, it's nothing to do with theory or far-seeing judgement. It's something personal.'

'As you said.'

'Very personal. Intimate. I said, if you remember, that it's some kind of deep fear.'

'For someone else?'

'Could be.'

Adamsberg leaned back against the upper steps and half closed his eyes, letting the sun shine on his face. Then he sat back up and called Froissy on his phone.

'One more thing, Froissy. If you don't mind, can you find out something about Danglard for me? He's got two sisters, one of them's about fifteen years older than him. She's the one that interests me.'

'Investigate the commandant's family?'

'Yes, Froissy.'

He pocketed the phone and slumped back again, face in the sun.

'What's that about?' asked Veyrenc.

'You said it yourself, Louis. Very personal. Intimate. And what's more personal than your close family? "Deep fear", you thought. On whose behalf? His family's. Never challenge a moray eel about his family.'

'Or a buffalo.'

'Or any creature. Look, the blackbird's getting tame, he's hopping over to us.'

'You're right, he is a bit thin.'

Froissy called back after six minutes. Adamsberg switched on the speaker for Veyrenc.

'I don't know how you knew this, sir. He has a sister, Ariane, four-teen years older than him. And she married a man.'

'Yes, all right, lieutenant. Who was the man?'

There was a pause.

'Are you still there, Froissy?

'Yes. She married Richard Jarras.'

'*Our* Richard Jarras?

'Yes, commissaire,' said Froissy sadly.

'And how old is he?'

'Seventy-five.'

'His occupation?'

'He was the one in hospital admin.'

'Meaning what?'

'Putting it simply, he was a buyer. That is, someone in charge of the chain of requirements and orders of medicines for the hospital.'

'Whereabouts?'

'At first at Cochin Hospital in Paris, and then in Marseille.'

'And where in Marseille?'

'He was employed for twenty-eight years at Sainte-Rosalie.'

'How is it you can tell me all this so fast?'

'Because I anticipated your questions. And yes, to the next one, it is indeed at Sainte-Rosalie that the Anti-Poison Centre is based. But still, they don't *manufacture* anti-venom there, if that's what you're thinking. They buy it in from pharmaceutical labs.'

'And those *do* have poisons.'

'Yes, but they don't sell them to private individuals. Give me another few minutes and I'll get back to you.'

'About what?'

'Your next question.'

'I've got a next question, have I? All right, Froissy, I'll wait.'

Adamsberg got to his feet and paced up and down in front of the steps, more or less followed by the blackbird.

'Shit,' said Veyrenc.

'You were right.'

'What made you think of the sister?'

'She lived with him for a while when his wife left him. She hauled him up out of the pit, she looked after the kids. Back in his childhood, she was already looking after him. Both parents were out at work so much the oldest sister had to mother the two younger children. I knew all that.'

'A mother-sister.'

'Yes. And you go troubling a moray eel's mother-sister at your peril.'

'Basic rule, Voisenet would say.'

Adamsberg walked round the yard again and returned to the steps.

'If Richard Jarras was bitten by a recluse when he was a child, along with ten other boys in the orphanage, it can't have been a secret to his family. Danglard must have already known the story of the Recluse Gang, by heart probably. Jarras may well have recounted his memories many times, repeating the names of the victims and the persecutors.

'Names most people wouldn't remember. But Danglard would.'

'And when someone called Claveyrolle and someone called Barral died, it must have rung alarm bells. It gets worse. His brother-in-law was a buyer of medical supplies for Sainte-Rosalie. Danglard panicked, he put up his defences.'

'And tried to block the investigation.'

'He bit.'

'Still, Froissy told you that in Sainte-Rosalie they only buy anti-venom, not poisons.'

'So Jarras would have had to go in secret to the manufacturers. Hello, Froissy?'

'Sainte-Rosalie orders its recluse anti-venom from a giant company called Meredial-Lab, and has contacts with its Pennsylvania factory. Because there are plenty of dangerous recluse spiders in the United States. Not just there, Mexico too.'

'Does Meredial have another branch?'

'In Mexico City. If someone's selling it, it could be anyone, an employee, a clerk, a carrier, a storeman, whatever, some man or woman not above selling stuff illegally for a good price. Those labs employ thousands of people.'

'And who would ever suspect that recluse venom would be sold on the black market?

'Exactly. And for what purpose?'

'And Richard Jarras,' said Veyrenc, 'who no doubt had access to the Meredial organigram, might have established a contact, and over the years acquired enough doses.'

'He couldn't have done it alone, Louis. The other victims must be behind him, maybe they shared it out.'

'But how did Jarras find a seller he could trust?'

'He could only do that on the spot.'

'Froissy?' Adamsberg called her back. 'Can you check whether Jarras has ever been to the US or Mexico? In the last twenty years.'

'All right. Wait and I'll call you.'

Adamsberg went back to pacing the yard.

'Nope,' Froissy reported in a few minutes. 'Never been to the US or anywhere in South or Central America. And I checked the passports of the other four, Quissol, Arjalas, Corbière and Escande. Same result.'

'So what does he do?' asked Veyrenc. 'He goes fishing? He telephones somebody over there at random, asking them to send him poison under cover? Don't like the sound of that.'

'Me neither, but it's our best lead, Louis. Injecting someone with a concentrated dose of venom makes a lot more sense than stuffing sixty spiders into someone's trousers at night.'

'But how does Jarras – or one of the others – manage to inject the victim? They were bitten on the leg. So, he pulls out a hypodermic needle and asks the man to please offer him his ankle?'

'No idea,' said Adamsberg, shrugging his shoulders. 'Posing as a doctor perhaps? Giving some kind of vaccination?'

'Against what?'

Adamsberg looked up at the clouds, then down at the blackbird which was hopping about.

'Bird flu?' he said. 'It's reappeared in the south of France.'

'And you think the men would fall for it?'

'Why not? We'll ask Retancourt to get on the case. Surveillance of Richard Jarras and René Quissol in Alès. What's the time?'

'Half past two. You should get those watches fixed.'

XXIII

LIEUTENANT RETANCOURT WAS FINISHING A SANDWICH AT THE DICE Thrower, the bistro at the corner of the street, not expensive but rather off-putting, on account of the grumpy attitude of the owner, a wiry little man locked in bitter social rivalry with the more upmarket Brasserie des Philosophes on the opposite corner. Adamsberg sat down at her table.

'There's a train at 16.07 for Alès. Does that give you time to fetch what you need from home?'

'Cutting it fine. What's the hurry for Alès?'

'Surveillance job. Two men to keep an eye on. You can take Kernorkian and four juniors.'

'So we have to watch them 24/7? Hired cars?'

'That's right.'

'Who are they?'

Adamsberg waited until they were outside the café to answer her question.

'René Quissol, but especially Richard Jarras. Two old men who were bitten by spiders as children.'

'Did they lose limbs?'

'No, these ones only had harmless bites.'

'Why concentrate on Jarras?'

'He worked for twenty-eight years as a buyer for the Sainte-Rosalie hospital in Marseille, the one where the APC is based.'

'And?'

'And this centre orders recluse anti-venom from a firm called Meredial-Lab that centralises collections of poison, in Pennsylvania and Mexico. Jarras would have had access to this circuit.'

'OK. And we know that Jarras went there, do we?'

'No, he never has.'

'So how has he found an accomplice across the Atlantic?'

'That's all we've got, Retancourt.'

'Right.'

When Retancourt was on a mission, and she had already embraced it, she didn't use many words, concentrating her energy on the object-ive. No chit-chat.

'This operation's top secret, lieutenant.'

'Why?'

'Richard Jarras is married.'

'Right.'

'To a woman whose name is Ariane Danglard.'

'*What?*'

'Yes. His sister.'

Retancourt stopped on the pavement, in front of the tall archway of the squad's building, blonde eyebrows puckered.

'So now we understand what it's about,' she said. 'Danglard hasn't gone soft in the head, he's scared.'

'The result's the same, lieutenant. He absolutely mustn't know.'

'Or he'd help this Richard to skedaddle. Tell Kernorkian not to waste time, I'll pick up his clothes for him.'

'The other officers will join you by late morning. Take care, Retancourt. A single injection and you've had it in two days.'

'Right.'

*

Adamsberg went round the squad distributing tasks. Kernorkian and the four junior officers were to leave for Alès, to keep an eye on Richard Jarras and René Quissol. Voisenet was to go to Fontaine-de-Vaucluse and Courthézon, accompanied by Lamarre, Justin and six colleagues, in order to watch Louis Arjalas, aka Little Louis, missing one leg, Marcel Corbière, missing one cheek, and Jean Escande, aka Jeannot, missing one foot. Froissy was to trace the GPS and mobile phones of Richard Jarras and René Quissol since 10 May, the date of the first lethal bite. Mercadet was to do the same for Arjalas, Corbière and Escande. And see whether they had in any way approached the remaining three stink bugs: Alain Lambertin in Senonches, Olivier Vessac in Saint-Porchaire, and Roger Torrailles in Lédignan.

Adamsberg sat in Froissy's office to watch as she tracked the movements of Jarras and Quissol.

'Far as I can see,' she said, 'your two guys don't go much outside Alès. They don't have GPS on their cars, and according to their mobile phones – just one in each household – I can only find short-distance trips in town. And that could be their wives. We don't suspect their wives, do we?'

'No. This is some kind of personal vengeance.'

'Both of them tend to use their landline mostly, in the traditional way. Ah, yes, on 27 May, Richard Jarras called his wife from Salindres, a few kilometres outside Alès, at 6.05 p.m. But that's not on the way to Nîmes. He was back in Alès by 9 p.m. No movement in the direction of the old men in the Recluse Gang.'

'Unless they left their mobiles at home, which would be prudent.'

'Essential, actually.'

Mercadet was having no more luck in Fontaine-de-Vaucluse, where Louis Arjalas and Marcel Corbière lived within a few streets of each other. Like the two spider-bite victims in Alès, they just seemed to move about locally, with the exception of one return trip to Carpentras. And

Jean Escande seemed similarly to stay put in Courthézon, apart from visits to Orange.

'Just shopping,' Mercadet suggested. 'Or going to the doctor, or some official business. Not one of them has gone anywhere near Nîmes. Unless they left their mobiles at home.'

'Which would be prudent,' Adamsberg repeated.

'That's what we all do.'

'You leave your mobile at home?'

'Correct, so as not to have the cops on my back all the time, commissaire.'

'So our five victims probably do the same then.'

'If it's them.'

'What about the rapes? Anything?'

'Too much,' sighed the lieutenant, 'and that's only the reported ones. For the 1950s, when women hardly dared go to the police, I've got two though.'

'In Nîmes itself?'

'Yes.'

'When?'

'One in 1952. When Claveyrolle and Barral would have been twenty, Landrieu nineteen, Missoli seventeen, Lambertin and Vessac eighteen and sixteen respectively. The first two, they're the ones who were caught in the girls' dormitory?'

'Yes.'

'I listed these names because the other boys seem a bit young for it: Haubert, Duval and Torrailles were fifteen and Ménard only fourteen.'

'It does happen though. Peer pressure.'

'The girl described older teenagers, not youngsters. The point in common with 1988 is the use of a van. And the fact that there were three of them. She was seventeen. It was her first time out at night, she'd had a bit to drink, she was walking home. She was only fifty metres away. Jocelyne Briac.'

'Landrieu, if he was involved, might have been able to borrow someone's van.'

'Jocelyne didn't dare tell anyone until two weeks later, so there was no usable evidence. One detail: one of the little pricks slipped up, because he said to his pal, "Your turn, César! The way's clear now." Because, you see, she was a virgin. Of course, there are plenty of boys called César in the south of France. Still, it could just have been César Missoli.'

'Claveyrolle was the chief, he would have gone first, then César Missoli would have followed him.'

'And the third?'

'She says he lay on top of her and wriggled about, but in fact didn't do anything and the other two mocked him.'

'Possibly one of the fifteen-year-olds, Haubert or Duval. I'm sure this was them, Mercadet, but we'll never be able to prove it. What about the second rape?'

'The following year, 1953, also in Nîmes. This was Véronique Martinez. One month before Missoli left the orphanage. This time, there were just two of them, on foot. They dragged the girl into a building. Again, no way of finding any evidence. And I should say, sir, that back in the day, the cops didn't bust a gut investigating rapes. I did note one thing. The girl said these boys smelled of bicycle oil.'

'Perhaps one of their chains came off a bike on the way.'

'Well, that's all we have. And these two girls, Jocelyne and Véronique, unlike Justine, didn't know their attackers at all. So why would they kill them sixty years later?'

'What if one of the boys was a suspect in a later rape case? And maybe one or other of the women saw his photo in the papers?'

'Possible, I suppose.'

'Yes, but we don't know. With all the work I've given Froissy, she hasn't been able to get round to the police records of all the stink bugs.'

'Why didn't you ask me?'

'It was before the meeting this morning. I didn't know if you would be on board.'

'The Recluse conspiracy,' said Mercadet with a grin. 'You and Veyrenc and Voisenet, and I know where you ended up in the evening. At La Garbure.'

'Have you been following me, lieutenant?'

'I didn't like the atmosphere in the squad. I envied you.'

'What for? The soup or the conspiracy?'

'Both.'

'You like garbure?'

'Never tasted it.'

'It's poor man's soup. You have to like cabbage.'

Mercadet pulled a face.

'That said,' he went on, 'even if I thought Voisenet's lecture about poisonous fluids was brilliant, I still don't believe a woman who had been raped would dream of killing someone with recluse venom. Why not use a viper? Because, yes, I can buy the idea of a snake rearing up and spitting fluid, it kind of figures. And it's relatively easy to extract venom from a snake. But a recluse spider? I just don't see it.'

'No, neither do I,' Adamsberg admitted. 'All the same, check whether among any of the women you've traced there might be a biologist or a zoologist, or someone who works in the Sainte-Rosalie hospital in Marseille. One of the kids who was bitten at the orphanage worked there for twenty-eight years. Our only lead, and not all that promising.'

'Which one?'

'Richard Jarras. But not a word about that, lieutenant. Retancourt is doing surveillance on him, and Voisenet on the three in the Vaucluse. We're doing 24/7 checking, to see if any of them moves.'

'And what if the killer doesn't attack for another month?'

'Then they'll stay on duty for a month.'

'Exhausting, that kind of work,' said Mercadet, puffing out his cheeks. 'Well, it doesn't apply to Retancourt, of course.'

Mercadet was himself ruled out from any surveillance operation. It wasn't practical to use a man who dropped off to sleep every three hours.

'So why is the Jarras lead useful, but not outstanding?' he asked.

'Because the APC in Marseille orders the stuff from the Pennsylvania branch of Meredial-Lab. Or else from Mexico City.'

'And they stock poisons, do they?'

'Yes, but Jarras has never been to America.'

'Not conclusive then.'

'Very thin, as Froissy might say.'

'About what?'

'The blackbird.'

'Perhaps he could have got a false passport. Not the blackbird, Jarras.'

'How could we find that out?'

'In the archives of fake passport issues.'

'But there are thousands of those, lieutenant.'

'Using his photo,' suggested Mercadet, who was not deterred by the idea of complicated internet searches.

For Mercadet, as for Froissy, the millions of routes through the internet were walkways he could navigate very fast, taking short cuts, diversions and so on, like a runaway cutting his way through barbed wire across a series of fields. He liked it. In fact, the more challenging the task, the better he liked it.

Adamsberg closed his office door to make some phone calls. With five lieutenants and ten junior ranks out on mission, the place was very quiet. Even if Danglard was sulking in his tent, Adamsberg didn't want to risk being overheard by him, as he enquired about official poison holdings in Paris.

After almost an hour of effort, while the various administrations passed him from one person to another until someone competent could answer his queries, Adamsberg went back to see Mercadet.

'Nothing,' he said, throwing his phone on to the desk as if it was the mobile's fault.

'You're going to break it at that rate.'

'The screen is already cracked – it's the one belonging to the cat. I just wanted to check other places: they don't keep any recluse venom in the Natural History Museum, nor the Pasteur Institute, nor in the centre in Grenoble.'

'Well, I did a little reconnoitre over the last twenty years. There's never been any whisper of a clandestine lab for spider venom, or indeed snake venom. And who on earth would try to extract it from a recluse anyway?' Mercadet said, pushing back the keyboard.

Adamsberg sat down heavily, running his hands several times through his hair. It was a habitual gesture of his, either to make his hair sit down, which didn't work, or to dispel fatigue. And you could see why, Mercadet thought: three old men murdered, five suspects from among the kids in the orphanage, not to mention the women who might have been raped, most of them unknown. Plus the fact that the murder method was still a mystery.

'Retancourt and Voisenet are tracking them,' Adamsberg repeated. 'One of these days, one of them is sure to make a move. Tonight, tomorrow.'

'Commissaire, why don't you take a rest? On the cushions upstairs? Oh shit!' Mercadet said, standing up, because mention of the cushions reminded him of the upstairs drinks room, and by extension the cat's feeding dish.

'An idea, lieutenant?'

'The cat, time to feed it. What if Retancourt was to get back and find the cat had lost weight!'

'He could do with losing weight.'

'Even so,' said Mercadet, going to fetch a tin of cat food from Violette's cupboard. 'I mustn't miss his afternoon feed, I'm already late.'

However great its hunger, and whatever its annoyance at not receiving dinner at the right time, the cat would never have dreamed of stirring itself – a mere seven metres – to ask for its food. It just waited calmly for someone to come and fetch it from the photocopier.

Mercadet came past again, with Snowball draped over his arm and climbed the stairs to the little room containing the drinks dispenser, the cat's dish and the three blue cushions.

Froissy appeared, with a little colour in her cheeks and followed by Veyrenc, just as Mercadet came down the stairs carrying a well-fed purring cat, which he gently replaced on the photocopier. The machine was pressed into service only for emergencies, because it was the creature's resting place. But they left the copier switched on so that the surface would stay warm. Fleetingly, Adamsberg thought that life in his squad was very complicated. Had he been too lax? Allowing Voisenet to litter his desk with magazines about fish, allowing the cat to dictate its own territory, allowing Mercadet to take a nap on the cushions whenever he needed to, allowing Froissy to fill her cupboards with food rations as if in wartime, allowing Mordent to indulge his love of fairy tales, Danglard to wallow in his encyclopedic erudition, and Noël to persevere in his sexism and homophobia? And allowing his own mind to be open to every wind.

He ran his fingers through his hair again as he watched Froissy approach, holding a file, followed by Veyrenc.

'What's going on?' he asked, in a voice that seemed to himself to sound tired.

'Something was bothering Veyrenc.'

'Just as well, Louis, because tonight, the wind is blowing through my ears. I feel like a damp rag.'

'I checked out the records of the bad boys in the orphanage who have already died,' Froissy continued. 'Remember them? The ones who were dead long before the recluse attacks?'

'Yes,' said Adamsberg. 'There were four of them.'

'César Missoli, Denis Haubert, Colin Duval and Victor Ménard,' Froissy listed them. 'Veyrenc thought it wasn't logical. If the boys who had been bitten had decided to take vengeance on the whole gang, it was unlikely they'd have allowed those ones to die in their beds.'

'Vengeance has to be total or nothing,' said Veyrenc.

'And?' said Adamsberg, looking up.

'César Missoli was shot in the back, outside his house in Beaulieu-sur-Mer, Alpes-Maritimes. They never got to the bottom of it. Since he was connected to mafia networks in Antibes, they assumed it was gang warfare.'

'When was this?'

'In 1996. Two years later, Denis Haubert fell off his roof, which he was repairing. The safety catch on his extension ladder gave way. Classified as a household accident.'

Adamsberg started to pace round the room, hands behind his back. Then he lit one of Zerk's last cigarettes, half emptied of tobacco. He was going to have to buy a few more for his son soon, so that he could steal them. He didn't like this brand, which was too bitter for him, but you don't look a gift cigarette in the mouth. Veyrenc was smiling, leaning back on Kernorkian's table, arms folded.

'Three years go by,' Froissy was saying. 'And it's Victor Ménard's turn, in 2001. He's a garage owner, likes powerful motorbikes. At the time he had a 630cc that he liked riding at top speed. A heavy machine if you hit a slippery patch on the road.'

'Slippery?'

'Covered in motor oil,' said Froissy, 'a stretch four metres long on a bend. He skidded at 137 kilometres an hour, fractured vertebrae, brake lever went through his liver, died. An accident of course. Then it's a year later, 2002, Colin Duval. He was a Sunday mushroom picker, also in the Alpes-Maritimes, knew all the good places. He was an expert, and what he did apparently was cut them into thin slices and hang them up to dry outside. Lived alone, cooked for himself. One evening in November, long after the picking season, he gets a violent bellyache. He's not too worried, he knows his mushrooms. Two days later, he feels better, so he relaxes. Then it starts again, and in three days, despite being in hospital, he dies of liver and kidney failure. The autopsy showed traces of both alpha and beta amanitins, the toxic element of the death cap mushroom – or *Amanita phalloides* to give it its Latin name. It has a white stem and flat top and looks like some edible species. It would be fairly simple to insert some, mixed up with others, in a basket out in the woods. But, since he was an expert, much more effective to add some slices to the string of dried mushrooms later on. You need to know,' she added, 'that half the top of a death cap is fatal.'

'Three accidental deaths, and one attributed to gang warfare,' said Veyrenc, 'that is, if we didn't know that all four belonged to the Recluse Gang. Not coincidence, not accidents. These were murders.'

'Bullseye!' said Adamsberg. 'So it means that the victims of the recluses didn't wait seventy years to get their own back, as we had assumed.'

'But then,' said Mercadet, 'they suddenly stopped. No more murders. When they'd wiped out four stink bugs, it was going to plan, nobody had suspected them. Because who would? But no, they stop for fourteen years before starting up again last month, with an infinitely complex method that we can't work out.'

'A very long period of latency,' Adamsberg agreed.

'But why?' asked Froissy.

'Maybe it was to devise an infinitely complex method that we wouldn't be able to work out.'

Froissy shook her head.

'That must be it,' said Adamsberg. 'Something about their modus operandi didn't satisfy them in the end. Remember, an eye for an eye, a tooth for a tooth. It's essential, this equivalence, it's as old as the earth.'

'And the equivalence wasn't right,' Veyrenc said. 'Yeah, the first four guys are dead all right, but if your enemy takes your eye out, you're not going to be satisfied cutting off his ear. Recluse venom against recluse venom.'

'So during those fourteen years, they're trying to accumulate enough of it to inject people?'

'It must be that,' said Adamsberg, 'or else it doesn't make sense.'

'So to do it, Jarras tries to get in touch with someone in Mexico City?' asked Froissy.

'Don't twist the knife in the wound. One way or another, they managed it.'

'And in fourteen years,' Veyrenc said, 'they collected enough poison to kill three men. And probably to kill another three?'

'Does this stuff keep?'

'I checked that,' said Veyrenc. 'Eighty years for some species, but it's better to freeze it. That's snakes – I don't know about the recluse.'

'We never know *anything* about the recluse,' said Mercadet with a sigh. 'That figures, they don't usually bother anyone.'

The commissaire stretched out his arms, feeling more satisfied. The wind had stopped whistling through his ears.

'Garbure?' Veyrenc suggested.

The interest Veyrenc had shown in this Estelle woman was more serious than he had realised, Adamsberg thought. With this lightly issued invitation, it was clear that the lieutenant didn't want to turn up there alone, but to have others around him. The previous time, Estelle had been playing hard to get.

'Yes, all right,' he said, although after these difficult days he would really have preferred to be stretching his legs out in front of his fireplace and trying to think. Or at least to read his notebook.

'Me too,' said Mercadet, switching off his computer.

'Is it nice, garbure?' asked Froissy, who was always concerned with the taste of food.

'It's excellent,' said Veyrenc.

'Well,' Adamsberg added, 'you have to like cabbage.'

XXIV

MERCADET AND FROISSY, AFTER GLANCING AT THE SOUP TUREEN brought over for Adamsberg and Veyrenc, had opted for the chicken casserole à la Henri IV. The clouds had cleared somewhat after Veyrenc's discoveries about the four other victims of the Ex-victim Gang, as they thought of them, who had been locked in combat with the Recluse Gang for twenty years. At last things were falling into place. Chronological elements, psychological elements and technical puzzles could all fit into an overall satisfactory explanation. The distress Adamsberg had felt whenever the word 'recluse' was uttered had melted away. All they had to do now was wait for the missions led by Retancourt and Voisenet to deliver results, and the end would be in sight. And for once, it was the commissaire who now cheerfully filled the glasses with Madiran.

Veyrenc had changed places again, and was sitting with his back to the counter. This evening, he would not get up to fetch coffee or sugar. Mercadet tasted the garbure, but passed it up without regret, and the conversations wandered, ranging in no particular order over the investigation, poisons, spiders, Mexico City, the fact that the cat wasn't interested in the blackbirds, stink bugs and the Miséricorde orphanage. Seven Recluse Gang members dead already, at the hands of the Ex-victim Gang.

'All right,' said Mercadet, 'so they had a hard time in the orphanage, but the poor little victims didn't turn into angels.'

'Someone who has suffered greatly will make others suffer,' Veyrenc said.

'I was getting fond of them. But in the end, they're murderers.'

'And very calculating. I've never come across such a long spell of obstinate determination. You'd think age would have made them less involved, but no.'

Estelle approached, and placed a finger, not a hand, on Veyrenc's shoulder, to ask if she should serve the Tomme cheese. Yes, of course she should.

'What's the time?' Adamsberg asked.

'Half past eleven,' said Veyrenc. 'You know, this is getting to be a pain, your asking the time.'

'Retancourt has been in position for three hours, Voisenet and his men two hours.'

'Jean-Baptiste, give it a rest,' said Veyrenc under his breath.

'Yes.'

Mercadet was dividing the Tomme when Adamsberg's mobile rang.

'Must be Retancourt,' he said, grabbing the phone.

Then he frowned, as he didn't recognise the caller's number.

'Commissaire? You weren't asleep, were you? I beg your pardon, I know it's very late, I'm really sorry. This is Madame Royer-Colombe, Irène Royer, Irène! Remember me?'

'No, I wasn't asleep, Irène. What's the matter? Has someone been throwing stones at your windows?'

'No, no, commissaire, worse than that.'

'I'm listening.'

Adamsberg switched on the speaker and the clatter of cutlery stopped.

'There's been another, commissaire! The web's going mad. Oh sorry, I didn't mean to be confusing, not a spider's web, the internet.'

'Another what?' asked Adamsberg.

He wanted to push her to tell him everything quickly, but he had realised that the more pressure one put on Irène, the less coherently she told her story. She had to be in charge of the pace and the digressions.

'Why, another *man* bitten!'

'Where?'

'That's what's so weird, not in our region, but in Charente-Maritime. Up in the west, that's not recluse territory. Still, the black widows have been going north, from the Mediterranean to the Atlantic coast. Why do they do that? Who knows? And last year, you know, a recluse bit someone in the Oise, up north. So you see, there must be some spiders who like adventure, something like that. Wondering whether the grass is greener somewhere else. Well, not literally.'

'Please, Irène. Can you give me the details?'

'Well, it's been all over Twitter for the last, what? Ten minutes. And I called you right away. They've taken him to hospital in Rochefort.'

'Is it certain this is a recluse bite?'

'Oh yes, because this man – it's another old man, commissaire – he recognised the swelling, there was a blister right away, and then a red spot, and what with all the panic at the moment, he went straight to hospital.'

'But how did the news get out so quickly on social media?'

'Must have been someone at the hospital, a paramedic perhaps, who knows? With all the scares at the moment.'

'And do you know the man's name?'

'Ah, commissaire, that's confidential, isn't it? They don't let you know that sort of thing. All we heard is that he was bitten after supper in Saint-Porchaire. Up there somewhere. He felt the bite.'

'Was he indoors or outdoors?'

'They don't say. What I wonder is whether this is a normal bite victim, or one of those special ones that you talked about.'

'I understand, Irène. I'll tell you when I know.'

'Wait, commissaire. Don't call me on my mobile – I forgot it at home on a chair.'

'But where are you then?'

'I'm in Bourges.'

'In Bourges?'

'Yes, because I pick a spot on the map and I go off there, it's for the antalgic posture, you understand.'

'Sorry?'

'Antalgic posture. Arms on the steering wheel, feet on the pedals, I can hardly feel my arthritis at all, see? I'd love to live like this, sitting at the wheel, on the road.'

'Well, do you have a hotel number?'

'This isn't a hotel, I'm in a guest house. It's very clean, I must say, and I've borrowed the owner's mobile. He's very kind, but I mustn't take advantage.'

Adamsberg switched off and looked round at his colleagues with a strained expression.

'This man is at Saint-Porchaire. Wasn't one of our stink bugs living there?'

'Yes, Olivier Vessac, age eighty,' said Froissy.

'I'm off then,' said Adamsberg. 'Our man's got only two days to live. I want to drag out of him the exact time of the wound and who or what gave it to him.'

'I'll come with you,' said Veyrenc, without moving. 'We could be in Rochefort in five hours. But what the heck would be the point of arriving in front of a hospital at half past four in the morning?'

Adamsberg nodded and called Retancourt, keeping the speaker on.

'Did I wake you, Retancourt?'

'Since when do I go to sleep on the job?'

'We've got another victim, Olivier Vessac, Saint-Porchaire near Rochefort. Bitten this evening, probably between eight and quarter to eleven. Any of your targets moved?'

'Negative. Richard Jarras and his wife went to a little restaurant in the town centre at 19.30 and left again at 21.30. Kerno says he's seen René Quissol and his wife in front of the TV, no movement there.'

'Kerno' was what they all called Kernorkian, turning an authentic Armenian into a Breton.

'You can leave Alès, lieutenant. Mission over. It must be someone from the Vaucluse that went. I'll get back to you.'

Adamsberg called Voisenet immediately.

'No, sir,' said Voisenet. 'Little Louis is right now sitting on a bench outside his house – it's still warm here. And what makes life easier for me is that he's playing cards with his pal Marcel.'

'Are you sure it's them, Voisenet?' said Adamsberg, raising his voice.

'Certain?'

'Absolutely, commissaire. Louis Arjalas and Marcel Corbière. Not difficult to spot, alas for them, because Louis has an artificial leg and Marcel is missing part of his cheek. He covers it up with a flesh-coloured dressing.'

'What about Lamarre? Has he seen any sign of Jeannot in Courthézon?'

'No, Jean Escande isn't there, the neighbours think he went to the seaside, to Palavas.'

'In his car?'

'Yes, he often goes there in fine weather.'

'And what about his mobile?'

'Nothing, no signal.'

'Very good. OK, get the whole team to move in on Palavas, and check the hotels, campsites everywhere. An old man limping about is easy enough to spot, especially if he's a regular. Find him, or better still, don't find him, lieutenant!'

'I've got his registration,' called Froissy who had consulted her phone, where she kept most of her current data. 'He drives a blue Verseau, five-door automatic, 234 WJA 84.'

'Got that, Voisenet?'

'Right, we're off, sir.'

Then back to Retancourt.

'There's only one of them missing, lieutenant. Jean Escande, who has apparently gone swimming in Palavas, but without a mobile signal. Voisenet's on to it. Can you go with your team to Saint-Porchaire, where Vessac was bitten? Jeannot Escande is seventy-seven. If he drove all the way from the Vaucluse to Saint-Porchaire, seven hours minimum, I doubt he'd be in much shape to set off straight back south, especially at night. Can you check the small hotels there and work outwards? An old man with an artificial foot should be easy to trace.'

'He might have slept in his car.'

'Here are the car's details: a blue Verseau automatic, five doors, 234 WJA 84.'

'Got it,' said Retancourt.

Adamsberg sat down again, holding his phone.

'If it *isn't* Jeannot, we're dished. Wrong all along the line. We've gone headlong into the sands, like Danglard said.'

'That's impossible,' said Veyrenc. 'It all fits. Let's snatch a couple of hours' sleep and then go to Rochefort. We can still be there by eight o'clock.'

Adamsberg nodded silently.

'No, it's gone dead, Louis. We're missing something.'

'You're the one who's gone dead. Get some rest. I'll see you at base at 3 a.m.'

Adamsberg nodded again. The word 'recluse' ran through his head once more, making him shiver. Veyrenc shook his shoulder, and pushed him outside.

'Look,' he said, 'Jeannot's disappeared, he's gone somewhere.'

'Yes.'

'It would be reasonable for just one of the Ex-victim Gang to do the job. They're not going to travel about in a group of five. They take turns, we can be sure of that. We'll get him.'

'I don't know.'

'What's the matter, Jean-Baptiste?'

'I can't see through the mists any more, Louis. Nothing there.'

XXV

ADAMSBERG PACKED A BAG IN HASTE, THEN SAT DOWN IN HIS KITCHEN, feet resting on the fender. For a moment, he had been on the point of going out to join Lucio under the beech tree in the garden, forgetting that his neighbour was in Spain. Nothing would have fascinated Lucio more than the terrible itching caused by the recluse spider.

And what would Lucio have said to him, in between swigs of beer under the tree?

'Go deep inside your fear, *hombre*, don't let it go, you gotta scratch it all the way, till it bleeds.'

'It'll go over, Lucio.'

'No it won't. Go deep, lad, you've got no choice.'

Yes, that's what he would have said, no question. He met Veyrenc outside the squad office at 3 a.m.

'You haven't slept, have you?' said Veyrenc.

'No.'

'In that case, I'll drive. I'll wake you in a couple of hours. If I was your mother, I'd tell you to shut your eyes.'

'I need to call her, actually, Louis, she's broken her arm.'

'Did she have a fall?'

'Yes, she tripped over the broomstick. She doesn't know whether the broom got in her way or whether she got in its way.'

'Important question when you think about it,' said Veyrenc, starting the engine, 'and it applies to quite a few things.'

'It's this very big broom she uses to chase spiders. Not recluses though, you don't get them round us.'

And Adamsberg, feeling a chill at the back of his neck, immediately regretted having pronounced the word. Or having associated it with his childhood home, and, even worse, with his mother. Perhaps Danglard's forebodings were finally worming their way into his thoughts.

Veyrenc pulled up just before 8 a.m. in front of the Rochefort main hospital and shook the commissaire by the shoulder.

'Good grief,' said Adamsberg, 'you didn't wake me.'

'No,' said Veyrenc.

The doctor on duty at Rochefort at first opposed any visitors having access to his patient, even the police. The man's condition had worsened overnight.

'How bad is it?' Adamsberg asked.

'The wound has spread too fast, it's already necrotic. We're faced with an accelerated reaction. He has a fever of 38.8.'

'Like the three patients in Nîmes.'

'That's what I'm afraid of, but I can't see what business it is of the police. Send us a specialist in poisons, that might make more sense,' he said, putting an end to the conversation and turning away.

'Where was he bitten?' Adamsberg asked.

'On the right arm. There's hope if we amputate.'

'I wouldn't be too hopeful, doctor. This man hasn't just been bitten by a spider. He's received twenty doses of venom. This is a murder.'

'Murder? By twenty recluse spiders?'

The doctor turned back to face them again, arms folded, legs apart, and smiled in a determined and defensive posture. He was a solid, efficient-looking man, authoritarian and tired.

'Since when,' he asked, 'have we been able to get spiders to obey orders? Whistle them up, get them into armies and send them to attack a victim? Eh? I ask you, since when?'

'Since 10 May, doctor. Three men have died and two more will die if you don't let us see your patient. I could get a warrant, if you insist, but I'd much prefer not to waste time and to be able to talk to him before his fever goes above 40.'

It would of course have been impossible for Adamsberg to obtain a warrant, since his superiors knew nothing about this investigation. But the word 'warrant' was enough to shake the doctor's confidence.

'All right, I'll let you have twenty minutes, no more. Don't get him worked up, we don't want his fever to rise any more. As for the wounded arm, whatever happens, he mustn't move it at all.'

'Where and when was he bitten? Was he indoors? Outdoors?'

'Outdoors – he was just arriving home with his lady friend. After dining out, they were coming back at nightfall. Room 203. Twenty minutes.'

The old man was not alone. Sitting in an armchair, where she seemed to have spent the night, was a woman of about seventy, with tear-swollen eyes, twisting a handkerchief in her fingers.

'Police,' Adamsberg announced quietly, approaching the bed. 'This is Lieutenant Veyrenc de Bilhc, and I'm Commissaire Adamsberg.'

The man blinked his eyes, seeming to say, 'Understood.'

'We are sorry to disturb you, Monsieur Vessac. We won't be long. Madame?'

'My lady friend,' Vessac introduced her. 'Élisabeth Bonpain. And she deserves her name.'

'Madame, I'm sorry, but I have to ask you to leave us. I need a few words alone with Monsieur Vessac.'

'I'm not moving from here,' said Élisabeth Bonpain in a faint voice.

'I'm sorry, it's just normal procedure,' said Veyrenc. 'Please don't hold it against us.'

'They're right,' Vessac said. 'Be reasonable, Élisabeth. Take advantage of the break, get some coffee and something to eat, it'll do you good.'

'But why are these policemen here to see you?'

'That's what they're going to tell me. Please go. Coffee, croissants,' Vessac said again. 'Do you good. Look at a magazine, get a change of scene. Don't worry, some piddling little spider isn't going to get the better of me.'

Élisabeth Bonpain left the room and Vessac indicated two chairs.

'You're keeping the truth from her, aren't you?' said Adamsberg.

'Of course. What else can I say to her?'

'And you're lying, because you *know*. It wasn't just a piddling little spider.'

Adamsberg was speaking gently. Stink bug or no stink bug, you don't bully a man who has two days to live and knows it. He tried to avoid his eyes being drawn to the wound, which already looked repulsive. Covering a patch ten centimetres by four, the necrosis was at work eating at muscle and vein.

'Nasty, eh?' said Vessac, following Adamsberg's gaze. 'But you've seen worse, as cops.'

'We've only got twenty minutes, Monsieur Vessac. So you know what's happened to you?'

'Yes.'

'You knew about the deaths of Albert Barral, Fernand Claveyrolle and Claude Landrieu, coming rapidly after bites from a recluse spider, last month in Nîmes.'

'Ah, you've worked that out, have you?'

Vessac gave a grim smile, and with his left arm signed to Veyrenc to pass him some water. His pronounced features had resisted the ravages of time, and even after so long, Adamsberg could recognise him from the teenage photos.

'We know about the orphanage, where the Recluse Gang attacked eleven children, leaving a couple of them as amputees, one impotent, another disfigured. And you were part of that gang, with eight other boys.'

Vessac did not look away.

'Little shits,' he said.

'Who, you or the victims?'

'Us, of course. We were total bastards. When Little Louis lost his leg, he was only four – four! What did we do? We laughed. Well, not me at that stage, I was younger, but I joined them soon after. Think that stopped us? No way. When Jeannot lost a foot and Marcel had his cheek eaten away – Christ, *he* was a sight – what did we do? We laughed some more. And what made us kill ourselves laughing was when one of Maurice's balls fell off like a walnut. Maurice One-Ball, we called him, and the whole of the orphanage knew.'

'Do you know who's done this to you?' Adamsberg asked, pointing to the wound.

'Yeah, of course. It's their revenge and no wonder. And I'll tell you something: I don't want to kick the bucket, but I get the message, I deserved it. At least they left it until we were old. They let us have time to live, meet women, have kids.'

'They didn't wait till all of you were so old, Vessac. Between 1996 and 2002, they killed four of your gang members: Missoli, Haubert, Ménard and Duval. Not with spider venom but with fake accidents.'

'Ah,' said Vessac. 'Still, I get it. What I don't know is how they're doing it. Takes a lot of venom to kill someone.'

'Twenty doses at least.'

'Well, beats me, but what do I care, state I'm in? Now look here!' said Vessac, suddenly raising his left arm. 'Élisabeth knows nothing about all this, she doesn't know I was a little ruffian when I was young. And she mustn't know.'

'There's an investigation under way,' said Adamsberg, 'and if it's successful, there'll be a trial . . .'

'Yeah, and the press will . . . All right. She'll find out in the end. But just don't let her find out before I die. So we can say goodbye without it hanging over us. Is that possible?'

'Yes, of course.'

'Word of honour?'

'Word of honour. But what about the rapes, Vessac?'

'No,' he said, 'that wasn't me.'

'Because they did rape girls, didn't they?'

'In Nîmes, yes.'

'Gang rapes?'

'Always. And it went on after the orphanage.'

'But not you?'

'No. Not because I'm good-hearted, commissaire, don't go thinking that. It was something else.'

'What?'

'If I don't tell you, you'll think I was in on the rapes too. But it's a bit complicated to explain.'

Vessac thought for a few moments, and asked Veyrenc for more water. His temperature was rising.

'Cops or no cops, this is between us men, OK?'

'Yes.'

'If I tell you, it won't go beyond these four walls?'

'No.'

'Word of honour?'

'Word of honour.'

'It was gang rape. Like you said. You had to prove to the others you could do it, you had to strip off. And I couldn't.'

Another silence, another sip of water.

'I thought, well, I knew,' he said, speaking with difficulty, 'my cock was too little. And that bastard Claveyrolle would have found some nickname for me. So I dodged it. You believe me?'

'Yes,' said Adamsberg.

'Doesn't make me an angel, make no mistake. Because I was still part of it. Looking on. Or worse, holding the girl down. That's being an accomplice, isn't it? Nothing to be proud of.'

The doctor opened the door.

'Three minutes,' he said.

'Let's be quick, Vessac,' said Adamsberg, leaning towards him. 'Who injected you with the venom?'

'Who? Nobody, commissaire.'

'Two of your ex-comrades are in the killer's sights, Alain Lambertin and Roger Torrailles. Tell me, and I might be able to save them. We've got seven deaths on our hands already.'

'Eight, counting me, cos I'm on the way out. But I can't help you. We were coming back from this café we go to, Élisabeth and me. I parked the car, I got out, I was just putting the key in the front door when I felt something sting my arm. Not a big sting. At about ten past nine.'

'You're lying, Vessac.'

'No, commissaire, word of honour.'

'But you must surely have seen the person, the one who injected you.'

'There *wasn't* anyone there. I thought maybe it was a bramble, there are some in the hedge, I meant to cut them back, oh well, it's too late now. No, I tell you, no one. You can ask Élisabeth, she was there, she'll tell you the same, that woman doesn't know how to tell a lie. It was only later I got to thinking, when I saw the swelling. Not that we get recluses round here. But as you might guess, I did a bit of research after the other three died. So I knew what to look for. Swelling, a little blister. And I told myself, your turn now, Olivier, they got you. But how they did it, commissaire? Fucked if I know.'

As the doctor opened the door again, Adamsberg got up and nodded. Then he put his hand on the man's left arm.

'Cheers, Vessac.'

'Cheers, commissaire. And thanks. You may not be a priest, anyway I'm not religious, but I feel a bit better after talking. But, hey, remember now, the pair of you. Word of honour?'

Adamsberg looked at his hand, resting on Vessac's good arm. On the arm of a stink bug, yes, but a man who was about to die.

'Word of honour,' he said.

They left the hospital building in silence and walked into its little garden.

'We'll have to check,' said Veyrenc.

'That there really was nobody there? Yes. We're going to have to torment Élisabeth Bonpain. Let's go to Saint-Porchaire. I want to see exactly where it happened, before any traces disappear.'

From the car, Adamsberg called Irène Royer at her guest house in Bourges. He was still affected by seeing Vessac's atrocious wound, and by hearing his admissions – word of honour – as well as by the dignity of the stink bug as he lay dying.

'Is that you, commissaire? You're just in time, I'm leaving. So was it just a normal bite victim?'

'No, not at all, Irène. It was another stink bug from the orphanage, a man called Vessac. But don't go putting this out on the internet, it's confidential, as agreed.'

'I promise.'

'But we still have the same problem. He says he didn't see anyone when he felt the bite.'

'Was he in the house or outside?'

'Outside, standing by his front door, just about to go in. I'm going to check that with his lady friend.'

'Where was he bitten?'

'Upper arm.'

'But that's impossible, commissaire, recluse spiders can't fly!'

'Well, that's where it was, on his arm.'

'Perhaps there was a big woodpile near his door. He might have brushed against it, and disturbed a spider just coming out for a walk.'

'I don't know. I'm going to check.'

'Wait a moment, commissaire. What was the name again?'

'Vessac.'

'Not Olivier Vessac, surely?'

'Yes, that's him.'

'Holy Mother of God. And his lady friend, that's Élisabeth Bonpain?'

'That's right, that's her name.'

'She's his lady friend and his partner. If you follow me.'

'Yes, I saw her, I've gathered that. And she's devastated.'

'Holy Mother! Élisabeth!'

'You know her?'

'She's a friend, commissaire. Kindest woman in the world, break your heart. I met her about, oh, eleven years ago. I went for one of my antalgic drives to Rochefort, that's where we met. I even stayed a whole week, because we were as thick as thieves, sorry, excuse me, shouldn't say that, we got on like a house on fire, oh dear, that's not much better, but we did.'

'Irène, would you be able to tell if she was lying?'

'Do you mean if she says there was no one there, but there was? But why would they want to protect a murderer?'

'So that people wouldn't find out about the past perhaps? And yet he did tell me about it himself. But then, it wasn't an official questioning under caution, it wouldn't count, as he knew perfectly well.'

'Oh. Maybe you're right. But I could certainly get the truth out of Élisabeth. We tell each other all sorts of things.'

'All right, come here then.'

'From Bourges?'

'Yes, why not? Is five hours in your anti-arthritis car too much?'

'No, commissaire, it's not that, it's this woman who shares my house. Did I not tell you about her? Louise, she's called. And she's, well, how shall I put it, she's a bit soft in the head. Well, really very soft. With the recluse business she's gone doolally, can't speak about anything else. Recluses, recluses. And what with all these deaths, when I'm not there she gets in a state, she sees them everywhere.'

'Look, Élisabeth's your friend, and quite apart from finding out whether she's telling the truth or not, her man Olivier is going to die in the next two days. Like I said, she's in great distress. She could be needing you.'

'I understand, commissaire, when you put it like that. I'll drive over – Louise will just have to suffer with her spiders.'

'Thank you. Where shall we meet? You know Saint-Porchaire, is there a café, or a restaurant?'

'Le Rossignol, not expensive and they let rooms too, so I could stay there. I'll try calling Élisabeth.'

'I'll meet you there about two thirty. Drive carefully, Irène.'

They were in sight of Saint-Porchaire when Mercadet called.

'We've got another bite victim,' Adamsberg said at once. 'Olivier Vessac.'

'One of the bastards?'

'Yes indeed. A repentant bastard, but apparently not a rapist. He was complicit though.'

'Not a rapist? And you believe that because he told you so?'

'Yes, correct.'

'Why?'

'Can't explain, Mercadet, I gave my word of honour.'

'Oh, OK, that's different,' said the lieutenant. 'Now I've got another one, too.'

'Another what?'

'Case of rape. In 1967. And this time, I've got the names: Claveyrolle, Barral, as usual, the terrible two, plus Roger Torrailles. A woman of thirty-two in Orange.'

'Well done, lieutenant. So how long did they get?'

'Nothing. There was a procedural irregularity. No trial. That's why it was hard to find.'

'What happened?'

'The clueless local cops forced confessions out of them without a lawyer present. They had the statement of the woman, Jeannette Brazac, and they just blundered straight ahead. Using violence, what's more. So that scuppered any chance of a trial. And Jeannette Brazac, well, she killed herself, eight months later.'

'Did you hear that, Louis?' said Adamsberg, ending the call. 'They really were a gang of rapists. And a woman died in 1967 because of them.'

'Well, stink bugs or rapists, we still have to protect the last two.'

Veyrenc braked as they reached the main square of Saint-Porchaire, while Adamsberg tried to reach Mordent.

'Keep going – Vessac's place is number 3 rue des Oies-Folles, the street of mad geese.'

'Do they exist, mad geese?'

'Of course. You said yourself we're all a bit crazy.'

'Wouldn't know about geese, though.'

'Mordent? Adamsberg here. Olivier Vessac is on his deathbed in hospital in Rochefort.'

'Oh shit! Are you there?'

'I've just left him. Listen, I need round-the-clock protection for the last two of the gang. Call up the gendarmeries of Senonches and Lédignan and ask them to send some men. Just say we have reason to believe they are being threatened. Uniformed cops, because they've got to be conspicuous.'

'What if Torrailles and Lambertin refuse?'

'Believe me, Mordent, with seven of their gang murdered and Vessac now dying, they'll agree.'

Veyrenc pulled up in front of 3 rue des Oies-Folles. The two men staked out the place, the earthen path, the little strip of woodland, the heavy wooden door of the house. There was no woodpile anywhere near.

Veyrenc slowly paced the short distance between the door and the car parked on the grass verge.

'No question,' he said. 'You can see their footsteps, Vessac and Élisabeth, as they walked across the wet grass. No third person behind them. No sign of anyone approaching from the other side.'

'Nothing here either,' said Adamsberg, crouching in front of the door, and feeling the top of the grass. 'Just the two of them.'

He liked grass. That's what he ought to do in the little garden he shared with Lucio, dig over the ground down to about fifty centimetres, take out all the Parisian stones, fill it with compost and sow grass. Lucio would love that.

Lucio: *Scratch that recluse, lad, scratch it till you draw blood.*

I don't want to, Lucio. Let me go.

You've got no choice, hombre.

Adamsberg felt the back of his neck tighten again, and his throat constricted at the same time as he suddenly thought of his mother. A passing vertigo made him put his hand on the ground.

'Shit, Jean-Baptiste, don't wipe out the marks.'

'Sorry.'

'Are you all right?' asked Veyrenc, seeing his friend's pale face. For a Béarnais with a dark complexion like Adamsberg, going pale was rare.

'I'm fine.'

No, Lucio, I don't want to.

Adamsberg went on automatically running his fingers through the grass.

'Look here, Louis,' he said, holding out an invisible object between his thumb and index finger.

'A little bit of nylon thread,' said Veyrenc. 'About twenty centimetres. Some local's fishing line?'

'People fish everywhere, but this was tangled up in a nettle.'

'Well, that wasn't what bit Vessac.'

'Still, get an evidence bag from the car, I'm afraid I'll lose it.'

Adamsberg and Veyrenc went on searching for another quarter of an hour among the plants, on the path, looking for anything, but finding nothing at all, except the fragment of fishing line. They got back in the car, Adamsberg driving now, both feeling dejected. Vessac and his 'lady friend' had indeed been alone, to all appearances.

'What do you want to do now?' asked Veyrenc, still keeping a weather eye on his friend.

'We haven't eaten since last night. Let's go to this Rossignol, get ourselves a Froissy-type breakfast and wait for Irène. Élisabeth Bonpain will be easier to question with her there.'

'Yes, I agree.'

'Where's the plastic bag?'

'In the case. Frightened of losing it?'

Adamsberg shrugged.

'It's all we've got,' he said.

'In other words, zilch.'

'You said it.'

XXVI

'ZILCH AGAIN,' SAID ADAMSBERG LETTING HIS MOBILE FALL ON TO THE table in Le Rossignol. 'Retancourt hasn't been able to trace any Jeannot Escande in the area, but she's only just begun her raids.'

'Raids?'

'When Violette goes on a search, it isn't a reconnaissance, it's a raid.'

'Jeannot probably slept in his car.'

'That would be sensible. And the Lamarre team hasn't found any sign of Jeannot in Palavas either. Which is *good* news. But again, they're just at the beginning.'

'Little Jeannot with one foot – who'd have thought it?'

'We don't have any hard evidence yet, Louis.'

'But he's the only one missing.'

'Yes.'

'And you have doubts about it?'

Adamsberg pushed away the remains of his breakfast, but poured another cup of coffee.

'You want some?' he asked Veyrenc. 'You've had hardly any sleep.'

'I'll take a nap in the car. We've got a good three hours to wait.'

'OK, Louis, I'm going to go for a walk, run a bit perhaps. I need to call my mother too.'

'You didn't answer my question,' said Veyrenc, standing up. 'You have doubts?'

'I don't know. I'm still waiting to see clearly, Louis.'

'Through your mists?'

'Yes.'

Adamsberg walked out of the village of Saint-Porchaire and found a forest path. Either his sense of smell or his desire made him capable of locating trees as accurately as elephants locate water. He sat down on a bank between two young elms, and called his home number in Béarn. His mother didn't want to talk about her arm and the broomstick, she wasn't one to complain. It was more important to have news of her Jean-Baptiste.

'What are you working on, son? You sound tired.'

'There are always difficult moments in an investigation, that's all.'

'What are you working on?' she repeated.

Adamsberg sighed, and hesitated.

'The recluse,' he said finally.

There was a short silence, then his mother spoke again, more hurriedly.

'The *recluse*, son? Which one? The nun or the creature?'

'Why did you say that? You know something?'

'Know what?'

'That's the second time someone has mentioned a woman, and I don't understand. A *nun*, you said?'

'No, no, Jean-Baptiste, I didn't say nun, I said "the man or the creature", the spider, you know.'

'No, I'm *sure* you said "the nun".'

'You must be tired, I said "the man".'

'What man, anyway?'

'Over Comminges way, there was this old fellow, he had a smallholding, and we called his place "La Recluse", because he didn't want to see anyone, and then in the end, he hanged himself. That's how people often end up, if they don't see anyone, they hang themselves. You know Raphaël has moved?'

'Yes, he's gone to live on the Île de Ré.'

'He's got a lot of work on his hands there, and guess what? He has a really nice seaside villa.'

His mother had changed the subject abruptly. Why did she mention a nun, and then backtrack and deny she'd said it? What was all that about a farm called La Recluse? And he knew it, that sick feeling was about to come over him again.

It didn't just come back, it enveloped him. He lay down on the bank, rubbing his fists into his eyes, feeling a chill down his back, and a stiffness in his neck. His mother. The recluse. Feeling shaken, he forced himself up and set off again, with hesitant steps, then broke into a trot, making his way along narrow tracks where the delicate branches of hazel bushes caught him in the face. He was brought to a halt in a clearing surrounded by thick undergrowth. How long had he been running? He looked at the time on his mobile. Only forty-five minutes before his rendezvous with Irène. He had no choice but to go back, at a brisk run now.

So he was dripping with sweat, his jacket knotted round his waist and his hair standing on end, but at least without any feeling of vertigo, when he burst into Le Rossignol. Veyrenc was sitting at a table with Irène Royer and Élisabeth Bonpain, who was holding her friend's hand. They had been eating lunch, except for Élisabeth, who was as if in mourning and had not touched a morsel on her plate.

Irène stood up at once to go and greet 'her' commissaire, assuming her position of privilege. She liked Veyrenc, but Adamsberg was the one she had chosen, over a hot chocolate in the Étoile d'Austerlitz.

'What happened to *you*?' she said, a little anxiously.

'I've been running.'

'But where were you running to, Holy Mother of God? And your cheek's bleeding.'

Adamsberg put his hand to his face and saw traces of blood on his fingers. The hazel twigs, he hadn't felt them at the time. Veyrenc discreetly passed him a paper napkin and Adamsberg went to the washroom to wipe his face and neck, emerging wetter than ever.

'I beg your pardon,' he said, sitting down.

'Understandable,' murmured Irène, 'all that emotion.'

'How is he?' Adamsberg asked Élisabeth Bonpain.

More tears, and Veyrenc at once offered her some paper napkins which he had asked for at the counter.

'Not so good,' he said.

Without Élisabeth seeing, since she had her head plunged in her hands, he wrote a few words on a napkin and passed it to Adamsberg. 'Haemolysis, necrosis of vital organs starting. Massive dose.' Adamsberg concealed the message, thinking once more of the last words he had spoken softly to the dying man: *Cheers, Vessac.*

'There's no hope, is there?' asked Élisabeth, raising her head.

'No,' said Adamsberg, as gently as he could. 'I'm truly sorry.'

'But why?'

'This year, the insecticides seem to have increased the power of the venom. Or perhaps the heat.'

Word of honour.

'Madame, I need your help,' he said. 'We need to check where these spiders are coming from. It was outside, was it, right by the door that Olivier felt the bite?'

'Oh yes. He just said "Bloody hell", and rubbed his shoulder.'

'And there was no one else around to see? Man, woman or child?'

'No, we were quite alone, commissaire. On that path, there's not a soul after the angelus.'

'One more question. Did Olivier like fishing?'

'Yes, every Sunday, he went to the lake.'

Adamsberg made a sign to Irène that he would leave the two women alone, and stood up, followed by Veyrenc. Le Rossignol was also a tobacconist's, so he bought a pack of Zerk's favourite cigarettes.

'You smoke that rubbish?' said Veyrenc, as they emerged on to the pavement, although he consented to take one himself.

'They're Zerk's choice.'

'And why are you buying them?'

'So I can steal them from him, because I've given up smoking.'

'I suppose there's a hidden logic in that somewhere. This woman seems to be sincere, doesn't she?'

'Irène will tell us. But yes, that's what I think too.'

Just then, Irène came out to find them.

'Yes, she's telling the truth, the whole truth,' she said. 'They were on their own. I wouldn't like to be in your shoes, commissaire. Very difficult.'

'Yes, very. Are you going to stay with her?'

'For a bit. Though I can't leave my daft Louise alone for too long, I think she's creating bloody havoc in the house, excuse me, but she is. She knows another man's been bitten and she's claiming she saw three recluses in the kitchen and another two in her bedroom. They're "multiplying", she says. That would make five new recluses in our house, walking about bold as brass.'

'Five? She's seen five?'

'She's imagining them, commissaire. Tomorrow she'll say there are ten, the next day thirty. I need to get back, otherwise I'll find her standing on a chair with three hundred recluses around her. She's soft in the head, that's all it is. That's the trouble with social media, they go on and on, everyone chips in and it blows some people's minds. And worse luck for me, that's what's happened to her.'

'How old is she?'

'Seventy-three.'

'I'd like to meet her,' said Adamsberg evasively.

'Whatever for? You must come across a lot of daft people in your work, surely?'

'I'd like to see how it is now that the recluse is blowing people's minds. Yes, that would interest me.'

'Ah, that's different. If you want to observe her, be my guest. We can pretend to squash recluses together. How long has he got, Élisabeth's Olivier?'

'Two days at most.'

Irène shook her head with a fatalistic expression.

'After the funeral, I'll ask Élisabeth to come and stay with me. There's a spare room, I could look after her.'

'Say goodbye to her for us,' said Adamsberg. 'Give her our sincerest wishes.'

'Commissaire, at the risk of shocking you, would you mind very much giving me a cigarette? I don't smoke normally. But with all this going on.'

'Feel free,' said Adamsberg, passing her three cigarettes. 'A gift from my son.'

They watched as Irène went back into Le Rossignol. Adamsberg stayed on the pavement, dividing Zerk's pack of cigarettes into two halves and thrusting them into his pockets.

'I don't like packets,' he said.

'As you wish.'

'Louis, I'm not going back to Paris.'

'Where are you going? Back to the Icelandic mists, to recover your sight?'

'My brother, Raphaël, lives on the Île de Ré now, and I haven't seen him for ages. Drop me off at Rochefort and I can get a bus to La Rochelle. I'll come back tomorrow.'

Veyrenc agreed. His brother and the seaside quite near at hand. Fair enough. But there was something else. Veyrenc couldn't see through the mists – who could? – but he was very good at interpreting Adamsberg's expressions.

'I'll drive you over to the Île de Ré, then I'll go straight back.'

'Drive carefully. You haven't had a lot of sleep. We're not Retancourt, you know.'

'Obviously not.'

'Ask the gendarmerie at Courthézon to alert us when Jean Escande gets back. Tell them not to call the squad, I mean not to call so that Danglard picks up. Just give them our two numbers.'

'Understood.'

'Tonight, you'd better have some garbure and then a good night's sleep.'

The two men from Béarn exchanged a quick glance as they got into the car.

XXVII

TWO HOURS LATER, ADAMSBERG WAS SLOWLY WALKING BAREFOOT ALONG an endless sandy beach, shoes in one hand, rucksack over his shoulder. From a distance, he made out his brother's silhouette, sitting on the terrace outside a tiny white building. Their mother preferred to believe Raphaël had a seaside villa, rather than a beach hut, and he did not care to disillusion her.

It would have been impossible for anyone else to recognise Adamsberg at that distance. But Raphaël turned his head, saw the man walking towards him and stood up at once. He went to meet him at a determined and almost as slow a pace.

'Jean-Baptiste,' was all he said, when they had hugged each other.

'Raphaël.'

'Come and have a drink. Will you have supper, or are you just passing through?'

'Supper. And sleep.'

After this brief exchange, the two brothers, who were strikingly alike to look at, went back to the house without a word. Silence had never bothered them, the way it is with all those who are practically twins.

Adamsberg decided not to broach the subject that was tormenting him until after their supper, which they ate outside, listening to the cries of the seagulls, with two candles on the table. He knew of course that Raphaël had at once sensed his anxiety and was waiting for him to be ready. They could read each other without having to think about it, and could almost have existed in their own self-sufficient world, exception made for women. Which was why they did not see each other so often.

Adamsberg lit a cigarette in the dark and started to recount to his brother everything that had happened since the very beginning of the investigation, an effort that was no simple matter for him, since he was not gifted for chronology or marshalling his thoughts logically. After twenty minutes, he stopped short.

'I'm boring you to death, I expect,' he said. 'But I've got to tell you all of it, not missing anything out. It's not just a moan about my life in the police.'

'You seem troubled, Jean-Baptiste. What's wrong?'

'Worse than troubled. It's this *damn* spider. And it gets worse still when I think about our mother. It's a kind of terror.'

'What's the connection?'

'There isn't one. It's just the way it is. Let me go on, I'm not going to spare you any details of the last week, anything that was said, just in case this terror is hidden somewhere under a floorboard, or in Froissy's cupboard, or in the jaws of that horrible moray eel, or in the lime blossom outside my window or in a speck of dust under my eyelid that I haven't seen before.'

Raphaël was not as vague as his brother. He was much more down to earth, better educated and more organised for the concrete world, despite finding that world and the way it was going intolerable. Raphaël was not Jean-Baptiste. But he had a gift no one else had: he could put himself in his brother's place, slip inside his skin to the ends of his fingers, almost being reincarnated in him, while preserving his full ability to observe.

Adamsberg took over an hour to finish his recital of the events, large and small, that had punctuated his pursuit of the killer. Then he paused to light another of Zerk's cigarettes.

'You smoke those things? I've got better ones if you want.'

'No, these belong to Zerk, he stayed back in Iceland.'

'I see. A glass of Madiran, perhaps? I get it delivered here. Or do you think that might muddle your ideas?'

'I don't have any ideas, Raphaël, the whole thing already seems a big muddle. So yeah, a glass of wine would be nice. We've just got this one man on the loose, Jean Escande. You picked that up?'

'I picked everything up,' Raphaël assured him, in the voice of a man who knows it hardly needs saying.

'All the arrows point towards him. Everything logically leads to him, as Vessac's murderer. The men in the Ex-victims Gang probably took it in turns to bump off their tormentors. It's perfect, it fits, the gang of boys who were bitten have launched a toxic offensive against the Recluse Gang. But I'm missing something here, I've got to probe deeper, I don't know what for. I don't *know*, because I can't *see*. And I can't see, because I can't *bear* this damned recluse, I can't even stand to hear its name any more, I don't want to hear it. It's eating me up on the spot, it's necrotic.'

'So you're stuck, caught in its web. And the investigation will run into the sands without you,' Raphaël concluded, pouring a glass of Madiran for his brother.

'And it'll leave me all alone, with what I haven't told you yet.'

'The terror. You said.'

With difficulty, stumbling over words, or avoiding them, Adamsberg described to his brother the growing malaise into which the recluse spider had plunged him, from the moment he had first seen its name on Voisenet's computer screen until this very afternoon, when after telephoning his mother, he had collapsed on the bank in the forest as if paralysed, and had then had to run in order to escape.

'So,' said Raphaël, when his brother had finished. 'You don't remember anything?'

'That's not what I said. I said "I can't *see* anything" and I'm empty-handed.'

'And I'm asking you: do you really not *remember* anything? When you mentioned a spectre just now, without even knowing what you meant, you really didn't remember? No image? No spectre? Jean Baptiste, don't you remember when you did see a spectre?'

'Never have.'

'Forget everything, yes, why not?' said Raphaël, in the same gentle low-pitched voice as his brother, although his own voice was usually sharper. 'Except when something absolutely refuses to be forgotten. Then it's warfare. And it hurts enough to make you fall down in the forest and then run like a madman without feeling the branches hit your face. You've got scratches on your cheeks.'

'It was just the hazel bushes, Raphaël.'

'You haven't lost the ability to see, Jean-Baptiste.'

And this time, Raphaël had really entered into the corners of his brother's mind. He rubbed the back of his own neck as if it was stiff.

'Raphaël, I just told you, I can't *see*,' cried Adamsberg, shocked by his brother's failure to understand. 'Are you listening, or have you gone as deaf as I'm blind?'

Adamsberg raised his voice very rarely and his recent outbursts, first to Voisenet because of his wretched moray eel, and then to Danglard because of his wretched cowardice, were unusual events. On the other hand, shouting at his brother was a habit and Raphaël was quite ready to shout back.

'You can see perfectly well,' yelled Raphaël, standing up and pounding the table. 'You can see as well as you see me standing here, the table, the candles. But some doors have shut, and put you in the dark. Can you understand that? And how do you choose the way out when everything's shut? In the dark?'

'What way out? How come these doors are shut?'

'You shut them yourself.'

'Me? *I'm* closing doors? When eight men have been murdered?'

'Yes, you, in person.'

'So I closed all these doors deliberately, so as to stay in the dark?'

'By dark, I mean profoundly dark. Like the interior of the earth, or inside a hole. Where the recluses hide.'

'I know all about the recluse spiders and they never frightened me.'

'I'm not talking about them, for God's sake, I'm talking about the other kind of recluse. The *women*. Holy women.'

Adamsberg shivered. The wind was rising on the beach. Raphaël did not say: 'It's getting cold, do you want to go in?' His brother had shivered. Good. He knew he was about to hurt him. He just pointed to Adamsberg's glass, which he had not touched.

'Drink up,' he said. 'So when I say "recluse" and "woman", that doesn't remind you of anything? Absolutely nothing?'

Adamsberg shook his head and sipped his wine.

'What am I supposed to remember? What do I have to break to get out of your black hole? Where do I have to go?'

'Wherever you like, you're the cop, it's your investigation, not mine.'

'So why are you bothering me with all these closed doors?'

Raphaël held out a hand for a cigarette, never mind that they were coarse.

'Why do you keep them loose in your pockets?'

'Don't like packets. Especially now.'

'I understand.'

There was a short silence, while Adamsberg located his lighter for his brother's cigarette.

'We're stupid,' said Raphaël, 'I could have lit it from the candle.'

'By the time you think of an idea, you know what it's like. Where were we?'

'We'd reached something I don't dare say to you.'

'Why?'

'Because I'm going to hurt you.'

'*You're* going to hurt me?'

'You don't remember a thing about it, and yet you were twelve years old. I was only ten. You were twelve! And you can't remember! That means it really has terrified you. I didn't see her. You did.'

'What are you talking about?'

'About the recluse for God's sake. A hideous old woman, hidden in the dark . . . You saw her. It was just off the road to Lourdes.'

Adamsberg shrugged.

'I remember the road to Lourdes perfectly well, Raphaël. The Chemin Henri IV.'

'Of course. Our mother forced us to walk along it every year, whether we wanted to or not.'

'Mostly not. But we didn't walk the whole thirty-five kilometres, all the same.'

'No, our father took us some of the way in the car, to a little wood.'

'The Bénéjacq wood.'

'That's it, I'd forgotten the name.'

'So you see, I do remember. And then we'd walk a few more kilometres, and our father would come back and take us the rest of the way to Lourdes. Every year, same thing.'

'Except this one time,' said Raphaël. 'That day, he drove us all the way to Lourdes. Our mother went to the grotto, bought her bottles of holy water and so on. Remember once we drank them? We got in big trouble.'

'Yeah, right, I remember that.'

'But nothing else?'

'Nothing. We went to Lourdes and we came back again. What am I supposed to say?'

Adamsberg felt better. He was listening to his brother, there was nothing else to be done. It must be that saint they worship at Lourdes who had kindly placed Raphaël near to him, on this sandy beach on the Île de Ré, not too far from Rochefort. And what was the saint called? Thérèse? Roberte?

'What's her name?' he asked. 'The saint, the one in Lourdes?'

'St Odette, no wait, St Bernadette.'

'So we didn't remember much about that bit of it!'

'No. Have some more wine.'

Adamsberg drank again, put down his glass, then looked at his brother, who continued:

'That summer, Mother had decided not to stop at Bénéjacq but to do five or six kilometres on foot on the way home from Lourdes. She had something she wanted to do. It was off the road, and she explained as we went along. You don't remember that either?'

'No.'

'Well, off the road,' Raphaël went on, 'up in a field, there was an old dovecot, you know, a place where they used to keep pigeons, built of stone. It was quite small, only about a couple of metres across. And the doors and flight-holes had all been bricked up. Except for one. I could see that.'

'And? What did she want with this dovecot?'

'There was a woman living there. She'd been there about five years, never came out.'

'What? You mean she lived there all the time, day and night?'

'Yes.'

'But how did she survive?'

'On charity, from people who were prepared to walk up the slope in the field and give her food and water through this window slot. They brought her straw as well for, you know, natural functions. Anyway, that's what our mother was going to do, take her some food. The locals thought she was a nun or a saint, who was going to protect them, like in the old days. The prefect didn't dare intervene.'

'I can't believe this, Raphaël.'

'You don't *want* to believe it, Jean-Baptiste.'

'But what was she doing there? Who'd locked her up?'

'I'm talking about a woman who'd cloistered herself up voluntarily, to stay there till death. Like in the olden days, medieval times.'

'Because there were women who did that then?'

'Yes, masses of women in the Middle Ages, and it went on until the sixteenth century. And they were called . . . recluses.'

Adamsberg's hand stopped in mid-air, holding his wine glass.

'Yes, recluses,' Raphaël repeated. 'And some of them survived in their cells for up to fifty years. Their hair grew like a wild mane, jumping with lice, their nails got so long they curved over like claws, their skin was ingrained with dirt, and their bodies smelled terrible, because their bedding was soaked with urine and crap. And this one, maybe the last recluse of our own times, you *saw* her, in the field: the recluse of the Pré d'Albret.'

'No, I did not!' Adamsberg shouted. 'Our mother would never have let me see her.'

'Quite right. When we were about ten metres from the dovecot, she made us stop and wait for her. But it was so mysterious, wasn't it? So you slipped behind her, and when she was on her way back, you ran like a hare and climbed up on to a rock, to peep in through the window. For a couple of minutes. A long couple of minutes. Then you screamed, you started screaming with terror, like a mad thing. And you lost consciousness.'

Adamsberg glared at his brother, his fists clenched.

'Mother tried to revive you by slapping your face and pouring Lourdes water over you. I ran back to the road to get our father. He carried you in his arms, and you didn't come round until you were in the back of the car. Your head was on my knee, and just from resting your chin on that window ledge, your face smelled of shit and death. And Mother gave you a shake and said, "Forget it, son, for mercy's sake, just forget it!" And you never mentioned it again. So that's the terror, that's the darkness, that's the recluse that's been gripping the back of your neck: the woman in the Pré d'Albret.'

Adamsberg stood up, his lips drained of blood and his body rigid, ran his hand stiffly across his face, and thought he could smell once more the atrocious odour of death and rotting. He could see his brother, the candles, the wine glass, but now he could see the claws, a shock of hair as grey as a cellar beetle, hair that was crawling with parasites, he could see a mouth opening slowly, wide open, full of rotten teeth, and the claws coming nearer, and he heard again the harsh terrifying roar. The recluse. Raphaël jumped up and dashed round the table just in time to catch his brother as he fainted. He managed to drag him to a bed, pulled off his shoes and covered him up.

'I knew I was going to hurt you,' he whispered.

XXVIII

ADAMSBERG NORMALLY SLEPT LITTLE, RISING AT DAYBREAK. RAPHAËL woke him at noon. He opened his eyes and sat up on the bed. He realised it was late, no need to ask the time.

'I'm taking over your bathroom,' he said. 'I haven't washed or changed in over twenty-four hours.'

'I've just got a shower.'

'OK, I'll take over your shower. Were there any phone calls?'

'Two.'

Adamsberg snatched up his mobile and listened to the voicemails from Voisenet and Retancourt. Voisenet was categorical. Jean Escande had arrived at Palavas two days before the venomous attack on Vessac. The old man with one foot, Jeannot, was well known in several small restaurants in the spa town, and they had finally tracked him down at the house of a woman friend, just as he was leaving. Adamsberg called Voisenet back.

'What'll I do now, boss?'

'Go home with the team, lieutenant. Did you have time to paddle in the sea at least?'

'For five minutes.'

'Well, that's something.'

Retancourt answered her phone at once.

'Thirty-eight hotels visited, commissaire.'

'We're not going to check the 17,000 hotels in all of France. Back to base, Retancourt.'

'He slept in his car then? That's what you think?'

'He slept at Palavas.'

'But if he was –'

'I know, I know,' Adamsberg cut her off.

'Are you still in Rochefort?'

'I'm on the Île de Ré, at my brother's. Tell Mordent I'll be back at base tomorrow. Mordent, not Danglard.'

Adamsberg rejoined Raphaël on the terrace, where lunch was waiting. Pasta and ham. Raphaël's cooking skills were no more advanced than those of his brother.

'We're dished,' he said. 'It wasn't Jean Escande who attacked Vessac. He's been located at the seaside, hundreds of kilometres from where the attack took place.'

'They might have sent one of their sons.'

'No, Raphaël, this kind of vengeance can't be done by proxy. It's got to be direct or nothing. The kids who were bitten *didn't* kill their tormentors. And yet there's no doubt, it was recluse venom. And it's still got to be that orphanage, La Miséricorde, that's somehow at the centre of this case. I'm sure about that, or nothing makes any sense. There's no other lead, but this lead is getting us nowhere. I've crashed head first into the sands, just like Danglard said.'

Raphaël passed Jean-Baptiste the bread, and the two brothers cleaned their plates with the sweeping gestures of country boys.

'But it's different now,' said Raphaël, throwing some crumbs to a few waders scurrying about on the beach.

'I have a pair of blackbirds at the squad. I feed them cake. The male is very thin.'

'Blackbirds are nice too. Are they nesting?

'The female's sitting on eggs. What's different?'

'Are you still blind?'

'No. I can perfectly well distinguish the recluse of the Pré d'Albret now. And I know why I screamed.'

'She came towards you.'

'How do you know?'

'I don't know, I just always imagined she had.'

'Yes, hands outstretched, and she shouted, no, she sort of roared. But I can look back at it now. I'm not afraid of her, and I'm not afraid of the word. Recluse, recluse, I can keep saying it all day without falling over.'

'So you can face it again. You're free. You can see.'

'If there's anything left to see now. Who on earth would kill using recluse venom, if not the boys from the orphanage? And it wasn't them.'

'Well, it must have been someone else, bro. You're free, you'll find them. You'll be there at eight.'

'Where?'

'Paris. I know you're going to jump on the next train.'

Adamsberg smiled.

Raphaël dropped his brother off at the station, after they had given each other a long hug.

'Oh dammit, Raphaël, I left my dirty clothes at your place.'

'That was the point, wasn't it?'

Like many people, Adamsberg enjoyed travelling by train, because it offers you a parenthesis, even an escape from the real world. Your thoughts can move around slowly, skirting difficulties. With his eyes half shut, his mind ranged over the painful shipwreck of the investigation and returned to the woman Louise, and her hundred imaginary recluses. He returned to the connections Voisenet had made between animal fluid and seminal fluid, and the women who had been raped.

He returned once more to the woman described as 'daft' who shared a house with Irène. He took out his phone and sent a text to Voisenet.

Thoughts on train. What you said: rape victim, control of toxic fluid, murdering an aggressor by turning fluid against him. Could a woman who was raped develop a phobia for poisonous creatures for same reason?

Thoughts in car, Voisenet replied. *Dictating to Lamarre, on way back to Paris. Certainly. Phobia of snakes scorpions spiders anything that injects toxin. Interesting but gets us nowhere.*

Never mind.

'Was that really all he replied?' Voisenet asked Lamarre. '"Never mind"?'

'Yes, that's all.'

Voisenet, who was tired out, wondered how the disastrous results of the investigation so far still left Adamsberg with the desire to go foraging on these distant paths. That was because he did not know that Raphaël had rescued his brother from the web of the recluse of the Pré d'Albret, restoring to him the aerial freedom of his movements and thoughts.

Adamsberg tried Irène next, having received permission to contact her on Élisabeth's phone, searching for an appropriate excuse to formulate his question. Without finding one, he decided to go ahead anyway and tapped:

Irène, what is full name of your housemate?

Louise Chevrier. Why?

That 'why?' was of course entirely justified.

I know a specialist on spider phobia. Could he help?

Not knowing if there was such a word as 'arachnophobia' he had avoided the word, so his message did not look as convincing as he had intended.

She won't see him. Hates men too, awkward, eh?

Just an idea.

I'm telling lies again, thought Adamsberg, pulling a face. Irène was replying spontaneously and he was deceiving her with other thoughts, train thoughts, that get you nowhere as Voisenet had rightly said. This time, he contacted Mercadet.

Check if Louise Chevrier, 73, was ever rape victim.

Urgent?

Need to understand something.

Adamsberg received the reply quite a while later, after he had dropped off to sleep again.

Raped in 1981 age 38 Nîmes!!! Rapist caught for once. Nicolas Carnot, got 15 yrs. Checked, but zero link to Miséricorde, either of them. Shit, missed her before. Trial held at Troyes, don't know why.

'Rapist caught for once.' Adamsberg understood what his officer meant. He was familiar with the damning statistics: a woman raped every seven minutes in France, and only one or two per cent of rapists sentenced. Might one of the victims develop a neurotic fear of poisonous creatures afterwards? So that she might imagine them coming after her from all sides on their hairy legs? Or on the contrary, might she do a deal with the toxin, get hold of it and violate the aggressor's life with it?

The hairy legs he had thought of might give an unquestioned advantage to the spider, if you wanted revenge for a rape, because they might suggest the arms of a man grabbing the victim. Well, the recluse spider wasn't actually hairy, but that was still an element in favour of arachnids – arachnodes? arachnes? – compared to their competitors, snakes, scorpions, wasps, hornets, etc. And there was something else too: in the spider world, the male was often killed by the female after mating, although again this wasn't usual for the recluse. But in its favour, the creature was timid, hiding away from humans, only venturing out where there was no threat. Yes, he said, trying to put himself in the mind of a woman who had been raped, the recluse could be a good companion for the rest of your life. And with its un-hairy legs, more feminine, in a way it might seem more approachable. At the same time, it was possessed of a venom that could destroy flesh and blood.

He turned away from the hills and clock towers speeding past before his eyes and texted Mercadet again.

Occupation of Louise Chevrier?

Via Froissy: childminder.

Where?

Strasbourg.

When?

1986 or so.

Strasbourg. He well remembered its mighty cathedral with its stee-ple. Which took him to another tower, a much more humble one, the one that must have been part of the Miséricorde orphanage. And that clock tower still loomed over their investigation. In his mind anyway.

Mercadet's responses had been slow, reminding him that his lieu-tenant was probably approaching his period of narcoleptic sleep. He closed his mobile, reckoning that the question of whether you called the spider family arachnids, arachnodes or arachnes could wait. And closed his eyes. Twelve hours' recovery time had not been enough.

XXIX

ADAMSBERG WALKED TO HEADQUARTERS NEXT MORNING, WATCHING A few seagulls that had accompanied him from the Île de Ré. He hadn't felt shaky at all, had not put his hand to his neck, or felt the presence of any kind of spectre.

But he was walking without haste, putting off the moment of arrival, wondering how to lead the meeting at which he would have to deal with the unquestionable debacle of this investigation, while facing all his officers, most of them exhausted. He was returning from an expedition on which he had sent everyone – Danglard excepted – like a defeated captain on a dismasted ship, driven up against the reefs of incontestable facts. After the uncertain start, his colleagues had believed him and followed him, and the return to port would be in silence, in the council chamber, on a calm sea. No Jeannot in detention, no charges against Little Louis, Marcel and the other ex-victims. He did nevertheless feel some satisfaction in having established that these men, who had been bitten by spiders long ago at La Miséricorde, and whom he had visualised as wounded children, had *not* actually killed anyone. And despite his professional disappointment, despite the investigation which had come to such an abrupt halt, the victory over himself that his brother had provided made him feel much more at ease and light-hearted. Scattered ideas without meaning came to play around in his head once more, like tiny bubbles, liberated to fill his mind with tumultuous gases, fizzing away without any concern for effectiveness.

Before he went through the archway of the squad building, he leaned against a lamp post and with a smile sent a text to Danglard:

You can go for dinner with your relatives now, Danglard, the coast is clear.

And in the office, faces did indeed look tired and sad. Veyrenc, to whom Adamsberg had delegated the task of dealing with whole sections of his speech, was concentrating on some notes. Retancourt remained imperturbable. This shipwreck of an investigation wasn't going to challenge her force of resistance. But like the others, she was afraid that Adamsberg would find this failure hard to bear, when faced with the bitter hostility of Danglard. The commandant possessed many linguistic resources with which to celebrate his victory, and he was facing a boss who, this morning, had no answers. And Danglard had still not appeared. Adamsberg went from desk to desk, making rapid gestures of reassurance, according to the character of each officer. For Retancourt and Froissy, he had picked in his own garden at dawn two handfuls of wild flowers, blue ones. He put one bunch on Retancourt's desk.

'Has Danglard come in?' he asked.

'He's in his office,' said Noël, 'hiding away like a recluse spider. Or perhaps he's glad we've hit the buffers.'

Adamsberg shrugged.

'Froissy – is she worn out?'

'She's in the courtyard.'

Adamsberg was about to go out and give her the fragile flowers which had already begun to droop in his hand, when she returned to the room, looking so happy that they hoped for a last-minute miracle. Perhaps there had been a Jeannot lookalike in Palavas, or perhaps the real one had turned up in Saint-Porchaire.

'They've hatched!' she said.

'The baby blackbirds?' asked Adamsberg.

'There are five of them and the parents are going mad trying to feed them.'

'Five is a big clutch,' said Voisenet, looking rather serious. 'Our courtyard is all cobblestones. And the bases of the trees have grids across them. They didn't choose a very good place, the parents. How are they going to find any worms?'

'Froissy,' said Adamsberg, taking a crumpled banknote from his pocket, 'there are some raspberries in the corner shop just now, go and get some. And a bit of cake. Voisenet, you can find them a dish for water, it hasn't rained for ten days. Retancourt, please keep an eye on the cat. Noël and Mercadet, could you go and take up the grids under the trees? Justin and Lamarre, can you water the earth there to make it soft? Anyone know where there's a shop that sells fishing supplies?'

'I do,' said Kernorkian. 'Ten minutes away by car.'

'Off you go then and buy some worms.'

'Big ones?'

'Little ones. Very thin ones.'

'What about the meeting? It's at 9 a.m.'

'We'll wait for you.'

Mordent stared at the scene before him, stunned. Adamsberg was distributing orders as though in the middle of a full-blown investigation, and all the officers were obeying at once, as if impressed by the importance of their mission. They seemed to be ignoring the failure they had all experienced, and the inexplicable quandary in which they were now placed.

Adamsberg went out into the courtyard and helped Noël and Mercadet to lift the grids. Then he took a look at the nest where five little beaks were gaping open non-stop. The parents were flying to and fro as fast as they could.

'Nobody get too near to the nest,' he said, going back indoors, feeling satisfied.

He bumped into Mordent and clapped him on the shoulder.

'Not so bad after all, is it?'

And when, in a rather agitated sequence, seven raspberries had been scattered, two slices of cake crumbled, and a dozen worms released on to the uncovered and softened earth under the trees, Adamsberg sent Estalère off to organise the coffees, a signal that the meeting would now begin in the council chamber, an hour late. Danglard's chair remained empty.

From his office, with the door closed, Danglard had heard the commotion from the squad, without knowing what explained it. When he started to listen properly, he gathered that all this fuss was about the hatching out of five baby blackbirds. Voisenet was no doubt correct that the nestlings were unlikely to survive in the paved courtyard and Adamsberg had taken the right steps to try to save them. But, anyway, what the fuck did the deaths of five baby birds mean to him, Danglard? Nothing. He looked again at the recent text he had received from Adamsberg:

You can go for dinner with your relatives now, Danglard, the coast is clear.

It was just as he had feared. Adamsberg had worked it out. The commissaire had been trying to discover the reason why Danglard was blocking the investigation and he had found it. Richard Jarras. Which was quite true. As soon as Danglard had had wind of the unusual deaths by recluse spider bite, he had known from which direction the attack might have come. And he had done all he could to place obstacles in the way, and to isolate Adamsberg from his colleagues. He had thought it would be easy to outwit the commissaire, but he had been wrong. Adamsberg had followed the trail leading to the orphanage and in the end he had persuaded his team to follow him. Now that the investigation had run into the sands, and Richard Jarras was no longer a suspect, Danglard was starting to realise the catastrophe into which his emotional reaction, his impulsiveness and his fear had led him. He had once more introduced discord into the squad;

he had decided to threaten the commissaire's career; and this time, deliberately, he had done all he could to shield a potential murderer. The offence would lead to punishment for complicity. He was done for.

And as sometimes happens when you think you are done for, and when the fault is entirely your own, Danglard's defence mechanism led him not towards contrition but towards aggression. If he was going down, well, he would bring someone down with him, namely the cause of his misfortune, Adamsberg.

In the council chamber, the commissaire was waiting for Danglard to deign to appear. The others all sat and watched him, anxious to know his decision. They knew that Danglard had encouraged dissent, and had intended to make a report to the divisionnaire. But Adamsberg had told only his three closest colleagues about the crime of which Danglard was guilty when he chose to shield a potential killer.

Adamsberg pursed his lips, and took out his mobile, listening first to the cheeping of the nestlings to moderate his irritation. Instead of sending a text, he called Danglard direct.

'Everything all right, commandant? You're ten minutes late,' he said calmly.

Danglard said nothing, as Adamsberg indicated by a gesture to his colleagues.

'According to the ethics of seaboard life,' said Adamsberg, employing, heaven knew why, a maritime metaphor, 'a senior officer doesn't leave a sinking ship.'

Commandant Mordent raised his head on hearing this noble pronouncement.

'So you are expected here at once,' Adamsberg went on. 'Are you coming, yes or no? I'm waiting for your answer.'

Danglard mumbled an indistinct 'yes' and hung up. Adamsberg looked round at the officers who were all dumbstruck with apprehension.

'There are more important things in life than Danglard's bad temper,' he said with a smile. 'The little birds for instance have nothing to do with the case.'

It was this last inappropriate sentence that Danglard heard as he opened the door. He went to his seat without looking at anyone.

'All right,' Adamsberg began, 'we're all present now, for me to tell you what we all know. The investigation is a total fiasco. We were wrong. Or rather, I should say, *I* was wrong. The lead looked like a clear trail, but it was a false one. The Gang of Ex-victims did *not* touch the stink bugs from the orphanage. We could go on pursuing them, but it would be a mistake. If none of them had anything to do with Vessac, then they didn't kill the others. But I am going to be obstinate on one point, one clock tower if you like. I am still *sure* there's a link between La Miséricorde orphanage and three deaths: those of Claveyrolle, Barral and Landrieu. Otherwise, there is no way to explain the outlandish method of using the venom of the recluse spider.'

He stopped since his phone had rung.

'*Four* deaths,' he corrected himself. 'Olivier Vessac died at Rochefort hospital, a quarter of an hour ago. There are two men left whom we need to save: Alain Lambertin and Roger Torrailles. At my request, they are at present under police protection.'

'That's good,' said Mordent.

'But this murderer has been on the go for fourteen years,' Adamsberg insisted. 'And if the trail leading to the boys who were bitten looked brightly lit and promising, I think the next one we have to travel will be dark and cold.'

'Why's that?' asked Lamarre.

'I don't know. We went astray. We followed the wrong route. One that was *too* brightly lit perhaps. It's not the first time that an investigation has found itself heading into, what shall I say, a dead end, a diverticulus? Is that the right word for it, Danglard? Leading nowhere. So we have to look for a different way, a channel, a strait, that will take us through to the killer.

'Oh, so easy,' said Danglard unpleasantly. 'And how do you think you are going to find this "channel", that you say is going to be dark and cold? You don't have any elements left that make sense. Unless you hope that your own belief, your own passion, and your own certainty, are going to guide you. Like Magellan, sailing into one false creek after another.'

'Magellan?' said Adamsberg.

And they all understood that Danglard was beginning to take his revenge, moving it on to his home ground of a war of words and encyclopedic knowledge. Magellan. Apart from Veyrenc, none of the officers in the room could have said who this Magellan was, or what he had done.

'Well, why not like Magellan, commandant?' asked Adamsberg, swinging round to face Danglard. 'I wouldn't dare compare our little expedition to his famous voyage. But since you insist, let's try it. I'm in a maritime mood after seeing Rochefort harbour.'

Adamsberg stood up and calmly walked over to a large map of the world which Veyrenc had one day pinned to the wall of the council chamber. He had said it was to give the squad a sense of the outside air. Like everyone, the commissaire knew perfectly well what Danglard was up to when he mentioned Magellan. He wanted to humiliate the commissaire in front of the team, to show up Adamsberg's habitual ignorance and demonstrate the inconsistency of his thought processes. But while Danglard knew plenty about Magellan, what he did *not* know about was the existence of a certain road mender in Adamsberg's native village. This old man had never left the Pyrenees. But he had had a passion for the voyages of sailing ships from long ago, making models of them which were the wonder of the whole district, as he reproduced in tiny detail all the intricacies of their rigging. Groups of children would watch in silence as the man's large fingers fixed delicate stays to the masts, and would listen to his often-repeated stories. So to Adamsberg, the tale of Magellan's voyage was entirely familiar. Once in front of the map, he put his finger on a point on the coast of Spain and met Veyrenc's eyes. Veyrenc, realising what was happening, winked to give his childhood friend the go-ahead.

'This,' said Adamsberg , 'is the port of Seville. On 10 August 1519, Magellan – real name Fernão de Magalhães – weighed anchor with five old and patched-up ships, the *San Antonio*, the *Trinidad*, the *Concepción*, the *Victoria* and the *Santiago*. As admiral, he sailed in the flagship, the *Trinidad*.'

Adamsberg then moved his finger down the African coast, crossed the Atlantic, and continued along the coasts of Brazil and Argentina, until he stopped at a point on the east coast of South America.

'This is the 40th parallel. A chart had indicated that the much sought-after channel through to a hypothetical ocean, the future Pacific, which would prove to the world in general, and the Church in particular, that the Earth was round, would be found at 40 degrees latitude. But the chart was wrong.'

All faces had now turned towards Adamsberg, showing both relief and fascination, as they followed his finger. Veyrenc was watching the change in Danglard's expression, especially when Adamsberg had listed the five ships and given the real name of the Portuguese sailor, Magellan.

'And Magellan kept going,' Adamsberg continued. 'He kept on going south. He explored every gulf, every inlet, hoping to find a way through to this other ocean. But they were all dead ends, leading nowhere. He wore himself out, he sailed on, through storms and tempests, he and his men were half dead from cold and hunger when they reached Puerto San Julián. He went on yet further, and finally, at the 52nd parallel, he found the channel leading through to the other side, the one we call today the Strait of Magellan. After him and his *crewmen*.'

The crewmen, the team, everyone understood. Adamsberg traced with his finger the long route, south of Patagonia, coming out into the Pacific, and let his hand rest there.

'We have to keep on going,' he said, finally letting his arm fall. 'We have to find the strait, as I was saying more simply, when Danglard interrupted me by his mention of Magellan.'

'About whom you seem to know a great deal, commissaire,' said Danglard, who from inside his personal abyss was still ready to bite.

'Does that bother you?'

'No, but it astonishes me.'

At this offensive reply, Noël leapt up, overturning his chair and moving in on the commandant, clearly on the attack.

'According to the ethics of seaboard life,' he said loudly and angrily, 'a senior officer does not insult the admiral. Take it back.'

'According to the ethics of seaboard life,' Danglard retorted, standing up in turn, 'a lieutenant does not give orders to a senior officer.'

Adamsberg closed his eyes for a moment. Danglard had changed, he had turned into a complete bloody idiot. And although the commandant was quite unequal physically to confronting a well-launched Noël – the latter having reverted to the cocky and dangerous streetfighter he had once been – he was still Danglard.

Adamsberg caught Noël's arm just before it connected with Danglard's jaw.

'Don't break the rules, Noël,' said Adamsberg. 'Thank you, but sit down.'

As Noël did, muttering, and as did Danglard, white-faced with shock, his sparse pepper-and-salt hair soaked with sweat.

'The incident is closed,' said Adamsberg. 'There were fights on board the *Trinidad* too. We'll take a break now,' he said. 'But don't all go trooping out into the yard to see the birds, you'd scare off the parents so they might not come back, and in that case, there'd be nothing we could do.'

XXX

DURING THE PAUSE, AS THE TEAM DISPERSED, AS RETANCOURT congratulated Noël on his attack, offering her professional appreciation of the intercepted trajectory of his right hook, and as Danglard slunk off to take refuge in his lair, Adamsberg escaped into his office. He took out the little plastic container, made the dead recluse spider roll over, and picked up his phone.

'Irène. This is Adamsberg. You know what's happened?'

'Vessac's died, yes, of course I know. I'm whispering because I'm with Élisabeth in the hospital corridor. I'm trying to get her to leave.'

'I wanted to know something. How did your Louise react? Have you been in touch? Does she know too?'

'Naturally she does. People are talking about nothing else in the whole region, back home. But look, nobody's suspecting any murders, I've kept my word, commissaire, I haven't told anyone. But the "curse" of the recluse is all over the internet. They all think its venom must have transmuted.'

'What about Louise though? Is she still seeing them everywhere?'

'She's getting worse and worse. She's locked herself up in her room, and she's vacuumed it all over, she says, I don't know how many times. She'll be vacuuming the walls next, you can bet. I need to get back home. And I tell you, with Élisabeth to look after, this isn't a good moment. Just my bad luck to have ended up with Louise. I didn't realise at first how batty she is. It began with the soap.'

'Soap?'

'Yes, you know, liquid soap with a thing you press and it squirts out in a jet. Well, I think it's more hygienic. But it makes her scream, she chucked it in the bin. I took it out again, I haven't got money to throw away.'

'What made her scream, the soap or the jet?'

'The jet. You have to have bats in the belfry, or maybe I should say spiders in the belfry, sorry, I shouldn't joke about it.'

'I don't mind your joking.'

'Good, I like my little jokes. Make the world go round, don't they?'

'Yes, that's the point of them, Irène. Does anything else make her scream?'

'Oh, any container with a thing to press, hand cream for instance. And oil. She can't stand oil being in the kind of bottle you have to press to make it come out. But how are we going to make our vinaigrette otherwise, eh?'

'Same with vinegar?'

'No, vinegar doesn't bother her. She's batty, like I said. And I can tell you that when I get groceries delivered, and it's always men who come, that isn't easy either. I have to warn her so she can shut herself in her room.'

'Do you know anything about her past life?'

'Nothing. Never says a word about it. I'd really like to kick her out, but I daren't do it. Who'd take her in, eh? And I'm not a nasty person, so I don't dare.'

'Does she ever leave the house?'

'On her own? You must be joking, commissaire. But if I go out on one of my arthritis trips, she'll get in the car with me. Even though I'd prefer a bit of peace myself. But again, it would be mean to refuse her so I don't. When we get somewhere, I drop her off at the guest house, let her find something to do, and I go for a walk with my camera. And I buy my snowstorms.'

'Snowstorms?'

'You know, those paperweights, like a globe, that make a snowstorm when you shake them. They're pretty, aren't they? I collect them, I've got over fifty. Look here, if you're keen on Bourges cathedral, I'll give you one of that.'

'Thank you,' said Adamsberg who liked his dead recluse spider a thousand times more. 'But I'd like to meet her.'

'To understand her arachnophobia?'

'Is that the word, "arachnophobia"? I must just write it down.'

'Oh, commissaire, if you want to see her, forget it, because you're a man.'

'I was forgetting.'

'That you're a man? That's not normal, commissaire, anyone can see you are.'

'No, I forgot she wouldn't want to see me. Well, we'll think about it, I have to go back to my meeting.'

'In my opinion,' said Irène, who despite her chatty and straightforward way of speaking, had no shortage of insight, 'you've got something else in mind, besides arachnophobia. After all, you are a cop.'

'And what might that something else be?'

'To see whether it's true or not that the recluses have multiplied.'

Adamsberg smiled.

'You're not wrong.'

He put the phone down, feeling puzzled. This Louise Chevrier, about whom so little was known, wasn't just 'batty', she must be totally neurotic. That is, if she had a phobia of liquid soap, a fluid substance squirting out, a recurrent image of the rape she had suffered. He had had to deal with a number of cases of women who had been raped. He had met some who couldn't stand to be in a room with a man, but he had never heard of terror extending to the sight of any kind of creamy liquid. Louise's phobias really did smack of insanity. But if he could, admittedly, see the link between liquid soap and sperm, he couldn't see how it extended to oil.

He closed his eyes for a few moments, then went and leaned his forehead against the window, looking at the lime tree. Oil. Now where had he heard the word recently? When he was crumbling the cake: 'Your trousers will be ruined'? No. The roar of a passing motorbike drowned out the chirruping of the nestlings.

Oil, yes, good grief, oil spilled on the road, the route that the third victim, stink bug Victor Ménard, would take on his motorbike.

Adamsberg ran his hands down his cheeks. No coincidence, since Mercadet would have found out about Louise being raped sooner or later. But why had this woman, so terrified of recluses, come to live with Irène Royer? When Irène made no secret of the fact that she didn't kill the creatures? It made no sense. Unless Louise had been lying all along the line. Unless she was really in that house precisely because she knew there *would* be recluse spiders there, where they were protected, like she was. Then in order to throw anyone off the scent, she pretended to be afraid of them, of being an arachnophobe. Whereas really she was an *arachnophile*, or even a reclusophile. He was pretty sure the latter term didn't exist.

But how would she have heard about an investigation? Irène had kept her word, because no news of it had got out on the internet. But they had spoken on the phone, and she regularly addressed him as 'commissaire', which was a giveaway.

Suddenly anxious, he stiffened his arms. Then he relaxed. Irène wasn't a man, and certainly not one of the Recluse Gang. She couldn't be at risk. Unless. Unless Louise was getting worried about the progress of the investigation, and unless Irène started to have suspicions about her housemate, about which she might, sooner or later, tell this mysterious 'commissaire'.

He called his arachnophile friend once more.

'Irène, this is quite urgent. Are you alone?'

'Élisabeth's asleep. What's happening?'

'Listen carefully. Don't phone me when Louise might be able to overhear us. Do you follow me?'

'No, not at all.'

'Never mind, I'm just asking you to promise.'

'But why?'

'Has she ever asked you about me? About the man you telephone sometimes?'

'No, never, why would she? With her spiders in the belfry, she's not going to take much notice of anyone else, I promise you that.'

'Well, that might change. If she does ask you about this "commissaire" you speak to, tell her this: I'm an old friend from Nîmes you met up with again by chance. And like you, I'm interested in spiders, in my spare time. I'm a zoologist manqué. That would explain our exchanges about the recluse and its latest doings. Understood?'

'Ye-es,' said Irène, for once at a loss for words.

'And I'm also a collector of snowstorms.'

'You are?'

'Of course not, it's a lie, Irène. You follow me?'

'No. You'll have to explain a bit. I'm not a mean person, like I said, but I'm not a puppet either, commissaire.'

'I don't think your Louise is just batty. I think she's deeply unhinged. And,' Adamsberg went on untruthfully, 'she might be capable of spreading any information she picked up from you about the investigation.'

'Oh, I see a bit better what you're getting at.'

'So she mustn't on any account suspect that I think these deaths are murders. For even a whisper of that to get out on social media would be a disaster.'

'Yes, I follow you.'

'All right, got that, Irène? Just an old friend, a frustrated zoologist interested in spiders and snowstorms.'

'Well, what I could do then,' said Irène, who seemed to have regained a little of her verve, 'I could buy *two* snowstorms here in Rochefort. And then when I get home, I could tell her I bought one for me, one for you, and that we met up in a souvenir shop. In Pau, for example. I've got a Pau snowstorm. That way it's me telling the lie.'

'That's perfect. And if you have a text message for me that mentions anything sensitive, send it then delete it.'

'I follow you. You think she might look on my phone?'

'And your computer.'

'Oh, well, in that case, we could take advantage of it. I could send you false messages! About snowstorms, with a photo, saying: "Have you got this one?" As if we were rival collectors. And then about the spiders, I could talk to you about house spiders, garden spiders and black widows, why not? Since you're a frustrated arachnologist, there's no reason you'd only be interested in recluses.'

'Yes. Excellent, do that, Irène.'

'There's a hitch though. If we're old friends who've met up again, and I like that idea, why would I call you "commissaire"?'

Adamsberg considered this for a moment, with a clear impression that Irène was a quicker thinker than he was.

'Well, say it's a joke. That you used to call me Jean-Baptiste, but when we met up again you learned I'd become a commissaire in the police, so you got in the habit of calling me that, just for a laugh.'

'That's not brilliant, commissaire.'

'No, it isn't.'

'I think I'll take turns. Sometimes I'll say "commissaire" and some-times "Jean-Baptiste". Or even "Jean-Bapt", it's more friendly, sounds more convincing.'

'You should have been a cop, Irène.'

'And you should have been an arachnologist, *Jean-Bapt*. Sorry, I'm just getting into practice.'

XXXI

'AS I WAS SAYING, BEFORE OUR VOYAGE TO THE PACIFIC,' ADAMSBERG began, once they were all back in their seats in the council chamber, 'we need to find another channel.'

'At the 52nd parallel,' said Mercadet seriously, and to himself.

'Commandant Danglard thinks we've nothing to get our teeth into. That's not quite true. Something else has been going on under our very eyes since the beginning. Something we haven't been looking at.'

'What?' asked Estalère.

'Not what, Estalère, who?'

'This is about the killer?'

'I think it's a woman.'

'A woman?' said Mordent. 'A *woman*? Who's supposed to have killed eight men over a period of twenty years? What's taken you in this direction, or rather into this . . . channel, commissaire?'

'The Recluse Gang mutated into the Rapists' Gang, we know that. Mercadet has been tracing cases of rape from when these boys reached adulthood until, let's say, the age of about sixty-five. Over a period of fifty years. It's a long job, and they could have been active further afield than the Gard département. Froissy will give him a hand.'

Adamsberg was trying to speak in a neutral way, to calm down the whole squad, but Danglard's attack had hit him hard. He was conscious that the commandant was on the edge of his own depressive abyss, and that his suicidal aggression could grow like briars over a demolition site. All the same, it was the first time Danglard had insulted him and knowingly spoken to him with such scorn in front of everyone. Adamsberg's natural suppleness inclined him to forget the incident. But it had cut him to the quick. Instinctively, what he wanted to do was leave the meeting and go for a walk. Not to have Danglard within sight, not to have to struggle to organise and justify arguments about the way of exploring this new but so far meagre lead. It was time to hand over to Veyrenc, who was quite at home in matters of logic.

'Any idea who this woman might be?' asked Froissy, who had been shocked by Danglard's intervention and intimidated by that of Noël, and now had her hands laid flat across her keyboard. Good posture against arthritis, Adamsberg thought.

'Just a few thoughts, nothing very original. But it's best to go back to the beginning when you've missed one way through.'

'Missed the straits you mean,' said Justin.

Magellan's voyage had certainly made an impression on them, giving them something of a heroic cast of mind which seemed to inspire them now. Despite the disastrous context of a voyage that had gone in entirely the wrong direction, Adamsberg noted that people were sitting up straighter than they had been when the meeting started, their attitudes looked more determined and their eyes turned now and then to the world map. Some of his officers were perhaps even imagining themselves far away from this room with its plastic chairs, hauling instead on the rigging during a storm, hanging on to the masts, plugging holes in the timbers and eating rotten ship's biscuit. Who knew? Some of them certainly looked as if they were somewhere else.

'Well, she has been on this killing spree for twenty years,' Adamsberg went on, 'with eight victims so far. Crimes like this, pursued over a long period, a programme of annihilation planned neurotically as a vital objective, must have their roots in childhood. There are no impulsive events, no slip-ups. So whoever this unknown killer is, she must have suffered very badly. That's the first and not very original idea I'm putting forward. It was something in her youth that transformed her into a determined criminal.'

'A difficult childhood,' remarked Justin. 'That won't help us narrow down the field much.'

'No, it won't. But we know she has been raped, which similarly does not help us much. Whether it was reported or not, followed up or not, this woman is carrying out her own justice. There is one element that might help us find her, and that is this bizarre choice of the recluse spider's venom. When she started, she didn't think about a spider. She used various means as they came to hand: shooting, interfering with equipment, a motorbike accident, and finally the poisonous mushrooms. That was probably the tipping point, when the idea began to take shape. For the fourth murder, she'd chosen a venomous substance. The name of the mushroom is significant: commonly called a death cap, but the Latin name is *Amanita phalloides*, so the phallic reference matters. And it links the two kinds of poison, one from fungi and one from spiders.'

'Correct,' said Voisenet, 'changing from a vegetal toxin to an animal one.'

'But collecting spider venom is a very different matter from finding death cap mushrooms in the woods. So she must have spent fourteen years with the obsessive desire to find a new type of poison. Remember what Voisenet told us about the links between venomous fluid and power. This woman has managed to dominate the spider and take over its powers. Since she was forcibly injected herself with animal fluid from a man, to devastating effect, she's turning it back as a lethal attack on her aggressor.'

'Yes, *her* aggressor,' Mordent repeated. 'So why not just take it out on the *one* man? Why go for the whole gang?'

'We don't know what has happened to her. She could have been raped more than once.'

'By the ten stink bugs?' asked Lamarre.

'The stink bugs, who were the ones who first managed to get the recluse to hurt people, are still our best lead. If this woman was raped by one of them – or even two or three, because we know they went in for gang rapes – she might have applied her vengeance to all of them.'

'*Love is a nettle that must be harvested every moment if one wishes to sleep in its shade,*' murmured Danglard. 'Pablo Picasso. Love, or passion.'

All eyes turned towards the commandant, since they had not expected him to speak at all. Was he coming back to them, beginning to rejoin his fellows? No, not at all. His pale face remained stony. Danglard was speaking only to himself.

'Well,' Kernorkian went on, ignoring the interruption, 'she would need to have known there *was* a gang, and their names.'

'Yes, obviously.'

'And also that they had this past history with recluse spiders,' Kernorkian persisted.

'Yes, that must be true,' said Veyrenc. 'One of them must have talked.'

Here the commissaire got to his feet, already feeling tired of sitting down, and began as usual to pace round the room.

'One rape case does interest me,' he said, 'though it has no direct connection to La Miséricorde.'

'I thought we had to stick to the orphanage,' said Noël.

'Well, I'm not forgetting it. But we're still in Nîmes, here's the story. The woman is called Louise Chevrier. She was raped in Nîmes in 1981, aged thirty-eight, and they caught the man. His name is Nicolas Carnot, and he's never been anywhere near the orphanage. They gave him fifteen years and he got out in 1996. Did he nevertheless have some connection with the gang? Mercadet's following this up. Froissy, can you check out Louise Chevrier? We need to know all we can about her. Meet back here at four.'

'With respect, sir, we won't have anything more by four,' said Justin.

'No, I know, that's not what we're going to discuss. At four o'clock, Commandant Danglard is going to give us a brief lecture on medieval recluses. The women, that is.'

'Medieval women recluses?' said Lamarre, looking stupefied.

'Yes indeed. Commandant, would that suit you?'

Danglard nodded. Four o'clock. That would give him time to pack up his things.

Adamsberg met Froissy as he crossed the courtyard.

'I'm going for a walk, lieutenant.'

'Yes, I understand, sir.'

'Walking, shaking the body as your feet hit the ground, shifts the tiny little bubbles of gas in the brain. They bump into each other. And when you want to get some ideas, that's what you have to do.'

Froissy hesitated.

'There aren't any tiny bubbles of gas in our brains, sir.'

'Well, since they aren't thoughts, what do you call them?'

Froissy did not answer.

'See, they *are* tiny bubbles of gas.'

XXXII

ADAMSBERG WALKED AS FAR AS THE SEINE, SOMETHING HE WAS IN THE habit of doing. In the city, he sorely missed the clear water of the Gave de Pau. He went down on to the quayside, to sit among the walkers, students and occasional strollers like himself. And like him, everyone was staring in consternation at about a hundred dead fish, floating belly-up on the slow-flowing grey-green waters of the river.

Feeling upset, Adamsberg went back up the steps and then along the embankments until he was level with Saint-Germain. As he walked, he put in a call to a psychiatrist he knew, Dr Martin-Robinson – by good fortune he had remembered his double-barrelled name. Adamsberg had met him as an expert witness on the degree of mental responsibility in a previous case. The doctor was at first sight what people tend to describe as 'a big teddy bear', with his beard and flowing hair, but in reality he was a man with inner depths, a professional who could be calm or talkative, jovial or sad, according to circumstances, or to whether the natural rotation of his soul showed you his beaming face or his overcast one.

'Dr Martin-Robinson? This is Commissaire Adamsberg. Remember me? The Franck Malloni case?'

'Yes, of course. Nice to hear from you.'

'I'd like to see you.'

'Another expert witness job?'

'No, I want your opinion about recluses, women who cut themselves off from the world.'

'In the Middle Ages? Not my field, Adamsberg.'

'I've got someone in my squad who knows about the Middle Ages. But not about in our own time.'

'There aren't any recluses around today.'

'I came across one when I was twelve years old. And I may be on the track of another.'

'Commissaire, I'm fighting a lonely battle with an over-fatty blanquette de veau, and I'm bored, which is not good for me. I'm in a little café on Place Saint-André-des-Arts, to the left of the tobacconist's.'

'I can get there in about ten minutes.'

'Shall I order you something to eat? I've only just started.'

'Yes, thank you, doctor, just choose for me.'

Adamsberg walked briskly along the quai de la Tournelle and the quai de Montebello, and up the rue de la Huchette to find the café, where the burly doctor stood up to welcome him with open arms. Adamsberg remembered that he always greeted you warmly, whether he was in an up or down phase.

'Hake with Normandy sauce all right?'

Adamsberg did not dare tell him that after what he had just seen in the Seine, eating dead fish did not greatly tempt him. He smiled and sat down and the doctor observed him with a quizzical look.

'Things not going so well? For you?'

'I've got this investigation that's taking us into the depths of the past and of the mind. Very difficult and I've just run headlong into the sands.'

'No, I'm talking about you personally. If I'm not mistaken, you've just had a bad experience. Very recently.'

'Yes, you're right, it was yesterday, but never mind about that.'

'But I do mind. I'll understand better why you've turned up here in such a hurry with your questions. So what happened to you yesterday?'

'My brother carried out the extraction of a tooth in my memory, on the Île de Ré. And this tooth was deeply embedded. It hadn't given me any pain until last week. But it's over now, it's OK.'

'So what was this memory? The recluse you saw when you were twelve?'

Dr Martin-Robinson was a man who got straight to the point, jumping all the in-between stages. There was no pulling the wool over his eyes.

'Yes, that was it. I couldn't remember having seen her, I couldn't remember anything. But whenever I heard the word "recluse", I started to feel ill.'

'Vertigo, dizziness?'

'Yes, and then when my brother pulled it out . . .'

'Because your brother was there, was he?'

'With my mother.'

'And your mother let you look at this recluse?'

'No, absolutely not, she just didn't see me creep up and take a peep, that's all. And then it was too late.'

'An inquisitive child, resistant to rules,' said the doctor with a grin.

'Then after the tooth was pulled, when it all came back, and I saw her awful face again, her rotten teeth, and breathed in that ghastly smell and heard her voice again, I passed out. Apparently when I was twelve, I passed out too. Before forgetting everything.'

'Repressing it you mean.'

'But I don't want to waste your time with all that.'

'Don't worry about my time, my first patient this afternoon has cancelled.'

'I'm worried about my time too,' said Adamsberg, 'and my murderer hasn't cancelled. Four deaths now, and two more expected. Actually ten, all told.'

The doctor took a little time to respond, pushing the meat to one side of the plate, and tackling the rice, which he covered with cream sauce.

'So these are the famous deaths attributed to bites from recluse spiders? They seem to be talking about the venom transmuting, because of insecticides. Personally, I don't believe that. Well, not in such proportions, not in a single year. Although these days, who knows?'

'I've just seen about a hundred dead fish floating down the Seine.'

'There'll be more. And we'll see the Mediterranean full of plastic. Practical, eh? – we'll be able to walk from Marseille to Tunis. So I suppose the fish dish wasn't really the best choice for you.'

'Oh, it'll pass,' said Adamsberg with a smile.

'But your pulled tooth won't. What I mean is, not as fast as you'd like. You'll need to sleep, you must accept that. Have a good sleep. You see, my professional advice isn't too hard to follow.'

'But I don't have time, doctor.'

'Tell me about your investigation and the recluse, then ask your question.'

By now, having had plenty of practice, Adamsberg was able to give quite a succinct account of the research trail, from La Miséricorde orphanage to the fiasco of the previous day and the new hypotheses he had suggested that very morning.

'I'm thinking it could be a woman who has been raped.'

Adamsberg broke off.

'When I say "I'm *thinking*" that's too strong a word, no, I'm stumbling about with this woman in mind, I'm blundering around empty-handed.'

'I can imagine the way you operate, Adamsberg. And any way of operating is a form of thinking.'

'Is it?'

'Yes.'

'Well, I'm thinking of a woman raped in the past, who might have somehow appropriated the power of the recluse, and in a sort of tit for tat, venom for venom, fluid for fluid, she's injecting it into her former aggressors.'

'Sounds a clever idea.'

'It's not my idea, actually, one of my lieutenants thought of it. A zoologist manqué. What I want to know, doctor, is what might drive a woman in this day and age to become a recluse. To shut herself up and disappear from the world.'

'Will you have some wine, commissaire? Keep me company, it's bad manners to allow a man to drink on his own.'

The doctor poured out the wine and looked at it through the clear glass.

'Why would one want to disappear from the world? There are the usual triggers: depression, bereavement. Traumatic experiences too, including rape, which is often followed by a period of withdrawal which may last some time. But in general, that tends to come to an end. Then if we go into nervous disorders, there's agoraphobia.'

'Which is?'

'A panicky fear of going outside. The state of terror can lead to staying at home all the time, except for special outings with someone reassuring.'

'Would that trigger aggressive behaviour?'

'No, I'd say rather the opposite.'

Adamsberg thought about Louise, shut in her bedroom, hanging on to Irène's arm for a few outings and pursued by her fear of men.

'This isolation can also be overcome, even if the subject still prefers on the whole to stay at home for security. But women who have actually been *sequestered* are very different. I've had to treat three cases of sequestration. Will you have a dessert?'

'No, just a black coffee.'

'I'll have both,' said the doctor, patting his stomach and laughing.

'And to think I'm meant to advise other people. Help them regain their balance.'

'One of my lieutenants says we are all neurotic to some extent.'

'You didn't know that?'

The doctor now ordered a fruit tart and two coffees, allowed himself to make a disobliging remark about the blanquette de veau, and turned back to his companion.

'These women you treated,' Adamsberg asked. 'Sequestered. Did they recover?'

'Insofar as it's possible. Three different girls, who'd been kept locked up by their own fathers since they were children. One in a cellar, one in an attic, the third in a garden shed. And every time, there was complicity, from the mother, which adds another dramatic element.'

'What did the mother do?'

'Usually nothing. These young girls who are sequestered, and there are more of them than you might imagine, are the exclusive property of the father, who constantly subjects them to rape. No exceptions.'

Adamsberg raised his hand to order more coffee. Dr Martin was right: he was feeling waves of drowsiness coming over him.

'You suddenly have a need to sleep?' asked the doctor.

'Yes.'

'That'll be the extraction. You'd do better to lie down than to drink more coffee.'

'I'll bear it in mind when this investigation's over.'

'*During* the investigation. What happened to you wasn't something trivial.'

'I hear what you're saying, doctor.'

'That's something. Well, in these cases of sequestration, you should know that there always comes a time when the tragedy is exposed. Some kind of liberation occurs – a brother escapes, a neighbour intervenes, the father dies. And then these poor little creatures leave their cages, much older perhaps, their eyes blinded by sunlight, terrified by the sight of the outside world, the main road, a cat. They're often unable to lead a normal life afterwards, as you can well imagine. They may spend years in some kind of psychiatric care before they can be gradually introduced to the flow of the everyday world. But sometimes, and I'm getting to your question, this "new life" might take the form of a second sequestration. Their life becomes confined once more, they're fearful and shut themselves in. The locked-in experience has structured their psyche and they reproduce it.'

'Like I said, doctor, I really *did* see an actual recluse when I was a child. She'd shut herself up voluntarily in an ancient dovecot, like in olden times. People brought her food and water, out of the goodness of their hearts, and passed them through a little window, the only one not bricked up. That's what I looked through to see this ghastly sight. And she stayed there five years. So what might have driven this woman to that place of reclusion? Instead of to a hospital?'

The doctor dug into his stodgy dessert and drank off his coffee in a single gulp.

'There aren't a hundred answers to that one, Adamsberg. I repeat: it has to be connected to a period of sequestration by the father in childhood, with frequent rape. When the woman – or rather the grown-up child – comes out, there's a strong risk she will reproduce the ill-treatment, the darkness, the lack of hygiene, the food eaten off the floor – the only things she has ever known, a past she has never been able to get past. She returns to the structure of her childhood, the exile from the world, and the desire for punishment and death.'

Adamsberg was taking notes and called the waiter to order a third coffee.

The doctor's large hand landed on his arm.

'No!' he said authoritatively. 'Sleep. It's during sleep that the unconscious will do its work.'

'It has work to do?'

'The unconscious never stops working, especially at night,' said the doctor with a laugh. 'And in your case, it's got plenty to work on.'

'What's it going to do?'

'It's going to dissolve the last traces of the damage done by the tooth extraction, tame the memory, make the recluse less threatening, and above all dissociate her from your mother. And if you don't let it do all this, the damage will return in the form of nightmares, at night at first, but then in the daytime too.'

'But I've got an investigation on my hands, doctor.'

'Your investigation won't succeed if you fall into a pit of your own making.'

Adamsberg nodded uneasily.

'All right,' he said.

'I'm glad to hear it. But now let me ask you a question. Why do you think your female killer could be someone who has been a recluse for a while? A real one?'

'Because of the choice of poison, the least probable in the world. I told you about the link between poisonous creatures and seminal fluid, and turning the power back on the aggressor, but I'm still not satisfied.'

'And you think . . . ?'

'If you can call it thinking,' Adamsberg reminded him.

'All right, you're hazarding a guess that if the killer uses the recluse to kill, then she must have been a recluse herself.'

'Not really. Because what do I know?'

'Because you happened to see a recluse when you were a child? But why not simply stick to a matter of vengeance? The bullies in the orphanage tormented other kids with recluse spiders. And someone is making them pay for their abject doings.'

'But the eleven kids who were bitten have been cleared.'

'What about some other kid? In the orphanage? Isn't there a man in the story?'

Adamsberg hesitated.

'Who is it?' asked the doctor.

'Well, there's the son of the former director. He became a child psychiatrist and he's still obsessed with the 876 orphans that his father took charge of, to the point his own son became invisible. He's a restless jumpy character, lives alone, eats sweet things addictively, and hates the Recluse Gang.'

'Whom his father also hated.'

'Yes, the father tried to get rid of them, but failed.'

'"Get rid of them" you say. So why might the son not try to finish the job?'

'I don't know,' said Adamsberg with a shrug. 'I haven't mentioned that lead to anyone. Until yesterday, we were just on the track of the boys who were bitten. And now, in my mind's eye, I see a woman.'

'A recluse. Have you talked about that to anyone?'

'No. I did talk about a woman who'd been raped, but not about a recluse.'

'Why not?'

'Because she's still in a kind of fog in my mind. Just a bubble of gas, not a thought. And I've already led my team into a dead end.'

'So you're playing it safe now, all of a sudden.'

'Yes. Should I stop? Or set sail, and hope for a favourable wind?'

'Which way do you incline?'

'I want to eliminate the recluse who's luring me into the mists.'

'Waste of time.'

The doctor pulled out his mobile, looked at it and burst out laughing again. Adamsberg liked people who could do that. He was incapable of it.

'The gods are with us today. My second patient has cancelled. Let me tell you something. I am very drawn to minds in which proto-thoughts are to be found.'

'Proto-thoughts?'

'Thoughts before they are thoughts, what you called bubbles of gas. Embryos that wander about, take time to develop, come and go, live or die. I like people who give them their chance. As for your recluse, if she's destined to fade away, then she will.'

'Really?'

'Really. But note I said "if she's destined to". So keep going with her, keep looking, because that's what your heart is telling you to do. Follow where the sails take you, even if they quiver and shake.'

'Because they're likely to?'

'Yes, indeed,' said the doctor, with his fourth hearty laugh.

On the way back, Adamsberg again followed the Seine, and found himself on the stone bench near the statue of Henri IV, where he had once sat talking with Maximilien Robespierre. He lay down on it, sent a message to the team putting the meeting off until 6 p.m. and closed his eyes. Doctor's orders. Go to sleep.

'And as for your recluse, keep looking, because that's what your heart is telling you to do.'

XXXIII

ADAMSBERG DARED NOT REFUSE THE COFFEE BROUGHT HIM BY ESTALÈRE as they began the second meeting of the day. It would have upset the young man greatly.

'Anything new, commissaire?' Mordent enquired with interest. 'Since you postponed the start?'

'I merely went to sleep, on my doctor's advice. Mercadet, did you get anything on Nicolas Carnot?'

'Yes, sir!'

Putting the meeting back two hours had allowed Mercadet to finish his rest cycle, and he was grinning broadly, as though sitting on an egg about to hatch.

'Apart from Carnot's chaotic case history, pickpocketing, car thefts – vans in fact – and minor drug dealing, I tried his school records, family, friends, and found – guess what?'

Yes, Adamsberg thought, Mercadet really was sitting on a big egg.

'He went to Louis Pasteur High School in Nîmes, where he was in the same class as guess who?'

'Claude Landrieu,' Adamsberg suggested.

'And therefore,' Mercadet continued, 'we've got a link between the gang of rapists from the orphanage with a second group of potential rapists in Nîmes, well, not a gang but a pair, Landrieu–Carnot.'

'Excellent work, Mercadet.'

'It gets better. I looked again at the Landrieu case, because he was an outsider when he met up with the Recluse Gang. How did they connect up? We hadn't worked that out.'

Oh, two eggs. The lieutenant had a clutch of two eggs and was beaming with pride.

'Go on, tell us!' said Adamsberg with a smile.

'This time, you'll never guess, sir.'

'No.'

'Landrieu's father, what do you think his job was?'

'Go on,' Adamsberg repeated.

'He was a janitor at La Miséricorde orphanage.'

The silence that followed enabled Mercadet to enjoy the full value of his findings. Commandant Mordent stretched out his neck, looking satisfied, but then frowned. He was a stickler for detail.

'That doesn't necessarily make him responsible for the sins of his son,' he said.

'Yeah, but listen to this, commandant. The father was a totally despicable adult stink bug. During World War II, Landrieu père lined up and shot fourteen Senegalese riflemen from his own battalion, and he's known to have raped women during the Allied advance into Germany.'

'So it was him!' Adamsberg murmured. '*He* was the one who opened the door at night to let them out on their spider trips, and later on their sex prowls. Excellent, Mercadet, now we know how these bullies managed to get into all the buildings free as air. And how the Recluse Gang could meet up with Landrieu's son and Nicolas Carnot.'

'Just doing my job,' said Mercadet modestly, though in fact he was as proud as Punch, or as the male blackbird in the courtyard. 'Shall I keep digging?'

'Just on one point. Let's concentrate on any girls who were raped, and who spent some time in a psychiatric hospital afterwards. A long time.'

'Why's that?'

Adamsberg did not at this stage propose to give up the bubble of gas, the quivering proto-thought as Dr Martin-Robinson described it, which had prompted him to think that in order to choose the extraordinary difficulty of getting recluse venom you had to have been a recluse yourself. And in order to turn into a recluse, you had to have been sequestered. And probably helped by a stay in a psychiatric hospital. No, he wouldn't reveal this yet, in the atmosphere Danglard had rendered so toxic and which was still fragile.

'I'll explain later, lieutenant,' he said. 'We need to hear what Danglard's going to tell us. Froissy, anything on Louise Chevrier?'

'Well, it's a bit odd. Nothing. We find her in Strasbourg, eleven years after the rape, working as a childminder. Then four years later, she vanishes. Before turning up back in Nîmes. She was fifty-three by then, and she took another job as childminder. But I can't find her birth certificate from 1943.'

'Is Chevrier her maiden name?'

'It must be, because in Strasbourg she says she's unmarried.'

'Are you thinking she might have been using a false name?'

'Not necessarily, she could have been born abroad.'

'Keep digging, Froissy, and check the psychiatric hospitals too.'

Adamsberg paused briefly, then smiled.

'Now,' he went on, 'regarding these women recluses of the Middle Ages, I'm well aware that you might not see the interest in them. Let's just say it's a matter of the word, the name. *Recluse*. It intrigues me. You're all free to stay or go, I know it's getting late.'

Only two officers left the room, Lamarre and Justin, one needed by his son, the other by his mother.

Danglard did not look up, keeping his eyes fixed on his notes. Since when had Danglard ever needed notes? The papers in front of him were only there, Adamsberg concluded, so that he need not meet the commissaire's eye.

'Although I have no idea,' Danglard began, 'why the commissaire wants information about women recluses of the Middle Ages, as they have no bearing whatever on the matter in hand, I will summarise what's known about them, since he has ordered me to do so. The phenomenon started in the early Middle Ages, let's say in the eighth or ninth century, expanded greatly after the thirteenth, then faded out in the seventeenth century. These women, often young, chose to be walled up alive for the rest of their days. They would be shut into a small enclosure or cell, sometimes so small that there was no room to lie down. The biggest ones were about two metres across. No table or writing desk, no mattress to sleep on, no pit for rubbish and excrement. After the woman had gone inside, the cell would be sealed up, apart from one small aperture, sometimes placed so high that the recluse couldn't see out or be seen. And it was through this little window that the woman would receive the charity of the local population: gruel, fruit, nuts, beans, water, which might or might not enable her to survive. Since there was usually a grid on the window, bales of straw could not be passed through to absorb the detritus. There are cases of recluses being knee-deep in a layer of rotten food and excrement. So much for the conditions of their "lives". Short lives often, because they mostly fell ill or went mad in the first years, despite the help of Jesus who was supposed to be their companion in martyrdom and who would surely lead them to everlasting life. But some women survived a long time, thirty or even fifty years. At the height of this practice, every town might have a whole collection of recluse cells, a dozen say, built alongside the pillars of bridges, or the town walls, against church buttresses or in graveyards, the most famous in Paris being those in the Cemetery of the Holy Innocents. As you will no doubt know, that cemetery was closed and evacuated in 1780 because of the noxious gases emanating from it. The bones of people buried there were transferred to the catacombs of Montrouge . . .'

Danglard was proceeding in a dry and pedantic tone, and Adamsberg forced himself to keep calm. The commandant's revenge had not yet been fully accomplished.

'Could we get back to the point please, commandant?'

'Very well. These women were respected, revered indeed, but that didn't mean they were properly fed, and the ordeal they underwent in the name of the Lord was considered a form of guarantee and divine protection for the town's population. They were the town's saints so to speak, quasi-nuns, in spite of their terrible appearance and degradation.'

'Thank you, Danglard,' Adamsberg broke in. 'What I would like to know now is the motives that drove these women into these deathly cells. Yes, there was a strong desire to cut themselves off from the world and serve God, but surely there were convents for that. Can you tell us about their reasons?'

'It was because they had lost all possibility of living a normal life on earth,' Danglard went on, turning over a page of non-existent notes. 'Because in fact even the convents' doors were closed to these women. They were seen as unworthy persons banished from society. These were women forbidden to marry, to have children, or an occupation, family, respect, even to exchange words with others, because they were considered impure. Either they had "gone astray" before marriage, or else their family had rejected them because they were unmarriageable for some reason – disgraced, handicapped or illegitimate. And the most frequent reason was that they had been raped. Women in that situation were considered guilty of having been soiled, having lost their virginity. They were pointed at if they went out of doors, they were fallen women, and all that was left to them was wandering the streets, prostitution or the recluse's cell. Where, since they had convinced themselves that it was their own fault, they were expiating their sins in the torment of isolation. I don't want to say any more about them. They're of purely historical interest, and apart from the name, these recluses have absolutely nothing to do with the matter currently in hand.'

'Apart from the name, indeed,' said Adamsberg. 'Thank you.'

Danglard shuffled his papers into a tidy pile and left the room. Adamsberg looked round at his officers.

'Apart from the name,' he repeated, and closed the meeting.

XXXIV

ADAMSBERG SIGNALLED TO MERCADET AND WENT UPSTAIRS TO THE
room with the drinks machine.

'One point I didn't mention in the meeting. When you're checking
rape victims who spent time in psychiatric hospitals, can you pay particular attention to cases of sequestration? By the father. Start with those.'

'And I don't tell anyone else?'

'Just Froissy, Veyrenc or Voisenet if you like. But keep it between
ourselves.'

Deep in thought, Mercadet watched Adamsberg go out. Why would
that make a woman want to kill people using recluse spiders? Even if
she'd seen some in her attic or cellar? After all, everyone's seen spiders.
But the loyal Mercadet was not about to question the commissaire's
instructions. He would have hated to be in charge of this infernal affair
of the recluses.

Adamsberg found Froissy sitting on the stone steps watching the nestlings being fed their evening meal. Not having forgotten her laptop,
from which she was never more than two metres away. He sat down
beside her.

'How are they doing?' he asked.

'Down to the last raspberry.'

'Have we got some more?'

'Yes, of course. What's going to happen now with Danglard?'

'Something.'

'It's a shame.'

'Not necessarily. Is there a way to find out the exact day and time of Olivier Vessac's burial?'

'We can check the local funeral directors. But we don't know if it will be in Saint-Porchaire. It might be in Nîmes, or somewhere else entirely.'

'We'd need to know where his parents are buried.'

'He was an orphan, commissaire. Both the father and mother were deported during the war, never returned.'

'Grandparents then?'

Froissy opened her computer as the female blackbird carried off the last raspberry, and Adamsberg watched Danglard out of the corner of his eye. At the other end of the courtyard, the commandant was loading a cardboard box into the boot of a car.

'They're buried in the Pont-de-Justice Cemetery in Nîmes,' Froissy announced.

'Well, that'll be it then.'

'I'll check.'

'What the devil is he doing, the bloody idiot?'

'Who?'

'Danglard. He's putting boxes into a car.'

'Is he going away? Got it, sir: Olivier Vessac, burial Friday 10 June, 11 a.m.'

'Tomorrow? So soon, only twenty-four hours later?'

'Well, that could be because it's more expensive on Saturdays, to put it a bit crudely. They'd have to put it off till Monday.'

'I suppose Irène pushed Élisabeth to get it over with quickly. But what the devil is he up to?' Adamsberg said again. 'Get me the number of the gendarmerie in Lédignan please, lieutenant. Not too fast, give me time to type it. Name of the commandant there?'

'Fabien Fasselac, he's a captain.'

'Another thing. Mercadet's got some info for you, but it stays between ourselves.'

Adamsberg stood up and waited for someone in Lédignan to answer his call. He crossed the yard diagonally, then with one arm pushed Danglard sideways from where he was standing leaning over the boot of the car, and read the labels carefully stuck on the boxes: 'Dictionaries and anthologies', 'Personal effects, 19th-century ornaments, Egyptian scarab', 'Personal writings, Essay on criminology, 15th century, Holy Roman Empire'.

Message received. Danglard was packing up for good.

'Is that the Lédignan gendarmerie? Commissaire Adamsberg here. Captain Fasselac please, it's urgent.'

A few clicks, several muttered oaths, and he finally got the captain.

'Still at work, captain?'

'Two sodding traffic accidents out of town. Be quick, commissaire, what do you want?'

'You've got two men keeping watch on Roger Torrailles.'

'You know that, you asked for them yourself. Which leaves me two men short, and I don't know how I'm going to manage.'

'You can't get reinforcements from Nîmes?'

'They're not rushing to help. They've got plenty to deal with too, a gas explosion on a housing estate, fair enough. Casualties. Possibly criminal.'

'I understand, Fasselac. I'll send you a couple of men tomorrow, they can take over from yours.'

'I appreciate that, Adamsberg.'

'What time does the first train from Paris get in?'

'One gets in to Nîmes at 9.05, almost on the hour, that's rare.'

'Leaving Paris at?'

'6.07. Why is it trains always leave at funny times, why can't they make it ten or ten thirty? Beats me. What's worse, they really do arrive at seven, eighteen, thirty-two, whatever, minutes past.'

'I've never understood that, either.'

'Not just me, then. That's reassuring. Thanks for the help.'

'I'm sending you a woman too, it'll be more discreet.'

'Why, what are you planning?'

'The funeral of the fourth recluse victim, Olivier Vessac, is being held in Nîmes tomorrow, 11 a.m., Pont-de-Justice Cemetery.'

'You think it might have been a murder?'

'Not a word about that.'

'OK. Wouldn't care to be in your shoes, Adamsberg.'

'It's possible Alain Lambertin and Roger Torrailles, because they're his two surviving friends, will come to the funeral. My men will be watching, and the woman will pose as a journalist to take photos of the people who attend.'

'In case the killer turns up at the burial?'

'Can't rule it out.'

'No.'

'They'll report to you when they get there. Can you give me the name of a local paper in Nîmes?'

'*Les Arènes*, that's the one takes most photos.'

'Important point, Fasselac: encourage the rumour about the spider's venom having mutated. No one must know we suspect foul play. Otherwise the killer could panic, and bump off the last two men before we get a chance to lay hands on her. She's *got* to finish her mission. And she's already got a lead of twenty years on us.'

'*She*?'

'Yes, I think so.'

'Weird business, commissaire. Twisted, vicious. Well, good luck, and thanks for the extra resources.'

Adamsberg put his hand on Danglard's shoulder. His colleague had been standing transfixed by the car.

'You, commandant. Don't move. You don't leave without saying a little word of goodbye, do you, after all these years? I'll be right back. What's the time?'

'Five to eight.'

Adamsberg went through the big room to find Retancourt, who was clearing her desk.

'Wait a sec, lieutenant. Who else is still here?' he asked, looking around the room.

'Kerno, Voisenet, Mercadet, Noël. Kerno and Voisenet are on night duty, Mercadet's asleep.'

'I need two men for tomorrow. And I need you, Retancourt. Train leaves for Nîmes at 6.07 – not 6.05, but 6.07. Is that OK?'

'Who with, then? Lamarre's got his kid.'

'No, don't bother him.'

'Justin's got his mum and dad.'

'Yes, we can bother him, he's always there with them.'

'Nothing wrong with that.'

'No, but call him, he's got to leave with you. If he wants to drag his mum and dad along too, fine. The mission's to attend Vessac's funeral tomorrow, 11 a.m. at the Pont-de-Justice Cemetery.'

'And you think Torrailles and Lambertin will be there, so we need more protection.'

One of Retancourt's other advantages was that you didn't have to spell everything out to her.

'Now you, lieutenant, are going to be a photographer for the local paper, *Les Arènes*.'

'I take snaps of anyone who turns up? Especially the women?'

'Take them all. She might even be disguised as a man. Even easier for someone old.'

'You think she's old?'

'Yes. In some ways she goes back to the Middle Ages.'

'Right.'

Adamsberg went upstairs to find Noël who was sinking a beer in the room with the drinks machine, alongside Mercadet who was sleeping.

'You're keeping watch over him, are you?'

'Meetings make me thirsty. Why did you stop me punching him on the jaw this morning? He acted like a swine, Danglard, I mean.'

'Correct, Noël, he was acting like a swine, but one who's in the depths of despair. You don't punch a swine who's in deep despair.'

'OK,' Noël conceded after a moment. 'Should have thought of that more often when I was younger. But how's he going to get back from this? I mean, how's the real Danglard going to come back to us, unless he's brought to his senses by a good sock on the jaw? I thought a punch would rearrange that stupid bloody idiot expression on his face. Well, I thought that afterwards.'

'Leave it to me, Noël. You're going to get a train to Nîmes tomorrow morning 6.07, with Justin and Retancourt. She'll explain. Before going to the cemetery, you need to report to Captain Fasselac in Lédignan.'

'Right you are, sir,' said Noël, pouring the rest of his beer into the sink. 'Know what? I liked that stuff Voisenet told us about poisonous creatures and what people thought they did.'

The lieutenant pulled up the sleeve of his T-shirt, revealing a blue-and-black cobra on his arm, rearing up, with its red tongue sticking out.

'Got this tattoo when I was nineteen,' he said with a grin. '*Now* I see a bit better what was going on in my head.'

'Yesterday, I understood something going on in my head too, but it started when I was twelve.'

'A snake?

'No, worse, a kind of spectre covered in cobwebs.'
'And now?'
'Finally made contact with it.'
'What about mine?' said Noël.
'Yours is different. You've tamed it.'
'And you haven't tamed this spectre?'
'No, Noël, not yet.'

XXXV

DANGLARD HAD SLAMMED DOWN THE BOOT OF THE CAR AND WAS sitting on it, shoulders hunched, arms folded across his chest. 'You don't leave without saying a little word of goodbye.' That was exactly what he had wanted to avoid this evening, to give himself time to make arrangements. Avoid having it out with the commissaire, avoid the lecture, and the letter of resignation.

And then the trial for 'non-reporting of a crime'. Danglard knew what the law said about this, and the punishment. *This misdemeanour applies to a person who has knowledge of a crime when it is still possible to prevent or limit its impact, or when its perpetrators are likely to commit further crimes which might be prevented, if that person does not inform the appropriate judicial or administrative authorities.*

For once, he would rather not have remembered the exact words so well. There would be aggravating circumstances, because of his job and rank: possibly five years in prison. He had gone off the rails, like a train without brakes plunging into the countryside. And he had given in to it. The commissaire would have no other choice than to dismiss him. If he was not to go down with him. It was sheer bad luck that Adamsberg had had the brilliant idea of exploring those horrible recluses. Who else would ever have thought of them?

He'd been hoping for time to make arrangements. What arrangements though? See the kids first, of course. But then? Should he run away? Enter a hermit's cell, like a recluse? Look at the world through a tiny window? Shoot himself? What good had it been, all his wretched encyclopedic and philosophical knowledge? What use had he made of it? Simply to mortify Adamsberg this very morning, acting in a more arrogant and wounding way even than that lawyer, Maître Carvin.

As he crossed the courtyard again, in failing light, Adamsberg took a call from Irène, who was using Élisabeth's mobile.

'I wanted to warn you, commissaire. The funeral's going to be tomorrow morning in Nîmes. Is it true what they say in cop shows on TV? That killers turn up at their victims' funerals?'

'Yes, it does happen, a final treat, so to speak, mission accomplished.'

'That's *disgusting*, isn't it? That's why I was calling. In case you wanted to send some policemen along, see what I mean?'

'It's already in hand, Irène, thank you.'

'Oh, sorry, my fault, of course it's in hand, you're a cop. But how did you find out so fast?'

'We have ways and means, Irène.'

'Oh, sorry, of course that's absolutely true, I should have known, but I wasn't sure. You know, the funeral being held so quickly after the death. But Saturday was all booked up. So I thought the sooner it was over the better, then I could get Élisabeth away from here.'

'By the way, Irène, was she with you just now when you mentioned "killers".'

'I'm not so daft, *Jean-Bapt*. I'm on my way to pick her up in Saint-Porchaire, she was going to fetch her clothes for the funeral. You'll see. We're going to drive down through the night.'

'Can she take turns driving?'

'No. Nice of you to ask, but we'll stop now and then. Another thing. If we're meant to be friends when Louise is around, when I'm calling you Jean-Bapt, we should perhaps call each other "tu" as well. It would be more plausible. But I'd need to get in practice. I'll start right now. *Don't you worry about me, Jean-Bapt, I'll make some halts on the way down*? Does that sound right?'

'Perfect. But with mobiles, the other voice can be heard as well. Goodnight, Irène, bon voyage to you. No offence, I'm getting in practice too.'

Adamsberg pocketed his phone and looked at Danglard, sitting on the dusty boot of the car, in his English-tailored suit. A very bad sign. The commandant, who had always tried to make up for his lack of good looks by wearing impeccable clothes of top quality cut, would never normally have dreamed of damaging the fabric by sitting on a dirty bench or stone steps. But tonight, the elegant Danglard was not giving a thought to the state of his clothes. That was all over, he'd given up on everything.

Adamsberg caught hold of his arm, and propelled him up into his office and on to a chair, for once shutting the door.

'So, Danglard, you were going to sneak away,' he said, once his colleague was sitting up more or less straight in front of him.

Adamsberg had remained standing, leaning against the opposite wall, arms folded. Danglard looked up. Yes, just as he had feared. A flame rising on his boss's cheeks, and reaching his eyes, where it left a threatening glint of piercing light. Like a shard sparkling in a tangle of dark seaweed, as a Breton fisherman had once said.

He stiffened.

'You didn't think you'd get away with it, did you?'

'No,' said Danglard, sitting up straighter.

'One,' Adamsberg went on, 'deliberate obstruction of an investigation. True or false?'

'True.'

'Two, inciting mutiny to the point I would find myself isolated in the team and forced to work secretly, in the courtyard, or a restaurant, or in the street at night. True or false?'

'True.'

'Three, protection of a potential criminal, who might already have been party to a crime, your brother-in-law, Richard Jarras. And four of his friends: René Quissol, Louis Arjalas, Marcel Corbière and Jean Escande. You know which article of the law applies to this offence?'

Danglard nodded.

'Four,' Adamsberg went on, 'this very morning, unworthy behaviour in front of the whole team. You were lucky I stopped Noël when he was going to punch you. Do you recognise that offence? Yes or no, dammit?'

'Yes, and since I agree entirely with this necessary and official (apart from the word dammit) list of charges, and all the offences you mention, you need go no further. If you would just hand me the document to sign.'

Danglard brought out his fountain pen from his inside pocket. He certainly wasn't going to sign this document with any old pen lying on someone else's table. The commandant was surprising himself. Lucid though he was about the seriousness of his actions, he nevertheless maintained a haughty demeanour, quite unlike his usual self, as if a layer of something foreign had become encrusted over his skin.

'Do you recall, Danglard,' said Adamsberg, coming nearer, 'that I asked you, twice, whether you had so easily forgotten what I'm like?'

'Yes, I remember it well, commissaire.'

'Well, I'm waiting for your reply.'

Danglard put down his pen, but did not speak. In an abrupt movement, Adamsberg swept his arm across the desk, sending the pen and various folders on to the floor. He seized his deputy in both hands by the collar of his English shirt, lifting him up gradually, so that they were face-to-face. With his foot, he kicked away the chair, leaving Danglard no choice but to remain upright, within his grasp.

'Have you so easily forgotten what I'm like that you bring out your fucking best pen and your fucking little speech? You pack your bags? You thought for a single second that I was going to fire you, and report you to the prosecutor? What has come over you? Have you really gone out of your mind?'

Adamsberg dropped his colleague, who staggered up against the wall.

'Did you think that?' Adamsberg insisted, raising his voice. 'Yes or no, dammit?'

'Yes,' Danglard said.

'Really?'

'Yes.'

And this time, Adamsberg's fist did lash out, catching the commandant on the chin. With his other hand, the commissaire held Danglard up as he collapsed, letting him down gently on to the floor, as if shedding a garment. Then he went back to the window, opened it wide, leaned on the rail and breathed in the scent of the lime blossom in the evening air. Behind him, Danglard was struggling into a sitting position, breathing with difficulty, and leaning against the wall. Those trousers will be ruined, Adamsberg thought. It wasn't the first time in his life that he had resorted to punching someone on the jaw, but he had never, ever, imagined that his fist would one day be raised against Adrien Danglard.

'Noël thought,' he said in a calm and steady voice, without turning round, 'he *really* thought that a good punch would rearrange that "stupid bloody idiot expression" on your face, as he put it in his inimitable way. So I have to ask you, Danglard, have you stopped acting like a bloody idiot at last?'

'I *have* to sign the paper,' said the commandant with difficulty, holding his jaw. 'Or you'll go down with me, for failing to report me.'

'By what miracle would that happen?'

'If you don't, others will.'

'The others whom you humiliated along with me, like a fucking pedant, by being "astonished" that anyone else might know anything about Magellan. Do you at least understand what you did to them?'

'Yes,' said Danglard, trying to get up, without success.

'So Noël was right. You're getting less like a bloody idiot. You're coming back to us. From far, far away.'

'All right,' said Danglard, 'but what's done is done. An offence was committed.'

'And do you really think all the others knew about your protection of Richard Jarras? No, they didn't, except for Froissy, Retancourt and Veyrenc, on whom I can rely absolutely.'

In a state of befuddlement – and pain, because the commissaire had not pulled his punch – Danglard looked at Adamsberg, still leaning on the rail, still with his back to him. Realising that the commissaire had not told the whole squad about his treachery. In his headlong rush off the rails, he had indeed forgotten what Adamsberg was like.

The commissaire closed the window and turned to face him.

'Are you back with me now, Danglard?'

'Yes, I am.'

Adamsberg picked up the chair and helped the commandant to his feet and then to sit down. He took a look at the bruise forming on the jaw.

'Wait a minute.'

He went out and returned five minutes later with a plastic bag of ice cubes and a glass.

'Put this to your jaw, and drink this. It's just water. Shall we go for dinner?'

As they were coming out of the office, they met Noël, also leaving, jacket slung over his shoulder.

'Can I have a word, sir?'

Adamsberg moved aside from Danglard, who was trying to cover the bruise with his hand.

'Make it quick, Noël, you've got to be up at dawn.'

'You really socked it to him, then?'

'Yes.'

'Did it work? He's getting back to normal?'

'Yes. But it's a method to be used sparingly, lieutenant. And only between close friends.'

'Understood, sir.'

XXXVI

AT ELEVEN IN THE MORNING, AT THE CEMETERY IN NÎMES, LIEUTENANTS Noël, Justin and Retancourt watched as the procession formed to follow Olivier Vessac's coffin.

'Lot of people,' Noël remarked.

'They can't all have known Vessac,' said Retancourt. 'It's the rumour about the recluse spiders that's brought them here. The sensation. It'll be in all the papers.'

'Suits us,' said Noël, 'we can circulate without being spotted.'

'Look over there,' said Justin, 'that woman, with two others. I recognise her, Froissy sent us her picture.'

'She's Louise something,' said Noël, 'the woman who was raped in Nîmes when she was thirty-eight.'

'Louise Chevrier,' Justin said.

'Oh shit,' said Retancourt, 'what's *she* doing here? I'll take her picture. Justin, text the boss. Noël, can you see if Lambertin and Torrailles are here?'

Noël took from his pocket the photographs of the two men, provided by the Lédignan captain. It wasn't going to be easy. Plenty of elderly men would be attending an old man's funeral. And to the lieutenant, all old men looked more or less alike.

Adamsberg had just reminded Lamarre of his duties – scattering some worms under the trees in the courtyard – when he received two text messages from Nîmes.

The first was from Irène:

Texting quietly cos rude to call during funeral. Some people haven't even turned phones off, what a din! Am here with poor Élisabeth. But guess what? Louise insisted on coming, didn't know him from Adam. Weird for arachnophobe to come to funeral for man killed by spider? Am I being silly?

No, Adamsberg replied. *Check what she does or says. Let me know.*

You're scaring me. Bye, just getting to grave.

The second message was from Justin:

Keeping it short, rude to text at funeral. Louise Chevrier here, why?

Adamsberg replied:

Her housemate Irène is friend of Vessac's partner, Élisabeth.

Louise knew Vessac?

No. Unless?

Unless she knew he was friend of Landrieu, so Carnot, so R. Gang? Bye, getting to grave.

Adamsberg went back to his examination of local maps of the Chemin Henri IV, scanning the zone between four and eight kilometres from Lourdes, on the right-hand side coming out of town. He hadn't been able to find anything on the internet about the recluse of the Pré d'Albret. Except that 'by prefectoral decree a woman had been taken without undue force out of the Albret dovecot', on the grounds of 'non-assistance to person in danger'. This dry note was all one could glean from the police archives of Lourdes. The secret of the saintly recluse must have been respected by anyone who knew her. He found a little green patch on the map where he thought he could see printed in tiny italics *Pré de J* . . . He picked up Froissy's magnifying glass and deciphered the rest. Yes, this was it: *Pré de Jeanne d'Albret.* He drew a circle round the green patch and looked at it in fascination.

He got up and walked across the room. Mercadet appeared in the doorway, looking extremely disturbed.

'Commissaire, I've got one. A sequestered woman. Two in fact!'

Adamsberg put a finger to his lips to remind his officer about being discreet, and motioned to him to fetch his laptop, and bring it into his office. Here, there were still folders lying all over the floor, witness to his dust-up with Danglard the previous evening. He had told the commandant to take two days off, to get over his worries and mistakes, and to allow time for the bruise – which had turned purple during the evening – to fade a bit.

Mercadet brought his laptop in, and put it in front of Adamsberg, looking as strongly affected as if he had laid another egg, but this time, it was a tragic one, and he still didn't understand why the commissaire was looking for sequestered women.

'This is one of the clearest photos,' he said. 'It was taken when they were brought out of the house. See the fat woman? That's the mother. And the two smaller ones, hiding from the photographers, with scarves over their heads? Those are the two girls who were sequestered. It's the first time they saw the outside world. The elder was twenty-one when the photo was taken, the younger nineteen. This is a truly terrible story, commissaire.'

'Go ahead, Mercadet. Where did it happen, that's the first thing.'

'About half a kilometre outside Nîmes,' the lieutenant declared triumphantly. 'On the road going south, La Route des Espagnols. An isolated farmhouse.'

'And when were they freed?'

'1967.'

'So,' Adamsberg said under his breath, 'the older sister was born in 1946, she'd be about seventy now and the other sixty-eight.'

'The father kept them locked in the attic all their lives. He systematically raped them for fourteen and sixteen years, both of them, starting from when they were five. There were six *babies* born, all buried behind the *fucking* farmhouse!'

'Calm down, lieutenant,' said Adamsberg who felt the same shudder come over him as well.

'Calm down, you say? But can you imagine it? Kept in an attic, just one skylight, and in two different places, what's more. They couldn't even see each other, just make contact through a wooden partition. The mother brought them food at midday and in the evening, and never intervened. Who the *fuck* are these monsters?'

'Gigantic stink bugs, I guess, Mercadet,' said Adamsberg hoarsely.

'And I'd have said "Bravo, kid!" I really mean it. But what did they do? Gave him twenty years. That's our shitty justice system for you.'

'Bravo who, Mercadet?'

'The son.'

'There was a son as well?'

'Called Enzo. And when he was twenty-three, he murdered his father. With an axe, three strokes and he decapitated him. And his private parts. I don't know what the word is for decapitating private parts.'

'So Enzo was the oldest child. Was he sequestered too?'

'Ah, no. He led a so-called normal life, he was allowed to go to school, but that was it. He was the face of normality for the neighbours. But he *knew*, of course. He'd heard the heavy footsteps on the stairs, his father's grunts, and the cries and tears of the little girls. He managed to sneak up to the attic and talk to them. He read them stories, pages from his schoolbooks, and he passed them pictures under the door, drawings and photos of what the outside world was like. He did what he could, poor kid. He even found a way of getting up on the roof and in through the skylight. Kids can be ingenious, God knows. But if he spoke a word to anyone, he'd been told he'd be killed, and so would his mother and sisters. So he kept his mouth shut all those years. And he grew up. Got stronger. And beheaded the old man.

Then he walked out on to the road, the bloody axe in his hand, and waited. When the cops got there, they found the mother prostrate by the body of the father. Enzo had lost the power of speech, and he pointed to the attic. That's when they went up and found the two sisters. In indescribable filth – the place had never been cleaned. Filthy mattresses on the floor with mice and God knows what running round, a bucket for a toilet, emptied once a week by the mother when they had a bath. Fair hair, hardly ever cut, and their nails practically never trimmed. They were dirty, thin, smelly. Wearing blue and pink dresses, but grey with dirt. When the sisters came out of the house, even though they stank to high heaven, Enzo hugged them for a long time, there on the pavement, against his bloodstained shirt. You can see that in the photos. And the cops didn't dare separate them. It was only after a bit that they handcuffed Enzo and took him away. And that's the last time he saw them before being chucked in jail.'

Adamsberg stood up and laid his hand on the lieutenant's shoulder. That seemed to help Mercadet calm down. It was said Adamsberg could send a child to sleep by putting the palm of his hand on its head. People claimed he could send suspects to sleep, and even himself, when sitting in his office.

When Mercadet had somewhat recovered, Adamsberg removed his hand.

'Got all that saved somewhere?' he said.

Mercadet nodded.

'Right, put your computer away and let's go and eat. Not the Dice Shaker and not the Brasserie des Philosophes. Somewhere else.'

'I'd like to go to La Garbure,' Mercadet said in a pleading tone, like a child.

'Fine, La Garbure it is.'

XXXVII

THE PYRENEAN RESTAURANT WAS NOISIER AT MIDDAY THAN IN THE evening, when the customers were fewer and mostly from the region. All to the good, thought Adamsberg as he steered his lieutenant, who was still shaken but a little calmer, towards a far table where they would not be overheard. At moments of tension, Mercadet's voice tended to be high-pitched and loud. The commissaire noted a flicker of disappointment on Estelle's face, but he had no inclination just then to concern himself with Estelle and Veyrenc.

He told Mercadet to eat some of his food, before they went any further.

'Is this all you have down there?' asked Mercadet. 'Pork and cabbage, cabbage and pork?'

'Oh, we have everything,' Adamsberg said, smiling. 'Chickens, sheep, goats, trout, honey, chestnuts. What more do you want?'

'Nothing. It's very good, all the same,' said Mercadet.

'So what were their names, lieutenant?'

'The family was called Seguin. The father was Eugène, the mother Laetitia, and the elder sister Bernadette.'

'Like the saint.'

'What saint?'

'The one in Lourdes.'

'Is there any connection?'

'A mystic one perhaps. The other sister?'

'Annette.'

'And what did the father do?'

'Officially a metalworker. But there seems to be a bit of a mystery. The boss of his workplace gave evidence, but there were only a few pay slips. Probably he worked for cash only. Seguin certainly had money, he'd made it during the war.'

'The mother?'

'She was at home. If you can call it a home.'

'You've accessed Enzo's trial records?'

'I haven't read them all yet, it's a huge file. Just enough to know the worst. Enzo gave the key evidence. The mother simply confirmed, after a fashion. The psychiatrists described her as amorphous, depersonalised. Enzo, though, was very bright. He was the one who provided the evidence about the younger girl, Annette.'

Adamsberg mashed up his potatoes to mix them with cabbage in the regional fashion, and waited.

'At first, Seguin raped her, like the elder sister, once she was five. Then he got tired of her. "His girl", his property, was Bernadette. And the other kid, well, he hired out the other kid, sir.'

'*What?*'

'Hired her out. To boys. From when she was seven until she was nineteen. Some youths he unearthed from somewhere or other. Enzo was asked to describe them but he couldn't, he never met them. On evenings when they "visited" Annette, he was locked up, by his father. He heard them talking and climbing the stairs.'

'Them?'

'Yes, because they came as a group. They asked Enzo how many youths had been in the house, in his opinion. If it was the same ones, or different. He said it was always the same ones, who had used his little sister over a period of twelve years. Twelve years. They asked him how many. From the voices, Enzo reckoned nine or ten.'

Adamsberg grabbed his officer's wrist.

'How many did you say?'

'Enzo thought nine or ten.'

'Nine or ten, Mercadet? And always the same ones? You realise what you just said?'

'What?'

'It's got to be those nine unspeakable youths from the orphanage. Work it out. Same dates, same ages, same place. The ones that the janitor Landrieu let out at night.'

'But, sir, forgive me, how would Landrieu have known that Seguin was hiring out his daughter like that?'

'They knew each other, Mercadet, they *must* have. I knew we had to keep concentrating on the orphanage tower. One of those two sisters has been eliminating the stink bugs for the last twenty years, one after another.'

'Maybe both of them.'

'Yes. Or maybe not. Not the older one, she wasn't raped by the same people. She would have had her revenge when the father was killed. Must be the younger one, surely. Annette's killing them. Or possibly,' he added after a moment, 'Bernadette.'

'Whichever of them it is, how would they know who all these youths were? Because Enzo never saw them.'

The two men thought in silence for so long, their food uneaten on their plates, that Estelle came over, looking anxious.

'Anything wrong with it?'

'No, no, Estelle, it's fine.'

And seeing their faces, looking tense and concentrated, she went quietly away.

'Annette would be sixty-eight,' said Adamsberg. 'That doesn't fit with Louise Chevrier, because she's five years older.'

'Easy to lie about your date of birth.'

'And where's Enzo now?'

'He got a sentence of twenty years. The mother got eleven for passive complicity and ill-treatment of the children. She died in prison. Enzo got out after doing seventeen years, in 1984.'

'And where's he now?'

'Don't know, sir, haven't had time to find that out yet.'

'And the daughters?'

'Same thing.'

'What a bastard!' said Adamsberg between clenched teeth.

'Who, the father?

'No, this time I mean the son of the orphanage director. Dr Cauvert. He *knew*, he must have known.'

'What? That Landrieu was letting the boys out at night?'

'That Eugène Seguin worked at the orphanage. But with the trial and the threat of scandal, his father, Cauvert senior, must have covered that up. And destroyed any records. La Miséricorde? Employing a man who imprisoned his children, a rapist, hiring out his own daughter? Oh no, that wouldn't do at all. That's *got* to be why there's such confusion about Seguin's work. He wasn't really a metalworker, he must have been working at the orphanage too. Probably as janitor along with Landrieu. And he took money from the young bullies in the Recluse Gang to rape his daughter.'

'What money would they have? They were orphans.'

Adamsberg shrugged.

'Pickpocketing round Nîmes was easy for them. Probably Seguin wasn't hiring the daughter out for the money, in fact. But for the sinister pleasure of prostituting her, listening, and watching everything. Then after they'd left the orphanage, it went on. It's *got* to be that, Mercadet, I can't see that it could be anything else.'

'You're going too fast, sir, we've got no evidence of that.'

'We've got a bundle of stuff: the connections, the dates, the number of boys.'

'You mean we're approaching the 52nd parallel?'

'Maybe we are.'

XXXVIII

'LIEUTENANT,' SAID ADAMSBERG, STOPPING UNDER THE ENTRANCE TO the squad headquarters, 'I need to find out more about the two women, Bernadette and Annette. Where they are now, *who* they are, everything. And about Louise Chevrier too.'

'Commissaire, if I could . . .' Mercadet began in embarrassment.

Adamsberg looked at his officer's face. His cheeks were drained of colour, his eyelids were drooping, and his shoulders were bent. His inescapable narcoleptic cycle was entering the sleep phase.

'No, no, you go and sleep, I'll ask Froissy. You can meet up with her later.'

Froissy listened intently as Adamsberg told her about the daughters of the Seguin couple.

'We can tell the rest of the team about them now. Make a full report on the imprisoned girls in Nîmes and send it out. Then see if you can find anything about the sisters, the brother, and Louise. Photos too, if you can, as recent as possible, but especially of them smiling.'

'For ID photos you're not allowed to smile these days. What was it you wanted to see?'

'Their teeth.'

'Their teeth?'

'Just an idea, a proto-idea.'

Froissy did not query the request. After a remark like that, there was no point trying to go further.

'A bubble of gas,' she said, nodding. 'In Louise's case, since she looked after children, I could look for some websites about former crèches and so on in the Nîmes and Strasbourg areas. But honestly I don't know if such sites exist. As for those two poor girls, did Mercadet say he couldn't trace them?'

'No, he just didn't have time. He's already done a lot of work.'

'And now,' said Froissy, consulting her watch, 'he must be asleep.'

'Correct.'

'He's a bit early.'

'The emotion.'

But Froissy had turned to her keyboard and stopped listening. He tapped her shoulder.

'Can you find me the time of the next train for Nîmes?'

After a moment:

'15.15, arrives 18.05.'

Adamsberg headed for Veyrenc's office.

'We're going back to Mas-de-Pessac, Louis. That bastard didn't tell us everything he knew.'

'Cauvert? A bit eccentric, but nice enough, I thought.'

'Nevertheless, he was protecting his father. We've lost days because of that. A train at 15.15, OK? We'll come back tonight.'

During the journey, Adamsberg filled Veyrenc in on the new material, the sequestered children of Nîmes and his conviction that Seguin must have worked in the orphanage. He also told him in total confidence about the tooth extraction on the Île de Ré. Veyrenc whistled, his way of showing feelings. According to the cadences, Adamsberg could guess which ones. This time a mixture: shock, stupefaction and thoughtfulness. Three tunes.

'So what we're going to do is shake down good old Dr Cauvert without any proof that Seguin worked there? That right?'

'Yes.'

'How will we do that?'

'We'll *tell* him he did. Your uncle worked there for a year, filling in for someone.'

'Oh yes? So what was his name?'

'Froissy found me someone who was a supply teacher. Your uncle's name was Robert Quentin.'

'All right. What subject?'

'Catechism class. That bother you?'

'That's the least of our problems. So I'm to say that through my Uncle Robert, I *know* Eugène Seguin was employed at La Miséricorde. But why would my uncle have told me that?'

'He just mentioned it, that's all. Don't fuss over the detail, Louis.'

'What if Seguin never worked there?'

'But he did, Louis.'

'If you say so. Are you going to sleep now?'

'Doctor's orders. No kidding, Louis, it's to allow scar tissue to form after the extraction. Apparently, if I don't do this, I'll fall into a pit. The doctor seemed pretty serious about that.'

Before obeying the doctor's orders, Adamsberg consulted his text messages. The psychiatrist didn't seem to realise that now people had mobiles it was impossible to go to sleep. Or to wander about watching the gulls fly over the dead fish in the river, or to allow the bubbles of gas to bounce around inside your head.

From Retancourt:

Lambertin + Torrailles turned up, now in café under watch Justin + Noël, I'm too visible. Eavesdrop result: Lambertin staying tonight with Torrailles.

OK, don't lose them.

From Irène:

At funeral Louise chuckling, esp. when earth hit coffin! Must like burials, some people do. She smiles a lot, little clicks, why? Not in the cemetery thank God. Can't stand her sometimes, feel mean. Have packed up yr snowstorm of Rochefort. L believes me but says why do cops waste time on that instead of protecting people? My answer: without hobbies or snowstorms, they'd go mad. Cheers, Jean-Bapt.

Cheers, Irène, and thanks.

From Froissy:

Nothing yet on the Seguin sisters, vanished. No record psych hosp. Same for brother. No photo of L Chevrier smiling on old websites. Trying dentists, Strasbourg, Nîmes, records easy but many dentists.

Don't forget evening meal.

Blackbirds?

Yes.

Think I'd forget?

Before dentists check any member Cauvert family suspected of war-time collaboration. Father, grandfather, uncle?

More family secrets?

Just so.

It was after six thirty when the two policemen rang the bell at Dr Cauvert's door. Adamsberg had deliberately not let him know they were coming and they disturbed him in the middle of working.

'*Now?*' said Cauvert, rather grumpily. 'You didn't even phone to say.'

'We were just down here,' said Veyrenc, 'and we thought we'd try our luck.'

'There's a detail we need to follow up,' added Adamsberg.

'OK, OK,' said the doctor, letting them in and disappearing into the kitchen, from which he emerged five minutes later looking more cheerful and carrying a laden tray. 'Ceylon tea, green tea, coffee, decaf, infusion, strawberry juice and, special treat, a Savoy cake! Whatever you like.'

To refuse would have distressed Cauvert, who was already putting out teacups and glasses, and plates for the cake. Once he was sitting in front of his coffee, Adamsberg got straight to the point.

'You must have heard, when you were young, about the two girls who were sequestered by their father in Nîmes, in the sixties.'

'That terrible case? Of course, everyone in the whole town, the whole region, knew about it! We followed the trial day by day.'

'So you knew that the father, Eugène Seguin, hired his younger daughter out to young local boys who raped her?'

The doctor shook his head, with the expression of a psychologist who does not think a young patient has much future. Adamsberg sensed he had flinched slightly on hearing the name Seguin.

'Yes, indeed, the brother's evidence was damning. What was his name again?'

'Enzo.'

'Enzo, that's right. Brave young man.'

'Unlike your father, who did all he could to conceal the fact that Seguin had been employed at La Miséricorde. That he sent the boys from the Recluse Gang off to have sex with his daughter. Aided by another janitor, Landrieu.'

'*What?*' said Cauvert, sitting up. 'What are you talking about?'

'I just told you. Seguin was working at La Miséricorde.'

'You dare to insult my father! In this room! Good Lord, if he'd known that a man like Seguin had any dealings with the Recluse Gang, he'd have gone straight to give evidence.'

'But he didn't.'

'Because Seguin was never employed by him!'

'Yes, he was,' said Veyrenc.

'Good Lord, man, my father hated that gang of little shits, as you well know. He was a good man, you hear me, an honourable man.'

'Exactly. And if he'd admitted that Seguin had worked for him, he'd be *dishonoured* and ruined, for lack of vigilance and professional shortcomings. But there was probably something else as well, so he couldn't bring himself to speak up. In the end, he kept quiet, and wiped Seguin out of the records. And after him, you've concealed the truth too.'

The doctor, by now perspiring with indignation, collected everything from the table in a hurry, before all the cake had been eaten, piling crockery on the tray and breaking a saucer. They were being asked to leave.

'Get out of here!' he said. 'Get out!'

'Seguin *was* here,' said Veyrenc. 'He was a janitor. The supply teacher for catechism, Robert Quentin, was my uncle. And he told me.'

'Oh, did he, indeed, and why didn't *he* speak up at the trial then?'

'He'd gone to live in Canada, he never heard about the girls who were locked up till much later.'

'And what about the other teachers, why would they have kept quiet, eh?'

'The teachers were only here during the school day,' said Adamsberg. 'They didn't have much to do with the daily life in the orphanage. None of them stayed more than three years. After the war, when more schools were being rebuilt, they left for better jobs. The janitors would only be known to them by sight, most of them probably didn't even know their names.'

The doctor got up and patted his cheeks one after the other, walking more slowly now.

'Can this remain between ourselves?' he said finally.

'Yes,' said Adamsberg. 'Word of honour.'

'All right, yes, Seguin did work in the orphanage,' he said, sitting down heavily. 'And yes, he did do favours for that gang, Claveyrolle's lot. Even as kids, we knew that. No point asking *him* to help us if you quarrelled with them. But sending them off to rape his *daughter*? No, my father *never* said anything about that to me.'

'But it *was* them, and your father must have realised that.'

'Surely not. He might have suspected them, but nothing more. It would have been wrong to denounce youths in his care without proof.'

'Oh, come on, Dr Cauvert. Your father wasn't stupid, and he knew all the boys like the back of his hand. He knew Claveyrolle and Co. were getting out at night. Because it wasn't just the once, was it? And he knew they went after girls, even inside the orphanage. And when the trial opened, and everyone learned that Seguin's own *daughter* had been raped by "nine or ten local boys", no more and no less, "always the same ones" and for several *years*, your father didn't immediately think of the Recluse Gang? When he knew they had been in cahoots with the janitor? He didn't just *suspect* them, Dr Cauvert, he knew.'

'My father respected the rule of presumption of innocence, and he was protecting the institution,' said Cauvert, twisting a delicate teaspoon between his fingers.

'No,' Adamsberg corrected him, 'he was protecting himself. It was his own professional fault, his past neglect coming home to roost. But it wasn't just that, was it?'

'You said that before. What on earth do you mean?'

'Why didn't he ever sack Seguin, if he was helping the gang that your father detested?'

'How should I know?' Cauvert cried.

'I'll tell you. Because the janitor was almost certainly blackmailing him. Seguin was deep into the black market and collaboration during the war, and so was your grandfather. If your father had laid a finger on him, Seguin could just have said "Son of a collaborator!" – words that at the time nobody wanted to hear, something that had to be kept quiet. So that explains what your father did, and why the Recluse Gang went unpunished.'

'No!' said Cauvert.

Adamsberg showed him in silence his message from Froissy, confirming that his grandfather Cauvert had indeed been a wartime collaborator. The doctor looked away, his features collapsed, and he swayed forward passively like a grass in the wind. His wandering gaze fell on his hand, where the teaspoon, now twisted out of shape, seemed to surprise him.

'I didn't know that,' he said in a dull voice. 'About the collaboration. So I didn't understand.'

'I believe you. And I'm sorry to have put you through this,' said Adamsberg, standing up quietly. 'But you must have suspected some dark secrets for a long time now. Thank you for being honest about this today.'

'Does my honesty wipe out my father's offence?'

'In part, doctor,' Adamsberg lied.

As they had the previous time, Adamsberg and Veyrenc went back up the long narrow street leading to the bus station.

'That was a good idea, the job in Canada,' said Adamsberg. 'I hadn't anticipated the question.'

'Ah, well, I did, I was his nephew after all!'

'The statue, the dog, St Roch,' Adamsberg murmured, as they went past the old sculpture in its niche.

'You were right, then. It was from La Miséricorde that Seguin was organising those gang rapes.'

'Which gives us the direct link between the killer and the death of the gang members. But Mercadet's question is still a fair one. How could *she* know that the rapists came from the orphanage?'

'Well, she must have known her father worked there.'

'Yes, OK, but out of two hundred orphans there at the time, how would she get their names? How would she know about the Recluse Gang? And the use of spider venom? Another *étoc* blocking our path, Louis.'

'Could the brother have told her?'

'But the father locked him up when the others came "visiting".'

Adamsberg turned round and glanced back one final time at the little weather-beaten statue of St Roch. All that was left of the dog was a ball of stone with two ears and a fragment of tail.

'But you know,' he went on, 'that *must* be it. The brother must have known their names, Louis. And he didn't tell the truth at the trial. He'd been all the time collecting information and taking it to his sisters when they were little, pictures from magazines – or perhaps the names of their attackers. Like St Roch's dog, bringing him some food. The necessary link between the dark forest and the outside world. Enzo was their saviour, the messenger. He must have known the names.'

'And then *he* killed them one after another?'

'No, I don't think that can be it. Enzo was the go-between. But I can't somehow see a man bothering with spider venom.'

'Well, you did when we thought it was Little Louis and company.'

'That's different, they'd been bitten. An eye for an eye, a tooth for a tooth, open warfare. But that isn't how it is for Enzo, I don't see the direct link.'

Veyrenc said nothing as they walked on, as if he was not listening. Then he stopped in front of a low wall covered in brick dust.

'Can you remember what the plan of the Seguin house looks like? Froissy put it in the file and I read it in the train. Look,' he said, tracing with his finger some lines in the dust, 'here's the entrance hall, and here's a little bedroom, Enzo's, and a downstairs toilet.'

'OK.'

'On the left is a door leading to the rest of the house. The door that takes you to the main room, and the stairs leading to the bedrooms, the bathroom and the attic. And we know that when there were "visitors", Enzo was confined to barracks.'

'In his room, yes.'

'Not exactly in his room, it was the door through to the main room that was locked.'

'Well, that means the whole house.'

'No, Enzo had access to another room.'

'No, he didn't.'

'Yes, he did. A room you never think of, because it isn't called a room: the entrance hall. And why don't we call it a room? Because it isn't one. It's just the place where the inside world and the outside world meet, a sort of airlock. Not really part of the rest of the house. Enzo's space.'

'What are you trying to say, Louis? That Enzo went to sit in the entrance hall, between the two worlds?'

'No, not to sit, but he could get hold of elements from the outside world there, that was his job, his mission. Like you said. The go-between.'

Veyrenc looked at his finger, dark with dust, and wiped it on the palm of his other hand. Adamsberg stared at the drawing on the wall.

'Elements of the outside world,' he repeated.

'Things people take off in an entrance hall, a vestibule.'

'A coat stand, hats, boots, umbrellas?'

'Think about the coat stand.'

'All right. Coats, caps, jackets . . .'

'You've got it.'

'The "visitors" left their coats there. All right, Louis. But do you think they'd leave their ID papers lying in their pockets when they were out on these trips? They'd have to be very stupid.'

'Their coats would be from the orphanage, Jean-Baptiste. Not only would they have the name of the institution on them, but most likely the name of the pupil, sewn on to a name-tape. In places with boarders, everything's labelled, from caps to shoes. Otherwise how do you give back the laundry or find the right coat?'

Adamsberg traced the diagram of the house with his finger and nodded, impressed.

'Good Lord,' he said, his finger still on the wall. 'The entrance hall. You never think of that.'

'No.'

'But it was all there. He had their names and the name of the orphanage. So why didn't he say anything?'

'Because his sister must have asked him not to. Well, one or other of them.'

'Yes, so that it would be *her* business, she'd handle that?'

'And all these years, the three of them have stuck close together and kept their counsel. Nothing has come out, no one has talked. But where are they now, the Seguin children?'

Adamsberg took his finger off the wall rather regretfully, and the two men walked on.

'According to Froissy,' said Veyrenc, 'it's impossible to locate them.'

'If even Froissy can't trace them, they must have changed their names, it's got to be that.'

'Like everyone does, Enzo probably found out to how to get hold of false ID papers when he was in jail. And as for the sisters, it's quite likely the courts granted them permission to change their names.'

'But how will we find two girls placed in psychiatric clinics forty-nine years ago, if we don't know either their names or what they look like?'

'Impossible.'

'Well, let's go and eat. The train leaves at 9 p.m. on the dot.'

'By the time we've got the bus into Nîmes,' said Veyrenc, pulling a face, 'we'll have to go to the station buffet. Which'll be closed. Instead of that, we could stay over, sleep in Nîmes, and take the first morning train. What difference would it make? None, you might say. And I'd say: everything. You'll be able to go to sleep sooner, doctor's orders, don't forget.'

'One should always obey them.'

'Just one detail, no luggage.'

'Never mind.'

'I dare say the shipmates on the *Trinidad* didn't have clean shirts either.'

*

So the two men found themselves at almost ten in the evening in a small hotel near the Roman amphitheatre, where food was still being served.

As they finished the meal, Adamsberg said:

'I think I know now what's been bugging me about that man's name, Seguin.' He waved his hand to order two coffees. The restaurant had officially closed, but while they were clearing the tables, the owner had let the two men carry on sitting there.

'Do you remember? It's a famous story: *La Chèvre de Monsieur Seguin*, Monsieur Seguin and his little goat.'

'We did it at school. She was called Blanquette,' said Veyrenc, 'and so pretty that the chestnut trees bent their boughs down to caress her with their branches.'

'And she wanted to run away and be free, didn't she?'

'Like the six goats before her.'

'I'd forgotten the other six.'

'Yes. Monsieur Seguin adored his little goats, but they'd all got away. Blanquette was the seventh.'

'I always thought Seguin himself was the wolf. And since his goat wanted to escape, he tethered her and ate her himself.'

'Or attacked her,' said Veyrenc. 'When they tried to run away, Seguin threatened his goats by saying they'd "see the wolf" – but you know what that expression means, "see the wolf"? See a man naked, lose your virginity. You're right. What the story really means is that Blanquette is raped. Do you remember how she "struggled all night" and at dawn she's lying on the ground with her white fur all bloodstained, because the pretty little goat was white, so a virgin – and is eaten up. So you're saying Seguin's name really suited him.'

'No, I'm saying Enzo read stories to his sisters. Since that's such a famous one, I think they must have known it.'

'Probably, yes, most people would have heard it in school in those days. But what's your idea?'

'Well, when you have to choose a new name, you'd almost certainly choose one that has some connection, some echo of the old one, or of your former life.'

'Agreed.'

'So think. Louise *Chevrier*, the story's title is "La Chèvre de Monsieur Seguin". Louise, the tethered goat, the victim who was devoured.'

'Louise Chevrier,' said Veyrenc slowly. 'Froissy couldn't find anyone born with that name in 1943.'

'A new identity then?'

'And she could have altered her date of birth.'

'Like Mercadet says, nothing easier than to fiddle a birth date.'

'It's too late to wake Froissy up, but the first name she chose, Louise, might have been one of her own other names, a second or third one.'

'Yes,' said Adamsberg as he started typing a message.

'Who are you going to wake up?'

'Froissy.'

'Oh for heaven's sake, she'll be asleep.'

'No, she won't.'

'But something doesn't fit here, Jean-Baptiste. Annette was freed aged nineteen – then fourteen years later, if we're right about Louise, she was raped again, by *Carnot*. Could that be some damned coincidence?'

'Who's talking about a coincidence? Carnot was friendly with the others, wasn't he? Annette was their victim, they might have latched on to her again.'

'I think Froissy's sleeping, you're a brute.'

'Talking of being a brute, Louis, I punched Danglard on the jaw.'

'Hard?'

'Quite hard, but just one blow on the chin. Not so much a blow as a rite of passage. A rite of return rather. Back to the team.'

The mobile on the table vibrated.

'See, she wasn't asleep.'

'She'll tell you some cover story.'

Sorry, sir, was having dinner. Elder sister Bernadette Marguerite Hélène, younger Annette Rose Louise.

Thanks, Froissy. Staying Nîmes overnight back 10am, goodnight.

'Annette Rose Louise,' said Adamsberg. 'Louise Chevrier. She must have chosen Louise deliberately and Chevrier unconsciously. The little kid goat, tied up by the father Seguin.'

'But how did Louise Chevrier manage to be on the spot for all those murders? She doesn't drive.'

'Let's just suppose she *does* actually drive.'

'And when she left for Saint-Porchaire, Irène didn't notice?'

'Irène was in Bourges at that time.'

The telephone pinged again. He'd missed a voicemail message and was anxious when he recognised Retancourt's voice.

'Commissaire, we were all three on duty around Torrailles's house in Lédignan. Easy, no need to hide, Torrailles knew he was under protection. He was finishing supper outside with Lambertin, at a little table, face-to-face, there was a lot of talk, belly laughs and revolting jokes, honestly, these guys have never stopped being stink bugs. There's a big courtyard, with a low hedge, it goes round all four sides. At 10 p.m. the street lamps went out but it was still quite light. There was a lamp over the door and a tea light on the garden table, quite visible, white plastic. It was attracting mosquitoes. They swatted them with their hands, slap, slap, slap. "It's only the females that bite, see, you gotta pay them back." About 10.15, Torrailles started to scratch his right arm. Here's their conversation: Torrailles: "Fucking female! One of the bitches got me." Lambertin: "That's your own bloody fault, turn off the light." Torrailles: "No, fuck's sake don't, can't see what we're drinking." Three minutes later, Lambertin starts to scratch his neck on the left side. They'd had enough of this, so they picked up the bottle and glasses and went inside. Then less than an hour later, out they come from the house, the pair of them, panicking, they beg us to get them to hospital, because the bites had swollen. I looked at them with a flashlight. There was already a swelling in both cases, couple of centimetres across, with a blister forming. Right now, we're all on the way to the hospital in Nîmes, they're up ahead with Justin and Noël, and I'm following in the other car. Right arm, left side of neck, so they must have been attacked from the same place. We were all three doing the rounds of the house all evening, no one could have got near, no one could have got in. Impossible – it's like it fell from the sky. We must have missed something. Terribly sorry.'

Adamsberg, his features frozen, let Veyrenc listen to the message. They stared at each other without a word.

'The last two standing, Louis, she's knocked off the last two,' said Adamsberg finally, swallowing his cold coffee quickly. 'In one go. With three cops doing the rounds outside. How in heaven's name could someone do that? Even if something falls from the sky, it should be visible, shouldn't it? What's the time now?'

'Ten past midnight.'

'Well, no point waking Irène to ask if Louise is there. They were "bitten" at about ten fifteen. It's not more than about forty-five minutes to get from Lédignan to Cadeirac.'

The hotel owner suggested more coffee. From their conversation, he had gathered a while back that they were from the police, and high-ranking, and on a case. When you've got the cops in your establishment, you try to be accommodating. Adamsberg accepted the offer of the free coffees, and went to fetch them himself from the bar.

'Retancourt? You're at the hospital?'

'Just getting there.'

'Can you come and pick us up, Veyrenc and me, at 7.30 a.m.?'

'In Paris? At 7 a.m.? Aren't there any cars there?'

'No, no, we're here in Nîmes, and without a car.'

'Where are you?'

'Hotel du Taureau, near the amphitheatre.'

'OK.'

'Lieutenant, have you got the evidence kit with you?'

'Doesn't leave my bag, sir. Haven't you?'

'No, we left without luggage.'

'I see.'

'Bring it along, plus your camera.'

'I want to repeat this, commissaire. *No one* went in, *no one* came out. Absolutely no one! And we could see quite well, the whole of the courtyard and five metres into the road. A shadow couldn't have got past.'

'Don't blame yourselves. Even you can't intercept everything that's spat from the sky.'

Adamsberg ended the call, drank his coffee standing up, and looked across at the wall of the dining room, where the owner had a display of guns. About fifteen lever-action rifles, old Winchesters, shining in the gloom.

'Spat from the sky. We're stupid, Veyrenc, *that's* what she must have done.'

'What, spat on them?' said Veyrenc, who was still stunned by the news of the two final assaults.

'Yes, that must be it,' said Adamsberg, pulling up his chair noisily and sitting back down.

'You're joking.'

'Drink your coffee, and listen. She must be using a gun.'

'To spit with.'

'Yes, liquid, fluid, a hypodermic gun. A tranquilliser dart, if you prefer.'

This time Veyrenc looked up.

'Oh. The sort vets have, to knock out animals? Stun guns? Tranquilliser darts, yes.'

'Exactly. With night-vision sights. They can shoot from forty, sixty metres away. On impact, the sheath of the needle comes off and the stuff's injected automatically.'

'How do you know that?'

'During my national service, I was a sniper, I still get the catalogues. This gun must be a category D weapon, openly available for sale with the syringes. Even though it could be lethal if people took it into their heads to fill the hypodermic with a solution of arsenic, say. Or recluse venom.'

'The venom of twenty-two recluses, Jean-Baptiste. Multiplied by six victims, and that means 132 spiders!'

'Forget the 132 recluses. She fired a gun, that's all that matters for now.'

'It doesn't figure. Nobody's reported having a dart or a hypodermic in their arm or leg. They'd have seen it. You feel a sting, you look to see, you put your hand there.'

'That's true.'

'Let's suppose for a moment that the hypodermic comes out and falls off, which would surprise me. We'd have found it in the grass at Saint-Porchaire by Vessac's front door. Unless the murderer comes along afterwards to collect it. Which would be foolish and very risky.'

Adamsberg leaned his chin on his hand, and looked down.

'We did find *something* in the grass at Saint-Porchaire,' he said after a while.

'Your bit of fishing line, dropped in there by the wind.'

'Not just dropped, Louis, it was caught in something. Help me here. Suppose I'm a murderer. I've absolutely got to make the hypodermic disappear.'

'But why? Does it really matter if someone finds the syringe? It gives less away than a bullet would. No traces from the gun's barrel. No way you can identify it. So why would you want to get the needle back?'

'So that nobody actually thinks for a *second* that these deaths are murders. If we hadn't discovered the links between the victims and the Miséricorde bullies, we'd still be back at the same place: the recluse spiders have just got more toxic and these old men have died simply because they're old. No murder, no investigation, the murderer has nothing to fear. And *I've* got nothing to fear. If I can get my hypodermic back, that is.'

'Well, how are you going to do that?'

'I'm going to pull it back. I get some nylon thread, fine but strong, 0.3 mm for instance, drop it through the muzzle, catch it at the breech and attach one end to the needle, which I then fill with venom. When the dart goes off, it takes let's say sixty metres of thread which unrolls from an external reel. Yes?'

'No. It'll pull on the roll and slow down the trajectory.'

'You're right. So before I fire, I unwind sixty metres, or thirty, whatever, the distance to the target.'

'So the thread goes off without being dragged back by the reel. OK.'

'When the hypodermic hits the target, I immediately pull hard on the thread, to extract it from the wound. By the time the guy has looked at his sting, or bite, the needle's vanished. Then I wind the other way, pulling the needle, and it comes back to me like a dog being whistled. What happened at Saint-Porchaire? Vessac was hit, I pulled on my thread, but the needle got stuck in the nettles. I make the reel work hard, and the thread breaks. Once Vessac's gone indoors with Élisabeth, I run over, cut the thread and recover my hypodermic. But a little bit of fishing line stays caught up in the vegetation. Who'd notice it? Or care?'

'You. But look Jean-Baptiste, a hypodermic needle is like a bullet, it has to fit snugly inside the barrel. With the thread there, it's going to hinder its trajectory, and it'll spin out of control.'

'The kind of gun they use, they're airguns, they have smooth barrels, so it won't twist. But yes, if you put a size 13 mm syringe in a 13 mm barrel plus the thread, it could get stuck. So I put a size 11 mm syringe in my 13 mm barrel.'

'With 2 mm extra, it'll be loose. And you won't be able to aim accurately.'

'Not if I wind something round my needle so as to make it 12.4 mm. That's what they used to do in olden times, with muskets and bullets that didn't fit properly, they rolled them in a twist of paper to make them a better fit. And you oil the whole thing, to make sure. And then, trust me, it would work. It's an old army trick. The advantage of these stun guns is they use compressed air, not gunpowder, it makes a plop, and at forty or sixty metres, or even much less, you can't hear a thing.'

'So how are you going to cart your gun around discreetly, even if it's dark, on a village road, or a street in Nîmes?'

'I use a folding model, they exist, and I carry it in a bag, with the reel and the telescopic sights.'

'It could work.'

'Louis, it *did* work. That's how it was spat from the skies.'

XXXIX

RETANCOURT WAS WAITING FOR THEM IN THE MORNING, LEANING against a bright yellow hired car, with the disquieting appearance of an angry giant.

'Ten!' she said, without greeting them. 'She's knocked off all ten of them!'

'She or he. Veyrenc sometimes thinks it could be Enzo, the brother of those sequestered girls. Did you get a chance to look at Froissy's material?'

'Just glanced at it, hard to read something when you're on watch. Well, Enzo or whoever, they got all ten of them! When you'd sussed out what was happening after the first two! And the squad was on to it by number three.'

'*Part* of the squad,' Adamsberg reminded her, as Retancourt let the clutch in furiously.

'Even so, sir. We worked on it, we checked the archives, we found the leads, we asked people, we tailed suspects, we travelled the length of the country, and this murderer's bumped them all off, almost under our very eyes. It just makes me mad, that's all!'

Faced with the latest failure, which had knocked out two men, Retancourt was furious, but also mortified. She'd been responsible for protecting them, and she'd failed.

'Take a right, Retancourt, we're going to Lédignan, and Torrailles's house. Yes, it does make you mad. But even if we'd had ten people on to it, we'd still not have been able to prevent it.'

'Why not? Because the murderer came flying through the air?'

'Well, yes, in a way. My fault, I ought to have thought of this sooner.'

Adamsberg leaned back in his seat, folding his arms. If only he'd been quicker off the mark. It was four days since he'd found that scrap of nylon thread. He'd picked it up himself, he'd insisted on keeping it. So he had indeed recognised its importance. And what had he done about it? Nothing. Violent waves had crashed over his head, carrying that fragile evidence far from his thoughts. The extraction of the tooth on the Île de Ré, the elimination from his inquiries of the boys who had been bitten, Danglard's rebellion, the discovery of that case of the girls imprisoned in Nîmes. And in all that, the little nylon thread had been forgotten.

'Here we are,' said Retancourt after a drive of forty minutes, screeching to a halt and making the handbrake squeal. 'Look how low the hedge is. It's the same all the way round. The street lamps were on until ten. Then their table light and the lamp over the door gave enough light to see them sitting at the table.'

'As you already told me, lieutenant.'

'So how did she get here then? By hot-air balloon?'

'Almost. With a dart.'

'You mean she fired some kind of shot?'

'Two shots, with a rifle and a hypodermic.'

Retancourt absorbed this new information, giving herself just time to haul her evidence kitbag roughly out of the boot.

'From how far away?'

'Without the street lamps on, and even with some night-vision telescopic sights, I'd say thirty metres, to be on the safe side.'

'But bloody hell! We were walking round the perimeter, commissaire. How come we didn't see her?'

'Because she wasn't firing from outside.'

'From the sky then.'

'No, from indoors, lieutenant. From the house. Where she'd gone to hide while the men were absent. She must already have been there when you came back with Torrailles and Lambertin.'

'God Almighty!'

'You couldn't have stopped it. You couldn't have seen a dark rifle barrel protruding from a darkened window.'

Retancourt nodded as she took this in, then drew the bolt to enter the courtyard. Adamsberg stopped at the table and looked up at the facade of the house.

'She can't have been on the ground floor, there must be a kitchen and another room. Too risky if they came inside. So she must have been upstairs, and then fired two oblique shots, on the slant, hitting them sideways on. From that room up there,' he said, pointing to a small, dirt-encrusted window. 'Retancourt, can you examine the whole surface that would be covered by a shot, between the house and the table?'

'What am I looking for?'

'A fragment of nylon thread maybe. The surface is concrete, but there's grass and thistles growing in the cracks. Try that. I'm going up to the first floor. Have you got those wretched foot covers?'

Adamsberg and Veyrenc took off their shoes and equipped themselves in the entrance hall. They looked all over the first floor, sliding about like patients in hospital, and rapidly inspected the two bedrooms, bathroom, lavatory and, overlooking the garden table, a small lumber room, full of suitcases, cardboard boxes and old boots. The floor was as dusty as one could hope for, made of grey speckled ceramic tiles.

Veyrenc switched on the light bulb dangling from the ceiling and sidled along the wall to the small window.

'Yes, opened recently,' he said. 'Scraps of paint here and there.'

'And some traces of footprints. You take that bit of the floor, I'll take the other.'

'These dappled grey tiles don't make it easy.'

'Now here,' said Adamsberg, who had crouched down near the window, 'we have a fairly clear footprint.'

'Tennis shoe,' said Veyrenc.

'Basic equipment, but a bit risky because of the pattern on the sole. The ridges look quite deep. See if there are any traces of earth, grass, vegetable matter in them.'

'No, nothing.'

'Me neither. Except for this.'

With his tweezers, Adamsberg held up to daylight a single hair about twenty centimetres long.

'She must have been waiting for them some time, rubbed her head or scratched it, a sign of stress. It wasn't going to be easy, was it, with three cops in attendance.'

'Reddish, with two centimetres of grey at the root. Curly. Permed presumably.'

'Here's another one. I'd be surprised if Enzo had long dyed hair, or ever had a perm.'

'No, it's got to be a woman,' admitted Veyrenc, 'and quite old.'

'Give me the magnifier. Yeah, we've got the root at the end. Total of four hairs,' he said, after they had searched some more. 'You can close the bag, we're rich now. Let's try for fingerprints.'

'Nothing on the glass, the dust there hasn't been disturbed.'

Veyrenc passed the dusting powder along the window frame and ledge.

'Wearing gloves,' he said. 'Well, who doesn't wear gloves? There's a scrap of paint here, on the sill. She must have rested the gun there.'

Adamsberg took two photographs, then two more of the partial footprint.

'Let's check the stairs,' he said, 'especially low down. It's when the sole bends that it might release its secrets. Like us when we crack and give way.'

The bottom few stairs yielded three pieces of gravel. They could have come from anywhere, the cemetery or the roadside near the hedge. And one crushed clover leaf, which, although not much help, seemed to be a final little offering.

'We'll take it anyway,' said Adamsberg, putting it into a last plastic bag.

'Why?'

'Because I'm fond of clover.'

'As you wish,' said Veyrenc, who often answered Adamsberg with these words, not that he accepted what had been said, but when he knew it was pointless to argue.

'So, Retancourt,' said Adamsberg as he joined her in the garden, where she was sitting on one of the plastic chairs and rubbing one hand. 'You're sitting in the middle of the crime scene.'

'Already checked. Nothing. No nylon thread. Nothing. And I got stung by a damn nettle.'

'Just vegetable poison, lieutenant.'

'So what did you get?'

'Four hairs, with their roots, DNA-worthy. And a clover leaf.'

'What good's that? The clover leaf.'

'To refresh us.'

Veyrenc took the second chair and Adamsberg sat on the ground, cross-legged.

'So,' he said, 'an elderly woman, grey hair dyed red and permed. Who goes round with a folding rifle, equipped with a hypodermic, stashed away in her travelling bag. And syringes filled with the venom of twenty-two recluse spiders. A woman who was raped, either in her youth or when she was older. But it has to be over twenty years ago, because that's when the first victim was shot in the back.'

'Not a lot, is it?'

'It's getting us closer, Retancourt.'

'Nearer the 52nd parallel. The name of the sailor, I've forgotten it, I mean Magellan's real name in Portuguese.'

'Fernão de Magalhães.'

'Thanks.'

'You're welcome.'

Adamsberg crossed his legs the other way and fished out two of Zerk's cigarettes, by now almost demolished. He passed one to Veyrenc and lit one for himself.

'I'd like one too,' said Retancourt.

'I thought you didn't smoke?'

'But these are stolen ones, if I've understood that right?'

'Absolutely.'

'Then I'll have one.'

They sat there, all three, in silence, smoking their cigarettes half empty of tobacco, in the early-morning sunshine.

'That was nice,' said Adamsberg, as he got out his mobile.

'Irène, did I wake you up?'

'I'm just drinking my coffee.'

'Have you heard? Two more, at the same time?'

'Just seen it on social media. That's infuriating.'

'Yes,' he said, picking up the same reaction of irritated anger as in Retancourt. 'All the more so as I had three officers on guard duty, keeping an eye on them at their garden table. They saw nothing.'

'I'm not going to be rude about the police, mind, I'm not saying it's easy, I'm not saying you haven't worked hard, commissaire, but there we are, he's got them all now. And we still don't know who's doing it. Infuriating. I'm not going to say these men were nice guys, from what you tell me they weren't, but still, all the same, it makes you mad.'

'Tell me, Irène, are you alone at the moment?'

'Yes, because Louise has her breakfast in her bedroom. She doesn't know yet about these last two, so I've got a bit of peace for the moment. And Élisabeth's still asleep.'

'I'm going to bother you again with some questions, about your Louise. Try and answer right away without thinking.'

'That's not my way, commissaire.'

'So I've noticed. What time did Louise go to her room last night?'

'Oh, she wasn't hungry after that funeral. The atmosphere. She had a bowl of soup at five and I didn't see her again.'

'Do you know if she went out after that?'

'What would she do that for?'

'How would I know?'

'Well, she does sometimes go and walk in the street when she can't sleep. Since there's no one about in our village then, she's not afraid of meeting a man, see.'

'Yes. So? Last night?'

'Hard to say, though it does get on my nerves. The thing is, she gets up practically every three hours to go . . .'

'To the bathroom?' said Adamsberg.

'Yes, you understand. And the door creaks, so it wakes me up.'

'And you heard the door creak last night?'

'I'm trying to tell you, commissaire, same as every night. But as for knowing if she went outside because she couldn't sleep, that I can't tell you.'

'OK, forget it, Irène. I'm going to send you someone, a woman. She'd like to photograph all the little lairs where recluse spiders hide in your house.'

'Whatever for?'

'For my report to the top brass. They want to know everything, check everything, it's the way they are. They want some visual proof that recluse spiders hide away.'

'So what?'

'So, *if you follow me*, the thicker the file, the better it is. And since the investigation has been a failure, I need to prove I've done a lot of work on the ground.'

'Ah, all right, I see.'

'Can I send her over?'

'But, oh! I didn't tell you!' said Irène, her voice suddenly rising an octave. 'I've got another one!'

'Another visitor?'

'Noooo! Hiding inside a roll of kitchen paper, I found it this morning in the kitchen.'

'A recluse, you mean?'

'Commissaire, who else would hide in the kitchen roll? Of course a recluse. A beauty! Adult female, but I'll have to get her outside, before she starts laying eggs. What if Louise was to see her? It'd be the end of the world.'

'Could you please not take it outside just yet? Wait for the photographer.'

'All right, I see, but hurry, because Louise now, she's into everything. And she uses the kitchen roll a lot.'

'In an hour and a quarter, OK?'

'Perfect, I'll be ready, because it's important I'm ready.'

'Of course.'

'Is she nice, this woman?'

'Very.'

'And what am I going to do with Louise while she takes photos?'

'Nothing at all, you invite her to have some coffee with the photographer, that'll distract her.'

'She only drinks tea.'

'All right, tea.'

'And what about the photos then?'

'You can tell her she's come to check on the disinfestation. That'll reassure Louise.'

'Because I've had the pest control round?'

'Exactly. Under pressure.'

'And when was that?'

'Early this morning.'

'Well, if you say so. It would calm her down, yes, I hadn't thought of that.'

Adamsberg ended the call, got up, rubbed the seat of his trousers, and smiled at Retancourt.

'I'm guessing this one's for me,' she said.

'Yes. A visit to my fellow cop and arachnologist in Cadeirac, Irène.'

Adamsberg explained briefly what her mission would be as a post-disinfestation photographer.

'But what really interests you is Louise Chevrier. You're going to have a cup of tea with her.'

'Is the tea compulsory? Can't I have coffee?'

'Yes, of course. Now I want to know three things: first does she look her age? Seventy-three. Or more like sixty-eight?'

'Not so easy if it's only five years' difference.'

'No, I know. Second, has she got hair dyed reddish, with grey roots showing, about two centimetres, and permed. Like these hairs,' he added, taking out the plastic evidence bag. 'Take a good look.'

'Understood.'

'And third, what are her front teeth like? Her own or false? You'll have to find a way, make her laugh or smile anyway. This is very important. Joking about Irène's collection might do the trick. Louise thinks it's hideous.'

'What's Irène's collection?'

'Snowstorms. Those things you shake and you get snowflakes all over some monument.'

'Understood.'

'And then ask to go to the bathroom, and try to get some of her hair from a brush or comb.'

'Which isn't allowed without a warrant.'

'Sure. There will be two hairbrushes. Besides Louise's there'll be one belonging to Irène, but she dyes her hair blonde. You won't be able to mistake them.'

'That's *if* Louise does dye her hair red. Which we don't know.'

'Precisely, and send me the result as soon as possible. Don't worry if Irène refers to me as "Jean-Bapt" in front of Louise. It's agreed between us. Oh, and one more thing, I told Irène you're very nice.'

'Oh for God's sake,' said Retancourt, losing a smidgeon of her usual confidence.

She thought for a moment.

'I'll manage,' she said finally. 'I think I can do it.'

'Who would ever doubt it, Violette?'

Retancourt dropped Adamsberg and Veyrenc at their hotel in Nîmes, and set off at once for Cadeirac, with her camera.

Adamsberg took the time to send a message to Froissy telling her to stop looking for pictures of Louise smiling. And another to Noël and Justin, to tell them to go back to headquarters.

'What I propose now,' he said to Veyrenc, 'is to eat a substantial breakfast and rest until Retancourt calls in.'

'You think she'll manage this visit? It isn't straightforward. She'll have to lie through her teeth, and be very tactful psychologically.'

'Retancourt can manage anything. She'd have been able to sail the *San Antonio* single-handed.'

'Perhaps you're pulling too hard on the rein.'

'Retancourt doesn't have one,' said Adamsberg, eyeing him. 'And if she did, she'd drag me right round the world.'

XL

VEYRENC TOOK THE TEXT FROM RETANCOURT AT ABOUT MIDDAY.

No response from boss, sent this earlier, can you pass on copy please? Louise has false teeth, complete set. Hair identical to sample. Looks 70. 'Used to drive.' Nothing in the bathroom, she has en suite bedroom. Couldn't get in there, creaky boards. Genuinely afraid of recluses. She started law degree Nîmes, gave up because of 'incident'. Spoke of labour law with authority. And as I might as well be hanged for a sheep as a lamb, I pinched a little teaspoon she used. I WAS nice. So were they. Irène's funny, but they're cooing and chattering all the time in that house, not my scene. She gave me a goddam Rochefort snowstorm for boss!

When Veyrenc went into Adamsberg's room, the commissaire was still fast asleep, fully dressed on the bed. He shook his shoulder.

'News from Retancourt, Jean-Baptiste. She's been trying to reach you.'

'Didn't hear.'

He smiled as he read the message.

'Yes, good idea the teaspoon.'

'Do you really suspect her?'

'False name, her age, her hair and teeth, for the moment everything fits.'

'What's all this about teeth?'

Adamsberg sighed and passed the mobile back.

'My recluse only had a few rotten teeth left in her mouth, Louis. Because of malnutrition. Once she was out of . . . shit! what's the name of that place, you know, where they keep those birds?'

'The dovecot, you mean? Doves, pigeons, same thing. Danglard would tell you it could be a columbarium, from columba, Latin for pigeon. Though when it's in a house, it could be a pigeon loft –'

'Just dovecot will do, not the rest. I must have slept too long,' said Adamsberg, smoothing his hair with his fingers. 'I'm forgetting words now.'

He stayed sitting on the bed for a few moments, then put his shoes on and opened his notebook. *Dovecot, I couldn't find the word.*

'It's just the extraction,' said Veyrenc. 'As the doc told you.'

'Yes, but still.'

'Forget the dovecot, back to Louise. Yes, all right, I agree, the name, Chevrier, Monsieur Seguin's little goat. And she was raped by Carnot, who knew Landrieu, who was linked to the orphanage gang. Yes, the hair, her phobias, soap and oil. But then again, she's terrified of recluses. And if she really started her law studies before the "incident" – which must be the rape – she can't be one of the sisters locked up in Nîmes. Froissy's probably right, she must have been born abroad.'

'She's having us on. Everything converges, everything *looks* solid. Apparently.'

'*Apparently*? You're sure you've got your killer, but now it's only "apparently"?'

'It's all these blind inlets, Louis. Maybe this is just one more. No,' he said, 'it's something else. A sort of itch that's bothering me, as Lucio would say.'

'Since when?'

'Can't say.'

'What kind of itch?'

'Dunno.'

'Come on then, let's clear the rooms and have breakfast.'

'*Drekka borða*,' agreed Adamsberg, getting up. 'And back to base. We'll send the hairs and the spoon straight to the lab for DNA testing. Then we'll know whether, yes or no, she was in that little box room with a gun and some venom. And we might find some link to the Seguin family.'

'Enzo can't have had his DNA taken when he got out of prison, they didn't do that in 1984. We'd have to exhume the parents.'

'Or find in police archives the axe that killed the father. Which might tell us if Louise was his tethered goat. Who, unlike in the story, got free and went around killing wolves.'

From the train on the way back to Paris, Adamsberg texted Retancourt: *Congratulations and end of mission. Leave spoon on my desk.*

Then he went into the corridor to phone Dr Martin-Robinson.

'Remember that recluse in the dovecot, doctor?'

'Yes, of course.'

'Well, today, I couldn't remember the word for "dovecot".'

'Have you been sleeping a lot, as advised?' the doctor asked.

'Never slept so much in my life.'

'Excellent.'

'If I've forgotten the word for dovecot, is that collateral damage from the extraction?'

'No, it means the scarring process is working. It's evasion. We all do it.'

'What do you mean, evasion?'

'You're failing to recognise something you do know, but you don't want to.'

'Why?'

'Because it hurts, it's a problem, we prefer to evade it, go round it, not say it.'

'But look, doctor, if it's the dovecot, I must be thinking about my recluse woman, mustn't I?'

'No. That chapter's over, and you've fully remembered it. Have you ever had anything else to do with doves? Or pigeons?'

'Pigeons? Six million Parisians see pigeons every day.'

'No, I don't mean that. Have you ever personally had any worry connected with a pigeon? Take your time.'

Adamsberg leaned against the train door, letting the motion of the carriage rock him.

'Well, yes, in fact I did once,' he said. 'With my son – we found this pigeon with its legs tied together. We took it in, looked after it, and it comes back almost every month to the house.'

'And you're fond of it?'

'I was concerned whether it would survive, yes. And I like it when it appears. Except the damn thing shits on the kitchen table every time.'

'That means it sees your place as a safe house. So it puts down a marker. Don't clean up its droppings in front of it, Adamsberg, you'd hurt its feelings, psychologically.'

'You can hurt a pigeon's feelings *psychologically*?'

'Naturally.'

'All right then, what about the dovecot? It was quite a while back that I rescued the pigeon.'

'It was probably the fact that its feet were tied together that affected you. The fact that it was a prisoner. So that relates to your investigation, and your search for any girls who had been sequestered. Have you found any?'

'Yes. We've discovered a horrific case. Dating back forty-nine years. And I do believe one of those two girls is the killer.'

'And you're feeling wretched at the thought of arresting her? Putting her back in a cage, or a dovecot, with your own hands.'

'Yes, precisely.'

'Quite normal. Hence the evasion. There is of course another possibility, less likely though. You know the slang meaning of pigeon? A sucker, a dupe, someone who's been tricked. Perhaps you're afraid that you're being taken for a ride, like a pigeon. In other words, someone's deceiving you. And since this possibility, in your unconscious, is hurtful, you're avoiding anything to do with pigeons, like the word dovecot, so it must be someone close to you. Someone who's fooled you. Maybe a colleague.'

'Yeah, as it happens, I was betrayed by my longest-standing deputy, but I've sorted it.'

'How?'

'By destroying the posture he'd taken up.'

'And how did you do that?'

'I socked him on the jaw.'

'Ah, that was a brutal method. Did it work?'

'Very well – he's returned to his normal self.'

'That's a style of therapy forbidden to me,' said the doctor, with one of his hearty laughs. 'But let's be serious. It's not your deputy, then. Think about the other members of your team. Perhaps you're afraid someone hasn't told you everything. Because after all, it would be *normal* for them not to want the murderer of these old bastards to get caught. To consider the vengeance well deserved.'

'No, no,' said Adamsberg. 'That's unthinkable for me.'

'I said there were *two* possibilities. Either you're bothered by the idea of putting the wounded creature, this woman, back in captivity, or by the thought that *you're* the pigeon, if someone's deceiving you. Think it over.'

'I can't think.'

'In that case, go back to sleep.'

Adamsberg returned to his seat, feeling worried. He wrote down the doctor's two theories. Putting back in chains the poor little girl who'd been locked up, even if she had become a demented killer? Sending her back to a cell, just like the one where she'd spent her childhood? Becoming her final jailer? Her final Monsieur Seguin? He tried to do his job, not think about it. Too painful. Evade it.

Then he thought about the second possibility. Was *he* the pigeon? Was someone in the team altering the vessel's course, as Danglard had already tried to do? Who had been in charge of processing information? Mercadet and Froissy. Neither of them had been able to find any trace of the Seguin sisters. Or so they had said. Voisenet, Justin, Noël and Lamarre had been on watch, and assured him that none of the boys who were bitten had gone missing at the time of Vessac's murder. So they'd abandoned that lead. There was Retancourt of course, who'd failed to stop the killer of Torrailles and Lambertin. Unusual for Retancourt to fail at anything. Why hadn't she thought of the possibility that the assassin was inside the house, rather than approaching it from outside? But then, he'd been slow off the mark himself, before he'd thought of the hypodermic. So he hadn't suggested anything of the sort to her. If he'd thought of it a few hours earlier, he'd have ordered them to keep Torrailles and Lambertin in a closed room under police protection. It was his own fault. Still, she had apologised and justified herself, she'd said 'I'm terribly sorry', which was unlike her. But no, not Retancourt, for the love of God, don't let it be Retancourt who's betraying me.

That evening, Adamsberg went into the almost deserted squad headquarters, to send a request to police archives concerning the homicide of Eugène Seguin in Nîmes in 1967. He didn't expect too much from the service, especially without some official backup from his superiors. To find an axe that had been packed away for forty-nine years was a very long shot. The hairs he had collected and the little teaspoon went off by special courier for analysis, with a personal request to make it urgent, addressed to Louvain, one of the senior staff in the DNA lab.

He left instructions to the duty officers regarding the blackbirds, and asked Veyrenc to draft a report for the team on the events at Lédignan. Gardon, who was on the desk, confessed shamefacedly that he really couldn't handle putting wriggling worms down in the earth for the birds. On the other hand, Estalère offered enthusiastically to do it. He was off duty next day, but he'd come in morning and evening to distribute the worms, cake and raspberries.

Estalère hadn't been in charge of any search for information. Estalère he could trust as if he were his own son.

XLI

ADAMSBERG WAS BECOMING AWARE THAT THERE WAS NOT JUST ONE single 'proto-thought' troubling him, but a whole disparate group of gas bubbles – and they certainly existed – some of them so small as to be barely discernible. He could feel them bouncing around in different directions, and their trajectories were wild. Facing two unresolved questions – and there were more, obviously – the bubbles had no more chance of finding their way than someone who was cross-eyed. Or that man in the story who tried to chase two hares at the same time – though why anyone would do that if they weren't completely stupid was anyone's guess. He lost them both, of course.

As if echoing the turbulence of his bubbles, as if watching their movements, spying on them, he was playing with his snowstorm, now on his desk. He shook it and watched the crazy whirlwind of white particles falling on the coat of arms of Rochefort: a star with five points, a tower, and a three-masted ship under full sail.

The ship again. What would that hardened mariner Magellan have done with a woman who had been first martyred then turned murderer? Would he have beheaded and dismembered her, as had been a custom at the time? Or abandoned her on a desert shore, as he had some of his shipmates who had turned traitor?

Two elements kept appearing on the path ahead. The clock tower of the orphanage La Miséricorde, and the cell of the recluse in the Pré d'Albret. But nothing, or virtually nothing, told him that the woman living there had the remotest connection to the killer who had managed to get rid of ten men in twenty years. Yet that 'virtually nothing' still preoccupied his thoughts. The saint of Lourdes was called Bernadette. And so was the elder Seguin sister. Had her despair at living sent her towards the territory of her patron saint to cloister herself in a cell? Or was it the younger one? Which of them? And how might Louise fit in?

Next morning the news from the hospital in Nîmes was not good. The doctors were giving the two men who had been 'bitten' only a couple of days to live. Blood tests, this time more detailed, apparently showed a dose of venom twenty times that of a normal recluse spider. Dr Pujol had been right. You needed at least forty-four venom glands to kill a medium-sized adult man, so you had to find the impossible number of 132 spiders, then get them to spit out their venom. And how on earth did you do that?

Adamsberg couldn't get his own recluse of Lourdes to spit out anything for him. The theory of venom for venom, fluid for fluid, didn't entirely convince him. With snakes, yes, why not? But recluse spiders? There must be some more powerful motive for someone to choose such a complex method of killing people. And since that hideous woman had surged up from the depths of his memory, only a real life as a recluse seemed to him to justify such an insane project. Only the status of being a genuine *recluse* could explain that this woman had become identified with the spider of the same name, one that lived with her in her dark cell. In the same way, her physical transformation – nails turning into claws, hair becoming a mane, making her more like a wild creature – could explain her metamorphosis into an animal, an animal with powerful, fluid, penetrating venom. That was her weapon, she had no choice.

This feeling was obsessive, but it was still exceedingly vague, with not the slightest factual proof to give it any substance. The sail was quivering in the wind – as Dr Martin-Robinson had said. Martin-Robinson – what a mouthful of a name!

It would be useless trying to find any clues on the spot. The woman had been surrounded by holy silence and remained so. Her identity and her secret had been buried deep in her hiding place, and she was no longer there.

Buried deep. Adamsberg looked up. What was the good of having a friend who was an archaeologist, if you didn't try to tease the truth out of the very earth where she had lived? He packed a bag hurriedly, put the snowstorm in his pocket, and caught the 10.24 Paris–Lourdes train. From the train, he called Mathias, the prehistoric expert he had consulted before, one of the so-called 'three evangelists' who shared a run-down house in Paris. They exchanged their news. Mathias was waiting to be hired on a dig that summer on a Solutrean site. Lucien was making a name for himself as a historian of the Great War. Marc, the medievalist, was still dividing his time between giving classes at university and ironing sheets. Marc's godfather, the ex-cop Vandoosler, was still alive and kicking, and as sarcastic as ever, and Marc was still addicted to stealing luxury food, especially hare and langoustines.

'I don't think he'll ever stop doing that,' said Mathias, 'but Lucien cooks it all beautifully. So what's this about?'

'A dig. It's not officially paid, but I'll see what I can do.'

'If it's for you, I'm not bothered about the money. Are you on a murder case?'

'Ten murders. Six in the last month.'

'So you want to look in some graves?'

'No, I want to look at the site of an old dovecot.'

'The soil underneath it? Pigeon droppings?'

'There was this recluse, who lived in it for five years, a long time ago, you weren't even born. I was a child myself.'

'You mean a *real* recluse?'

'Yes, real, like in medieval times.'

'But what do you want to find by excavating it?'

'Her identity. I need your help. I can get some of my men to dig up the turf and the humus. But then what? To examine the soil of her "habitat", who am I going to ask? The cops? It's quite small, can't be more than four square metres.'

'No, that makes sense, she wouldn't have had a three-bedroom flat if she was, like you say, a genuine recluse.'

'But I need to go through the stuff with a toothcomb. So that we can get some uncontaminated DNA from hair or teeth.'

'No problem,' said the phlegmatic and reliable Mathias.

'There's probably a lot of hair, but after years in the damp, the roots will have gone, and even the hair will be damaged. I'm banking on the teeth with soft tissue still being there.'

'What makes you think there'll be teeth?'

'I saw her.'

'You *saw* her?'

'She had her mouth wide open. Just a few rotten stumps.'

'Scurvy, perhaps? What sailors used to get on long voyages.'

'Yes, well, I'm on a long voyage too.'

'When is this for?'

'As soon as you can. I'm on my way now to reconnoitre the place. I know where the field is, but it covers about four hectares.'

'The dovecot's been demolished?'

'Knocked down, immediately after she left.'

'Now, if you're trying to locate it in a field, here are some tips. If the soil occupied is not very deep down, that has an effect on the way the vegetation grows and what it looks like. Even two thousand years later.'

'Yes, you once told me that.'

'Under the humus, there will be the remains of stones from the perimeter walls of the dovecot, and the grass won't grow so well there. You might find brambles, nettles, thistles. Look for a circle of what most people call weeds.'

'Right.'

'And *inside* the circle, you'll have a lot of organic matter, rotten food, excrement. So there, the vegetation should be very rich, nice juicy grass, very green. Got the picture?'

'A circular patch of rich grass, surrounded by nettles.'

'That's it. Don't just look down vertically at the field, but crouch down and look along the surface horizontally. You'll find it. I'll come by road and meet you with my gear. So where is this?'

'About six kilometres outside Lourdes.'

'In the van, let's say it'll take about ten to twelve hours. I'll set out tomorrow.'

'Thanks, Mathias.'

'No problem, it really interests me.'

It was almost 8 p.m. when Adamsberg drew up outside the Pré d'Albret. He had tried to find a room for the night, but Lourdes and the surrounding areas were booked out. People apparently reserved months ahead. He called Mathias.

'I'm on the site. Can you bring some camping equipment? There aren't any rooms to let.'

'For how many people?'

'You, me and two of my men. Or rather you, me and two of my team, one of whom is a woman who's worth ten men. If they come.'

'All right, will organise. Can you arrange anti-contamination suits, gloves and all that stuff? Seen anything yet?'

'I've just got here and I'm hungry. What are you eating tonight?'

'Jugged hare and langoustines, I dare say. What about you?'

'Spinach boiled in Lourdes holy water, I expect.'

'Why are you on your own, without anyone helping?'

'Because I haven't told anyone. Yet.'

'Ah, you haven't changed, I see. Suits me.'

Adamsberg decided to divide the field into eight strips, by sight, and began staking it out, crouching down often, as Mathias had advised. The grass wasn't tall, since there had evidently been a flock of sheep there recently, leaving plenty of droppings. That reminded him of the Icelandic ewe that had trodden his mobile into its dung. He halted his search at 9 p.m. since the light was fading, and set off towards Lourdes, where he found a truckers' café, neglected by the pilgrims. He ate a solid meat stew with some sharpish Côtes du Rhône, still wondering whether his impulse that morning to come and search the remains of the recluse's cell was in any way justifiable. He called Veyrenc, so that at least one team member should be aware of his absence. When Louis answered, he could hear sounds of a restaurant in the background.

'You're in La Garbure.'

'Come and join me, I've only just started.'

'I'm a bit far away, Louis. I'm in a truckers' café just outside Lourdes.'

There was a silence. Estelle was bringing the lieutenant's food.

'You're on the trail of your own recluse?'

'I've been pacing out her meadow, four hectares of it.'

'So how do you hope to find where it was?'

'By looking. The grass won't have grown where there are buried stones from the building, but it will grow strongly on earth enriched by organic matter.'

'And how do you know that?'

'I have an archaeologist friend.'

'Because you're going to dig?'

'Yes.'

'What for?'

'Teeth.'

'Have you told anyone?'

'No.'

'Worried about Danglard?'

'No, I'm just worried that they're all exhausted. We've had a double failure so far. The first time was when the trail leading to the boys who were bitten collapsed. If it has collapsed. And then these last executions using spider venom, which we've been unable to prevent. So I'm not about to ask their permission to go digging around in the relics of a recluse that *nothing* connects with the murders, on the pretext that I saw her as a child. Nothing except two words: Bernadette and recluse.'

'All right. What did you mean by "if it has". About the boys who were bitten.'

'Danglard was capable of obstruction to protect his brother-in-law. What if someone else is doing the same thing? Are we really so sure none of those men went missing when Vessac was murdered?'

'Someone else? You mean our fellow officers?'

'I have to think of them.'

'Danglard had one of the suspects in his own family. That's unlikely to be the case for anyone else.'

'I don't mean a family motive, but an ethical one. People don't want to arrest the killer. I'm obliged to wonder about that, because I'm wondering myself what I'll do when I find her. *If* I find her. If this turns out to be another blind inlet, we'll have to go back to those boys who were bitten. Because Little Louis and the others will certainly have realised what's going on, right from the start. But none of them has ever contacted the police with a view to saving the last of the old gang.'

'Because they were protecting one of their group?'

'Or the woman who has been doing the killing. They might know who she is.'

'Well, no point putting them through it, they'll all keep their mouths shut. There's nobody else left to kill. The trail's gone cold.'

Adamsberg paused, then took out his notebook.

'What did you just say?'

'That the trail's gone cold.'

'No, before that. Something quite ordinary – can you say it again please?'

'They'll all keep their mouths shut. There's nobody else left to kill.'

'Thanks, Louis. Don't tell anyone about this for now. No point until I get permission from the local authority to do the dig. Which might not be straightforward because it's a protected place, undisturbed. I suppose no one wanted to buy the land at the time and make money out of holy terrain. And they haven't since either. They seem to let sheep graze there, but I guess sheep don't offend holy ground, being the Lord's flock or something like that.'

Adamsberg had no wish to drive to Pau to find the hotels there closed to him. He parked his hired car on the verge near the Pré d'Albret and tipped the seat back to form a makeshift bed. He took the snowstorm from his pocket and made it dance in the light of the waning moon. He repeated again the last sentence that had pierced one of his bubbles of gas: 'There's nobody else left to kill.'

As for the other little thing that was troubling him, he had worked that one out, and it was of no importance: the name of the psychiatrist, Martin-Robinson. Two birds in his name, but neither of them pigeons: a martin and a robin. Of no great significance.

He settled down as best he could in the car, feeling depressed and besieged by the bubbles bouncing around relentlessly, unprompted and unwanted, along various secret routes. Yes, there were those hairs from the box room. And yes, there were certainly signs that could link Louise to the murders. But for two days now, something had gone missing in his thought processes, undermining his conviction that he was on the right track. And that something was hiding in the bubbles, he felt sure. But that was as far as he got. When had his certainty started to wobble? After Retancourt had been to see Louise? No, before that. But Retancourt had written something in her text message that had prompted some disturbance. He reread her last message, which Veyrenc had forwarded to his phone. *Couldn't get in there, creaking boards.* He shrugged his shoulders. Yes, of course, creaking boards. One of Magellan's ships, the *Santiago* had come to grief in a storm. Its timbers and masts must have creaked mightily, before it was wrecked on a dark cliff in yet another blind inlet. But still, nothing to lose, he opened his notebook and wrote down: *creaking boards.*

There'd been something else as well: *too much chattering and cooing, not my scene.*

Cooing. That brought him back to pigeons. He copied that out too: *too much cooing.* Then he closed his notebook, feeling ill at ease.

XLII

AT 6 A.M., FEELING STIFF ALL OVER AFTER HIS NIGHT IN THE CAR, ADAMSBERG set off to find a stream which his map showed to be nearby. He passed a café where the iron blinds were just being lifted, but thought it better to wait until he had washed and put on some less crumpled clothes.

The water was icy cold and clear, but he liked clear water and didn't mind the cold. Once he was clean and properly dressed, his hair still wet, he ordered breakfast in the same village café, where he was the first customer. His dip in the stream had washed away his darker thoughts, but he still sensed, through the snowstorm in his pocket, that the bubbles of gas were waking up, stretching and getting ready to start their erratic waltz again. He wrote in his notebook: *Martin-Robinson: just two birds, not a problem*, and underlined it. Veyrenc sent him a text as he was on his way back to the car at seven thirty.

Need help? Can get to Lourdes by 14.22.

I'll pick you up. Charge your mobile battery. Nowhere to stay, sleeping in car, washing in stream, eating at truckers. OK?

Fine. Will bring some extras.

Bring two anti-contamination suits and the usual stuff.

And clothes?

Yes please.

*

At 8 a.m. on the dot, Adamsberg walked into the town hall of Lourdes, which was the local authority for the Pré d'Albret. Two hours later, he was no further forward. They understood his request and his problem, but it needed the personal approval of the mayor. And the mayor was not available. Monday morning, creaking machinery. The commissaire explained politely that he was quite willing not to disturb the mayor, but in that case, his staff should contact the prefect of Hautes-Pyrénées département, to explain that while the mayor of Lourdes couldn't be found, a senior policeman wished to lodge an urgent request in connection with an investigation relating to the deaths of ten people, so far. At that point, things moved quickly, and ten minutes later Adamsberg was walking out with the document in his hand.

He drank another strong coffee on the way back, bought some water and a sandwich, and started prospecting the field again, tackling the first quarter of the second strip. By 1 p.m. he had finished the third strip, but without finding any anomaly in the vegetation. Perhaps, since he had been capable of forgetting the word 'dovecot', he was also subconsciously failing to see the site, and looking at it without perceiving it. He sat in the shade to eat a lunch of which Froissy would have disapproved, especially the apple full of pesticides. His thoughts returned to Louise Chevrier. He called the lab and asked to speak to Louvain.

'This is Adamsberg. Look, I know you're overworked, Louvain.'

'Nice to hear from you. What are you on to?'

'Ten murders.'

'*Ten?*'

'The six most recent in the last month.'

'I've heard nothing about them. I'd have been told, wouldn't I?'

'You're being told now. It's those deaths by recluse spider venom.'

'The old geezers in the south? Are they *murders*?'

'Keep it to yourself.'

'Why?'

'Because so far, nobody's prepared to admit it's possible to kill someone with recluse venom. The only way I can prove they're murders is via DNA tests.'

'You mean the hierarchy doesn't know about your investigation?'

'Correct.'

'So the samples you sent, the hairs and the spoon, you got them illicitly?'

'Correct.'

'And you want me to do an illicit test? That I can't write into the report?'

'Remember a few years ago, you had a secret paternity test done on yourself in your lab, to investigate claims for child support from a mother who was threatening you with mega problems. As it turned out, you weren't the father. So, wasn't that an illicit test?'

'Yes, of course.'

'Well, just suppose my hierarchy is like an inflexible and recalcitrant mother, which it is. I have to take a short cut.'

'Well, OK, since it's for you, and because the mother is recalcitrant. We registered the samples this morning, but I'll take them off the register. I might be able to give you a partial result tonight. It would give you an inkling.'

As he drove towards the station in Lourdes, Adamsberg hoped that Louvain's willingness to process the samples quickly would dispel the worrying ballet of gas bubbles. Nothing of the kind happened though, and he had to try to expel them deliberately, as he saw the train enter the station. Veyrenc's arrival was welcome: the terrain was much more complex to search than he had foreseen, and being able to discuss things would help. To all appearances, Veyrenc's approach to a conversation sometimes seemed banal, negligent, even obtuse, but this had the subtle effect of uprooting Adamsberg's thoughts from where they had lodged. Either Veyrenc simply agreed, especially if he could see no way ahead, or he contradicted and argued, forcing Adamsberg to go back over simple elements, and make more of an effort to dislodge his subterranean thoughts. There was a Greek word for that approach.

The lieutenant got down from the train with two large suitcases and a bulky rucksack.

'Here we have the luxury bedroom and bathroom,' he said, pointing to the luggage. 'A de luxe bar and grill. I didn't bring any bedside tables. So what's new?'

'Tonight we might know more about the DNA.'

'How did you manage that?'

'Louvain's on to it. I just gave him a bit of nudge, that's all.'

'*Though crooked grows the tree / The fruit might luscious be.*'

'Louis, now that Danglard is off duty, don't start quoting stuff at me, I'm tired of it.'

'I made that up, not that Danglard would approve.'

'Danglard says your versification is faulty.'

'He's right.'

The two men loaded the extremely heavy bags into the car.

'Sure you didn't bring bedside tables?' asked Adamsberg. 'Or wardrobes?'

'Nope.'

'Have you had some lunch?'

'Just a sandwich in the train.'

'I did too, but under a tree. Tell me, what's it called, that way of talking that consists of making the other person feel really stupid, by asking questions to make him say what he thinks he doesn't know, but he really does.'

'Maieutics.'

'And who invented it?'

'Socrates.'

'So when you keep asking me questions one after another, that's what you're doing?'

'Wouldn't you like to know?' said Veyrenc with a smile.

They both attacked the field right away, one on the fourth strip, one on the fifth, once Adamsberg had explained to Veyrenc the method of looking along the grass horizontally. At 7 p.m. Adamsberg was starting the sixth strip and Veyrenc the seventh. An hour later, Veyrenc waved his hand. He'd found the circle. Mathias was right. A circular patch of very green and thick grass was surrounded by a mixture of thistles, nettles and barren grasses. The two men did high fives like idiots, since Veyrenc had never wanted to dig out the recluse's cell, and Adamsberg had been afraid of it. He stood beside the circle and looked around.

'Yes, this must be it, I recognise it now.' He raised his arm and pointed. 'My mother must have been standing there when I peeped in through the window, the *pigeonhole*. I'll alert Mathias and Retancourt.'

'What do you want us all to do?'

'Simple. You, Retancourt and I will do some digging to get the surface soil up. Then Mathias will search the soil underneath, for traces of occupation.'

'Can't say fairer than that. Is Retancourt really going to come?'

'No idea.'

'Well, you sort it out. I'm going to organise our dinner.'

'We're not going to the truckers' café?'

'No.'

Without being fussy about food, Veyrenc did not share Adamsberg's almost total indifference to it. He had come to the conclusion that everyday life was quite bad enough to get through as it was, without having to forgo the transitory well-being brought by a good meal. Adamsberg sent a text to Mathias.

Found the place. 5.2 km out of Lourdes on C14, goes by Chemin Henri

IV towards Pau. Field's name Pré Jeanne d'Albret, 4 hectares, should be on your map. Look for my car, bright blue.

The reply was immediate.

Have loaded gear. Leaving now, taking 5h rest overnight, with you c11 tomorrow.

One man with me already. Woman arriving tomorrow 14.38.

The one worth 10?

Polyvalent goddess of team. Tree of forest. Shiva 18 arms.

8 arms you mean. Good-looker?

See what you think. Bark of magic trees an obstacle sometimes.

Adamsberg texted Retancourt next, to save his battery.

Archaeological dig. Am here with Veyrenc. Can you lend us a hand?

Lending a hand, he thought, was the kind of invitation to tempt Retancourt's surplus energy, always needing an outlet. But she was by no means simple-minded and he had to get past the bark first.

What kind of dig?

DNA of potential killer.

Louise? What about spoon I pinched?

I know.

A laconic reply, which to the best-informed members of the squad really meant Adamsberg's habitual 'I don't know'.

Dig for what then?

He couldn't avoid the question now.

Ancient recluse cell. Woman lived here for 5 years after being locked up and raped.

When?

When I was a kid.

That's why you asked Danglard to talk about women recluses?

Partly.

But why would recluse you saw as a child be ours?

You know many recluse cells used in our lifetime?

Know zilch about them.

Bernadette Seguin or sister Annette, also named Louise, could have been in one. Only 3 of us here + mass of earth to shift.

Train time?

It wasn't the weak argument about the Seguin sisters that had tipped the balance for Retancourt, Adamsberg realised. But the mass of earth to shift with only three men.

09.48 arrives Lourdes 14.38. You can meet my pal Mathias prehistoric expert.

Good-looking while we're at it?

Yes. Man of few words. Outer bark to get past.

His satisfaction at discovering the dovecot ('dovecot, dovecot', he said to himself several times) had calmed down the bubbles of gas. Adamsberg went off to find some wood for a fire. Then he built his fireplace, surrounded by stones, a good distance from the dovecot. You had to give time for the embers to form. Because he was pretty sure Veyrenc wouldn't be arriving with sandwiches, but with something to grill.

As he watched the fire take, he opened his notebook. The relief had been only short-lived. He reread in order the notes he had made in the hope that one of the bubbles would burst. Like when you revise something for an exam, but don't take in a single word.

Dovecot: couldn't find the word.

Evasion: anguish at someone being tethered (pigeon feet tied) or being pigeon myself (doctor).

There's nobody else left to kill (Veyrenc).

Creaking boards (Retancourt).

Too much chattering and cooing (Retancourt).

Martin-Robinson: just two birds, not a problem, resolved.

In fact, this list was more like an esoteric incantation, a mantra, than a search for meaning. Maybe his bubbles were simply random particles looking for mystic wisdom, nothing to do with a pragmatic solution to a police investigation. Maybe they were little sparks of madness. Maybe they didn't give a damn about his work. Or any work come to that. They just enjoyed frolicking and dancing, and like a schoolboy who's daydreaming instead of studying, they were pretending, so as to fool anyone spying on them. And the spy was himself in this case, thinking the bubbles were working when they were really bunking off.

The embers were glowing by the time Veyrenc came back from his shopping trip and set about preparing a meal.

'Nice fire,' he approved. 'What matters with an open fire is balance, makes it more efficient.'

He then set up a big barbecue on the embers, laid out some chops and sausages, and lit a small camping stove to heat up some tinned haricot beans.

'Sorry about the veg,' he said. 'But I wasn't going to shell peas and chop up bacon.'

'It's perfect, Louis.'

'And I didn't bring proper wine glasses either with stems. No point spilling our wine on the grass.'

Apart from the worry about his list of esoteric mantras, and the bubbles that had gone off playing truant, Adamsberg felt blissfully content to smell the meat grilling and to look around the encampment. He let Veyrenc set out the plates and cutlery, just as Froissy would have, and bring out of his backpack two tumblers which he placed firmly down on the grass, before uncorking a bottle of Madiran.

'To the almost-excavated cell,' he said, filling the glasses.

Veyrenc produced salt and pepper and served out the meat and beans. The two men ate their meal in silence for a while.

'To the almost excavated cell,' Adamsberg repeated. 'Because you believe in it?'

'Possibly.'

'You're being Socratic.'

'The trick is you can never know when I'm doing it or not.'

Adamsberg's mobile buzzed in the grass. A text. It was nine thirty. He leaned over in the darkness to pick it up.

'You say we're all neurotic, but our mobile phones certainly are.'

He picked up the phone and lifted a finger.

'It's Louvain,' he said with sudden excitement. 'The DNA result.'

He looked at the phone for a moment before pressing the button. Read it in silence, then passed it to Veyrenc.

Partial analysis of representative but fragmentary samples of hair and spoon. No correspondence. Tomorrow, with more tests, we might find some link, cousin to cousin to cousin. Any use or not?

As I expected, replied Adamsberg, typing in the failing light. *But thanks.*

He passed the phone to Veyrenc. The pale light from its little screen illuminated his colleague's face, which was looking more granite-like than ever.

Adamsberg took out his notebook and by the light of the fire which he had rekindled, wrote down: *After the negative DNA result I said to Louvain 'As I expected'. No idea why.*

Veyrenc got up without speaking, collected the plates, cutlery and pan, which he then stacked with exaggerated care.

'We can wash it all in the stream in the morning,' he said in a studiedly neutral voice.

'Yeah, fine, we don't want to do that in the dark,' replied Adamsberg in the same distant tone.

'I brought some washing-up liquid. Ecological.'

'Better for the stream.'

'Yes, good for the stream.'

'We can go after our morning coffee, and clear everything in one go.'

'Yes, better than two trips.'

Then Veyrenc sat down cross-legged and the two men remained silent.

'Who's going to start?' asked Veyrenc.

'Me,' said Adamsberg. 'It was my idea and I was wrong. To the second blind inlet,' he said, raising his glass.

'Wait a moment, Jean-Baptiste. There's still the possibility Louise did do the shooting, but deposited someone else's hair.'

'No, you're right. The analysis doesn't quite rule her out.'

Adamsberg sprawled on one elbow to feel around in the grass. The moon, veiled by cloud that night, was no help. He found his jacket and brought out another two crumpled cigarettes, which he repaired with his fingers. He gave one to Veyrenc and lit his own with a twig from the fire.

'But why would she pick hair that looked so like her own?'

'Bad question. Lots of women her age dye their hair.'

'But why did I reply to Louvain that it was as I expected?'

'Because you did expect it.'

'It was sort of coming apart.'

'And I'll ask you the same question I asked when we were in the Hotel du Taureau. When did it start, your doubt?'

'Two days ago?'

'And why?'

'I don't know. It's these bubbles of gas dancing inside my head. They tell each other stuff, they whisper. And I can't get any sense out of them.'

'Bubbles of gas?'

'Proto-thoughts, if you prefer. Nonsense. I think of them as bubbles of gas. Whether they're at play or at work, I don't know. Do you want me to read out the words that seem to trigger or disturb them? Not that they make anything clearer to me.'

He did not wait for Veyrenc's approval to open his notebook.

Dovecot: couldn't find the word.
Evasion: anguish at someone being tethered (pigeon feet tied) or being pigeon myself (doctor).

There's nobody else left to kill (Veyrenc).
Creaking boards (Retancourt).
Too much chattering and cooing (Retancourt).
Martin-Robinson: just two birds, not a problem, resolved.

Veyrenc nodded and raised a hand. Adamsberg could see the hand moving by the light from the tip of his cigarette.

'When did you write "*Martin-Robinson: just two birds, not a problem, resolved*"?'

'This morning.'

'Why, if it was resolved?'

Adamsberg shrugged.

'Because one of the bubbles fussed about it, that's all.'

'Well, I'd say you wrote it because the matter *wasn't* sorted.'

'Yes it is.'

'I don't think so. Was it the doctor himself that got the bubbles bothered?'

'No, it's just his name, that's all.'

'A lot of *birds* in there as well as pigeons: a martin, a robin . . .'

'Yes, cooing as well. Do you believe his second theory?'

'About there being a traitor?'

'Suppose,' Adamsberg began, reluctantly, as if about to pronounce a sentence he should not be saying, 'just suppose, that someone is fooling us. With those hairs. And when I say "suppose", that isn't right, actually I feel certain. It was a decoy. I said we were lucky to have found four. I said we were rich. Too rich of course.'

'Four isn't just too many, it's improbable. Our killer isn't a beginner. He or she would have taken the elementary precaution of wearing a cap or a hood. I say he or she, because we can't rule out it being a man now.'

'But who, Louis, could have been able to place those hairs in the box room in Torrailles's house?'

'Only one person, the killer.'

'No, two: the killer or Retancourt. I wondered how, being in charge of guarding Torrailles and Lambertin, she hadn't imagined the attack might come from inside the house. When the whole of the outside was being patrolled by three cops. She must have thought of it.'

'Or not. You hadn't thought of it yourself. Nor had I. Or anyone else.'

Veyrenc threw his cigarette stub into the fire.

'Look,' he said, 'Retancourt's far more subtle than that. She'd never have left *four* hairs.'

'Just the one,' said Adamsberg, looking up again.

The lieutenant picked up the bottle for their last glasses of the evening.

'At the stage we've reached . . .' he said.

'At the stage we've reached,' said Adamsberg, pointing in the dark towards the site of the dovecot, 'the answer's got to be there. In the territory of the recluse. Where we'll find her teeth.'

'But a *woman*'s teeth,' said Louis with a slight demur.

'I know.'

'Enzo. He had the list.'

'So did Cauvert. I'm not forgetting him, Louis.'

Veyrenc moved off to distribute cushions and blankets in the car. It would be a bit of a tight squeeze. But when you've known each other as children, anything goes.

Adamsberg covered the fire, scattering ash over the embers. He opened his notebook one last time, by the light of his mobile.

After '*Martin-Robinson: just two birds, not a problem, resolved*', he wrote: '*Or not.*'

XLIII

ADAMSBERG AND VEYRENC HELPED MATHIAS, WHO ARRIVED AT THE Pré d'Albret shortly before 11 a.m., to unload his materials. It was the first time Veyrenc had met the archaeologist, and found himself faced with a man of few words, well-built and with long, thick blond hair. He wore sandals on his bare feet, and his canvas trousers were kept up with a length of rope.

With the rapidity born of long practice, Mathias pumped up four inflatable tents in a ring around the now cool fireplace and installed mattresses and camping lamps. He set up a field latrine behind a large tree, then, essentials completed, went to inspect the circle and returned looking pleased.

'Will this do?' asked Adamsberg.

'Yes, that's it all right. I don't think the occupied area is very deep down. Fifteen to twenty centimetres. So we should use pickaxes but not the point, just the blade.'

'Right away?'

'Right away.'

'We've saved you some hot coffee.'

'Later.'

Since the circle was too small for two people to attack it with picks, the three men took turns for the first hour, one digging while the other two shovelled bucketloads of earth and emptied them out. Mathias was more efficient at digging than either Adamsberg or Veyrenc, so they modified the rota.

'Here!' said Mathias suddenly, kneeling down and with his trowel clearing a patch of twenty square centimetres of dark brown, packed earth, which contrasted slightly with the surrounding humus. 'This is the level of occupation. Seventeen centimetres down.'

'How can you tell? asked Adamsberg.

Mathias looked at him in puzzlement.

'Can't you see the change? We've reached a different layer.'

'No.'

'Never mind. This was where she walked.'

The three men ate a hasty lunch, Mathias because he was in a hurry to get back to the site, Adamsberg because he had to go and pick up Retancourt from Lourdes.

When they returned, the prehistorian was still digging, but now taking much more care, while Veyrenc emptied out the soil, both of them shirtless and sweating under the hot June sunshine.

The sight of Retancourt made Mathias stop in mid-swing, and he let the pickaxe fall to the ground. The lieutenant, whom Adamsberg had described as the magic tree in the forest, was as tall as himself, Mathias noted. And this woman, who would have looked fully armed even if naked, had a very interesting face with finely drawn features. But despite her faultless lips, straight nose and tender blue eyes, he could not have said whether she was pretty or attractive. He hesitated, suspecting she could probably change her appearance at will, veering from harmonious to off-putting whenever she wanted to. And what about her power? Was it simply muscular or psychological? Retancourt defied description and analysis.

He climbed out of the pit to shake her hand, wiping the earth off on his trousers first, and looked her in the eye.

'Mathias Delamarre,' he introduced himself.

'Violette Retancourt. Don't stop on my account, I'll watch what you do and pick it up. The commissaire told me you'd reached the level of occupation.'

'Here it is,' said Mathias, pointing to a cleared patch which now measured almost a square metre.

Adamsberg offered Retancourt bread, fruit and coffee, but she refused, putting down her bag, taking off her jacket, and at once taking her place in the chain emptying out earth. Her arrival speeded up progress, so by seven in the evening Mathias had been able to clear the entire earthen floor, inside the circle of stones remaining from the ancient foundations of the dovecot.

'This is where she lived,' said Mathias, standing up – after several hours without speaking at all – as if inviting visitors to inspect a property, while he leaned on his pick handle. 'There,' he said, pointing to some splinters of wood, 'was a plank she must have sat on to keep off the cold and damp. She must have eaten here. There are fragments from the plate she used. In this area here, where it's less brown, without organic matter, will be where she slept. There are traces of two post sockets. So she had one advantage, and one only, over the recluses of the Middle Ages, she must have had a hammock, so she could sleep in the dry. Here we have a pile of food remains. You can see some fragments of chops, chicken wings, cheap cuts people must have given her. And here, maybe it was Christmas, is an oyster shell. She was very organised and careful, as far as possible in the circumstances, she didn't let herself go. She'd made a walkway of thirty centimetres wide – can you see it? – from the hammock to the window where people put their offerings. And she didn't drop anything along that path in five years.'

'How do you know the window was on this side?' asked Retancourt.

'That path and this stone. She would have stood on it to receive the food. So with some old photographs of the dovecot, one could estimate her height, Adamsberg. And here,' he said, 'this zone with lighter-coloured earth, already becoming rather powdery in bits, was her privy.'

'You'd never guess,' said Retancourt.

'Surprising, isn't it? You might think it would be a heavier kind of loam. But no, it gets to be light and crumbly, it's quite nice to handle. Look.'

Mathias scooped up some finely powdered earth and put it in Retancourt's outstretched palm. Adamsberg gave a slight start as he watched the archaeologist concentrating so hard that he didn't seem to realise he was giving a woman a handful of shit. Retancourt crumbled the sediment in her fingers, impressed by the way Mathias had brought the living habits of the recluse to life: following in her footsteps, imagining her activity in this reduced space, even her character – clean, organised, determined – and her efforts not to be wading through her own rubbish, to 'keep house'.

'As for teeth,' he said, turning to Adamsberg, 'there are certainly some there. I can see some cusps – the tips of molars,' he explained.

Mathias spent the next two hours erecting his hoist, a triangular apparatus for setting up a sieve.

'We don't have water,' he said, 'so we'll have to fetch some in buckets from the stream.'

That night, from his tent, Adamsberg could hear Mathias and Retancourt chatting round the fire. Retancourt *chatting*.

A text from Froissy woke him at two o'clock. Both Torrailles and Lambertin had died that day, a few hours apart. Full house.

XLIV

UNDER THE ADMIRING GAZE OF RETANCOURT, WHO WAS ABSORBING these skills that she did not possess, Mathias, wearing an anti-contamination suit, spent the second day of the dig silently excavating the occupied surface of the cell, and sifting out all the material. He placed in containers the various objects he had collected: fragments of china from a single plate and a water jug; some metal objects – knife, fork, spoon, a small mattock and a crucifix – all encased in rust; scraps of fabric from a blanket and a hammock, some shreds of leather (from a Bible); and finally a few animal bones, evidence of the rare gifts of meat, as well as some fish bones, eggshells and oyster shells (four of them or one for each Christmas spent there). The rest of the food received – gruel, soup, bread – had disappeared. No seeds from fruit, except for seven cherry stones. No bucket for a toilet. No comb, no mirror, no scissors. People might be pious and revere this holy woman, but they seemed to have been grudging with their offerings. Mathias often shook his head, disillusioned. When he dug out the latrine, a metre deep – she must have spent a long time digging it herself with the little mattock she'd received as a charitable gift – he nevertheless found five layers of straw, which meant she had been able to cover it over once a year. But there had been no straw elsewhere on the ground, which would have made the cell healthier.

'All the same,' he said, having dug out a total of fifty-eight plastic roses, '*someone* must have brought her a rose every month, and she stacked them against the wall. All the same,' he repeated. 'Out of a hundred men just one who thinks differently. Here, for you,' he said, passing a bag to Adamsberg. 'Six incisors, three canines, twelve premolars and molars. She'd lost twenty-one of her teeth.'

Adamsberg went closer, feeling suddenly hesitant. The identity of the recluse was within reach. He took the bag, carefully, almost intimidated, put it away, then took his place without speaking alongside Retancourt, as they continued to fetch water non-stop, while Veyrenc sieved the sediment. Mathias pointed out the objects to pick up, the bones of mice, rats, a weasel, and countless scraps of chitin, the remnants of beetles and spiders. They also found long fragments of curved and broken fingernails, and quantities of hairs, blonde and grey, about four handfuls.

Mathias inspected many of them under a magnifying glass.

'The roots have gone, Adamsberg, you won't get any DNA out of them. She came in here with blonde hair and went out grey. God Almighty, whatever happened to this woman?'

'If she was Bernadette, the older sister –'

'Bernadette, like St Bernadette?' Mathias interrupted. 'That's why she came to Lourdes?'

'Possibly. She was locked up until she was twenty-one by her father, raped from the age of five, ill-treated, badly fed, not cared for.'

'One tooth lost for every year of suffering. And plenty of hair.'

'If it was the younger sister, Annette, she was shut up until she was nineteen, and she was hired out to a gang of ten young boys who raped her between the ages of seven and nineteen. Whichever one of them it was, she couldn't return to normal life. She did the only thing she'd learned to do, shut herself up in a cell.'

Mathias twisted his trowel in his hands.

'So who got her out of it?'

'An order by the prefect of this département.'

'No, I mean from her father's house.'

'Her older brother. At the age of twenty-three, he cut his father's head off.'

'And what do you suspect this woman has done?'

'Murdered the ten rapists.'

'So what are you going to do now?'

By nine o'clock that evening, they had completed the work, after thirteen hours of solid effort. Only Retancourt was still busy, washing tools, dismantling the hoist, loading containers into the van. Mathias watched her, wondering if the power of the tree might be able to take a break.

'Don't put the shovels in the van, Violette,' he said. 'We'll fill in the dig tomorrow.'

'No, I thought of that.'

'I'll keep the plate,' said Adamsberg. 'Can you put the pieces on one side for me please, lieutenant?'

'You want to stick it together?'

'Yes, I think so.'

'When we seal it all up, we'll put the roses back in, shall we?' she asked.

Adamsberg nodded and went off to help Veyrenc prepare their supper: Louis had decided this should be a really satisfying one.

'What do you think of Mathias?' Adamsberg asked him.

'Talented, subtle, a bit farouche. But I think your prehistoric man appreciates Retancourt.'

'What's more worrying, I think it's mutual.'

'Why is that worrying? For her?'

'Because someone who becomes human loses their divine faculties.'

As they ate their roast beef, potatoes baked in the ashes, and cheese, washed down with Madiran, Mathias nodded his thanks to Veyrenc several times. Adamsberg leaned on his elbows in the grass. Why was it that Veyrenc thought that the Dr Martin-Robinson bubble had not been resolved? He had been so pleased to cross it off the list. He thought about martins and robins. Small birds, nothing to do with the investigation. And the bubbles didn't react when he thought about either of them, although the word 'bird' itself did seem to make the bubbles vibrate. Well, there were of course a lot of pigeons in there too.

He sat up and wrote 'Bird' in his notebook.

'What are you writing?' asked Veyrenc.

'Bird.'

'As you wish.'

Lying in his tent in the dark, his back stiff from lugging pails of water, Adamsberg thought about pitching a tent like this in his small garden, if Lucio would let him. He liked it here, it was a bit like time out travelling by train, noticing all the sounds of nature clearly, some distant frogs, the whoosh of bats flying low, the snuffling of a hedgehog outside his tent, and the sound of a male wood-pigeon which instead of going to sleep like all the daytime birds, went on making its mating call. It was June and he hadn't found a mate. Adamsberg wished him luck, sincerely. There were some human noises too. The rasping sound of a tent being unzipped, a few metres to his left, footsteps in the grass, then a second zip being opened on the right. The tents of Retancourt and Mathias. Good Lord. Were they going to go on chatting, like the night before, sitting cross-legged in the tent by the light of a lantern? Or something else? Adamsberg had the uneasy feeling that his property was being stolen . . . He had by some unspoken Freudian slip allowed himself to think his property had been violated. Violate, Violette . . . He opened his own tent and peered out into the night. Yes, there was a lamp lit to his right. He lay down again and forced himself to think of something else. Mission accomplished, he had found the teeth of the recluse.

So what are you going to do now?

XLV

THE MORNING WAS SPENT FILLING IN THE EXCAVATION — WITH THE fifty-eight roses buried inside – and striking camp. Adamsberg packed up the teeth and the fragments of the china plate. Mathias put the rest of the equipment in the van.

He left at two o'clock, after shaking hands with the two men and kissing Retancourt under Adamsberg's watchful eye. He had been wrong to describe his lieutenant as being 'worth ten men'. She was worth one woman, and she was a woman. And he couldn't help his feelings cooling towards her, as if she had in some obscure way betrayed him.

Retancourt decided to drive the hired car with the baggage all the way back to Paris, which would take twice as long as the train, and dropped Veyrenc and Adamsberg off at the station.

'She's running away,' said Adamsberg.

'You were sulking, so she's running away,' said Veyrenc.

'I was not sulking.'

'Yes you were.'

'Did you hear, last night? The tent zips.'

'Yes.'

'Well?'

'Well, what?'

'Oh, all right,' said Adamsberg, knowing that in this matter Veyrenc was right and he was wrong.

At nine in the evening, back in Paris, he had the new samples sent to the lab with a note for Louvain. This time, the DNA of the teeth would surely correspond to Louise, contrary to the false trail of the four hairs from Lédignan. Veyrenc had put it simply, and convincingly. Louise might well have put the hairs there. The crumbling of his own certainty, caused by the fruitless tumult of his thoughts, was based on nothing solid.

He did not need to open the fridge or the cupboard to know that there was nothing to eat in his house. He set out without any destination in mind, his mood gloomy and his body tired. After a quarter of an hour of aimless walking, he headed back to his former neighbourhood and an Irish bar he used to go to, where the loud voices of the customers didn't bother him since they were speaking English. In this incomprehensible hubbub, he could try to concentrate better than if he were alone. Back there, he sometimes managed it by small steps, feeling his way.

He opened his notebook as he walked through the night, and looked at the crazy sequences of words, feeling discouraged, then clapped it shut again. How had he even dared read them out to Veyrenc? Louis had been Socratically annoying, by remarking that he had not crossed out the note about Martin-Robinson. And he had added that there were 'a lot of birds in there'. Especially pigeons. Well, of course there were, but these feathered creatures could be chucked out with everything else. The bubbles of gas, the martins, robins, pigeons and creaky sounds could just be dispensed with, they were unwanted. His slight and enigmatic bitterness towards Retancourt was actually stopping him thinking about the bubbles. The previous evening was blocking his thoughts, that instant when the sound of the tent zip had felt like an assault. He kept running the nocturnal sounds on a loop through his head, the bats, the hedgehog, the bird desperately calling its companion to which he'd wished good luck.

Then Adamsberg stopped short in mid-pavement, his notebook in hand, and stood still. This time he must not move an inch. A snowflake, a bubble, a proto-thought was stirring somewhere. He recognised the slight tickle as it made its way up, knowing he should not make any movement which might scare it off, if he wanted to see it clearly.

Sometimes he didn't have to wait long. This time, it seemed an eternity. And it was. A heavy bubble, a clumsy one perhaps, finding it hard to manoeuvre, or find the strength to rise to the surface. Passersby in the street avoided this man standing there, or bumped into him, by mistake, but no matter. It was imperative not to take any notice of them, not to move or say a word. He stood as if transfixed.

Suddenly, the bubble reached the surface explosively, making him drop his notebook. He picked it up, found a pen and wrote in shaky handwriting:

The male bird in the night.

Then he reread the list.

Out of breath now, more than after ferrying hundreds of bucketfuls of water, he leaned against a tree and called Veyrenc.

'Where are you?' he asked him.

'Have you been running?'

'No, no. Where the hell are you? At La Garbure?'

'No, at home.'

'Get over here, Louis. I'm on the corner of the rue Saint-Antoine and the rue du Petit Musc. There's a café here. Get a move on.'

'No, you come over to my place. Earth, buckets, I'm dropping off to sleep.'

'Louis, I can't move.'

'Have you hurt yourself?'

'Something like that. Listen, I'm reading the name of the café, Le Petit Musc. Jump in a taxi and get here fast, Louis.'

'Should I bring a gun?'

'No, just your brain. Run.'

Veyrenc never neglected this type of appeal from Adamsberg. Voice, tone, rhythm of speaking, all were different. Wide awake now, he managed, by running as requested, to catch the first passing taxi.

Even from a distance, from the door of the café, he could see the brilliance of Adamsberg's eyes, which seemed to concentrate all the surrounding light, instead of diluting it as usual. He was sitting in front of a sandwich and a coffee, but neither eating nor moving. His notebook lay on the table, with his hands flat down either side of it.

'You need to follow me carefully,' said Adamsberg, before Veyrenc had even sat down. 'Follow me carefully, because this will come out jumbled. You'll be able to sort it out. Last night, before we heard the tent zip open, I was lying in my tent, listening to the sounds of the night. Are you with me?'

'So far, yes. Mind if I order a coffee?'

'Go ahead. There were frogs croaking, the wind in the grass, the flutter of bats swooping low, a hedgehog, and a wood-pigeon *cooing* all the time, trying to attract a mate.'

'Right.'

'And none of that reminds you of anything?'

'Just one thing. The wood-pigeon. Which is a species of pigeon.'

'And that explains why the bubbles got excited about the pigeon. Like you said, we've mentioned pigeons quite a lot.'

Adamsberg pulled the notebook towards him and read phrases out:

' "*Dovecot: couldn't find the word / pigeon feet tied / being pigeon myself / too much chattering and cooing*." But it's not just pigeon I should have written down, Louis, but "*wood-pigeon*".'

'It's just another kind of pigeon, different from the town ones.'

'But then what? Shit, Louis, where does that take us?' said

Adamsberg, shaking his notebook. 'What does the *wood*-pigeon connect to? It was you that told me.'

'Me?'

'Yes, you did. Look, I had to write it down. "*Martin-Robinson: just two birds, not a problem, resolved. Or not.*"'

'What I said was that if that thought had really been dealt with, you wouldn't have read it out to me.'

'And why *wasn't* it dealt with?'

Adamsberg broke off to drink some coffee.

'I'm tired,' he said.

'You too? The buckets, eh?'

'No, not the buckets. Now don't say anything, or you'll confuse me. So what's the connection between Dr Martin-Robinson and a wood-pigeon?'

'Easy, you've got two names of birds in there, martin and robin.'

'Yes, but as well, they're *double-barrelled* names, Louis. Double! See now?'

'No.'

'Then there were the two things Retancourt said: "*too much chattering and cooing*" was one of them. Pigeons again, they coo, don't they?'

'Yeah, you read that one out too.'

'And the other thing's connected, too. Everything's connected, Louis. My bubbles are dancing round, holding hands, and I can't ignore them. The other thing she said was "*creaking boards*". Now what links those two sentences?'

'Look, I'm sorry,' said Veyrenc, by now worried about the apparent confusion of Adamsberg's thoughts, 'but I'm going to need a glass of Armagnac.'

'All right, get me a glass too.'

'Are you sure?' asked Veyrenc, a little anxious about his boss's apparent state of mind.

'Yes.'

'A glass of what?'

'Anything. See what links them? It's the *place*. The place it happened, the place where the *cooing* went on, the place where everything was *creaking*. Creaky, not right, doesn't hold water.'

'Well, Retancourt was talking about Louise's house.'

'Yes indeed, Socrates. See, where we're going now, if you connect it to the *wood-pigeon*, and the *double-barrelled* surnames.'

The waiter put their glasses on the table and Veyrenc drank off half of his at once.

'To be quite honest, no,' he said.

'Yes. It's linked to the names in that house. Their meaning. Remember we went astray, because Louise had the surname Chevrier, and it tied up so neatly with that story, *La Chèvre de Monsieur Seguin*, Monsieur Seguin's little goat?'

'What's to say it's a mistake? We haven't got the DNA from the teeth yet. For crying out loud, Jean-Baptiste, it was *you* that insisted we dig to find them.'

'There's another name that's creaking and flying around in that house and it's *Irène's*. She's got a double-barrelled name too, Louis, like Dr Martin-Robinson. She doesn't use it much but it's Irène Royer-Colombe.'

Adamsberg stopped, picked up his glass but did not drink from it.

'So now you know everything.'

'No, I don't. Irène's got a double-barrelled name, lots of people do.'

'Good grief, have you forgotten that the Seguin sisters will certainly have had permission to change their names? And that when you do that, you are almost bound to keep some link with your previous life.'

'So why would a Seguin girl choose the name Royer-Colombe?'

'Royer, forget it, means nothing. But *Colombe*. Because that's where she had escaped from. You told me yourself, remember, when I couldn't recall the word for dovecot, you told me other names. One was *columbarium*, because you said *columba*, Latin, *colombe* in French, was another word for pigeon. She's given herself the name *Colombe*. And another word you gave me was *pigeon loft*. So now. What's the definition of a pigeon *loft*, not a dovecot, look it up on the internet.'

Veyrenc took out his phone and after a minute said : 'A little space under the eaves, to keep pigeons in. OK, it's like an attic. The pigeon loft where she was sequestered.'

'Then there's the *actual* dovecot, where she shut herself up.'

'Yeah, right.'

'And now think about her first name, Irène. Remind you of anything?'

'Yes, there's a St Irénée, second century, first real theologian.'

'Try for something more simple and onomatopoeic.'

'Don't see.'

'Wait.'

Adamsberg pulled out his phone, faster than usual, and chose a name. He put it on speaker and waited. The ringtone was repeated, no answer.

'I'll start again, he's a heavy sleeper.'

'Who are you calling? Don't you know the time? Nearly midnight.'

'Never mind. Who'm I calling? Danglard, that's who.'

This time the commandant answered in a sleepy voice.

'Danglard, did I wake you?

'Yes.'

'Tell me, Danglard, what are the old words for spider. We say *araignée* today, but before that?'

'Pardon?'

'What was the word for *araignée* in the olden days?'

'Just a sec, commissaire, let me sit down. Wait a minute. Well, it all started with the young Greek woman, Arachne, who was a gifted spinner. Athene turned her into a spider out of revenge. The Greek word for spider is *arachne*. She'd challenged Zeus's daughter to a competition –'

'No, no, just the names please,' Adamsberg interrupted.

'All right. In old French, we get various versions, *aragne, araigne* and *yraigne*, from the twelfth century or thereabouts. That's all I can think of.'

'How do you spell the last one, *yraigne*?'

'Y-r-a-i-g-n-e.'

'Did it go on being used?'

'Yes, you get variants of it right down the ages, in the seventeenth century for instance, you find Aragne in the fables of La Fontaine.'

'Fables for children?'

'Well, the one I'm thinking of isn't much read today. But recently, I've seen people use Yraigne as a first name on social media. The La Fontaine verse goes like this: *La pauvre Aragne n'ayant plus / Que la tête et les pieds, artisans superflus.* And poor Arachne was bereft / Head and legs were all she had left.'

'Many thanks, Danglard, go back to sleep. *Yraigne,* Veyrenc, say it out loud,' repeated Adamsberg, stressing the word. 'And it's almost the same as *Irène.* The spider. The ones she lived with in the attic – the *pigeon loft* – the spiders that the stink bugs used to torment boys, the spiders that kept her company in her cell, the ones she ended up identifying with, the recluse spider. Irène-Yraigne Colombe-Pigeon, the sequestered child of Nîmes, the recluse of the Pré d'Albret, the older sister, Bernadette Seguin.'

'The *older* one. But she wasn't raped by the ten bullies.'

'She wasn't doing it for herself, she killed them to free her sister.'

Relieved and now out of breath, Adamsberg leaned back. Veyrenc nodded his head three times.

'Right,' the commissaire continued, 'in the list of bubbles, there was something *you* said as well: "There's nobody else left to kill." Well, you know my bubbles crash into each other, and that one met another, same kind, something Retancourt said first: that all ten men had been murdered and we hadn't been able to stop it, and she was angry about that.'

'Yes, I remember.'

'But it bumped into something *Irène* said very soon afterwards, the morning when we were searching Torrailles's house after the double attack. I called her to ask if Louise had been out that night. Remember, I told you my certainty was wobbling a bit, something wasn't right? That's what it was, Louis. Irène already *knew* about the two last murders. Of course, because she'd committed them herself. She told me the news was out on social media, which was true. And like Retancourt, she also added right away that it was infuriating that the killer had "got them all" and that the police still hadn't got anywhere. And I didn't react. I was too used to her chatter, to her "cooing", too trusting. If anyone was making a "pigeon" out of me in that sense, it was her, and brilliantly so. One has to admire her.'

'You didn't react to what?'

'You're tired, Louis, but mainly you still trust her too, you *like* her, same as me. But tell me this. How could Irène ever have known that he'd "got them all"? I never told her that the Recluse Gang consisted of precisely nine members plus Claude Landrieu? Ten names to wipe out. And the killer'd got them *all*. How did she know that once Torrailles and Lambertin went, there'd be *nobody else left to kill*? She should have said "another two", not "he's got them all". And I didn't react.'

'Well, you did in a way. You lost faith in the idea that Louise was guilty.'

'Yes, just at that point, without understanding why. But it was only tonight, after the bubble – a very big bubble, Louis – exploded and told me to think about Irène, that I heard again in my ear that sentence from the phone call when I was sitting on the ground in the courtyard in Lédignan. "Got them all." She'd finished the job. That alone is proof of her guilt. Her only mistake.'

'That's not like her. To make a mistake.'

'But she must have totally identified with her role in relation to me, and she handled it in a masterly way from the start. She was to be one of my "helpers", apparently spontaneous, efficient and looking out for clues, taking care even to seem a little stupid or naive at times. That was remarkable, Louis, the impersonation, a work of art. And that morning, she had entered entirely into the role of being that character, so she expressed the same anger that Retancourt felt. She forgot for a moment to be Irène. And she dropped a stitch.'

'No. I can't think a woman like her would really have done it by accident. And why did she leave those hairs there? Why not some real hairs belonging to Louise, which would have been very easy?'

'Because her moral code is stainless steel. She would never have wanted another person actually to be charged with the murders.'

'So why the hairs then, if they were just like Louise's? For a joke?'

'To discourage me. She'd picked up that I suspected Louise. And with those hairs, I was going to go charging off in that direction. Leading to another dead end.'

'No. Because why did she take the trouble to connect with you in the first place? Why not stay unknown, in the shadows? There was no risk.'

'Why, why, you're being Socrates again!'

'I want to understand her. So answer my question, why did she attach herself to you?'

'She had no choice. We met at the Natural History Museum, remember. She found out that I was actually investigating the deaths by spider venom. That someone, and worst of all, a cop, was doubtful about the first deaths. That was a serious blow. She adapted immediately, and made friends with me so that she could follow the course of the investigation. And influence it or send it into a blind alley, like with those hairs in the box room.'

'But why had she come to the Natural History Museum?'

'Along with that slip-up over the phone, I think that was her only real mistake. She was too zealous. She wanted to ask a specialist if there was any chance people might actually suspect these deaths were murders. She would have been able to go away feeling reassured. Except that while she was there, she bumped into a cop.'

'But it was thanks to her, and what she told us about the conversation in the café between Claveyrolle and Barral, that we followed the lead to La Miséricorde.'

'She's very subtle. She sensed I wasn't going to give up on my investigation. So right away, when we were in the Étoile d'Austerlitz, she sent me off towards the orphanage. She knew we would follow the trail about the boys who were bitten. That would give her the necessary time to get on with her programme. Three left to kill, she needed to get the job finished at all costs.'

Veyrenc frowned.

'But all this is only circumstantial. Her first name, Irène-Yraigne, and her second name Royer-Colombe, a court would never wear that. There's her mistake on the phone, agreed, but what's to say you didn't mishear or misquote what she said?'

'If I had, Louis, the sentence wouldn't have stuck to a bubble.'

'I'm looking at it from the point of view of the judge, the lawyers and the jury, and they're not going to take any notice of your bubbles. If you hadn't known about the Lourdes recluse, she'd have got away scot-free.'

'No, Louis. It would have taken much longer, that's all. The psychiatrist put us on the right track. Look for a young girl who was sequestered and a contemporary recluse. If we'd launched a media appeal, someone would have put us on to the recluse in the Pré d'Albret, and we'd have done the dig.'

'Well, so what? Her DNA isn't on record.'

'Even without the dig, with ten murders to account for, we would have managed in the end – yes, all right, with great difficulty – to convince an examining magistrate, and activate all the cogs in the story until they came up with the new name of the Seguin daughter. Until the archives turned up the axe that killed the father. We'd have got there, sooner or later. We've found a short cut, that's all.'

'All right, we'd have found out she was Seguin's daughter. But which one? What's to say it wasn't Annette living in the cell at Lourdes?'

'It's the names she chose, Louis. The pigeon loft where she spent her childhood was so embedded in her psyche that she gave herself the name of the bird, Colombe, as an identity. When she was originally freed from the house, she must have gone to Lourdes often, to get help from her patron saint, Bernadette.'

'So she'd know about the dovecot in the Pré d'Albret.'

'Where there are a lot of *wood-pigeons*, taking refuge in the woods. A columbarium. Her ultimate refuge.'

'So she shut herself up there.'

The two men remained silent. Adamsberg raised the glass from which he had yet to drink.

'She's a remarkable woman, Louis. I'm not ashamed to have been deceived by her. But I was so slow, so slow.'

'Why was that?'

'Because, Socrates, it's the way I am.'

'That's not the real reason.'

It was past 1 a.m., the café was closing and the owner was putting upturned chairs on the tables. Veyrenc raised his glass as well.

'*A child when you saw her, you feared this wretched soul,*
The recluse in a tomb, in poverty and dearth.
Grown up, did you know her, when she returned to earth
And set about reaching her terrifying goal?
Did you slow your footsteps, to let her show her worth?'

XLVI

ADAMSBERG DELEGATED TO VEYRENC THE TASK OF EXPLAINING TO THE squad the motive for the excavation of the recluse's cell in the Pré d'Albret, and the almost certain identification of the killer, even before they had the DNA results or could compare the exhumed molars with the axe used by Enzo Seguin forty-nine years previously. Veyrenc could not, of course, go into details about martins, robins, wood-pigeons and so forth, but he worked out a brilliant way of presenting otherwise the assumptions that had led the commissaire on the trail of Irène Royer-Colombe. Irène or Yraigne, he said, meeting Danglard's eye. Danglard, this time, nodded sagaciously.

Everyone understood. They all held their breath: after the many false trails, the blocked inlets, after sedition by one of the ship's commanders (Danglard), after the deaths of ten men, the flagship *Trinidad* was entering the narrow mouth of the straits, beyond the 52nd parallel.

As they all knew, this strait represented triumph, but it was icy cold. Because arresting this suspect would be one of the most painful tasks Adamsberg had ever had to undertake. The commissaire was duty-bound to wall this woman up for the third time in her life.

An urgent request had been made to police archives to produce the axe wielded by Enzo Seguin, this time through official channels.

And while the squad was buzzing with both excitement and anguish, Adamsberg had slept for eleven hours, after which, sitting at his kitchen table and moving his chair to follow the sun around, he pieced together the broken plate: a traditional white porcelain plate, with three blue flowers in the centre. He stopped only to drink some coffee and send a message to Froissy.

Can you get recent photos of all the victims? Urgently. From their families perhaps? Ask Mercadet to help and print them out on paper.

Want them at work tomorrow, or get delivered to you now?

Send to my home address. I'm doing a ceramic jigsaw.

Pretty?

Very.

In fact, the jigsaw was a desperately sad one. But since Froissy liked the word 'pretty', Adamsberg didn't want to disappoint her.

At about 9 p.m., hunger finally caught up with him and he called Retancourt.

'Lieutenant, can I rely on you one more time?'

'You want me to fly the flag for you?'

'I want to send you one last time down to Cadeirac.'

'Oh, no, commissaire,' said Retancourt with determination. 'I'm not going to arrest that woman. Out of the question.'

'No, no, I wouldn't ask you to do such a thing, Violette. I just want you to steal another teaspoon. From Irène this time.'

'All right, I could do that. But what excuse am I going to use this time? I'm going to photograph the ceilings?'

'I haven't thought of that yet. Do you by any chance have any snowstorms?'

'I don't have "*snowstorms*", no,' said Retancourt, rather tetchily, 'but I do have *one*. After I dropped you at the station at Lourdes, I went past this shop full of tacky religious souvenirs, including snowstorms. I bought one. Not St Bernadette, no. A rather podgy cherub flying about in the snow.'

'Would you be prepared to give it away?'

'Yes, of course. Why would I care about a snowstorm?'

'So take it to Irène as a mark of thanks in return for her hospitality.'

'And as another mark of thanks, I pinch her teaspoon.'

'Exactly.'

'I'm not keen on this, commissaire. But I'll do it. I'll go there and back in a day and you'll have your spoon by seven tomorrow evening.'

Adamsberg took out his little snowstorm with the Rochefort ship and shook its flakes. He liked this silly toy as much as he liked intelligent Irène. He put it in his pocket and went out into Paris in search of food and a walk.

The last DNA test, comparing the molar and the second teaspoon, arrived three days later, at three o'clock. Yes, Irène Royer-Colombe was indeed the recluse of the Pré d'Albret. Although it did not surprise him, this news affected Adamsberg deeply. Everything that took him nearer to arresting Irène plunged him into a very dark place. An hour later, confirmation arrived at the squad from the judicial records. Bernadette Marguerite Hélène Seguin had legally changed her name to Irène Annette Royer-Colombe, while her sister, Annette Rose Louise Seguin, had changed hers to Claire Bernadette Michel. Each sister had borrowed a first name from the other, and Annette had chosen as a surname one of her brother's first names.

This time, it was Adamsberg who announced the news to the squad. The die was cast, the cards had been dealt. All that remained now was to go to Cadeirac.

He went out into the courtyard, where the blackbirds had been regularly fed, and spent two hours there, walking around, or sitting on the stone steps, then pacing about again. No one dared go and disturb him, since they all knew that at this painful stage in the passage of the strait, no one could help him. He was desperately lonely, in sole charge of his ship. At about 7 p.m. he called Veyrenc, who came out to the courtyard.

'I'm going down there tomorrow. Will you come with me? Not to do anything, I won't ask that of you. Just to be a witness. When I'm speaking, don't say anything. And don't tell anyone.'

'What time train?' was all Veyrenc said.

XLVII

IN THE MORNING, ADAMSBERG HAD SENT A FRIENDLY TEXT TO IRÈNE.

Am in area with red-haired colleague checking details on site. Might we call for coffee?

With pleasure, Jean-Bapt. But two men means I must get Louise away. What time?

After lunch? About 2.30?

Perfect. She has siesta, I clear up! Coffee hot when you arrive.

Putting away his phone, Adamsberg bit his lip, disgusted at his own hypocrisy.

Six hours later, he was pacing about outside the neatly kept front door of the small house in Cadeirac.

'The last waiting room,' he said to Veyrenc.

Irène had put on her best clothes in their honour, after her own fashion, a dress with a flowery pattern so gaudy that it could have been wallpaper. By contrast, she was still wearing the inappropriate trainers, because of her arthritis.

'Louise has been snoring away for a good fifteen minutes,' she said cheerfully, as she invited them to sit down.

Adamsberg sat at one end of the table, Irène on his left, Veyrenc on the bench to his right.

'Forgive me, Irène, but I haven't brought a present. I'm really not going to give you a present today.'

'Goodness, commissaire, we don't have to give each other things every time we meet. It loses its charm in the end. And you know what, your colleague who takes photos, *she* brought me a gift. A snowstorm from Lourdes. Religious tat, I've actually had enough of that in my life. But she has subtle taste, doesn't she, that woman? You wouldn't think so, what with her size. She's chosen a little cherub, looks like a child playing in the snow. I'll show you, and bet you think it's sweet.'

Irène went to fetch the new snowstorm from the collection displayed on the sideboard. Adamsberg had not been inside before: the house was full of knick-knacks, but all very tidily arranged. A place for everything and everything in its place. 'She was very organised and careful,' Mathias had said, and so she had remained. Tenacious too, brave and determined.

Irène put the Lourdes globe down in front of Adamsberg, and he took his Rochefort one from his pocket.

'Oh, you're not going to give me it back, are you? It was a present.'

'And I'm very fond of it. I like to watch the bubbles of snow dancing.'

'They're called snowflakes, commissaire, not bubbles.'

'It was just to show you that it never leaves my pocket.'

'But what's the point of having it tucked away in your pocket?'

'It helps me think. I shake it and then I look at it.'

'Oh, well, if that's what you like. To each his own,' said Irène, as she poured out the hot coffee. 'By the way,' she said sternly, 'I'm missing two teaspoons. And they disappeared after each visit from your woman colleague. It doesn't matter, I've got plenty more. And she was very nice. But all the same, I'm missing my two spoons.'

'She's a bit of a kleptomaniac, Irène, *you follow me*? Picks up a little souvenir every place she goes. I'll get them back from her. I'm used to it.'

'Well, I wouldn't say no. Because it's a set of twelve, and they have plastic handles, all different colours. So of course, it makes a gap in the set.'

'I promise, I'll post them to you.'

'That's kind of you.'

'Today, Irène, I'm not going to be kind.'

'Oh, really. That's a pity. But go ahead. Coffee all right?'

'Excellent.'

Adamsberg shook his snowstorm and watched the flakes falling around the Rochefort ship. The *Trinidad* was sailing through the icy cold strait. Veyrenc remained silent.

'You too?' said Irène, with a nod towards Veyrenc. 'You don't look too happy either.'

'He's got a headache,' said Adamsberg.

'You want something for it?'

'He's already taken a couple of pills. When he's got a migraine, he can't talk.'

'Oh, you'll find it goes over with age,' said Irène. 'So what are you going to be unkind to me about, Jean-Bapt?'

'This,' said Adamsberg, opening his bag. 'Don't say anything until afterwards, please. It's quite hard enough as it is.'

He lined up on the table the photographs of the nine Miséricorde stink bugs, plus Claude Landrieu, all aged eighteen. In the chronological order of their deaths. Then he put down another row underneath the first, the photos of the same men, forty or sixty years later.

'It looks like you're playing patience and it's all come out right,' remarked Irène.

'All dead,' he said.

'That's what I said. For the killer, it came out right.'

'Absolutely. Starting with this one, César Missoli, who died in 1996, and ending with these two, Torrailles and Lambertin, who died last

Tuesday. The first four were either shot or had fake accidents, between 1996 and 2002. The other six all died from a high dose of recluse spider venom in the last month.'

Irène imperturbably suggested another cup of coffee.

'It's very good for headaches,' she said. 'They've proved it.'

'Thank you,' said Veyrenc, holding out his cup. Then she served Adamsberg, then herself, in polite succession.

'After 2002,' Adamsberg went on, 'there's a gap of fourteen years. We must assume the murderer spent that time perfecting a new method of killing people, a very complex method, but one that suited the perpetrator infinitely better: recluse venom.'

'Yes, that's possible,' said Irène, looking interested.

'But that *wouldn't* be a possibility open to just anyone. It's a long process and an inventive one. But this killer did manage it, and executed six men one after another. *You follow me?*'

'Yes, of course.'

'But why choose a recluse spider, Irène? Why choose just about the most complicated method anyone could imagine?'

Irène waited for him to go on, looking him in the eye.

'Finding the answers, that's *your* job,' she said.

'Because only a recluse, a genuine recluse, could become a recluse spider herself, and kill with her poison. Because of this, Irène,' said Adamsberg, bringing out a package in bubble wrap, which he opened carefully and respectfully. 'Because of this,' he repeated, putting on the table the white plate with blue flowers, glued together by himself.

Irène gave a thin smile.

'This is her plate,' he went on at once, to avoid her having to speak. 'The one she used to eat off for five years, any food she had, whatever people gave her through the high little window, the *pigeon-hole*, in the old bricked-up dovecot in the Pré d'Albret. I ordered a dig there, and we've covered it back over. I replaced the fifty-eight roses, where she put them, month after month, against the wall.'

Veyrenc was looking down, but not Irène, whose gaze moved from the plate to the commissaire's face.

Adamsberg felt in his bag again and put on the table two newspaper cuttings from 1967, one showing the mother and her two daughters, and another showing Enzo, hugging his sisters in his blood-soaked arms.

'Here they are,' he said. 'The older one, Bernadette Seguin, and her younger sister Annette, who was raped over a period of twelve years by the stink bugs from the Miséricorde. Where the girls' father was a janitor. And then,' he went on, as nobody spoke, 'they changed their names, and they disappeared from sight. It was hard to go out into the world after such suffering, so they were placed in a psychiatric clinic, where they stayed for a few years. From 1967 until some later date, I don't know when.'

'1980 for the younger one,' said Irène calmly.

'But Bernadette walled herself up in the old dovecot, which she turned into a recluse's cell. She had a crucifix, and read the Bible. She was expelled from it after five years by the prefectoral authorities. She came back to the clinic, and this time, she was able to adapt, to learn, and read books. She found her sister, still prostrate and unable to live without Enzo's care. But she was fading away. Nothing helped. Bernadette decided to jettison her religion, which had only ever taught the girls to obey and bow the head. Her mission took shape, irrevocably. She alone would be the one who would free her sister from the men who had destroyed her. She didn't act entirely alone though. Enzo provided her with the names.'

'Enzo's clever.'

'You both are. He found out that nine of them had been in the orphanage.'

'Where my father –'

But here, Irène interrupted herself and spat on to the immaculate tiles of the floor.

'I'm sorry, excuse me, but it's a vow. Every time I say "my father", I have to spit on the floor, so that the words don't stay in my mouth. Sorry.'

'Go ahead, Irène.'

'– recruited them.'

'From a group known as the Recluse Gang. Enzo had begun searching and he finally found out everything about them, those unspeakable stink bugs, including their use of the recluse spiders.'

'Good word for them, isn't it? Can you imagine? Putting a spider inside a four-year-old's shirt? Tells you a lot about the road to hell, doesn't it? And when those snakes got into Annette's attic, my father –'

Here she spat again.

'– stayed at the door and watched.'

'But Enzo had the list. You were going to be able to bring Annette back to life.'

'Now look here, commissaire, don't go bothering her. She's got nothing to do with it. But when those accidents happened, and the first four bit the dust, she already started to feel better. And don't you go bothering Enzo either. All he did was he gave me their names,' she said with a smile.

'But he knew what you were going to do with them.'

'No, he didn't.'

'Well, he could see what you *were* doing.'

'After the four accidents,' Irène went on without replying to this, 'I took some time out. Yes, I could have saved her much more quickly. But to make the recluse venom get into their bloodstream and destroy their bodies, that looked so desirable, and that's what I had to do. I just had to, commissaire. And I promised Annette they'd all be dead within ten years. That'll keep her hanging on in there, I thought. And you can't get anything on her, commissaire, or on Enzo, I've done my homework.'

'A person who knowingly fails to reveal a crime about to be

committed, can be imprisoned. Unless that person has a direct family connection to the killer. Neither a sister nor a brother can be touched by the judicial system.'

'There you are then,' said Irène with a smile. 'So it was a week ago today that Annette was finally free. And she will be even better when I've written the book with their names in. Enzo told me that yesterday she ate almost an entire meal. He wanted her to drink some champagne, but she wouldn't, then in the end she did drink two-thirds of a glass. And she almost laughed. Hear that, commissaire? *Laughed*. One day she'll be able to come out, and she'll be able to speak. Maybe even drive a car.'

'In an antalgic position.'

'Oh, see here, commissaire, I'm no more arthritic than you or the next person! But I needed an excuse for travelling about. So I began doing that well before I started eliminating the vermin, to make it look like a regular habit, get it? Of course I had to go on a lot of pointless trips, except I'll say this, they did help me to collect snowstorms. So I also mixed them up with real journeys like the one to Bourges, when I called you. I hadn't been in Bourges all the time of course, I was on my way back from Saint-Porchaire.'

'With your stun gun.'

'It's an excellent model. You can order them from the internet. One click. Very practical.'

'Did Enzo do that for you?'

'Enzo did nothing.'

There was a sound from upstairs. Louise was waking up.

'One minute, commissaire, I'll make her go back in her hole. Never a moment's peace here.'

Irene climbed halfway up the stairs, lightly and without using her walking stick, and called:

'Don't come down, Louise, my dear! I've got two men here! That should do it,' she said, as she sat down, and they heard Louise shutting her bedroom door. 'Easy. Poor woman, don't repeat this, but she was raped when she was thirty-eight.'

'Yes, I know. Nicolas Carnot. Who knew Claude Landrieu. And the Recluse Gang.'

'That was why you suspected her.'

'You understood that, Irène.'

'It wasn't very difficult.'

'It was because of her name as well: Chevrier. I thought she'd chosen it because of the story about Monsieur Seguin and his little goat.'

'You're allowed to spit, because you mentioned that name.'

Adamsberg obeyed.

'Was it to take us first towards her then away from her that you left those hairs in the box room in Torrailles's house?'

'Yes, I wanted to send you off on a wild goose chase. Sorry, commissaire, I really like you, I do, but all's fair in love and war.'

'What I've never worked out is the business about the venom. How did you collect enough? All right, it took you fourteen years. But how? You had to find the spiders, then make them spit out their venom.'

'Ha! Have to be pretty smart to do that, don't you?'

'Yes, indeed,' said Adamsberg with a smile. 'And the idea of the nylon thread as well. Tell me, did you really load a 13 mm rifle with 11 mm syringes? By packing them in something?'

'Yes, of course, or they'd have got wedged. I put some sticky tape round them, then oiled them. You have to think of tricks. It's like the recluses. Know how many I collected? Five hundred and sixty-five, counting the ones that died.'

'But how?' Adamsberg repeated.

'To start with, I used a vacuum cleaner and sucked them out of their holes. What with the woodpile, the cellar, the attic and the garage, I had plenty, believe me. Then I emptied out the vacuum bag and caught them with tweezers to put into a little container, well, the proper name, you know, is a *vivarium*. And one vivarium each, because what do they do if you put them in together? They eat each other, that's what. Because what do they see in anything else that moves? A meal, that's all. No more complicated than that. Well, I had up to sixty-three little containers. I can't show you, because I chucked out the bloody things, oops, sorry, language, I chucked them out with the rubbish. A vivarium sounds grand, but it's just a little glass box with a lid and holes in, some earth at the bottom and bits of twig so that they can hide in there and put their cocoons in there, plus some dead insects like flies or crickets for them to eat. When the time came for mating, I put a male in with a female and hoop-la! Then I gathered the cocoons and waited for the babies to hatch out. Then I put the new ones into special little vivariums, otherwise they'd eat each other. And I'll tell you something, commissaire: catching a baby spider without injuring it, that takes practice. What I was doing really, I was breeding them.'

'What about the venom though, Irène?'

'Ah now, what they do in labs is they give them an electric shock, makes them spit it out. But they have very sophisticated equipment. What I had to do was a bit of DIY. You get a torch, see, the kind you just press for half a second to make signals.'

'I see.'

'Good. Well, you attach some copper wire to the conductors on the battery, that's not rocket science either. And you apply the end of the wire to the spider's body, the cephalothorax. *You follow me*, Jean-Bapt?'

'I'm listening, anyway.'

'Then you press the switch on the torch very quickly, it sends out a tiny charge and the spider spits out the venom. But careful, you need a 3-volt battery, otherwise it's too much, it kills them. And you only press it for a fraction of a second. I killed masses of them till I got the technique right. I put the creatures in a little shallow dish. I'd make, oh, let's say a hundred of them spit venom, one after another, then I sucked it up with a syringe and stored it in tiny test tubes, well sealed. Next stop, the fridge. Well, in fact, the freezer, because you have to store it at minus 20 degrees, so you have to have a good 4-star one. Then you can preserve the venom as long as you want.'

'Wait a second, Irène, how did you stop the recluse running away when you put it in a dish?'

'A tiny puff of gas from the cooker, not too much. You have to have the knack, I tested it on some small house spiders, a centimetre long, and I killed a lot of them too. Well, I got the knack in the end. A teeny puff of gas, not everyone can do that, you need practice. Well, you find a way if you have to. Now my recluse is away with the fairies, she won't budge, I make her spit. Of course, it takes thought, and it means a lot of work. I'm not saying that to boast. It took me four years before my vivariums were functioning properly. I lost a lot of spiders, sorry, I already told you that. You need to know that a recluse can replenish its venom glands in a day or two. I always preferred to wait three days, so as to be sure to get a full dose. I measured twenty-five doses per syringe, so as to be certain they'd work. So I had to prepare a hundred and fifty doses, to account for the six bastards I still had to deal with. Plus another hundred, in case I missed with the gun. Two hundred and fifty doses. Plus another two hundred and fifty kept separately, in case the freezer broke down or there was a power cut. Oh yes, you have to think of everything. So that meant five hundred doses to collect, I rounded it up to six hundred, because there's always some dried venom you can't get up out of the dish. So you see, Jean-Bapt, I had to think ahead about all that. I've got a spare freezer in the woodshed, and I kept all my vivariums with spiders in the same place, behind the logs, because who's going to go and move a lot of lumps of wood? And my spare freezer, locked up, with its own generator, could keep going for four days. It's just like everything else, you want to do it, you find a way.'

'As I said, you thought fourteen years ahead.'

'That's why you couldn't prevent anything, commissaire. Don't blame yourself. But still, you did find me in the end. So bravo, congratulations! But I don't care two hoots, let me tell you, because the job's done! Yours is too. I like it when a job's finished properly.'

Adamsberg pulled together the photos and put them back in his bag. He pointed to the plate with a gesture suggesting 'Do you want to keep it?'

'What use is that to me?' she said. 'It's all cracked. And they won't let me use that to eat from in prison, will they?'

Adamsberg put the bubble wrap round the plate and carefully replaced it inside his bag.

'What are *you* going to do with it then?' she asked.

'Put it back there, I think. In the earth from the recluse cell.'

'Yes, I'd like that.'

'And now, Irène,' he began, standing up and glancing across at Veyrenc.

'Oh well, can you let me have a few minutes?' she interrupted. 'I need to clear away the coffee cups first, then pack a bag.'

'You can have as long as you like. Get lost, Irène!'

Adamsberg pulled on his jacket, pocketed his snowstorm, shouldered his bag and made for the door. Both Irène and Veyrenc stood still, looking at him.

'*What* did you say?' asked Irène.

'I said: get lost, Irène. Pack a bag, take some money, if you've got cash. And disappear. By tomorrow. I'm quite sure Enzo will be able to provide you with a new identity, as he did for himself. And an untraceable mobile phone.'

'No, no, commissaire,' said Irène, as she began collecting up the cups. 'You don't understand. I *want* to go to prison, that was always part of the plan.'

'No,' said Adamsberg. 'Not another cell, not for the third time.'

'But that's just it. I'll be perfectly all right there. For reasons which you seem to have guessed. I've completed my mission, I'm going back inside my four walls. I respect what you're doing there, Jean-Bapt, I respect it, and I thank you. But let me go to prison. And since you did offer me a bit of time, can I take two days, just to get my affairs in order, and go and see Annette and Enzo? Thank you very much for the delay. I don't like unfinished business. And whether you like it or not, on the third day, I'm going to walk into the gendarmerie in Nîmes. Because it would be best if it's them that put me away. Not you. If it was you, I get the feeling you wouldn't like it very much.'

Adamsberg had put down his bag and cocked his head, staring at her as if to consider her resolution.

'I can see you get the point, commissaire.'

'I'm not sure I want to.'

'Come on, you don't have to try hard. What will they give me? At my age? With all the "special circumstances" as they say? Ten years perhaps. Then after four, they'll let me out. Just the right amount of time to write my book on the stink bugs of the Miséricorde. And that, I can only do in a prison cell. *You follow me?* But I have another thing to ask, this is a bit tricky. I'm sorry, I'm a bit embarrassed.'

'What is it?'

'Can you see if there's some way I could have my collection of snowstorms in prison? They're light, they're made of plastic, no danger to anyone, and I haven't got anyone else to kill now.'

'I'll see what I can do, Irène.'

'Will you manage it?'

'I'll bring you the lot.'

At this Irène smiled more broadly than he had ever seen her do in the past.

XLVIII

ADAMSBERG SLEPT CONTINUOUSLY FOR THE THREE AND A HALF HOURS OF the train journey, leaning on his side with the snowstorm digging into his ribs, but without moving it. Veyrenc shook him as the train pulled in to the Gare de Lyon with a screech of the brakes which had failed to wake him.

Back home, in crumpled clothes, and still feeling some inner turmoil, he put his bag down carefully on the floor in the kitchen – so as not to break the plate – then went into the little garden, sat down under the beech tree, lit one of Zerk's cigarettes, and stretched out on the dry grass, watching the clouds pass across the stars blocking out any light from the moon. Just as well – it corresponded to his state of mind. He wasn't hungry or thirsty.

Propping himself up in the dark, he sent a message to all his officers:

Attention all crew members. 52nd parallel reached. Embargo on news for two days. Take time off, keep basic team on guard, feed the birds. Details Friday 2 p.m.

Then he lay back down, thinking that when Magellan discovered the strait, the ships had fired their cannon in victory. He did not wish to do anything of the sort.

And his phone's buzzing disturbed him.

A text from Veyrenc.

Am twenty metres from La Garbure, still open. Waiting for you. Have a question.

No, Louis, sorry.

I have a question.

Adamsberg understood that Veyrenc, knowing about the icy waters of the strait, was calling to take him out of the frozen shades of the recluse's cell. He saw once more the worn statuette of St Roch. The man was deep in the forest, where the dog, the messenger from the external world, had found him.

On my way, he replied.

'Are you hungry?' asked Adamsberg as he sat in front of a dish of garbure.

Veyrenc shrugged.

'No more than you.'

'So?'

'You must swallow and I must swallow. That's how I see things.'

They both conscientiously swallowed their soup in silence, as if they were two workers concentrating on their task.

'Did you plan in advance to do that?' Veyrenc asked as, their task completed, he filled their glasses with Madiran.

'Was that your question?'

'Yes.'

'We've drunk a lot of Madiran these last two weeks.'

'It was probably necessary to fight the cold and the wind driving us from one cliff to another.'

'Yes, it wasn't warm, was it?'

'So answer me. Did you plan to do that? To let her go?'

'Yes. Only towards the end. But yes.'

Veyrenc raised his glass and the two men clinked glasses on the surface of the table, taking great care not to make a noise.

'But she's going back, she's returning to her cage,' said Adamsberg.

'If you hadn't found her, she'd have set you on her trail anyway.'

'You did suggest she'd done it on purpose. The mistake. On the phone. "It's infuriating, the killer's got them all." '

'That woman doesn't make mistakes. It was over, and she was expecting you.'

'But why didn't I react?'

'I think I already told you that.'

'Oh? When?'

'In my bad verses.'

'Ah,' said Adamsberg after a pause. *'Did you slow your footsteps, to let her show her worth?'*

'See, you do remember. But if you want to memorise something, choose some real poetry next time.'

'Thank you, Socratician,' said Adamsberg, leaning back half against the chair half against the wall.

'At the risk of sounding like Danglard, you don't say "Socratician".'

'What then?'

'Socratic philosopher. But I'm not a philosopher. Are you going to try and get the snowstorms to her in prison?'

'I'll try, and I'll succeed, Louis.'

Adamsberg raised his hand and read the message that had just arrived on his phone.

I salute the navigation of the strait, and present my humble compliments.

'Who do you think that's from?' he said, showing it to Louis.

'Danglard.'

'See, he's stopped being a bloody idiot.'

Adamsberg glanced over at Estelle who was sitting at a distant table, pen in hand. She should have been checking her accounts, but was not doing so.

'This is your last chance, Louis.'

'But my mind is in Cadeirac, Jean-Baptiste.'

'How could it be anywhere else? But you're forgetting two things. If you go on doing nothing, you end up doing nothing.'

'Should I write that down?'

Adamsberg shook his head. Veyrenc had succeeded in distracting him.

'Absolutely not. You should only write down things you don't understand.'

'And the second thing?'

'This is our last meal at La Garbure. You won't come back here, Louis. And nor will I.'

'Why's that?'

'There are places like this that accompany a voyage. The voyage is coming to an end and this place has to end too.'

'The ship's weighing anchor.'

'Exactly. So you see you haven't much time left. Had you thought of that?'

'No.'

This time it was Adamsberg who filled their glasses.

'Well, think about it now. While we finish our wine.'

Adamsberg remained silent, accompanied by Veyrenc. Yes, it was the last evening, no doubt about it. After a long moment, Veyrenc put down his empty glass and acknowledged it, with a slight movement of his thick eyelashes.

'Don't just chat,' said Adamsberg, standing up and throwing his jacket over his shoulder. 'You've done too much of that.'

'Because if you keep on chatting, you'll do nothing but chat.'

'Exactly.'

Adamsberg went back along the streets towards his house, taking unnecessary detours, hands in pockets, and gripping the snowstorm. Yes, the ship was weighing anchor, the ship would be carrying off

Yraigne, the spider. Tomorrow, Lucio would be back from Spain. He'd tell him all about the spider, as they sat outside on the tea chest. And Lucio wouldn't be able to order him to do anything: all the bites and stings and wounds had indeed been scratched until blood ran.

He remembered Lucio's voice as it had come to him, outside Vessac's house in Saint-Porchaire. A voice that had pushed him to keep on digging, when he had been tempted to give it all up. What old Lucio had said was:

'You've got no choice, *hombre*.'